monsoonbooks

SNOW OVER SURAB

Nigel Barley was born south ~~~~~~~~~~~ 1947. After taking a degree in modern languages at Cambridge, he gained a doctorate in anthropology at Oxford. Barley originally trained as an anthropologist and worked in West Africa, spending time with the Dowayo people of North Cameroon. He survived to move to the Ethnography Department of the British Museum and it was in this connection that he first travelled to Southeast Asia. After forays into Thailand, Malaysia, Singapore, Japan and Burma, Barley settled on Indonesia as his principal research interest and has worked on both the history and contemporary culture of that area.

After escaping from the museum, he is now a writer and broadcaster and divides his time between London and Indonesia.

ALSO BY NIGEL BARLEY

The Innocent Anthropologist
A Plague of Caterpillars
Not a Hazardous Sport
Foreheads of the Dead
The Coast
Smashing Pots
Dancing on the Grave
The Golden Sword
White Rajah
In the Footsteps of Stamford Raffles *
Rogue Raider *
Island of Demons *
The Devil's Garden *
Toraja *

(* published by Monsoon Books)

SNOW OVER SURABAYA

NIGEL BARLEY

monsoon

monsoonbooks

First published in 2017
by Monsoon Books Ltd
www.monsoonbooks.co.uk

No.1 Duke of Windsor Suite, Burrough Court,
Burrough on the Hill, Leicestershire LE14 2QS, UK

First edition.

ISBN (paperback): 978-1-912049-00-4
ISBN (ebook): 978-1-912049-01-1

Cover design by CoverKitchen.

A Cataloguing-in-Publication data record is available from the British
Library.

Printed in Great Britain by Clays Ltd, St Ives plc
20 19 18 17   1 2 3 4 5

Kepada Malcolm McLeod, teman yang setia.

Introduction

Although it deals with real events, this is largely a work of fantasy but provoked by another work of fantasy that it may well bring closer to the truth. All one can be really sure of – we have the pieces of paper – is that a girl to be named Muriel Stuart Walker was born in Glasgow in the year 1898, where she first embarked on that circuitous perambulation that we term a life. The nature of that life is subject to conflicting accounts, deliberate manipulations, forgettings, subjectivities and the myriad uncertainties that post-modernists and theoretical historians wallow in so luxuriously. Muriel would grow up to be a deliberate chamaeleon, wandering from continent to continent – Europe, America, Asia – frequently changing name, profession, identity, in short completely reinventing herself in various tongues and accents so that it is legitimate to wonder whether, at the end, anything at all remained of the larrikin original. In the course of it she moved, most improbably, from being a Scottish schoolgirl to a heroine of the Indonesian Revolution and took the name K'tut Tantri.

Many of her romantic tales are obvious inventions, the work of a proxy Baroness Munchhausen, yet some have a ring of truth about them and are firmly rooted in reality. She gathered her biographical tales all together in a book published as *Revolt in Paradise* published in 1960 both as an account of her past within the Indonesian Revolution after WWII and a blueprint for what she wanted to become, since there can be no doubt that – like all good fantasists – she came to believe many of her own fabulations.

Needless to say, she has been 'rediscovered' several times by the West, by the East, by the sceptical and by the credulous. Special thanks are due to Tim Hannigan whose original suggestion this book was and, more generally, it is truly a child of *Biku*, that unique Balinese mixture of tearoom, restaurant and literary salon, presided over by the inimitable Jero Asri Kerthyasa.

We are also fortunate to have another excellent work about Muriel Walker, Timothy Lindsey's *The Romance of K'tut Tantri and Indonesia* (1997) where her imaginings and psyche are forensically dissected and held up to the light. As Lindsey points out, the reason for the neglect of K'tut Tantri's rôle in Indonesia's independence struggle lies not so much in the relation between her story and truth as in the manner of its telling – falling between the genres of war story, biography, romance and travel book. As his title indicates, it is perhaps closest to what was once termed 'romance' (less politely 'shopgirl fiction' or more modernly 'chicklit') and he argues that the whole purpose of her life was to construct, defend and live that romance.

A further work sheds light on Muriel's later life and character, when she had decided to give her story to the world both as a book and a film script: Michael Campbell's, *The Princess In England* (1964), based on his experience of the difficulties of working with her as a (soon to be betrayed and discarded) ghostwriter.

But frankly, K'tut Tantri's fantasies are not very good fantasies, being limited by the conventions of the oversyrupy romance genre as it developed after WWII. At times she reads like a Barbara Cartland impersonator to whose bizarre and stilted sense of sexual propriety she is eager to conform and in her prose, as in her visual art, she is chocolate-boxy even in an imagination that is firmly rooted in conventional, Western notions of the Orient as an exotic paradise. The result is an account of stirring times that impoverishes rather than enriches them. Previous discussions of K'tut Tantri have sought to free her from her fantasies. This book is an attempt rather to free the fantasies from the limitations of the chocolate box – a sort of 'K'tut unchained'.

For those who know little of the postwar events that led to the birth of a free Indonesia, almost nothing here is pure invention though links have been deliberately made and liberties taken that historians would consider outrageous. The Hollywood film of her life that Muriel dreamed of making never quite happened. She insisted that it should feature neither sex nor smoking and – at that time – a film without smoking was unthinkable.

Chapter One

'Muriel Walker, come and get yer piece ye wee bastard!' The voice of love. In Glaswegian. The voice of my mother, Ma, calling from an upstairs window, echoing around the close, summoning me to what I have now learned to call 'lunch'. And, for those who do not know, a 'piece' is more technically a 'jeely piece', a doorstep-thick slice of bread, smeared with butter or margarine and then spread dripping with tinned jam. It is the original and authentic fast food of the Glasgow poor, the preferred dessert course, the explanation for their rotted teeth and one of the ancient wisdoms of my people. Except, of course, they are *not* my people. Everything denies it, even Ma's use of that word 'bastard'.

It is 1910 and my eleven-year-old allegedly 'female' brain already feels alienation and revulsion from the surrounding grey depression of a Glasgow tenement with its weed-sprouting, flagged yard and leaky, brick privy. My flaming red hair, so different from my mother's mousy mop, cries out a secret ancestry, as do the almond eyes that earn me the nickname of 'Chinky' at school and the short stature that stands in contrast to the lankiness of all my so-called kin – to say nothing of their ghastly taste in soft furnishings. To anticipate the song, I am a lonely, little petunia in an onion patch.

On a scholarship to the local girls' grammar school my English is being starched, pleated and pressed, while I am acquiring the practical skills that will help me to survive in the modern world – such as being able to talk to the Ancient Romans and calculate the volume of a pyramid – but the Bible is already being drummed into my pliant mind by the busy agents of the Wee Free Kirk, greedy for my soul, and it has absorbed the tale of Moses in the bulrushes as my own secret biography – only reversed. I am an exotic princess found by slaves, stripped of my birthright, and raised to hardship and poverty and mean thoughts. In the pocket atlas of Great Britain that forms the rest of our library up on the third floor, the object of constant, dreamy study, I am drawn to islands, islands off islands, islands in the middle of lakes in islands off islands. The Isle of Man is my first discovery, a distant foreign land, a fortress surrounded by sea, home of Vikings and elfin seers and monstrous creatures with three legs but no bodies – as far as my baby brain can reach. As an only child, I live in my own imagination. And from the top floor I imagine I can almost see it through winter mists. It is the first of many candidates to be considered my real home in a search that will consume my life.

'For the last time of telling, come and get yer piece, or yer da will give ye a belt!'

Concern for well-being is equated with the threat of physical violence, just part of the crazy logic that governs the link of parents to children. The single privy that is shared by all the families – what I would now term a 'non-suite bathroom' – echoes to the sound of gasps and groans, the simultaneous, tearing evacuation of gas from both ends, to be followed by the ripping of newspaper and the Christmassy jangle of the cistern chain like a dog rising reluctantly to its feet. I get myself up off the sandstone step, its dished centre the perfect shape to cup young buttocks – product not so much of feet as of a thousand sharpenings of Sunday carving knives – and go in the back door and back to the prison of my 'family' home. I steel myself against the grinding sense of them watching me and intuitively know it is essential I do not betray my secret knowledge of who I really am – especially to the man there in the privy who calls himself my 'da' and whose boots I can hear clattering on the stairs behind me and cutting off all retreat.

Mr. Walker is a boilermaker in the shipyards – a dangerous and demanding occupation that is often solitary and leaves him ingrown and moody and turns his hands into shaking, scarred crab's pincers incapable of gentle touch. It is a Saturday so there is no sit-down midday meal or mother's godfearing – they are for tomorrow – but later he will be off to football and rambling trade union talk in the pub afterwards. Mr. Walker is strong on the union. It's workers this and workers that and behind it all the evil conspiracy of the English employers who are somehow the same thing as the Jews of his rarer but longer anti-Semitic rants. He is not a very warm father to me – though perhaps that has something to do with the fact that I call him very determinedly 'Mr. Walker' to his face. Perhaps I am being unfair to him. After trying all methods known to civilised man to bring a child to gentle reason and light – shaking, smacks, punches, strappings, starvation, doses of castor oil, half-drownings, incarceration in a light- and airless coalhole that swarms with cockroaches – he has given up and contemplates with blank resignation the presence of this exotic cuckoo in his nest.

* * *

1915 brought us the continuing distraction of the First World War that few in Glasgow felt to concern them. It was an English war that was of interest only to the employers and their men with the soft hands in Edinburgh and the buzz of propaganda blurred into the background of fuzzy, patriotic noise coming from the south that was a constant of empire and simply ignored. Far more important to us that year was the attempt by our landlords to hike the rents of the poor and evict vulnerable war widows whose noble sacrifice was being trumpeted elsewhere. Mary Barbour, the leader of the resulting rent strike, was a friend of my mother and helped her organise a general refusal to pay the increase demanded. All the women banded together to pay only the old rate. Attempted evictions followed but we all had a grand time pelting the sheriff's men with flour bombs and then posing as wee, starving bairns thrown out into the snow for the newspapermen, many of whom were elbow-patched sympathisers. There are few walls more formidable than a row of self-righteous Glasgow mothers with their arms folded, closing off the street. Hadrian could have saved himself a lot of trouble and expense. When the owners moved to the courts, only munitions workers that the government needed desperately to fill shells turned up to be jailed and I was proud to be one of the 10,000 that marched on the assizes and terrified the government into freezing rents by law. A great victory for the workers – except that the men were unsettled to see their women taking on the High Hiedyins, the big cheeses, and beating them – which they never had. A rash of itchy strikes broke out all over Scotland.

But it was not so much raw, socialist zeal as the attractions of the tram itself that drove me to the strikebound shipyards on that balmy autumn evening when golden sunshine coaxed poignant beauty even from the skeletons of the derricks and the rags on the washing lines. Trams were still new enough to have a wonder of their own, the novelty of horseless carriagery, the modernist rumble and thunk of steel on bare steel. As a young woman in ungainful employment – I now worked in a city office with evening classes in the fiendish new technology of the typewriter – I was part of the modern age and acquired a new, more English, accent appropriate to my new position. For some education is heaven, for others hell. For me it was at that moment the only route of escape on offer.

But it was not the beauties of Nature that had charmed my girlish heart. It was the young conductor. I had seen him before on this run as he danced between the benches or twirled his hips up the spiral staircase. Our eyes had met over the dispensing of tickets and a whole encyclopaedia of forbidden knowledge had flashed between us in one bat of his long eyelashes and the almost accidental passage of silken heat from his hand into mine as he counted out change. He was simply the most beautiful thing I had ever seen. To look at him made me want to cry and Muriel Walker is not a girl much given to crying. Now, he came down the stairs in one glamorous slide, supporting his weight on the handrails, crutch thrust out, converting an act of labour into how I imagine a ballet to be and stood in the stairwell with his eyes boldly blazing into mine. And what eyes! Dark, smouldering, with a curious lilt to them like a grace note in a melody. I stared back entranced, breathing heavily as he shifted his moneybag deliberately from side to front and seemed to undergo a sudden, significant rise in the size of his takings.

The tram juddered round a corner with bacon-slicer noises of resistance between rail and wheel and there came the din of another kind of resistance screamed from a thousand angry mouths as the pickets – pinned between dockyard gates and a line of police – greeted our arrival as if we were a blockade-busting battleship and surged forward. A banner made from an old sheet on broom handles wavered towards us, Mr. Walker grim-faced beneath it like a coffin-bearer. 'Fair Wages for Free Men.' My conductor stood firm, a captain on the bridge of his orange ship in the full glamour of his uniform as the driver pushed on slowly through the tide of confused bodies, waving and shouting to clear the tracks. The police were bemused, unsure whether freedom of passage was one of the things they are supposed to be protecting here or whether this was simply a vehicle bringing reinforcements for the enemy. And then the matter was sharply resolved. With one leap, my conductor grabbed the door rail and swung outside with waving fist.

'Down with the Keystone Cops!'

With cheering laughter, the strikers rushed forward again, the whole thing now become carnival – knocking off helmets like coconuts at the fair – and a fat sergeant went down, notebook and truncheon trampled pitilessly underfoot. Others stumbled, tripped over the greasy tramlines. Law-enforcing backsides were roundly kicked with stout, steel-tipped dockyard boots. Placards and banners rained from above on the police like the eagles of Roman legions and suddenly I am there at the door too, body pressed hard against my hero, eyes shining, as the structures of capitalism tumble around us in the heady screech of police whistles.

Breaking glass, blood, broken heads, screaming and bellowing, a maelstrom of anger and despair, revenge and terror! There is a wonderful excitement and creativity in the smashing of things. Every shattered window draws a line through time. That night, we presented ourselves at home, myself and Mr. Walker, he clutching the trophy of a police helmet like a taken head – bound in unwilling comradeship, both stained with the blood of martyrs – and surrendered ourselves to dabbing rags dipped in disinfectant for our wounds. There was something horribly akin to paternal pride in his face. I shuddered as he said, 'She's a braw wee lass, mother. Ye should ha' seen the way she heaved a brick at yon black Maria.'

Except the blood all over me isn't just martyr blood. This

is the day of my fulfilment as a woman – behind a blackberry hedge that is heavy with the symbolism of late-ripened fruit in the midst of thorns and with the strident shout of battle in our ears. It comes through the good offices of a derailed and flyly unbuttoned employee of the Glasgow Tramway and Omnibus Company with beautiful, dark eyes.

* * *

Sin was to be found everywhere in Glasgow, almost without looking, and especially on a Sunday, for it had been drummed into me that there was nothing on earth more wicked than sinning on Sunday – a proposition I have spent my life disproving. It hung in the air and dripped down the walls like condensation on wash day. It was in the breath of the horses and the scent that ladies dabbed behind their ears. It was in the drinking in the pubs around Sauchiehall Street and the painted women of easy virtue who lurked there. Sometimes it was visible only to the godly for it festered in the churches of any denomination but your own and the damned, hell-bound devil-worshippers that frequented them and their smoking altars. For the very pure, it was even to be found in the swings in the parks that must be chained up on a Sunday to prevent the evil of children's laughter on the Lord's Day. It is the last of these that I am about – not swings but roundabout pleasure – in the comely form of Hamish Friend, 17-year-old incarnation of the sins of the flesh and the primal fall of Eve and part-time tram conductor. Ironically, it was the strictures of the godly that made all this possible. Ham knew how to tickle open the lock of a nearby sports pavilion secure in the knowledge that God would strike down anyone else using it on the Sabbath. So it was here amongst the decayed smell of sweaty armpits and unwashed feet that we made the beast with two backs on a splintery pine floor, with undarned socks abandoned in corners like forlorn hopes. This association of lust and male dirt, once established, is very convenient to a young girl in a world where women make love while men merely grab grubby sex. I chased away the thought that Ham might have been here before and done more than unlace and dubbin his football boots in all-male company.

Not being a visitor of the art galleries, I had never seen a completely naked, male body before. In those prudish days, many men had probably never seen one either and the finally revealed secret of what human beings really look like was astonishing to me. I explored and probed his body deliciously and shamelessly as he blushed coyly – the unexpected pubic hair, the outrageousness of the old man's scrotum between smooth, young thighs all challenged me like the three-legged monsters of the Isle of Man. I had missed out on a lot by avoiding art galleries and this was the moment when I decided to take up painting. I told him my true origins, that my father was a Manxman by birth, an African archaeologist, dead to a tropical fever – no – eaten by cannibals after the discovery of a lost city in the jungles of the Sahara. Most people found this astonishing. But there was more to Ham than met the eye. His skin had a beautiful olive softness unlike the uncooked pastry appearance of most Glaswegians. That on the shaft of his penis was definitely brown. Perhaps he is one of the 'Sons of Ham' that the Wee Free thunder against. My fair, dark Ham tells me a romantic story to explain it away in a voice with the soft accents of the far west, a voice that breathes of peat and malt whisky.

'Once upon a time there was a great laird in India. He ran the whole country for John Company. One day, the King of Bally, a beautiful island in the South Seas, sent him two fine boy slaves as a present. Their fathers were also great men of the country but the wicked King of Bally had killed them and taken their lands and now wanted to be rid of their sons by sending them far, far away. So they entered the service of the great laird of India and he, not knowing what else to do with them and being a godly man, had them sent to school there and baptised them Edmund Friend and Francis Mann to remind himself that – though once slaves – they were his friends and fellow men. And they lived in a great palace with fountains and peacocks and a harem of lovely ladies. But the laird's enemies were plotting against him at home and he was recalled to Scotland and the boys they came too as just part of his luggage, along with the silk umbrellas and the gold robes and the feathered hats. The peacocks came too but they lost their voices when they left India and became mute for the rest of their days. But the great laird died on the way home and so the lads were left to run wild in the family castle in the north of Scotland. There they learned Scots and hunted and fished and finally married local women – though these were far beneath them – and raised families of which I am the latest, fairest fruit. The two families have always kept in touch. My father was a Friend. My mother a Mann.'

The last line made me giggle, being so unlike my own life, but I found it hard to believe a word of all this. People make up such silly tales. A fairy story, then. But why tell the ugly truth when something else can be so much more lovely? I looked at him again. I would definitely take up painting.

*　*　*

1919 and the Great War is over. Too late for me. Poor Ham lies broken and buried somewhere in Northern France, conscripted on his eighteenth birthday as a fresh sacrifice to the profits of the international arms industry and dead on his third day at the front. It is a year before I know – the news broken casually by a fellow tram conductor as he reshuffles his ticket rack – with me screaming and wailing in the tram's rattling stairwell and comforted by patting women who have seen it all before as some perky, young telegraph boy skips whistling up to their door bearing news from the War Office of their father, brother, husband or son.

There were strikes everywhere, docks, railways, shipyards, a heaving underswell of turbulence and disaffection was passing through the nation as a swallowed goat passes down a snake, stretching the seams. The streets were dotted with broken windows. The Battle of George Square led Winston Churchill to order the army into the city and there were tanks and soldiers billeted in all the parks with Lewis guns mounted on street corners and nervous, wall-eyed Englishmen in khaki clutching them as though for comfort. Glaswegian troops were shipped south and safely out of the city. The High Hiedyins were terrified of a Bolshevik uprising like the one they were having in Russia, but this is still Britain and the sheriff's bumbling attempts to read the Riot Act are prevented by the simple expedient of Mr. Walker and other members of the Workers' Councils hitting him on the head with it and tearing it up. This is Mr. Walker's moment of glory but shortlived like himself, for, as the court officers turn, hitch up their robes and flee womanishly up the town hall steps, he clutches at his heart and goes down. An unsuccessful life crowned by a successful death. But then the last thing he sees is the words, 'unlawfully, riotously and tumultuously remain' blowing on a paper fragment of the Riot Act and plastered to his face by the wind, to be followed by a triumphant 'God Save the King'.

I will never know what led my mother, a most unadventurous

person, to up sticks at her time of life and move to America. Certainly, it could be nothing that I had said or done. America was very far from my dreams. Yet, there hung around us all, a sense of things coming to an inevitable end, something that was no more to be resisted and the passing of Mr. Walker seemed to draw a line under a whole section of her life. So there she sat after the extravagant trade union funeral with its clenched fist salutes, with all her worldly goods tied up in the curtains as though for a moonlight flit from a pressing landlord. Only when we were well down the road on the back of a fish truck – we were travelling in style, really poor people went by horse and cart – did I even discover that we were indeed leaving without bothering to pay the rent or the gas. Perhaps that was Ma's way of having the last word. It taught me the lesson that not everything in life has to be faced. It's not a form of weakness to simply walk away. It takes real moxie.

Chapter Two

Joseph Kennedy was a big beanpole of a man with one of those Boston Irish cabbage faces and finally starting to slap on some weight around the belly. He leaned back in his chair and drew fragrant breath through his cigar, said, 'Of all my female employees, Manxi, I guess you're about the only one I've never tried to screw.' He scratched his crotch thoughtfully as though I was ruining his collection. You had to admit that fancy education and Harvard fraternities had not quite rubbed off all of his rough corners. Joe was a serial fornicator who brought his business methods to his love life. I once heard him explaining to someone on the phone, 'Never settle for a workaday fuck before four in the afternoon. You might still get a better offer later before close of business and come up short before you can restore liquidity.' Rose, his poor wife dumped back in Boston, was about the only other woman in the States not to be on the receiving end of his attentions – but somehow maintained a mysterious state of constant pregnancy. Perhaps Joe could fornicate even over the phone.

I asked, 'Is that meant as a compliment or an insult, Joe?' I had asked Gloria Swanson the same question once when she had remarked that, in bed, Joe was a total animal.

He laughed and flicked ash, waggled his blazing red tip at me. 'Maybe a little of both, honey. After all, I like 'em dumb, scrawny and obliging.'

New York had been a terrible place, an ugly, cruel city – even worse than Glasgow since Ma was scared of the black men – never having seen one before – and no one could understand a word she said. I, of course, had long acclimatised to American and assumed its modalities just as I borrowed Auntie BBC's English back in Glasgow for office use. Joe sometimes joked that mine was an accent I had picked up from the silent screen. California was better – much better – though I thought at the start I was getting the fuzzy end of the lollipop again. I took an office job with a small motion pictures outfit, Film Booking Offices of America, a shoestring operation that churned out cheapie movies, mostly Westerns. The horses cost more than the actors who were just cheap camera fodder and often a little too quick on the draw with the office help. Then it seemed that FBO was going AOT and I had already started scanning the wanted ads. At the last minute, Joe turned up, bought out the operation, brought in his boys, refloated, refinanced, flipped some companies, did some shouting down the telephones, cut some deals and suddenly the money was pouring in. Joe's real business, of course, was knowing people. His father was in the saloons trade which exposed him to a wide range of contacts. The result was that Joe ended up married to the mayor's daughter while being well-connected with the absolute cream of organised crime – bootlegging across the Canadian border being his most profitable activity. At the same time, he had enough contacts in the trading rooms to be the first to get inside information or be able to fix the markets so that no investment ever turned bad for him. I suppose he should have set my socialist principles on edge but he was less a stodgy financier than an outlaw, bringing ever nearer Mr. Walker's inevitable destruction of late capitalism. I ran the local office and answered the telephone to Rose, always having a new story to hand to explain Joe's non-availability. Mostly, his non-availability was owing to his close-ups with Gloria Swanson. Gloria, at that time, was at the height of her fame but spreading her legs for a studio director was a good way for a girl to make sure she kept all her options open. She was spending $12,000 on a dress, $6,000 a year on perfume but the real extravagance must be the $10,000 a year she splashed out on knickers that she hardly ever had on. To be blunt, one way or another she was working her arse off so I invented a whole network of secret government projects to take Joe out of town to unknown, undisclosable locations – especially around five in the afternoon. You would often see Gloria's Lancia – upholstered in fabulous leopard skin – outside the same addresses. Joe called me his 'head scriptwriter'. That was all before they fell out, of course – him and Gloria – when she discovered she was the golden goose being systematically plucked as well as … I also wrote for the scandal rags under another name but I never blabbed on Joe, he had too many friends who could make you fall off the end of a pier.

'I've got a little job for you, Manxi. Right up your alley.' We were in his private office, sour LA sunshine leaking through the Venetian blinds and he had both feet up on the desk, clad in great Irish boots and the thick navvy's socks that made him feel secure. All Kennedy boys had flat feet and big noses to grab as much free earth and air as possible. He sipped coffee from an army mug and looked at me hard. I chugged illegal Scotch, poured from the office bottle, one part of my cultural heritage that I still embraced. Joe saw the Irish whiskey-swilling thing as a cliché and refused to go to hell on a cliché, so he seldom drank. Movies people! 'The key to making money in the movies business is to control both the film production and the movie theatres that show them. Then you can load the dice against the competition and crowd them out with your own cut-price films. There's a business I've had my eye on, Pantages Pictures, with a holding of 84 houses up and down the West coast and Canada – all making money. I've offered that little Greek shit Alex Pantages 8 million bucks and he's turned me down flat. I've cut off our films to him. Since we control talkie copyrights through RKO, we're squeezing his balls from all sides but still he won't budge. That's undemocratic, unAmerican. I reckon it's time for him to suffer a little misfortune with one of his dancers. It seems Alex is going to attack poor, innocent, little, Eunice Pringle – great little mover – in a broom cupboard at the theatre and make her do a jolly jig against the wall. Being, as she is, an untouched virgin from convent school this will lead her to run out into the street, screaming, blind with distress and her clothes all torn.' He chuckled. 'Reporters will happen to be there. The Hirst newspapers have been fixed to be sympathetic to our – poor Eunice's – cause but she'll need coaching so she can tell a good tale at the trial and give the journalists what they want. Pretty little twat she is, a brain she ain't. Do you reckon you could do that for me, head scriptwriter? Needless to say, I'll show myself very, very grateful.'

I meet 17-year-old Eunice in a hotel down on the Strip and explain to the management that we're rehearsing scenes from a movie – not exactly a lie. I'm a method perjurer. Eunice was a beauty all right with lots of thick, dark hair and lips like a boiled clam. We act out her violation, fix times, responses, escape routes, what drawers she was wearing, decide which questions she will answer in shocking detail, which she will demur at with maidenly modesty, when she will cry and at what signal she will finally break down and swoon, making sure she shows her legs. We rehearse her screams and pleadings and discuss the advisability of a failed suicide attempt before the hearing – finally deciding against it. On the whole it's hard work but a hoot. And then, when they put her on the stand, beautifully prepared, and ask her to tell, in her own words, what happened, she just says, 'Aw gee, he schtupped me but good, honey, with this fat Greek schlong.'

Never mind. The judge clearly thought she was too dumb to lie. After his first conviction, Partages is ruined and has to sell up to RKO for a knock-down $3.5 million. Sure he gets off on a retrial having learned his lesson and hired a lawyer who can read and write. Needless to say, I'm not the one who gets the missing $5 million but then neither is dear Eunice.

* * *

Mine was what you might term a 'marriage of inconvenience'. I had suffered a mismarriage. Karl Pearson was not the world's greatest catch – tall, skinny, the trout-like suspicion of a wall-eye – but Ma liked him, which got her off my back. He lived in the same building and Ma dragged him home one day with a leg of lamb and the rest of the shopping but more like a cat would a rat and dumped him on the doormat. Sure, he was irritating but it was not all bad – like all men who work with wood, he was good with his hands. He also had a cute smile and an American passport and I had a use for the latter. Karl made a nice, steady living refinishing old furniture that he sold around the new developments shooting up all over LA. I am not a beautiful woman but I know how to be exotic and exotic gets men every time. I cooked him a few traditional Manx dishes as learned from my Viking forefathers and he was hooked like a Manx herring so that, in a few short months, I had him wed, pussy-whipped and sleeping in separate beds with the wedding photos safely stowed on the secondhand piano. Let him find relief in French-polishing his big chests and rubbing up his tallboys. A husband who smelled of fish glue and sawdust was not what I was used to in the movie business.

Karl began to hit the bottle like Mr. Walker before him. I didn't mind that until it started, in turn, hitting the finances. Booze was illegal and expensive and Joe Kennedy didn't give discounts to his workers. Then Ma took up the habit and I would come home to the pair of them passed out with stupid grins pasted on their faces and something that looked and smelled like a speakeasy at daybreak and with enough empty bottles up and down the hallway to set up a bowling alley. Something had to give. I sat down and started to write a movie script about a woman who plans to murder her dypso husband in a faked car crash and frame her own mother. It came easily and flowed from my pen. If I say so myself, it was brilliant.

* * *

Unlike Randolph Hearst's yacht, Louella Parsons, queen of Hollywood gossip, was totally unsinkable. Not that their fates were not firmly entwined. The *Oneida* had once been the German Kaiser's gin palace until newspaper magnate Hearst bought it and had the final, lingering marks of good taste expensively removed to please his starlet mistress, Marion Davies. And Louella happened to be on that yacht off Catalina, with her busy, little pencil, when the cowboy star, Tom Mix, mysteriously died of acute indigestion following a shot to the head that somehow escaped notice in the medical examiner's report. What followed immediately was a fat syndication deal for her Hollywood gossip column with Hearst Newspapers and the rest was silence. Not that, at parties, she didn't do a brilliant and vicious impersonation of Marion in her silent movie days when she was afflicted with a terrible stammer. Hearst claimed to have cured her through some Italian speech guru who put marbles in her mouth. Louella always said it was Charlie Chaplin who popped in something much more challenging and t-t-t-tasty. And there she sat over the other side of the room, prune-faced and wearing a silly hat like a strawberry pavlova on her head and a cross round her scrawny, hypocritical neck big enough to nail a bishop to.

The Depression had hit Hollywood hard. People without enough to eat didn't think about popcorn. The studios had cut back on the falling stars, many were teetering on the edge of bankruptcy and at parties both diamonds and caviar had been replaced by different kinds of cheap paste of fishy origin. Worse still, the moral strictures of the Hays Code had made the films boring and actors were now following in their footsteps and losing the wild eccentricity that had once made them such fun. All over town the gilt was peeling off the cherubs and official Hollywood henceforth only existed above the waist.

Louella – Lolly – had written the odd movie script and was a fellow journalist so we were old friends. I carried over one of her favourite triple martinis and joined her on the sofa.

'Hi, Manxi. What's cooking?'

I settled in snugly. Louella was kind of touchy. With her it was never love at first slight. But she and I had an old sparring-partner relationship. 'Well, Lolly, I can give you an exclusive. Joe Kennedy and I are planning to marry as soon as his divorce from Rose on the grounds of her adultery with the Pope is final. We have to act fast because I'm due in two months with twins. If they turn out to be white, we'll keep them and tell everyone they're Joe's rather than name them after the whole basketball team that fathered them.'

She made a sour puss. 'Don't joke about tragedy, honey. You should never joke about your bread and butter. The Good Lord doesn't like it and neither do I. If any of that was true you could name your own price for the story and you know it.' She gulped and her eyes became moist at the thought of losing so much money that never was.

'Lolly, you're so right to remind me that we live beneath the sway of a benevolent deity. Why! Only this morning I had a terrible pain in the arse and the Lord, in his infinite mercy, gave me a greater pain in the neck to help me get my mind off it.'

I looked around. It was another of those endless Hollywood cocktail parties that are all surface gloss and peanut brittle bitchiness – like walking on broken glass – and I was, I guess, a little overtired and sad. I had made an effort to look my best lest my enemies carry away the news of my total collapse into frumphood. But there were somehow always too many competing bodies in Tinseltown. No one had looked up when I came in and, as dear Gloria used to say, every girl appreciates a big, warm hand on her entrance. I didn't do too well at glitzy places with all these heavy-breasted showgirls fluttering their eyelashes and gasping at the fascinating chatup lines of fat moguls. Some silly blonde girl was throwing herself into appreciating George Cukor's jokes, leaning backwards and giving him a faceful of hot cleavage at every guffaw. She must be new not to know George was a 'Twilight Gentleman' and as gay as a naval parade. A nice young waiter bent and replaced his empty glass with a full one, a twist of lemon and a twisted smile as George slipped a patting, fatherly hand on his pert backside and squeezed – one of Hollywood's less unpleasant forms of feeling the pinch. George enjoyed a certain immunity from Louella, being on her kiss-and-tell informants' list following an indiscretion with a sailor at the YMCA that went heavily unreported in all the newspapers some time before. Both their backs were well-scratched.

Louella scowled at the impiety, then her thoughts turned back to business. 'Of course, Manxi dear, if I could ever persuade you to open those tight, little lips of yours about your employer and name some of the names of his toasty teatime treats, it might be worth some folding money from me. But then maybe you're on that list too.' She appraised sharply over the infinity pool of her martini glass. Louella had a whole economy of scandal going – what a story was worth to the papers, what it was worth to a star *not* to publish it, what a small favour to a studio now might be worth in future returns when some erring lamb made it big. Her little, black book held the number of every studio exec. and bent cop in LA. Come to think of it, it was a *very big*, black book.

'Actually, Lolly, I'm writing a film script and I wondered ...'

Her whole face collapsed and she turned away in disgust. 'Oh, darling, who isn't?'

Outside by the fish-shaped pool, the new hottie, Mae West, had been poured into some tight, shiny sheath dress like a performing seal and excessorized with the sort of jewellery you might hang on a horse. She was in characteristic, narcissistic pose, patting her hair, other hand on hip, leg thrust out, surrounded by lapping gigolos and ogling some dark hunk of chuck steak in tight trunks, an English boy called Archie Leach, who had made a bit of a name in a bit part in a film called, oddly, *Singapore Sue*. They both looked overblown in every possible sense. Not surprisingly she snapped him up for her big hit *She Done Him Wrong*. From what I saw that night, omit the last word and you've got it right.

* * *

I didn't often go down Hollywood Boulevard, a place of flaking stucco and ravaged hookers even in broad daylight. Another prime feature was those medical practices where the doctor slipped you something that accidentally got rid of unscripted babies or where he was known to be usefully quick with the needle for those patients of a nervous disposition. Louella's own husband was a studio doctor specialising in much the same line with a little bit of celebrity clap on the side. I always wondered how that squared with a wife who dealt in celebrity claptrap professionally. They must have a 'no-talking-in-bed' rule. It was mid-1932 and I was feeling, as usual, a little depressed and hung over and a rare chill rain was blowing down from the hills, stirring up muddy dust and memories. Down on Hollywood is a friendly hair salon where a lot of the struggling actresses go to get a cheap makeover. In fact plenty of the girls who go there have given up struggling altogether and decided to just lie back and accept the inevitable but they do you a good Marcel wave which I always find lifts me like a Hollywood happy pill. And then, as I am passing an obscure film theatre on the way home, I see a poster for one of those odd, little movies that never make the main circuit, *Bali, The Last Paradise*. In RKO I am a pro in that off-piste area of the cinematographic art and I am intrigued. I buy a ticket and go in.

I suppose it's a silly film really – all love under the palm trees – but to those of us who have known real love under the palm trees and the jolly dancing of ripe coconuts, it's the only love there is. But the sheer beauty of the place and the people – both men and women wandering bare-chested and innocent as Adam and Eve – blow me away in that sleazy fleapit, full of coughing cigarette-smokers and saliva-slurping afternoon adulterers. The music, the dancing, the cascading streams carry me away to the place of my dreams. And then the penny drops. Bali. Bally! The ancient island home of poor, dear Ham and his ghost looms up again in the full, barbarous splendour of the Glasgow Tramway and Omnibus Company uniform of so many years ago and tears

served both colonial officials and tourists. I had never felt safer or freer and was enchanted by the politeness of everybody after the constant crude pushing and shoving of America as hustlers bellied up to the Hollywood trough. I have always appreciated politeness, the virtue that immediately makes you smile and say sorry when someone treads on your foot in a tram. Javanese had it in spades. Every night, I teased my palate with delicious, local delicacies, spiked with chilli and felt my soul expand as the moneybelt shrank. Even my taste buds were being spanked into new life. As in that movie back in LA, I once more gazed in wonder at the beauty of the jungles and mountains, the streams and valleys and the incredible comeliness of the natives, feeling myself bloated and clumsy in comparison. Wherever I felt the urge, I could just stop and paint. A large crowd always gathered round and I swiftly made friends with them as they stared in wonder at the vast, layered images I coaxed out onto a small, flat canvas. My imagination was fired. Yet here it was all for real and I had less a sense of novelty than one of finally coming home and my whole body tingled with excitement as I approached Banyuwangi and the narrow, storm-lashed straight that divided Java from Bali.

I pulled up at the harbour front, a ramshackle dockside of picturesque rocks, warehouses and a couple of leggy cranes. The thrum of the engine still echoed in my ears and warred with the gusting wind and the chatter of excited natives but soon I was haggling and bargaining over the sea crossing and found the street drama refreshing as I shamelessly simulated astonishment, outrage, womanly fear, attraction and disdain with a melodramatic range that would have cowed Clara Bow. The adoption of an actor's role seemed like a preparation for my new self, the first trying on of a new hat. The sailors laughed back at me but we agreed on a price that struck me as impossibly low. Perhaps I was being carried off by pirates into the white slave trade. But no. After a storm-tossed night, I and the car arrived in Gilimanuk and one of the crew helped me from the boat with the charming civility of an 18th-century marquis taking my hand for a minuet. As agreed, I crossed the palm of that hand with gold that it clutched to its heart. I would have to learn that, in the Indies, blue collars did not necessarily produce red necks. As Ma would say, I felt like Lady Muck from Turd Hill.

My drive across the island was another enchanted journey beneath the whispering palms but the magic faded as I approach Denpasar with its cheap Arab and Chinese shops, its crowds of overdressed Dutch and Eurasians and white walls stained with blood-red betel juice, damp and urine. It was as if the famous massacre of the Dutch invasion had just happened and the reddened walls cried out its lingering shame to the world. I shall *not* speak droolingly – yet again – about the bare breasts of the Balinese women. This will distinguish me from every other writer who has ever visited the island – mostly men, of course. Let me comment instead on the beautifully sculpted, bare chests of the local men who certainly had more to offer than Karl Pearson even after a few drinks on Thanksgiving.

I have only been staying at the Bali Hotel for a few days when the Dutch leeches begin circling. Can leeches circle? All right then, the sharks, in the form of the Assistant Controleur – all blue eyes and blond hair of which he is so enamoured that he constantly touches it with wonder just like Mae West. In his white ducks and gold epaulettes, he must be as catnip to the bored, local wives. First, he blusters, there are taxes and permits to be paid. I tell him I have already dealt with that in Batavia. Well then I must register as a foreigner. I must visit the office in person within three days or face deportation. What is it I am after in Bali? It is a common ploy of those who have no real work to do to go round demanding that others justify their existence. I learned that one from Joe Kennedy. I tell him I am an artist which enables him to pigeonhole me and soothes his frustrated administrative zeal. My proposal to go and live in a village is greeted with hilarity and condescension, which tells me it is something really worth doing.

Bali encourages a mystical frame of mind. The Balinese do not live in a random, statistical universe. Everything happens for a reason and fate governs all. I had seen those famous Balinese photographs from before the First World War, published to wide acclaim by the German doctor, Krause, of the innocently naked fauns and nymphs of the villages but then again I had also been to the New York nightclub called *The Sins of Bali* where it seemed these were pretty much the same as the sins of old New York. Now, I know photographers are simply morons who open a hole in a box and point it at someone yet they claim to be artists so I decided to simply drive out into the countryside to see reality for myself. Dr. Krause had worked for the Dutch in Bangli and that would be a good place to start.

I drive and the enchantment of the countryside enfolds me in a gossamer web spun from silver and gold. Time slows so that chickens seem to flash past in the honeyed air. I follow the signs to Bangli but it never seems to get any closer and I begin to fixate on the fuel gauge that shows empty. Finally, when I begin to think that I have a magic car that runs on air, the engine coughs and dies and I coast to a stop. A magnificent split gateway with spread wings beckons me up some steps. From within comes the gentle wail and tinkle of Balinese music. I set off towards it. A child encounters me at the top, screams and takes to his heels. A slightly older lad appears and gives a look, howls something and runs too. I pause and cough politely, clap my hands to attract attention.

Perhaps this is a forbidden place. Then a bent, old man peers round the corner, looking worried, gasps and takes off swiftly on knobbly legs. Finally, a beautiful young man with a fine, bold face and long, wavy hair, gloriously dressed in an iridescent, green and gold sarong – colours of a dragonfly – and a headdress teased up into a nodding flame, comes to the top of the steps and ... laughs at me.

'Do you know what they were saying? No? They said a demon was coming. Our demons all have red hair like yours. Proper human beings all have black hair. Please come in, lady demon.' He has a smile that lights up the whole courtyard with its ancient, mossy statues and fragrant flowers – the courtyard has them, I mean, not the smile. My first real encounter with Bali and it goes far better than I could ever have dreamed. This is Anak Agung Nura, handsome son of the Rajah of Bangli, a sweet and refined man who is to become the brother I never had. Educated in Holland and well travelled, he speaks English and will be my bridge into Balinese culture. I tell him my tale of running out of petrol, of being sent by fate, the gods, anything but that I had read Krause and come quite deliberately. To make it short – he introduces me to his father, a simply wonderful, gentle old man – an old gentleman. His father accepts my coming as a present from on high and I'm invited to join the court as a divinely bestowed gift. There is general rejoicing. I have a family. I am a princess, living in a glittering palace that looks down over the river where the locals come and bathe every evening in fairyland enchantment just as in Krause's photos. The next morning, after the servants have organised my bath and served my breakfast while crawling on their knees, I set up my easel and start to paint again! The Balinese are angels and make simply heavenly hosts.

That's my version and I'm sticking to it. Of course, I could tell a different story. I could say, I was put up in a guest house a bit like a garage, with cockroaches, and they charged me rent. I could say that I paid the rent in kind – or kindness. That's what the Dutch say. But then a Dutch woman would have been obliged to put down her riverside binoculars and start screeching in outrage about the naked bathers. All women will understand the delicious torment of sweaty, tossing sleeplessness, of wondering whether the Rudolph Valentino of their compulsive thoughts was coming or not, the hope that he would and yet the fear that he might. Then the faint, erotic whisper of bare feet and the rustled dropping of a sarong. Perhaps he came, we saw, I concurred. Perhaps.

I dyed my hair black, I learned Balinese and Malay and took to the Balinese sarong. I became a proper human being. In return I was comprehensively shunned by the Dutch who circled their wagons against me and spoke of race treachery. This troubled me not one iota. I spent my time with the Balinese and travelled all over the island with my new family, took part in all kinds of ceremonies straight out of a Hollywood movie and gained a deep knowledge and respect for Balinese ways. Finally, I am given my Balinese name in a special ceremony by a Brahman priest and become K'tut Tantri. K'tut means fourth-born, the rajah accepting me as his latest daughter and Tantri, the heroine of an ancient Balinese tale. I feel the whole of Bali has embraced me and I sink down gratefully into that warm embrace.

* * *

Much of my time in Bali was spent with Nura and his friends. Open-minded and politically advanced, they let me join in their discussions of the best route to a free Indonesia. The only Westerners that I was friends with were my fellow artists for

Bali hosted a community of progressive thinkers and brilliant intellectuals with whom I could feel at ease and who were as much the object of colonial disapproval as myself. There was Le Mayeur, a member of the Belgian royal family who married a beautiful, young Balinese dancer and painted her obsessively like Degas his tiny ballerinas. There was Theo Meier, a Swiss who became Balinese to the point of marrying two Balinese and having a child by each. And there were others, who just passed through, having drunk and refreshed themselves at the unpolluted well of Balinese nature. But above all there was Walter Spies, a German who had escaped from an oppressive Europe and installed himself in a fairyland setting by the river surrounded by his animals and admirers – surprisingly many of them female. I guess Walter was what would be called, in later times, a 'hag fag' since he adored adoring women. With his blonde hair, blue eyes and dancer's body he would have made a fitting model for one of the Führer's Aryan god statues but had declined that honour by just running away – a kindred spirit then. Walter and I were firm friends and met frequently, spending hours discussing together painting technique and art and enjoying the free play of our bubbling ideas as we stared down into the crystal water that flowed from the mountains and past his doorstep.

'It has always seemed to me, Walter, that painting and music are one. What was it Kandinsky said? "Colour is the keyboard, the eyes are the hammers, the soul is the piano with many strings. The artist is the hand which plays, touching one key or another, to cause vibrations in the soul."'

He made a soft farting noise, 'Pfui! Manxi. I had to listen to so much of that stuff back in Germany. Our eyes and our ears are stuffed up with big thoughts till we cannot see and hear and feel any more. That is what we come to Bali to unlearn. We must stop putting ourselves at the centre of everything and be what we were meant to be, just part of the enduring whole. Does this drink taste right to you?' We were sitting in the swimming pool that Barbara Hutton, the original 'poor, little rich girl' who owned Woolworth's, had excavated for him, and drinking his house cocktail, the Baboon's Arse, named from its glowing red colour that derived from a shot of grenadine to liven up the mix of whisky, tea and grapefruit.

'But surely, Walter, you as a musician must agree ...?'

'You know. I think the boys must have got the bottles muddled up again. They do that. Usually it's not dangerous as they stick to the bottles on the sideboard but once I put down a bottle of Collis-Browne's compound – you know the thing for diarrhoea with morphine in – and it got stirred in. It tasted simply heavenly and the immediate effect was terribly liberating but none of us went to the shithouse for a fortnight. We were as constipated as bicycle tubes.'

'But the notion of harmony in music surely must carry over ...'

'There was a bottle of paraffin by the back door this morning but it doesn't smell like that. It's sort of heady and perfumed.' He sniffed and frowned. 'I could ask them, I suppose, but it always gets so complicated when you have to explain this and that and the other ... and they are having so much fun in the water that it seems a shame to bother them.'

Two young men of Walter's staff were taking turns to leap off a high rock into a deep spot in the river below, turning somersaults in midair, screaming in delicious anticipation and disappearing into the water for what seemed an age before they burst back through the surface in a splashy explosion of joy. Domestic staff turns into pure geometry. They were simply lovely, coltish creatures of nature, slim, muscular, long, black, wavy hair and perfect teeth and so completely, almost tragically, happy and able to live wholly in the moment. Surely they were the way God intended Man to look and feel. I shut up about art.

Another figure slipped into the water beside us, blonde, body well-maintained, in the latest style of swimsuit, and bobbed up, smoothing back her hair. I never put my head under water. Ma convinced me that water leaks in through your ears and rots your brain. 'Hello, darlings.' It was Vicki Baum, Austrian author of *Grand Hotel*, the international bestseller, that had gone on to grace the stage around the world before becoming the movie that carried off the Academy Best Film Award of that year. She stared down at her arm and flexed it the way Westerners do when they suddenly discover they have bodies in a tropical climate. She had arms and shoulders like a basketball player and I remembered that she had practised boxing at the same Berlin gym as Garbo. That would have made a match you could sell tickets to. 'I hope you don't want to be alooone,' she cooed huskily, as if reading my mind.

'Was that line in the original book, Vicki? Or did the scriptwriter just stick it in?'

'Stick it in? In Garbo you mean? What? Oh, I see. Sorry darling I have a dirty mind. Oh, to tell you the truth, I couldn't tell you any more what's mine and what isn't. As you know, in the Hollywood writers' buildings a hundred other guys are borrowing your toothbrush and every sheet of toilet paper has been used at least twice over before by someone else. Anyway, it was poor, old Garbo that got stuck with the line. It saved her thinking one up for herself, I suppose.'

Walter grinned across. 'Actually, I remember her saying it was a running gag from her early silent pictures between her and a cameraman and then the studio decided to use it and play it up to make her into a woman of mystery rather than someone just tired of talking to fools. They say she has given up the movies and is collecting art. Is that true? She hasn't asked for one of mine.' He pouted and sulked.

'She's got some movie coming out soon – I forget what. You know she loves to work with George Cukor. They just adore each other – real soul sisters. But it's true she's gone big on art and bought a load of Renoirs and Bonnards and Kandinsky's and nailed them up all over the walls of her place. She said decorators were so expensive that it was cheaper in New York than having the walls repainted. Don't worry darling I'm sure she'll want something from you even if she has to build more walls.'

'Talking of Kandinsky and art ...' I said.

'Oh and you too, Manxi. Hey! Can I ask you, Walter? I've lost a great, big bottle of eau de cologne somewhere. I thought I left it on the sideboard last night after dabbing my fevered temples after dinner. Any idea where it could have gone?'

Walter lay back in the sunlight filtering through the tall bamboo and smiled lazily. 'Aha! Don't worry about it. It'll turn up. In time all mysteries sort themselves out. Unless of course the monkeys have got it, in which case it's gone for good. Why not have a drink? A great, big Baboon's Arse for you, darling? The boys have given its tail a new tweak.'

* * *

I sometimes accompanied visitors who wished to get to know my own Bali, quite different from the version they received from the Dutch hotels. From me they got dances, weaving, rituals – all in the actual villages. And it is on these travels around the island that I discover the fabulous beach of Kuta, a swathe of brilliant sand untouched even by fishermen and I know with the certainty of a Muslim hearing the call to Mecca that this is to be *my* place. The Dutch did not allow foreigners to buy land but the poor villagers were happy to lease it to me at a price I could not believe. It was just enough to pay the taxes that the Dutch squeezed out of them so I was happily able to free them of that burden. Of course, I realised that in opposing the Dutch I was still fighting the English shipyard owners of my Scottish childhood, Mr. Walker's exploitative curse of foreign capital turned on its head. There on that beach, one day, I planned to build my own hotel for discriminating guests of all races and religions and be free of my own. Artists would stay free of charge.

This happened sooner than I imagined. One day, I was showing the beach to a visiting Frenchman, a man of great exploitative foreign capital and telling him of my dream. 'Let us do it, Tantri,' he says simply. 'Let us do it together.' And so my hotel is born, the Bali Beach Hotel, with nothing but the finest craftsmanship, an Arabian Nights fantasy. I know all the greatest Balinese carvers and painters and hire them to construct a shimmering jewel that calls like a lighthouse to kindred spirits from afar. It has ancient doors of gold carving, is enbosomed in banana and palm groves and has a rough white, coral wall with inset statues and lamps that separate it from the beach of everybody's dreams. Inside, the staff are all accomplished dancers and weavers and artists. I quote, of course, from my own brochure.

But, while building a hotel may be a matter of taste and artistic flair, running one calls for other, meaner skills and the sort of low, commercial grind I have always abhorred. It is at this point that I fall foul of Bob Koke and his wife, Louise. My French patron has faded away as patrons always do and I am desperately short of money. Bob insinuates himself into my affections and finances by playing the Hollywood card. He claims to have worked on *Mutiny on the Bounty* on Catalina Island and be a friend of my old chum, Clark Gable, he surfs, he is a tennis coach, a master of all the gigolo arts. Before I know it, the Kokes have declared themselves my partners and – like cuckoos in my own nest – they start to elbow me out.

* * *

'Godammit Manxi you can't go on fighting with the Dutch like this!' Bob Koke, red in the face, slamming his fist into his hand, shaking with rage. Louise nodding over his shoulder with an I-told-you-so smirk on her fat face. I have just sent some Dutch packing, off to the rival Bali Hotel, for being rude to the staff who had laid out their clothes without putting on white gloves first. Balinese are the cleanest people on earth, like cats they are always washing. The gloves had nothing to do with actual dirt. They had everything to do with insulting the locals. This had been coming for a long time. The Kokes and I had argued over everything, the potato peelings in the kitchen, the amount of salt in the food – Asians like it salty and the chef dumped it in by the handful – Louise's taste in lampshades …

'Why shouldn't I fight with them? It is a matter of pride to me that I am banned from the Bali Hotel. Have you heard the stories they tell about me? They say I'm running a knocking shop for the Dutch airforce just up the beach. They accuse me of sleeping with any Balinese man they see me out with whereas I live the life of a nun. The closest I get to physical excitement is cutting my own toenails.'

'Yeah, well. Whatever … Frankly, Manxi, I don't care if

you're easier to make than a peanut butter sandwich. But that reminds me.' Bob looking at his wife's face for support. 'We seem to be having some problems with the accounts. These claims for mileage. Private shopping trips are not strictly deductible. And fees for tours should be paid to the hotel, not into your private account. You can't keep all the income and shuffle off all the expenses onto us.' Louise smirking over his shoulder again. God how I'd love to smack her in the kisser.

'The hotel is mine. The land is mine. The original idea was mine. You can scarcely expect to be regarded as my equals in the business.' Harsh words lead to more harsh words. Louise, the witch, pitches in. She has one of those droning, nagging voices that make you want to do anything just to stop her talking – marry her, kill her – anything. Things that should never be said are shouted out in front of astonished guests and staff.

I withdraw to my bungalow and weep to see the hotel, my lovechild, debauched and debased with Louise's bad taste and Bob's money-grubbing. The staff desert and come to live with me, providently bringing much of the linen and china, though I warn them that I have no money to pay their wages. I have no means left, no prospects, no hope.

Then, one morning, they are there, gathered together on my veranda and, laughing, they gently push towards me a cloth knotted at the top. 'For you, *nyonya*.' It is full of ancient, silver dollars, shining in the sun!

'But how ...? Why ...?'

They are in tears. I am in tears. 'We are simple farmers who have little and live by the rhythms of nature. We have mortgaged our ricefields with the Chinese. Now you have the money to build your dream without a partner. Everybody in Bali loves you, *nyonya*. Everyone has given. You are our mother and we your children. Everyone would lay down their lives for you, *nyonya*.'

And so it goes. We rebuild over the other side of the road in the staggered bungalow style of Walter Spies's hotel up in Campuan and my establishment slowly begins to flourish again with the crème de la crème of world society patronising our ballroom and dining rooms. Every night, they glow with fine silks and sparkling jewels but always in the heat of Dutch jealousy and hatred. We replant the garden thickly with banana and papaya and coax enchantment from the soil so that, after dark, little lamps wink among the greenery. But I'm damned if I'm giving up the name of my hotel to Bob and Louise, so now there are two Bali Beach Hotels side by side and not talking to each other, which I hope causes Bob and his bookkeepers a little more of that administrative difficulty.

Our greatest triumph is the visit of Lord and Lady Duff Cooper, the British plenipotentiary and his wife, the society beauty Lady Manners, on a tour of British installations in the East. They have booked to come to us but the Dutch will not have it. First the authorities try to hijack them at the airport in a fleet of limousines – all shiny and black like scrabbling cockroaches – to carry them off to the Residence. As they stand outside, bowing and grimly beard-wagging at the couple, their speeches of welcome grasped in their hands like undertakers presenting their bill, we draw up honking and laughing. We have decked out our old convertible with garlands of flowers and the prettiest girls and boys all waving and smiling. The Duff Coopers take one look and throw their luggage at us and we flee, giggling like naughty schoolchildren. The Bali Hotel, the 'official' Dutch hotel, pulls strings to try to stop the best Balinese musicians and dancers from coming to our establishment to entertain them, threatening to blacklist any who do. They laugh and come anyway. 'You, nyonya,' they say, 'are one of us.'

After the stuffiness of officialdom, the Duff Coopers were delighted with the elegant simplicity of our hotel, the beach, the bamboo bar, the fresh seafood lavishly served on a shell. We drank cocktails from half coconuts and listened to the crash of the surf on the flawless beach. Only the conversation was gloomy.

'The East is about to blow up, K'tut. Singapore is impregnable, of course, and the Japanese will not dare bypass it to get here but they will try and in their attempt some very bad things will happen.'

In thanks for the success of their visit, the Dutch Controleur then tries to deport me but I appeal over his head to the Governor General via the American consul, who is an art lover and a friend of mine. The order is rescinded. The local Dutch hate me still more.

Steadily and unstoppably, the war clouds gather and clot. Pearl Harbour. The Japanese invasion of Malaya. The fall of impregnable Singapore. Japanese forces spread like a great bloodstain over the map and pour down towards the Indies. Allied navies clash and gore at the Japanese advance and Western imperial pride goes down in a great gurgle of lost tonnage. The Dutch are a little less arrogant nowadays. Prince Nura is frantic with fear for me. He offers me marriage, as do many of the very highest aristocrats, anxious to make me safe. I tell them, 'I shall never marry except for love. I hold an American passport, an ally of Holland, the more outside enemies cluster around the safer I am. What could possibly happen to me here?' More to the point, there is always the problem of husband Karl, still in LA but still doggedly alive and dog-in-the–manger married to me.

Then, one morning, Bob Koke is there, banging on my door in his absurd, California leisure wear, pineapples swarming all over his back in garish colours, the first time he has ever set foot in my Bali Beach Hotel. 'I just got a message from the American Consul. All Americans should get the hell out and I guess you qualify. The Japs will be here in days.' He turns and strides away, crunching purposefully across the sand. The war will be good for people like Bob, lending them an importance they lack in everyday life. From over the road I can hear Louise wailing like an air raid siren. She always loved drama.

taken me down to the Dutch Controleur's old office in Denpasar and registered me as an adopted member of his family. I got a life-saving pass and a rising sun armband that kept me out of the prison camps, where most of the Dutch were to be penned up, and allowed me to move about. Many of the most arrogant members of Denpasar's white community had been at the office too, humbly queuing in the corridors and suddenly vaunting some obscure touch of the tarbrush that they would have fought tooth and nail to deny a week ago so they could be classed as Eurasian. We were all learning to be someone else in order to survive and we all bowed low – really low – to any passing Japanese soldier to show we accepted our new, lowly place in the order of things.

Nura and the other locals – soon to be Indonesians – are confused by the Japanese battlecry of 'Asia for the Asians!' Can the announced Greater East Asia Co-prosperity Sphere really mean the end of the hated Dutch occupation of their islands after hundreds of years? Are the Dutch East Indies really to become the single, free state so long dreamed about by a few scruffy intellectuals and religious madmen in Java? The ancient prophecies of the 12th century seer Joyoboyo are dusted off – that the Europeans would be driven out by a race of yellow dwarves from the north whose own rule would last for the time of just one maize crop before the day of the Ratu Adil – the Just Ruler – would finally dawn.

At first the Japanese were like kind, old uncles and sweet-faced nephews. They arrived more like policemen than an army. No rapes. No looting. In Bali not one shot was fired. They were all smiles and tousled the hair of blond children. Here they were smart navy men, anyway, not soldiers hardened by jungle combat. Then they began to turn the screw, turn after turn after turn, until the Indonesians realised that the Japanese were even more brutal than the Dutch in their exactions. They seized food, manufactures and demanded women for their brothels. Any resistance was met with death. Nura and his friends were disillusioned. They had long supported the principle of being free of the Dutch but never really agreed how this was to be brought about in those long and rambling conversations where we took the ideas of the day and discussed them far into the night. That I was privileged to listen in and offer my advice shows how far they had come towards accepting me as one of them and, as a Scot, my whole being resonated to our shared experience of being colonised persons. Yet there were bitter arguments even among the leaders of the independence struggle. On posters everywhere, Soekarno's sunlit face beamed down and urged the people to support the Japanese to win the fight against the Dutch and thousands of ardent, young volunteers, *romusha*, were shipped off to work for them in the forests and swamps of Burma, building railways and such. We see their happy faces and pumping fists in the newsreels as they leave but none ever come back.

In the newspapers, Hatta, the intellectual of the group, carried his ventriloquist-dummy grin and sweaty brow from rally to rally and meeting to meeting while Sutan Sjahrir went underground and joined the anti-Japanese resistance. It is he who becomes our inspiration and makes us realise that soft words are all very well but we need arms to make sure the Just Ruler doesn't turn up to find us empty-handed. Which is why I am in Java, flaunting my pass and my armband in a borrowed Buick and trying to get travel permits. The idea was to establish a travelling group of Balinese dancers that would freely tour Java to entertain the Japanese and also transport arms and information behind their backs while making a little money on the side. People in Bali were starving with the exactions of the occupying forces. I had to force myself to play the part of a good-time girl, mixing and flirting with Japanese in all the smartest clubs though secretly I hated them for what they were doing to Bali. Even my beautiful hotel had been levelled to the ground.

The officer came out to the car and clicked his fingers to a soldier, dressed in the usual flour-sack uniform, to open the trunk. There was the box – books on top all right but the real stuff – grenades, small arms, dynamite – underneath. He flicked disdainfully through the titles. Books on Japanese art, history, culture, the photo of the weedy emperor on horseback – an amulet lovingly propped upright with a flower at its feet and not lightly to be just grabbed and displaced. He pouted approvingly, saluted, nodded to the flour-sack who slammed the trunk shut and stalked away. I started to breathe again. I slid behind the wheel, shaking, barely able to see, the whole world spinning and was a hundred yards down the road towards far Banyuwangi and the wild sea-crossing back to Bali before I realised where I was and what I was doing and my own unruly feelings overwhelmed me. I pulled in by the roadside and burst into quivering tears.

* * *

I made other trips. It all became routine. The guards at the roadblocks came to know me, waved me through, even smiled and I slipped into sloppy habits. One night, as I was preparing for bed in Surabaya, there came a hammering at the door. It was of course the Kempeitai, the feared Japanese secret police that even their own people were scared of, checking up on guest houses. The sloppy habit I am in at that late hour is a thin nightgown. At first, their visit seemed fairly routine. They went in for the usual business of slaps and insults and upending suitcases on the floor and trampling the precious contents, laughing, under their boots – the silly, schoolboy stuff you expect from all armies of occupation. And then one of them sneeringly lifted up my nightie in gratuitous humiliation and they all froze. At first I took it as a compliment, then grabbed the hem back and pushed it back down but it was all too late. Carroty pubic hair is an undyed, red flag to them. Sloppy, as I said. The dark glasses were knocked from my nose to reveal even more incriminating blue eyes. My cover as an Indo-Balinese was blown. A more thorough search revealed the concealed American passport afforded by my marriage to Karl Pearson, stupidly tucked inside the pillowcase. Even out here, Karl is still giving me grief. I was beaten to the ground, dragged outside to a car and whisked off to headquarters as an American spy. Kempeitai headquarters was a terrifying, blank-faced building that people didn't even pass without crossing over the other side of the street. I never saw anyone walk into that place. I never saw anyone simply riding there in a car. More to the point, no one ever walked out either. They always had to be, in some sense, just an unconscious body being dragged. As a fancy, foreign spy they clapped me up for two days in a deluxe cell like an oven with bare concrete walls and an iron door before they moved me to an economy semi-detached of rusty bars with a woman who screamed all night at the demons in her own mind.

From that day on, I woke every morning with the wish for death. This is no melodramatic exaggeration. The return of consciousness brought me nothing but despair. I lay naked on a scrap of filthy matting and felt vermin crawling over my body in the dark. At dawn, inasmuch as we ever saw dawn, a dollop of foul slop was thrown at me on a banana leaf and then I cowered and waited for the inevitable sound of approaching feet and the jangle of keys. Yet, every day, I still hoped that today at least they would not come. If I was on the floor they kicked me to my feet. If I was on my feet they beat me to the ground. Then I was dragged to the interrogation room and it was always the same questions. 'Who are you? What is your mission? Who are your contacts?' Questions I could not answer so each one was followed by a punch, first to one side of the face, then to the other. I found it oddly upsetting when my torturer lost the rhythm and got the order wrong. The world made that much less sense. When I finally blacked out, they threw water over me and then they started again. 'Who are you? What is your mission? Who are your contacts?'

With their rifle butts, they drove me naked across the town square, paraded me in front of jeering troops, hoping to break my spirit but my body no longer belonged to me. It was outside me, a separate thing, something out there. They could do anything with it that they wished. On one wonderful day, they told me I was to be shot and I was hauled to a yard with big, high walls topped with barbed wire and tied to a bullet-chewed post and blindfolded. There followed the sound of troops being shuffled into a line in the dust and the purposeful click of shells being loaded into rifles. 'Take aim! Fire!' There came the crash of gunfire and an enormous force thudded into my chest and then I was floating, floating, finally free. So there is life after death! Joy, liberation. The Wee Free Kirk was right! Who on earth would have thought it? In that moment I understood that fear of death is simply fear of losing the story in our heads that is ourselves, it is fear of losing the end of that story. And then the grinning officer was there, tearing off the blindfold, holding the rock he had just hurled into my chest and they were all leaning on their rifles and laughing. And I felt no relief to be still alive, just the greatest possible disappointment. I wept as they dragged me back to the interrogation room and 'Who are you? What is your mission?

Who are your contacts?' And then, one day, they turned me loose.

* * *

My reprieve was short-lived. Perhaps it was a deliberate, vicious tactic to make me think the agony was over just so they could renew it. There is nothing crueller than hope. After two days, the Kempeitai returned in their costume of trench coats and felt hats. I was bundled into the back of a car with two agents suffering from a fishy halitosis of such monumental pungency that it momentarily dispelled my fear. This time, it is the Ambarawa concentration camp in Central Java where some 24,000 white women are kept. But, oddly, they didn't put me in with the others. Instead, I was kept in a cell completely on my own, totally bare except for a sleeping mat, and with bars high up to allow in a little light and air. So not a single person knew I was there. At first, it was horribly lonely but, quite frankly, I could do without the kind of human company I had been enjoying recently and it offered me a wonderful sense of peace to try to knit together my shattered body and spirit. A trustie brought me rice and gruel and water once a day. I tried desperately to engage her in conversation, anything that would confirm our common humanity. She opened her mouth to show a gaping, scarred hole and the absence of a tongue. She was mute. The Japanese had ripped it out. There would be no small talk.

I entered a world of silence. There were no visitors, no interrogations. I felt like a file that had been misplaced and forgotten. I watched the *cicak* lizards hunting bluebottles. One night, the cell was invaded by fireflies that danced and turned like wayward fireworks. The next night they were replaced by squadrons of mosquitoes that dive-bombed throughout the hours of darkness. In daylight, there was a little square of blue sky that could just be seen from high in one corner, like the sea view of a cheap boarding house. Prisoners are always supposed to be obsessed with recording the passage of time. I surrendered to it blindly. I have no idea how long they kept me there. Waking and sleeping blended into one as when, back in Glasgow, mothers would quieten fractious children by slipping the gas ring under their blankets and turning it on for a couple of minutes. After a while, the silence, the lack of food and stimulation, released me from my own body. I felt myself begin to float once more. I knew that one day soon I would float away like a helium balloon and never return.

My salvation is a pack of cards. Their creation is a work of absolute genius. I unpick some bands of dried leaf from my sleeping mat and snap them into squares, make paint of ground red tile from the floor and white plaster from the wall, create black from a scrap of charcoal and paint my own playing cards. I play patience, recreate games of bridge from the past and rejoin the rich and elegant people with whom I played in the long, velvet evenings of Bali. I hear again the crash of the swirling surf on Kuta beach and the tinkle of civilised laughter over drinks. I read my own future in the cards, the interplay of fate and design, purpose and randomness, whirling me away. I laugh when they tell me I should prepare for possible bad changes in my circumstances.

And then the Kempeitai came back. It was the usual routine of beatings, insults but, by now, I was inured to pain. I stared at my feet and refused to speak or even cry out in agony. Sometimes, as their most famous prisoner, they dressed me up and painted my face and made me pose with Japanese officers, forcing me to smile in some ghastly caricature of social life. I knew they would use the pictures to try to convince my friends that I was collaborating and so persuade them to confess in turn. What could I do? I tried to look as unhappy and unattractive as possible but they knew what I was doing. More clever than the rest, one of them drove me one night to a pretty little villa with a beautiful bathroom and locked me in with a wonderful bath filled with scented oils and the sound of Rachmaninov pulsing through the wall. I knew that if I refused, they would throw me in and scrub me against my will. Food, I could reject but the thought of immersing my tired and tortured body in clean, healing water was more than I could withstand. As I lay cossetted by silky warmth, the aches, the pain, flowed out of me and I dissolved in tears in the bathtub, silently asking the forgiveness of my comrades. I became one of Charles Kingsley's water babies. I dried myself in a cool, fluffy towel as soft moonlight streamed through the window and I thought of all the scenes in art and music – Anthony and Cleopatra, Romeo and Juliet, Rosalka – where parted lovers gazed at the moon and thought of how it was the same moon that their loved ones were staring at – and so they were brought together.

The thought and recalled sensation of that bath might have strengthened me through the weeks that followed but it had done something terrible to my brain and also restored to me the sense of having a body at all so that the kickings and beatings suddenly had a renewed power I thought had gone for ever.

And then something changes. It is like the first stirrings of the spring thaw in the new year, a strange sensation in the air, a surreptitious crackling spreading through the ice underfoot, an awareness of motion and unfreezing. Suddenly the endlessly trumpeted series of Japanese victories is no more. The faces of the officers register unusual emotions – doubt, worry, fear – and they are less harsh, less ready with the boot and the fist. The food improves. I am allowed exercise. One day, as I walk in the dusty yard outside my cell, I hear the sound of a prisoner in the neighbouring compound softly singing some old, Dutch song, carried away in it, gently humming those bits where she has forgotten the words. Normally, any such sign of simple, human joy would be a provocation that the guards would slash to the ground with bamboo clubs. Now one of them taps his fingers against the wall in time to the song and looks the other way. The hair on my neck stands on end. And there are conversations with other prisoners exchanged in rasping whispers. We have all heard crazy rumours before and had our hopes dashed and cannot believe what we are hearing now. This is surely the craziest of all. The war is already over! There is a magical, new weapon that turns people to dust and the Japanese have surrendered to it. Their army is just waiting to be shovelled away by the victorious Allies. Can it possibly be true? What of their threat that in defeat they will kill all prisoners and then themselves?

One cold, stiff morning, I awake to a strange howling on the wind and gunfire. My first thought is that the feared massacre of prisoners has started and I sit quietly in one corner with my hands in my lap and wait with calm resolve for the end. There is a crashing of iron on iron at the far end of the corridor as the door is flung open, the sound of my approaching executioners' boots coming to take me. And then the key turns in the lock and it is not a pinched Japanese face that looks in at me but a beautiful Indonesian one with wide, brown eyes, all smiles.

'Si K'tut? I have been sent for you. *Merdeka*! Freedom!' Other young men crowd in, shouldering guns, laughing, waving fists in the air. I am carried on their joyous, strong shoulders out to liberty and into the sunshine, dazzled like a pit pony brought up from the mines. The war is over. My life has begun again!

Chapter Five

The kaleidoscope has been given another twist, rearranging the same, familiar pieces into strange and unfamiliar patterns. The Surabaya docks swarm with Japanese, but no longer proud conquerors. Japanese arrogance has collapsed like a badly made soufflé and been blown away by an atom bomb. Now they are reduced to being Asian coolies, crouched shivering in the rain, stripped to ragged *fundoshi* loincloths and odd, squelching, rubber boots that have a separate big toe, hissing like polite geese and hauling the luggage of white faces off and on the ships that are coming in from Singapore and the wider world. To someone, somewhere, they must be a fetishist's wet dream. Surabaya is one great waiting room. Westerners with fresh uniforms and plump, pink faces, are waiting to get in, other Westerners from the camps – mere yellow-skinned bags of bones – are waiting to get out, and everyone is waiting for some clear pattern to emerge from the dust and rain and heat haze. Drooling, toothless mouths to feed, bemerded backsides to wipe and clean, the world is reduced to its Marxist fundamentals. And everywhere is the rubble of the war, gutted factories, once-trim villas with tarpaulins for roofs and walls daubed with a red hand, gripping a wavy dagger dripping with blood and that single word *Merdeka*, 'freedom,' that is to be the solution to everything. And the sign is everywhere.

The new Republic of Indonesia is independent – in name at least. Soekarno, the collaborator with the Japs, the hero, the heretic, the apostate, the betrayer and defender of the people has been forced by enthusiastic students to hop off the fence and read the fatal words of the Freedom Proclamation and now that he has been acclaimed President there is no stuffing the genie back in the bottle. The date 17th August 1945 will never be the same again. In the British Consul-General's former villa in far Batavia – renamed Jakarta – as Rear Admiral Tadashi snores in cherry blossom, Japanese dreams upstairs, downstairs they haggle over who is to sign the Proclamation of Independence and what it should actually say. Other Japanese are against the act and so it has to be done in public – but secretly – like something carried out in a public lavatory. After all, just two days before, in Tokyo, the army attempted a coup to stop another radio broadcast from the Emperor, so that his surrender had to be smuggled out of the palace on a gramophone record in a laundry basket like a royal bastard child. The solution to the conundrum is obvious. An outside broadcast. The nimble technicians from the Batavia – sorry now Jakarta – *Hoso Kyoko* radio station have set up the microphone. The new flag of the nation – the old flag of the Javanese Majapahit empire – proud red and white – is unfurled. The passage from Netherlands to Indonesian rule can now be neatly and economically marked all over the archipelago by simply ripping off the third blue strip of the Dutch flag – a most parsimonious proceeding that one might have otherwise expected to find favour in provident, Dutch eyes. The intellectual Hatta stands beside wavering Soekarno. And behind stands sharp-eyed Adam Malik, ever watchful lest the other, slippery pair slide away again leaving the fateful deed still undone.

In Surabaya, the Pemuda young bloods are thrilled. Only in the young does hope ever really completely triumph over fear. 'K'tut, this has to go out to the world or they will try to hush it up. Can you translate the Proclamation into American and read it out over the radio? We need you, K'tut. You must be our voice to the world.'

I shrug. I am staying in an exploded Dutch house with a bunch of students, surrounded by jettisoned Japanese military hardware and only gradually getting used again to human kindness. Like real food to a starving body, it can overwhelm you, make you worse, I think you can even be killed with sudden kindness. I am walking in a dream as if permanently stunned. Boxes of grenades are stacked against one wall, rifles against another but all good Javanese boys dream of tanks. Someone, at some stage, has fired a mortar through the roof. Dutch? Japanese? British? No one knows. Violence is random. Poignant reminders of gentility haunt the building – shattered paintings, a headless cherub and the vast garden is a tangle of roses run wild. The students and freedom fighters who inhabit the building have planted yams among them and stocked the weed-filled pond with strictly practical fish, the garden become a battleground between native, economic necessity and foreign self-indulgence. My white face is now a military asset again, a passport that allows me access to places that my local friends cannot visit. I carry messages, count ships, pick up gossip in the bars and pass it on to my contacts in the Pemuda. On the other hand, I can no longer wander at will and alone in the outer suburbs. Something has changed. There, my white face would lead me to be spat upon, even attacked. It is all out in the open now.

The British are here. Since the Dutch are in no position to take back their eastern empire, they have tricked the British into doing it for them. Officially, they are simply here to maintain social order and free the internees and arrange for their safe transport back to so-called civilisation but their relations with the Pemuda are just short of open hostility since both sides know they are merely keeping a place warm for the Dutch to slip their fat backsides into again. Apparently the British Commander in Chief told the head of the operation, 'We don't have the forces for anything but a gentle occupation. It's pussyfooting, old man, and you're the pussy.' Their position isn't helped by the fact that they are being boycotted by the local Dutch who reproach them for not launching an open attack on the rebels. Yet the Dutch burghers are clear which side their bread is buttered on. Wits among them have replaced their 'Beware of the Dog' signs with 'Beware of the Ghurka.' As for the Brits, the poor ninnies were told to expect their foremost problem to be the damping down of the wild enthusiasm of the Indonesians at having the Dutch back, that they would snuggle under the Dutch flag as a tricolore treat – but then the Brits also always blindly insisted that – deep down – the Indians *really* loved them too. No one seemed to realise that, with the sudden, official outbreak of peace, the real war would not end but be displaced, have to go somewhere else and be internalised.

Meanwhile the young freedom fighters rage in frustration against a cautious, older generation who fight with pieces of paper and votes in unrecognised forums but a lot of their own conflict is carried out in slogans and flags. The Japanese refuse to haul theirs down, the Indonesians rip down that of the Dutch, the Brits modestly fly theirs in miniature form, on the front of their trucks as if to pretend that is all the territory they claim for themselves and every night heroes from all sides switch the flags around on the public buildings and trip over each other in nasty, little firefights. In technologically sophisticated Jakarta, the students boobytrap the flagpoles by electrifying them but it is my country boys who overrun the fancy Hotel Yamato and join in a pitched battle with Dutchmen and the Japanese guards who are trying to change the sign back to 'Hotel Oranje' under a flagpole where the hated symbol of oppression has been raised once more. In the scrap that follows, any kind of weapon will serve. One man does great damage with a well-used bicycle, spontaneously dismantling it and converting each part into an implement of offence. One of the lither boys climbs up, gripping the pole with his hands and shreds the blue strip from the Dutch flag with his teeth – a fine image of patriotic hatred. Some describe the Dutchmen as wearing dinner jackets and being well-oiled on Bols which makes attacking them an act of worker solidarity as well. According to others they are just a bunch of hysterical Dutch kids fresh back from the camps, an experience that has understandably shortened their tempers. Of course, many thousands of the Dutch were never in the camps at all, being members of the pro-Nazi NSB but after the war, they and all official mention of them evaporate into thin air and everyone becomes a free-Dutch patriot who spent the war singing the popular song, 'We are not afraid'. In revenge for the hotel incident, shortly afterwards, pro-Dutch Eurasians hideously murder a harmless Chinese hairdresser in silk pyjamas for flaunting a politically ambiguous red and white barber's pole outside his shophouse.

Lanky Lukman walks around the garden in his Japanese-style uniform, shaking, puffing cigarettes, still high on Oranje adrenalin, with blood left proudly on his face – actually his own – someone has accidentally elbowed him in the nose. He usually spends most of his time fighting the good fight with a screwdriver, unblocking wireless sets that the Japanese had fixed so they could only pick up their own stations. 'The old men in Jakarta just talk and give away everything we have gained by fighting. They want the Dutch to still be their friends and tell us to sit on our hands. Well we won't. You can never have too many enemies, K'tut. They help you know who you are. Love may lie. Enmity never does.'

Gentle Reza disagrees, pouting like one of the practical fish. 'The future of the revolution is to bring people together. For example, there is no conflict between Islam ...' He plucks a white rose. 'And socialism.' He plucks a red, holds them together and offers them to me blushingly like the corsage a boy gives to a girl before her first prom. There is great tenderness in the way he touches the flowers. He is the principal planter of yams. 'The imams have declared this a holy war. Most of the boys here are from Islamic schools. I was at an agricultural school.' Red and white roses. Hadn't I done all this in my own education? Part of English history? The Wars of the Roses. Had that ended well? I couldn't remember but I rather doubted it. But it was all very Indonesian. The arrival of a new belief – Hinduism, Buddhism, Islam, Christianity, Socialism – did not entail the jettisoning of the old that it conflicted with. You just added another layer and ignored the contradictions as part of the rich tapestry of life.

Then little Uki with the soft brown eyes that would melt any heart speaks up. 'We need you, K'tut. You must be our voice to the world. Tell them in English about our Proclamation of Independence. On the radio.'

I look at those shining, happy faces and feel a greater love than I have ever known, maternal, self-sacrificing but tinged with a sad awareness of its own, inevitable evanescence. In my life I have often had to fight against my better instincts. I tell myself that experience of the world will soon snuff out that wonderful innocence of theirs in a few short weeks, but for the moment let them enjoy being young. With a unique wisdom, words for 'love' in Indonesian are based on roots of 'pity' and 'compassion' and I have always found it hard to fall in love with abstract nouns, for me they have to become people I meet before I can really commit to them. These three hopefuls *are* freedom. Side by side they look like a series of fine wood samples my husband Karl kept nailed to the wall of his workshop – glowing mahogany, delicate rosewood and smoky, burred walnut. It is odd that war, that engenders violence, hatred and inhumanity, also gives birth to so much compassion, love and self-sacrifice.

We set off in an old Panhard, once some Dutch burgher's pride and joy but now a smoky wreck with rustholes in the floor and a cracked windscreen. There can be nothing sadder than a patched whitewall tyre with its mixture of pretension and confessed poverty, like a doilie on a tin plate. The British have established a strong, defensive perimeter around the centre of Surabaya, centred on Rembrandt Square, using the Indian army – all mugs of *chai* and big, tombstone teeth – whose black skins and hairiness scare the Javanese but it seems we are not heading that way and lurch away from the city through a blasted landscape of flattened huts and pools of industrial waste. The Japanese radio studio in the city is not our goal then but an abandoned cement factory that boils with mosquitoes even at midday. We round the corner of some sort of silo and there is a Japanese truck like a huge steel box, bristling with aerials and covered with cement dust for camouflage and with great holes where something like tracer fire has passed clean through it. For some reason, they are known as 'banzai boxes'. If it had been a chest of drawers, my husband, Karl, would have described it as 'well loved'. It is the work of a few minutes to hydraulically raise the main aerial and crank up the generator. As the boys grin their encouragement and light each other's celebratory cigarettes, a young Madurese Marconi technician slaps a pair of headphones over my ears and I am live, on air – walking on air – speaking to the world, the first-ever English-language broadcast of Rebel Radio Indonesia.

'We the Indonesian people hereby declare the independence of Indonesia …' Not much to the Independence Proclamation really. Sjahrir – soon to be Prime Minister – had written something much fancier that the others had hacked to pieces. Reviewers are hell. Certainly not a lot to show for a whole night's wrangling and rewriting. Just a couple of lines more about the rest being sorted out as and when and then that's it. Nowadays it sounds all a bit slapdash. Typical politics, I suppose. A brave, sweeping declaration followed by a load of vague mumbled ifs and buts that can't be pinned down and so make it unenforceable.

We can't leave it like that of course. I think of what the boys have just been saying in the garden with blood on their faces and roses in their hands so I have to make up some sort of speech about the glorious struggle that is to come and the two colours of our new flag symbolising just about anything you care to hold dear – earth and sky, martyrs' blood and innocence, socialism and Islam, body and soul, female and male, some stuff I half remember about Diponegoro fighting under red and white of the old Majapahit Empire during the Java War that so nearly chased the Dutch out in the last century. I'm not sure whether it's true and Diponegoro was a religious lunatic anyway that any decent Indonesian government would end up shooting but it sounds good so I mix it all in any old how, my audience are hardly going to rush off and look up the references in a library. I have always been the sort of cook who just throws everything into a pot and stirs, hoping a handful of chilli will cover up the cracks. I confess, I get a little carried away. But my muddled news bulletin is a great success. It seems that clarity of thought is not required in this job, being a terrible obstacle to both oratory and to patriotism.

At the end of it, the boys hug me and fist the air, exuding the sweet-tea odour of Asian sweat. A wrinkled old woman dressed

same three wizened biscuits from the 'banzai-box'. He ignores them, crossing his legs vampishly and letting his clove cigarette curl lavishly away in smoke. I have not allowed for the club's change in circumstances – seized by Pemuda with the Dutch all chased away – and am overdressed in my one good frock. Western dress always makes me look out of proportion. I should have worn my batik sarong. I look him over and slip off my earrings.

He bears a handgun glamorously strapped on his hip, creaking with shiny leather and has the long, untamed hair that is the mark of the young 'extremists'. Many have vowed not to cut it until Indonesia is free, a further blow to those poor barbers with red and white poles that have been victims of the Eurasian 'dogs of the Dutch' as they are called in Soetomo's fiery speeches. Lukman has told me that is part of his being a *jago*, a village 'cockerel' with superhuman strength and magical powers. Lukman goes misty-eyed whenever he talks of Soetomo. He gets a lump in his throat and maybe in his trousers. But the *jago* is just a stage presence. In person, Soetomo is no wild man, rather shy and with the smile of a choirboy, forever pushing or tossing his wind-blown hair out of his eyes. They call him Bung Tomo, 'big brother Tomo', but he is more 'little brother' being only 25 years old and sparely built but then many of his forces are literally schoolboys – or would be if they were ever allowed to go to school by the colonists. He has eyes that burn like hot coals and a mouth made for kissing babies, the sort that reunites, in women, their two strongest urges, that to breastfeed and that to have sex. He is simply beautiful despite the scraggy beard that so contrasts with the small, almost girlish features. What a shame that being a *jago* involves forswearing all sexual contact with women! But then, perhaps it is as well. Men always reduce all the different kinds of love to mere grunting, ferrety sex so that they all quickly come to the same sticky end.

'Sister K'tut, I have heard your talk,' he says, 'on my Rebel Radio. I could not follow all of it. What, for example is an *eejit*? But I especially liked the bit about Diponegoro. You know I am a descendant of his?' He preens briefly. 'It is from him I have my powers. You are a fellow artist, a true orator, and I admire you. Thank you for bringing the news of our freedom to the world. From Surabaya it has echoed around the islands and the planet. They have staged Proclamations in all the major cities.'

'I'm not a dog of the Dutch then?'

He laughs, waves the suggestion away in clove-scented smoke. 'Nooo. You are a tiger of the Indonesian people. You know that in the old days, the kings organised fights between tigers and buffaloes for entertainment. The tigers were supposed to be the Dutch and the buffaloes our own people. Tigers were fierce and cunning and had great claws but buffaloes were strong and patient and waited till the tiger had worn himself out with its roaring and clawing before impaling it on those great horns and stamping it to death. The buffalo *always* won in the end. All those *eejits* who were so keen to be of mixed blood when the Japanese arrived and dodge the camps are now of pure, Dutch blood again and some of that blood will have to be spilt to purge our land of lies and betrayal. The mist of resistance has condensed into solid form. Ours will not be a freedom won under a full moon and in the perfume of roses and jasmine. It will not be won around a polished conference table in a palace but over a Dutch butcher's block. And there will be accounts to settle with the Timorese and Ambonese who have thrown their lot in with the Dutch.'

A truck rumbles past, bearing cheering adolescents with raised fists and bamboo spears, boys simply enjoying smashing things up. I remember only too well the pleasures of the Glasgow tram riots and the ghost of Ham swims fleetingly into view. The air around them boils with a sweaty haze of cocked testosterone that could take fire at any minute. Bung Tomo smiles and waves back, looks embarrassed at his own celebrity. The gleaming, white walls of the club building are a provocation to youth and they have been daubing them with slogans in the red paint that they have all over their hands and clothes for lack of accessible, Dutch or collaborators' blood. A dusty banner across the entrance reads, more demurely, 'Once and forever the Indonesian Republic' like a Californian advertisement for diamond engagement rings. From round the back, come screams of laughter from the men washing in the river, splashing each other and joining in rough boys' games. Bung Tomo looks wistfully in that direction then turns back to me. He wants to go out and play.

'I want you to work with us, to go on the radio. Women are as just as good revolutionaries as men. The whores and pimps on the docks are already all loyal workers for the revolution, luring the troops away from duty, so why not you?' He laughs.

'You mean, in the revolutionary struggle, women are just men with knobs on – or rather off?' Many of the dockside whores were really men anyway – that fine old, Asian tradition of transvestism.

'What? Perhaps. Now we have access to new, shortwave equipment, we can reach far out. It is not like the old days in Jakarta. There they only had a rickety old transmitter hidden round the back of the hospital mortuary and used the stink of the corpses to keep the Dutch away. Even in death the patriots fought on over the air for the cause. But it took a week before some of the outer islands and the British Parliament knew of the Proclamation. The Dutch can use such delays against us. Moreover, the British and the Indians are in our city and we must divide them, weaken them, get them out. Many of them do not want to be here at all. The Indians are throwing the British out of India and everyone is tired and wants to go home. You speak their language. You will know what to say.'

'Bung. All my life I have been the friend of oppressed peoples. It would be an honour. The British cannot win. They are like men trying to sweep up leaves in a gale.'

'I like that. I will use it. The old men like Soekarno and Hatta say it is unreasonable for a mob like us to fight an organised army but the Japanese taught us that reason is a Western idea not an Asian one. More important is spirit. The Japanese had it and now we have it too.' He pushed something across the table. 'You had better wear this. It may save your life.' It was another armband, this time red and white and bearing the words, '*Merdeka atau mati*', 'Liberty or death'. As employment contracts go, it left a lot to be desired. 'It's from the same factory that used to make armbands for the Japanese. As we speak, we are moving against them and taking over their installations and stores. By the end of the day, we will have tanks!' His bright, young face glows with excitement. There it is again. Every growing boy wants to have his own tank. 'You must excuse me. I have to go and see Moestopo.' His pained face is eloquent. Moestopo is the former dentist now in charge of the Japanese-trained regular forces. Moestopo was said to like the idea of inflicting pain, a professional hazard perhaps. He teaches the militias to dip the tips of their spears into horse dung to create infected wounds and to eat cats so they can see at night – a visionary of sorts then. As well as pimps and whores and schoolboys, cats too can be heroes of the revolution and the uneaten parts receive honourable burial. Why shouldn't I join them? What else had I to do?

I move into the Oranje hotel and keep my ears open, cat-like. At the very least I steal copies of foreign or divisional newspapers and scan them for information to be used on the air.

The strange sort of truce that was brokered between the British and the local Pemuda after the flag incident – by no less than Soekarno and Hatta themselves – is still just about holding but every night is punctuated by gunshots and the reverberation of distant explosions. By agreement, the Japanese guard has been replaced by a tense Indonesian one. He has been tipped off. When I walk past he winks in a most obvious manner that the whites see – fortunately – as the sort of impertinent, sexual harassment they are protecting their own women from.

At the bar is mostly a mix of Dutch and Americans, the former from the camps, the latter from various newspapers – the Antara news agency is just across the street and newsmen are lazy but ever-thirsty creatures. That is almost certainly why the flag incident was blown up into an iconic event to mark the start of the fighting. If they'd had to walk to the end of the street to see it, it would have gone unnoticed. With the first I flaunt my Japanese scars and with the second my American accent. They relax around me and flap their mouths loosely over Skat and poker.

The Dutch rage against the British for not attacking the rebels so they can go back to their whitewashed lives of polite lawns and neatly trimmed servants but if you listen carefully it is clear that even those that have survived as married couples know there is no going back. Relationships have shrivelled and died, feelings become numbed by all that has happened under the Japanese. Everywhere life has become a temporary expedient, stripped of all sense of permanence, and everyone is just getting by. One evening, an American chain-smoker with an economics degree drops the information that the amount they give the Dutch in Marshal Aid exactly balances what they are spending to recoup their colonies. The land of the free is paying to hold the East in subjection. The fact sticks in my mind. I file it away. That will come in use much later.

'It is nothing but a few hotheads,' one Harlem banker maintains cigar-puffing. 'The Javanese are like children, easily led astray by a few bad apples. But they soon smarten up their ideas when the headmaster cracks his cane.'

Van Mook, the Dutch governor had said much the same thing. In fact, he said all sorts of dumb things about how the Indonesians were 'too nice' to fight him. And when he stumbled off the boat from Australia at Batavia – sorry Jakarta now – without his glasses, he saw the crowds holding up banners and was touched by such a warm welcome. 'What do they say?' he asked tearfully.

'Death to Van Mook, Your Excellency,' came the answer.

That night at a rally at the Simpang Club I see these 'few hotheads'. I slip away from the Oranje and rendezvous with Uki and Lukman who drive me there. The gardens are lit up with a thousand blazing, resin torches. The Japanese blackout is ignored. The speech will be carried echoing out into the streets on the loudspeakers they set up through the city to spread their own propaganda. The torchlights gleam on a vast, bobbing sea of shiny brown skin, white teeth, flashing eyes, excitement radiates out from their faces, happiness. How many thousands more tailing away into the darkness? I cannot tell. Perhaps it is the whole of Indonesia here this night feeling their essential humanity restored. Uki and Lukman sandwich me on either side as we ease into that hot, human maelstrom and I feel myself gripped by its tides and eddies and sucked into the swaying rhythm of that great, primeval force, a part of it, its blood my blood, its breath my own and I surrender to it as it boils through my lungs and veins. 'Merdeka! Merdeka!' Merdeka is not a philosophy or a set of arguments, it is a dizzying drug, a visceral mutation as irreversible as the caterpillar becoming a butterfly and I feel my own bones abruptly dissolve, reconsolidate and click into new, immutable forms designed for a different purpose in a different world. There can be no going back now – for Indonesia or for me.

Bung Tomo is in fine form. He stands high on an improvised stage behind the big, square box of the microphone waving his wiry fist into the night sky. The British have dropped leaflets demanding that the Pemuda lay down their arms and surrender, thus abrogating the agreement they have just made. The city is erupting in rage. His fury rolls out in fine, thundering phrases. 'As long as the wild bull buffaloes of Indonesia have red blood capable of making a scrap of red and white cloth, that long shall we refuse to surrender to anyone.' The wild bulls around us roar and paw at their native soil, full of red blood. The ground shakes with their stamping feet and their bellowing throats. '*Merdeka! Merdeka!*'

Chapter Six

You remember that iconic black and white photo of Bung Tomo? Everyone knows it. The one where he looks like one of those paintings from the French Revolution? He's in uniform, one hand raised to the heavens, the famous thin moustache and flying hair, mouth crying out to the world against injustice. It's the picture of a man so charismatic he could have started his own mass movement in an empty room. He's shot from below and over him is a visually interesting umbrella swirling in what you know must be red and white raspberry ripple and the eyes are blazing into the crowd. Everyone assumes it was taken on November 9th when he made that stirring speech about the wild bulls. Actually, it was taken much later when we were in a little mountain town and by me. For months, there would be no time for speeches or photographs after that last night. Out of the blue, under the red and the white, the issues had suddenly become black and white and we were fighting for our lives.

Matters first came to a head on the 30th October. In the finest traditions of the British army it was a five-star, gold-braided, world-class cock-up. In fact it was a combination of more cock-ups than a chicken farmer sees in a year down on the farm.

At the Oranje hotel, I was booked in under the name of Miss Manxi, an homage to my Isle of Man origins – well – alleged origins. The hotel had had its ups and downs. First the Pemuda had come and dragged everyone away for interrogation and stripped it bare, then the Dutch had turned up with a truck and it had been freshly furnished with goods taken from some magical, mystical Japanese Ali Baba warehouse rumoured to exist down by the docks. Most of the stuff must have been looted by them from the houses of rich Chinese – all dragons and silk tassels – so that the whole place looked like a tart's parlour in flickering candle- and lamplight. A snazzy, walnut radio set with gold knobs stood on the bar, leaking Western music that sounded like an orchestrated stiff upper lip. I was drinking with a Dutch liaison officer, Wim, who was getting a little too friendly. He was young, blond, probably missed his mother and his pink, pig-faced girlfriend back in Leiden. I peeled his hand from my arm like a slug off a leaf.

'You're drunk.'

''Course I'm bloody drunk, Manxi. What else is there to do in bloody Surabaya? Listen to the bloody wireless?' He nodded at the bar-top god.

I laughed. 'It depends what station you listen to.' It was silly of me but I couldn't resist it.

He scowled into his glass of beer as into a crystal ball. 'I have to spend half my day reading reports on that damned Rebel Radio. It's stirring up the young bloods, whipping them up to god knows what atrocities. Thank God those collaborators Soekarno and The Mad Hatta went on the government station and tried to calm them down but they won't listen to them. It's that extremist Bung Tomo they heed.' The old men in Jakarta still trying to keep their hands clean, sitting on the fence, helping the Dutch to build yet more fences. For Wim all Indonesians were either Jap collaborators or extremists – both excluded as fit partners in any negotiation. 'Yesterday, one of Tomo's gangs threw hand grenades into a convoy of trucks transporting starving women and children to a feeding station. The Mahrattas, the Indians, fought to defend them till their last bullet but it was a mob of hundreds of crazed people shouting for blood, fighting their way over the bodies with knives and guns and spears to get at them. One of them was swinging a swordfish jaw over his head as a weapon for Christ's sake! And they've started chopping up the Indians they take prisoner – alive. We found a bunch of them, roped together with British troops, floating in the river with their eyes gouged out and their dicks chopped off. And I won't tell you what they did to the survivors of a forced landing of one of our planes out in the countryside.'

'Is it fair to blame the radio for that?' I stirred a little more Scots into my accent, twanged an American vowel or two. You could never be too careful. There would be no more sloppy, red flags from me.

He gulped beer, belched, wiped his mouth on the back of a hand and shook his head wearily. 'You haven't read the transcripts. And they've got this new woman – Surabaya Sue they call her – who pours out the most poisonous filth in English. We've put a price on her head.' He looked at me with incredulous, drink-bleared eyes. For a moment I thought the penny had dropped. But no. He went back to his beer and looked vacantly through the window.

Surabaya Sue! I had my own call sign just like Tokyo Rose. I would use it on air tonight. I had a broadcast in two hours.

'How much?'

'What?'

'The price on her head. How much?'

'Ten thousand guilders.'

It was a fortune! I thought what I could do with it and drifted off into daydreams of cashing myself in. But then, of course, I would be dead.

'You know why this revolution will fail?'

I sighed, called back to dull reality – very dull reality. 'Please enlighten me Wim dear.'

'Well it's because – in every successful anti-colonial rebellion there's ever been, the occupiers always assume the educated and Westernised locals will support them because they have more in common with them than with the unwashed natives. But they never do. You see, they're the new elite, the ones with most to gain from independence so they can get their own hands in the till. Look at America. The revolution was all about a bunch of greedy, local lawyers not wanting to pay their share of taxes and getting a bigger cut of the graft. The extremists have made a fatal mistake by alienating just those people, the Chinese, the Eurasians, the mulattos, the – what do they call them? – *blasteran*. By attacking them and killing them in their thousands they've made sure they're a hundred percent with us. We can't lose. We've got the elite. We've got all the brains.' He drank contentedly. 'Another thing. We're not supposed to bring in Dutch troops but I've got a little plan.' He tapped the side of his nose squiffily.

'Do tell, darling.' I put his hand back on my arm. It was like lifting a dead dog.

'What I'm gonna do, see, is bring in Dutch troops, black them up like Indians and pass them off under the noses of the rebels as Mahrattas. They won't even know we're here till it's too late.'

'Isn't that a bit daft? Why not just slip them into British uniforms? Wouldn't that be easier? Isn't that what you are, Dutch in a British uniform?'

He paused, mouth agape, eyes swimming, blinking. 'Bloody hell, you're right! I hadn't thought of that.' One of the elite with brains – he swivelled and blinked out through the window, rubbing his eyes and squinting. 'Snow?' he said suddenly, rising unsteadily to his feet, pointing out into darkness in trembling disbelief. 'What the hell? It's snow.' He turned to the crowd. 'Snow in Surabaya! It's a miracle! It's an omen of our restoration!'

It was impossible yet true. Great, white flakes were twirling down past the glass into the tropical garden, pale ghosts in the weak light. Out he rushed, the rest of us following to see this wonder. We looked up into the night sky, the whole, surrounding city velvety dark from the lack of reliable electricity but the hills aglow with a sliver of moon. The stars were that odd golden colour they sometimes have in Java but now we were smacked in the face by – not snow – but another drop of onion-skin leaflets, more like lavatory paper than snow, toppling down from on high, out of the heavens, riding the breaths of wind from the sea. Moonlight and snow was a romantic combination, moonlight and toilet paper lacked the same appeal. From overhead came the drone of a circling aircraft. Wim crouched to pick up a leaflet and nearly toppled drunkenly onto his front. He wheezed back up on his knees and held it to the lamplight leaking out through the window, struggling to read the print. A great grin lit up his flushed face.

'It's a final ultimatum from the Brits. They've given the rebels 48 hours to disarm and surrender or they will attack. No more buggering about. They're finally going to fight the natives for us!' He broke into a little dance of joy, lumbered around in an elephantine jig. The other Dutch hugged each other and laughed beguiled – no doubt – by those visions of houses and estates restored and pattering, newly deferential servants. This was a journalistic scoop falling right into my lap so I bent and scooped and sidled off, unobserved, into darkness clutching a sheet, Indonesian one side, English the other. There at the end of the road a rickshaw was waiting, pulled up in the shadows under a mango tree, the driver lolling in the seat with his feet up on the handlebars, his presence betrayed only by the glowworm circle of his cigarette.

'*Merdeka atau mati*,' I murmur.

There is a line of white teeth. '*Merdeka atau mati*. Climb in sister.' Uki flings aside the cigarette, clambers into the saddle and leans down on the pedals and we whisper away towards Rebel Radio. He is dressed as a rickshaw driver in old shorts and a torn vest and has very fine thighs filmed with sweat. My appreciation is purely aesthetic, not sexual. An artist learns to grab such glimpses of beauty in an ugly world.

It seems that, while local commanders had negotiated a perfectly satisfactory ceasefire with the Indonesian forces to allow the evacuation of prisoners of war, the brass in India and Jakarta had arranged for more leaflets to be dropped demanding their immediate surrender and didn't think to tell anyone in Surabaya. This looked like treachery to Bung Tomo and the result was renewed attacks on the Indian troops stationed at various strategic but isolated points around the city. Posts were overrun. People were butchered in the streets. The British commander, Brigadier Mallaby, drove to the International Building which was one such hotspot and tried to stop the fighting as had been negotiated with Soekarno and Hatta, bringing news of the latest ceasefire agreement. There are various accounts of what happened next. I know now that everyone lies in official reports. But I was there the next day with Uki and Lukman getting copy to pass on to the international press. I *saw*.

* * *

It was a hot day by the Red Bridge and everyone was trigger-happy. The Indians were scared. The Indonesians were furious. There had been a lot of potshotting about and the fronts of the building were all pockmarked with bullets but now things had settled down with the Indonesians all busy eating rice behind their sandbags and the Indians drinking tea inside the office block behind theirs. The sun on the square in front of the Dutch buildings hit you like a flatiron and to be caught on its exposed emptiness was certain death. Mallaby drove up with some local liaison people, a little Union Jack fluttering on the bonnet of the car, and parked right under a sign that said, 'Once and for ever the Indonesian Republic'. I don't know why he did that. Drivers are taught to always park in the shade and maybe that was it. Not a great slogan but it was an even worse choice of parking spot. It meant that every time someone looked at Mallaby, they saw the sign, saw his English flag and got all riled up again. His car was immediately surrounded by a mob, pushing and shoving, shouting and waving banners and he didn't help by poking at people with that silly, little stick English officers carry. I don't think he was in any danger but perhaps the Indians couldn't see that because of the sign being in the way. Anyway, the opening shot didn't come from either them or the Indonesians. It came from one of the other buildings. A white man was skulking along one of the upper balconies, taking advantage of the height to get a free line of fire. I quite clearly saw him rise on one knee and shoot at the Pemuda forces, bringing down a youth at the front then swivel and fire at the Indians, toppling a trooper behind a machine gun before throwing himself down behind the balustrade. He must be one of the Dutch vigilantes, shooting at both sides, as they often did, hoping to get something going. Well it worked. The Indians panicked and fired – some say into the air but I saw men falling and screaming, a young boy shot through the leg, blood pumping like a geyser. I will never forget the look of sheer terror on his face, astonished at the sudden revelation of his own mortality. And then all hell broke loose.

Lukman grabbed me and dragged me behind a car, bullets pinging over our heads and glass cascading down from the shot-up windows. Uki was face down in the dust but – with relief – I saw him move and make a successful dash for a pile of sandbags at the edge of the river as someone behind us opened up with a heavy machine gun and soon bits of the International Bank Building – a nice, modern piece of cast concrete – were flying in all directions. We made our way to join Uki in the long grass and, as the firing died down again, all settled in for a long wait, Lukman pulling his hat down over his eyes and taking a nap with creditable aplomb. Then, as in a dream, a young schoolboy, carrying a rifle and wearing some fantastical outfit of red and white and with a headband of silver lamé ripped from some lady's best frock, walked out from cover and slowly swaggered up to the British car – bullets from the Indians flying around him but he immune. This did not surprise the Javanese in the least. Everyone knows there are people who have magic, *ilmu kedotan*, that makes them bulletproof and that they were doing a good trade in the city. A great cry of 'Wah!' went up in admiration of him. The slim boy gripped the doorframe and swung light-footed in the window of the car as you might to have a cheery conversation with a neighbour then suddenly stepped back and raised his rifle one-handed, let off a few casual shots and turned balletically on one heel to walk away, holding the gun high in the air. A hand appeared at the window, groped blindly and tossed a grenade out of the car towards him and there came a great explosion that humped the whole vehicle off the ground and – as the smoke cleared – flames licked out at the rear with a great Whoosh! The back door towards us opened with a screech of metal, falling off its hinges as in a circus act for clowns and two British soldiers stumbled out, coughing and crawling with comically smoke-blackened faces. Uki raised his rifle to fire and took long, careful aim but I pushed down the barrel, leaving the squint still on his surprised face. The men scrambled down the riverbank and waded out into the corpse-strewn river, sweat running down their foreheads and blank terror in their eyes. Soon they were gone, doubtless incredulous to be still alive.

'No, Uki,' I said. 'Let them go. Otherwise they will say it was a cowardly ambush. Information is everything in a fight like this. Let the truth be known.'

* * *

'It was an ambush,' whined Wim, my Dutch 'friend'. 'A bloody cowardly ambush. You know they chopped the head off poor Mallaby's corpse? The Brits keep trying to spread oil over troubled waters and the rebels just keep setting fire to it. They're just a bunch of gangsters using the revolution as an excuse to go round killing and robbing people. Anyway, the whole Republic thing was just an invention of the Japanese to cause trouble because they lost the war. Sour *sake*. And the Brits have always envied us our Indies possessions, which is why they do nothing. They try to keep things from us but all their secretaries are good Dutch girls so we get to know everything the bastards are up to. Not English are you?

'American.'

'There you are then.' He signalled the Oranje barman for a refill. 'There's a hundred thousand troublemakers flooded into the city from all over the island just in the past two weeks. Kids,

Muslim lunatics. I've read the reports. The imams have declared it a holy war, all good Muslims must kill and maim and so on. They knew damned well Mallaby's team were unarmed, insisted on it, except for allowing them a grenade each.'

'Why a grenade each? Doesn't that sound a bit odd to you for a mission to announce a ceasefire?'

He stared at me blankly across the table, put his glass down and grabbed as it toppled on the edge, proud with raised, carved dragons. Chinese furniture is made for intimidation not comfort or convenience. 'What? Well that's hardly the point now is it? Do you know I passed by the Red Bridge with a patrol today. Mallaby's car's still there all burnt out but, would you believe it, the thieving buggers have already stripped it bare – wheels, tyres, bulbs from the headlights – all gone. They'd nick anything round here.' He sat back in the uncomfy chair nicked from the Japanese warehouse that had nicked it from a Chinese merchant's house in a whole country the Dutch had nicked and lit another cigarette. 'The good news is that the British are coming. It seems that for once they actually meant what they said in that leaflet drop. Had it from my friend Derek today. Do you know Derek? Ripping chap. Artistic, like you. Tried to show me his etchings but they were wasted on me, I'm afraid ...'

I had met him all right, at the Oranje Hotel, a failed actor, who had told me the dunderhead, British commander in Jakarta was drunk all the time and his chief interest was in staying as close to the bar in the Officers' Mess as possible, only being enticed away by the stream of women he had to procure for him as his ADC. Derek was a sweet-faced man with what I thought a typical Javanese Eurasian face – a cute little nose and that unmistakable, thick, black, Indo hair that fell over one eye in a delicious cowlick. And a fellow artist to boot. His name was Derek but I heard that he afterwards changed it to Dirk – Dirk Bogarde. It was the first time a man had invited me to his room to see his etchings and actually shown me etchings. They were curiously old-maidish sketches of quaint little buildings with the odd local with a 'good face'. And some constipated-looking male nudes.

'... Anyway, the Brits've finally decided to do the right thing. Another week and they'll have 25,000 troops, naval vessels and the air force – all on their way from Singapore. Those rebel bastards will get what's coming to them. Boy will they be surprised.' He smiled and blew smoke in satisfaction, seeing them going down like ninepins in his mind. 'Then we'll put the whole so-called government on trial as collaborators with the Japanese and shoot the lot of them.'

'Really?' I said, putting my hand on his arm like Mae West and a 'my hero' gleam in my eyes. 'How wonderful, Wim darling. Do tell me more.'

* * *

The heavy, naval bombardment from the offshore fleet began at dawn and, as the guns boomed and shook the city like an earthquake, the British bombers came in over an inappropriate rising sun – Mosquitoes and Thunderbolts – raining down not leaflets this time but death and destruction south of the river. They say some 500 bombs whistled down onto undefended Surabaya and ripped it apart in flowers of flame. Then tanks and armoured cars lumbered off the ships and snarled down the wide Dutch avenues from the docks and into the narrow maze that was the native town. Everyone grabbed the children and the old ladies and poured out into the streets that were immediately clogged with screaming, panicking people, falling on each other and trampling everything underfoot except the urge for self-preservation. This was the Japanese invasion all over again and, now the Japs had surrendered, no one had imagined to go through it a second time. The British had expected to take the Indonesian forces by surprise and cut them off in large numbers but it was as if they somehow knew all about the Allies' plans and kept open the routes for a staged retreat into the hills. Battle-hardened British troops followed in the shelter of the advancing Shermans and then it was hand-to-hand fighting – dirty, messy and vicious – as they cleared the city street-by-street and house-by-house at bayonet point. Both sides had scores to settle. The Indonesians fired back with captured Japanese artillery but no one had shown them how to set the fuses on the shells first and they just bounced off. The Brits joked that their orders must be 'Ready, Fire, Aim.' Ironically, Moestopo, the notional Indonesian commander, had gone off to Gresik in a huff because the old men in Jakarta wouldn't let him fight the British and stopped him every time he tried. Now such a fight would change from being an unauthorised ceasefire violation to an act of national heroism. The British had Dunkirk as their own heroic defeat. We would have Surabaya. After such an effusion of blood there could be no turning back and every death fertilised the blooms of freedom. That's from one of my broadcasts by the way. Rather fine I thought.

It took three weeks for the British to drive the rebels and most of the starving, civilian population from the city. Out at the cement factory, fuelled by an unbroken stream not of ADC-procured women but of warm, weak tea, we gave it back to them hot and strong over the airwaves. The tea was brought by the same little, old lady who had brought the biscuits after my first broadcast. No one knew who she was or where she got the tea from.

'Hundreds upon hundreds were killed. Streets ran with blood, women and children lay dead in the gutters. *Kampongs* were in flames, and the people fled in panic to the relative safety of the rice fields. But the Indonesians did not surrender.' It was getting a little hard to find anything fresh to say but that, I suppose, is the nature of war. It seldom pleases by its sheer novelty.

The boys, Uki, Lukman and Reza, were fretting at being assigned to guard the radio station instead of flinging themselves, outgunned, on the Indians in some pointless act of sacrificial courage. This was seen as all my fault of course. Occasionally they would fire in frustration at aircraft overhead, far out of range but attracting their unwelcome attention, or chase away refugees desperate to get any sort of roof over their heads. Mostly, they just sat slumped against a wall and gazed glumly at the pall of smoke rising in the distance as if watching their own youth blowing away and listened to the dull crump of artillery and the rattle of machine guns that made such an evocative background to my own broadcasts. They dreamed of bigger weapons and to compensate for the lack of them, began to draw them intricately on the walls in an act of military masturbation, like the boys the Japanese allowed to parade around with solid wooden rifles on their shoulders during their own occupation. It struck me how very much better we had got at killing people during the few years of the war with all sorts of new tricks. What was needed was anti-aircraft guns, anti-tank weapons, mines. What they sent us was a writer. It is sometimes hard not to suspect the military of having a wicked sense of humour.

He wandered in after about a week, a thin, dark man of about twenty holding a notepad, dressed in an immaculate shirt and with shorts whose creases were sharp enough to hone the pencils in his top pocket. The whites of his eyes were beautifully clear, unlike our own, yellow from fever and dirt. He said his name was Idrus from the new revolutionary government office of literature and his accent said he was a Minang from Sumatra. He had a clear and polished way of speaking – an intellectual – and he spoke Javanese in the polite and elaborately embroidered *kromo*, form that the revolution had almost outlawed as hostile to its egalitarian spirit – as well as very good English. The boys were intrigued, never having seen anyone quite like this before and gathered round to peer at him.

'You are young like us,' they sneered. 'Not old like sister K'tut. Why do you not pick up a gun and fight?' Reza waved his rifle in demonstration. 'You use a lot of Dutch words. Are you a friend of the Dutch?'

The writer looked around at the snug and peaceful installation we had created beside the crazed concrete wall, the colourful awning set up against the sun, the cushions to rest on, the mugs of tea brought by the shuffling old lady, the card game abandoned on the table in boredom and said mildly, 'We all do what we can with what we have been given by God. I fight with words.'

'We too fight with words,' insisted Lukman, chest-beating and shrugging his rifle over one shoulder. 'We have written "*Merdeka atau mati*" on at least a thousand walls.'

Idrus smiled wanly. 'I congratulate you, brother. You might say then that all our writers struggle to emulate your own achievement.'

Lukman glowed and swaggered away to ask what 'emulate' meant but froze when he heard, over his shoulder, 'Of course. We should remember that you did not actually make up those words. The alliteration, the vocalic ending, the balance on either side of 'atau', all suggest a man who had a way with words and a piece of paper to hand. He might even have had to put away his rifle for a minute or two to write them down.'

Lukman turned back with a loud sigh, hands dangling loose by his sides like a gunfighter. He pushed out his chin. 'We have been warned to look out for spies and to shoot them on sight. How do we know you are not a spy? To me you look like a spy.'

'You are a journalist, you say?' I intervened, hastily, pulling Idrus into the shelter and gesturing towards a cushion. He remained standing as the boys stared in coldly from outside. I remembered that Lukman liked to have nice, clear enemies. We were all a little paranoid.

'No, not really. I work as an editor in Bata– ... Jakarta. I also write. It seemed to me that this fight would be something worth writing about, swordplay turned into wordplay.' Offensively good English then.

'I imagine you will want to go to the front right away,' I urged, offering a cigarette then turning him round and pointing. 'You will want first-hand experience, to see the facts.'

He smiled again as he waved out the flame of the match and inhaled in a smooth, aristocratic gesture and turned back. 'Maybe that would be just the pornography of violence. The facts are not the same as the truth, sister. The truth lies beyond the mere facts and all good fiction is a lie that tells the truth. Perhaps there is more truth to be found here than at the front. But then the whole world lives by stories so perhaps even truth is not enough. In the final analysis, it is only the stories we tell ourselves that keep us going. Politics is always ultimately about either hope or fear. We do hope. The Dutch do fear. That is why we shall win.'

'But you would not want people to say that you had never really been there, that you did not know.'

The old woman shuffled in with tea, yet more tea. Idrus thanked her politely and settled back on a cushion. The setting sun was drawn into the cracks in the wall above his head, transforming them into bloody arteries. 'They will say that anyway. Your young friends seem very eager for a fight – any fight. It is always easier to know what you are fighting *against* rather than what you are fighting *for*.'

'When you are fighting an army of Indians, it is hard not to behave like cowboys.'

His face lit up. 'That's good! Do you mind if I use that? Perhaps that's the sort of truth I have been looking for. After all, even a true story is still just a story. It needs shape. Point. A dominant image. Cowboys and Indians.' He leaned forward and grasped my hand softly between his two. 'Thank you, sister.'

Chapter Seven

The order to retreat to Malang came three days later. The boys returned from a briefing in town with the news and an American jeep, roaring into the yard in a cloud of dust with great grins on their faces. It was not quite a tank, but still …

'Where did you get it?'

Uki blushed. 'Oh, umm. We found it. It didn't seem to belong to anyone. So …' He shrugged. 'We've got petrol for it,' he pleaded. It was the way a little boy would justify bringing home a stray puppy that he desperately wanted to keep.

It was the work of minutes to pack up the few things we owned and a mere half hour more for the boys to decorate the jeep with red and white flags and ribbons to their satisfaction. The 'banzai-box' would follow at its own speed. Black rain clouds were fermenting overhead and unleashed themselves as we set off. I shall never forget that drive in the rain. The road was clogged with terrified civilians, bullock carts of wounded, rickshaws, grinding army trucks, heaving over the potholes. There were little groups of deserting Japanese and mutinous Indian troops with '*Merdeka atau mati*' armbands. Occasionally, enemy planes would be heard circling overhead, triggering a new panic and a stampede for trees and ditches. A near-naked woman ran by, screaming and clutching a baby covered with blood. And it went on and on for mile after weary mile with the rain licking at the refugees' trembling legs and shoulders and endless honking to get them out of our path. We were soon all soaked, beyond caring, hungry, exhausted. And the eyes of those people on foot, tramping through the mud, seared through my heart like daggers – envious but uncomplaining, registering my white skin and my privileged seat in a jeep as a sign that nothing had changed. Yet everything had changed. I wanted to shout it out against the cynical gaze of the old women and the hurt, reproachful eyes of the sobbing children. And then another plane would come overhead and people would start running again, wild-eyed, banging against the jeep, nearly falling under its wheels in their terror, hearing the whistling bombs once more in their heads. It's not true that you never hear the bomb that kills you. I've seen it happen.

And then we began the long climb from the hot, coastal plains up into the hills and mountains, volcanoes belching smoke on all sides as if eager to join in the destruction. The air cooled and thinned around us – becoming what Ma would call *dreich* – and we started to shiver in mist as we crawled through abandoned tea plantations, the neglected bushes already sprouting into lovely but unproductive trees, the gullies full of possessions that the fleeing had simply jettisoned in despair as impossible to carry any further. And now the rain had stopped, you could see the tears on the people's faces. Going downhill is at least as onerous as going up as all the weight has to be constantly braked by the legs and by the time Malang came into view, laid out before us, we had gathered up half a dozen more lost souls in various stages of physical and mental collapse, arranged on the edges and the bonnet of the jeep, so the driver could barely see the road ahead. One man was clutching two cheap Balinese carvings, one under each arm, the standard tourist rubbish, depicting a man in a headcloth and a woman in a dance headdress. What did they mean to him? Home? A memory of love? He hung on to them as if they meant life itself and shook and shook and shook.

Malang had become one great encampment of tents and strings of washing, hiding under a layer of swirling woodsmoke. Flocks of wild children fluttered amongst the ruins like swallows, briefly coalescing into packs that would swirl and swarm with sudden purpose. We drove through the centre, dropping off our passengers to wander in lost confusion and out the other side into one of the neat clutches of Dutch villas that crawled up the hillside. A white bungalow with pointed gables, its door smashed down and contents looted, suited us best. One of the rooms had been set up as a strongroom with a great steel door that had resisted amateur attempts to gain entry. Reza had at it more professionally with a will and a sticky tank bomb in the hope of treasure. The blast was misjudged and brought down part of the kitchen wall but what he found was much better than treasure, sacks of rice and an incongruous, slightly singed fur coat that they insisted I wear at night against the mountain chill, turning me into a moth-eaten bear. All quite unnecessary, I thought. In the climate of revolutionary Malang, many are cold but few are frozen. The garden was thickly planted with dense mango trees that would help to hide our radio mast. In case of circling Mustang spotter aircraft we could quickly down-scope like a U-boat captain in a crash-dive. It took the technical crew a day to reach us but two more days to find us in all the chaos, then Rebel Radio went back on the air. 'Indonesia – once free, forever free.'

* * *

Broadcasting can be like shouting down a well and receiving no answering echo. Yet two incidents showed the value of our work. Given that we dared have no fixed abode, we scarcely expected fan mail. But one day, despite the capricious functioning of the mail service, Uki rushed in with an envelope with the name 'Surabaya Sue' on it. It was no ordinary envelope, thick and creamy and full of military self-confidence. In the top, left corner, it bore the name of the Republic of Indonesia in simple classic script, final concrete proof of the existence of that mystical object of our desire. At that stage we had not yet got around to having overwrought Garuda birds plastered over everything official. The boys gathered round.

'Open it K'tut. It must be from Gnub Onrak.'

'Who?'

Reza grimaced. 'Bung Karno. That is what he is called here in *boso walikan*. All the Pemuda use it here in Gnalam. You turn words back to front. It confuses spies.'

'Well, it confuses me too, so stop it. Perhaps we should leave it until this evening when I can read it in private,' I teased, laying it, unopened, in my lap like a ticking time-bomb. 'It is addressed to me. It might be something personal – a marriage proposal for instance. Is General Soedirman married?'

'Open it! Please!'

'... or perhaps it is a command for me to leave Indonesia. My travel documents are a little out of order, you know.'

'Please.'

'... or it could be a tax demand. Can they send you a tax demand when you don't get a salary?'

'Sister K'tut, pleeeease!'

I eased open the flap gently. Dutch envelope glue had never worked very well in the steamy tropics and, anyway, it seemed a crime to tear it in a world where so few things were crisp and new and unsullied. They all stared breathless and unblinking at the folded sheet of plump paper inside that I teased out to spring back into shape. I had seen that spellbound expression before. It was like the men in the speakeasies back in America when the bump and grind dancer was finally getting down to shaking the real nitty gritty right in their faces.

I glanced at the signature. 'It's not from Bung Karno.' They groaned in disappointment. Reza slapped his thigh and turned away. Little Uki pouted. 'It's from General Namridoes.' I watched, grinning, as they rolled it around backwards in their heads. Soedirman, the new commander-in-chief! Their mouths gaped.

'Whaaat?' They had all perked up again. 'What does he say? Is there anything about us?'

'Dear Miss Surabaya, I am writing to thank you and the team of Rebel Radio for your fine work during the Battle of Surabaya that shares its name with you ...' – It was the first time we had heard the expression. We had become part of history. The Battle of Surabaya. '... and your services to the Indonesian people. I would wish you to know that your work has not gone without good effects. Although some 15,000 of our people were lost in the fight against the aggressors and only 600 Allied troops, more than 700 Mahrattas deserted, many citing your broadcasts as the reason. In addition, a contingent of Scottish gunners have come over to our side and are now working as artillery trainers in the Siliwangi Division. Please use this information in your future broadcasts. We wish you every, continuing success.' I scanned quickly. The rest was all verbiage, 'our victory certain', 'our cause just', 'given our people a new sense of purpose and self-respect', '*Merdeka*!' – in fact the sort of stuff I churned out myself by the yard. 'Right, boys,' I said. 'Too long have we lived like mice. This evening we do a special broadcast – one of victory – the victory of the Battle of Surabaya.'

That night, we walked back from the studio box in darkness, mango leaves rustling under our feet, still pumped high with excitement. The boys wanted to go off and look for girls in the town, feeling their oats and the urge to sow them widely. There were plenty of girls around nowadays, selling the only thing they had to sell and, of course, the boys – who had no money – would try to replace cash with charm. They had plenty of that. The girls loved their long, patriotic hair and tight uniforms. Young blood called out to young blood and male muscle under stretched fabric has a mute appeal all of its own. Some boys claimed to have magical, warrior powers so the girls wouldn't get pregnant. Occasionally, girls would come to me from the town, as the repository of all western scientific knowledge, and ask me what was the most effective form of contraception. In our circumstances what could I say? 'A sour face,' was the best I could offer them. It was just life reasserting itself and no one could think any the worse of either side.

'You should come too, sister,' giggled Lukman. 'Perhaps it is time you had a man. Not one of us, of course, we are too young. But perhaps we could find you one of those Indian deserters, all black and hairy.' He shuddered and dropped his voice to a panting whisper. 'They are very beeeg,' he grinned and gestured with his hands two feet apart, popping his eyes naughtily as in a Balinese dance. 'But they smell bad.'

'Yes,' grinned dark, little Uki. 'But you know they say men are like fruit. The black ones are juicier. There is that Captain Rashid who has deserted from the Indians and is on the radio in Bandung. Perhaps you could get together and … broadcast something. They say he has a beautiful moustache like the handlebars of a bicycle.'

'A kind thought, Lukman, Uki, but I have taken a holy oath of chastity.' Everyone stopped, suddenly solemn. Javanese view such things seriously.

'What oath is that, sister?'

'I have sworn an oath not to sleep with Bung Tomo until

Indonesia is free. It is a great disappointment to him.' *Then* they laughed.

That exultant broadcast raised our stock to such a degree that, a few days later, I was kidnapped. Kidnapping was fashionable at the time. Hatta and Soekarno had been kidnapped by the Pemuda to force the Proclamation of Independence. The Prime Minister, Sjahrir, was kidnapped by a rival faction until they were made to let him go. The Dutch would kidnap the whole republican government and be made to give it back. But most people who were kidnapped did not come back – ever. The rivers were clogged with the bodies of kidnapped Ambonese killed by republicans, Christians killed by Muslims, Muslims killed by communists, rebels killed by Dutch and Chinese killed by just about everyone. Most trigger-happy were members of the colonial army, newly freed from the Japanese camps and sadly embittered. Up around Tegal, there were rumours of kidnappings and massacres of the aristocrats and government officials who had sent the people's sons away to be slave labour for the Japanese and almost certainly to a horrible death – having been encouraged by Bung Karno to do so. I was unbelievably lucky. I was kidnapped by people who were fans of a sort.

They turned up one morning in a jeep, dressed as three young men from one of the Pemuda groups. In those days there were so many splinter groups on both sides and everyone was playing alphabet soup what with the SEAC, NICA, RAPWI, PETA, BKR, TKR, PNI, PKI, PPKI, PPPKI and all the groups changing their names and merging and resplitting like Hollywood couples. The names, of course, had promptly spawned more demotic interpretations among the determinedly monoglot British soldiery in their world of *jankers* and *fizzers* – Screw Every Asian Cunt, Nutless Idle Crap Army, Rape All Pretty Women in Indonesia and so on – an outpouring of foul schoolboy wit. The point is you never quite knew who anyone really was. The British and Dutch had got some of their vehicles straight from the Americans and not bothered to paint out the stars so that many of the Pemuda actually believed they were at war with America. They had come, they said, to take me to Bung Tomo's headquarters for a meeting. And no one thought anything more of it. But when we got to the centre of town, they suddenly swerved off in another direction.

'What's this?' I asked. 'This isn't the way to Bung Tomo's HQ.'

'It's moved,' they grinned at each other evilly. 'Security.'

That kept me quiet for another few miles as we headed off into the hills and then I really began to smell a rat as the town fell away and even bamboo huts became scarce as the vegetation closed in from either side of the road until it brushed against the flanks of the jeep. Perhaps they thought I was Dutch and intended to do something about it. I slithered the *Merdeka atau mati* armband out of my pocket and slipped it on, reached forward and tapped the driver on the shoulder so they would all see it. There were two ways to go. I could use the hanky-waving skills I had taught young Eunice Pringle back in LA or stamp my foot like a *grande dame*. I decided the latter would make me look too Dutch so I turned on the waterworks. I flung myself at the young captor to my left and began to wail.

'Oh where are you taking me? I'm a poor helpless woman. So alooone.'

They were appalled and exchanged horrified looks. 'Please don't distress yourself, mother. We are taking you to Tretes, to the radio station there. We have no one who can broadcast for us in English and everybody wants to listen to you. You will be safer there. You have been kidnapped by admirers.'

'Mother?' I shrieked, deeply insulted, and clipped him sharply round the ear. 'Mother? How old do you think I am? At the very most I am "big sister" to you boys.'

They laughed. We were friends.

* * *

The radio station was a real guerrilla *kampung* up in the hills, a filthy tangle of shacks and camp fires and tough, little horses coming and going at all hours bearing food and ammunition. Java, at that time, was riddled with different factions with separate militias who were under no central control. Some were loyal to particular political parties. Some fought under the banner of Islam or Christianity or Communism or Socialism. Some were loyal only to their local leader. They were fighting to create a new world and no ideas were too crazy to command belief somewhere.

This one was led by a self-styled colonel – mid-fifties, body rapidly turning pear-shaped, mulish but with little, piggy eyes – red-rimmed like piss holes in the snow – and a worrying facial twitch. He had a fat lower lip that was permanently wet, like a great, slimy slug.

'*Merdeka*!' I shouted, always a good bet.

'*Bebas*!' he replied, finger-wagging and giggled. Ah! Now that wasn't a good sign. *Bebas* is 'liberated'. Only the communists answered like that, making a pedantic distinction between independence and liberation – implying the former was just the start of the latter, a bloody, social revolution to follow on the heels of the political one with social hierarchy and privilege put to the sword. Then he confirmed my assessment with the words, 'Welcome comrade. Have you heard the great news? The parasitic rajahs of East Sumatra have all been executed in the just wrath of the proletariat and their wealth liberated for the people! Come and eat.' He gestured at a table where rice, fish and other, half-forgotten pleasures were laid out, liberated no doubt from the parasitic, local farmers. I could see my broadcasts would be moving strongly to the left and the red and the white would be pure red from now on. For the moment, I accepted it. Life is too short for the making of puff pastry or worrying about those things that cannot be changed. At least the food was better here than the endless plain meals of gritty rice and raunchy chilli of the Pemuda. No wonder many more died of the shits than the shells but such food was the red and the white, the blood and the bone of Indonesia. All these fearless defenders of the proletariat looked sleek and well-fed and the colonel contemplated the men around his table smugly.

Before the revolution, Colonel Soejanto had lived mainly by plying his crowbar around the back windows of his neighbours' houses and his forces still got cash mostly by plundering the wealthy Chinese of his patch. The fact that his men now wore nice, matching, black uniforms was neither here nor there. They were clearly bad boys and he was probably both mad and very dangerous. I soon learned that if he was crossed to the slightest degree, petulance would flicker across his jowls and people would start running before the fragile dam of his rage burst. My first broadcast that night was adjudged insufficiently socialist in tone.

'So what are you going to do,' I asked, 'shoot me?'

For once, he was stunned. Then. 'Look at it this way, K'tut,' he whispered gently, hissing like a snake, 'unless you can learn to fit in, we shall take away your armband – maybe we could even paint you up in the Dutch colours – and dump you in the middle of republican territory. I don't think you'd last very long out there. It could be very nasty.' He giggled again. The sound made the hair stand up on the back of my neck.

The communists had always enjoyed using sticks more than carrots. So I learned to fit in. I made it a grim joke. The Americans and British became 'the imperialist forces of reaction'. The Dutch became 'the running dogs of the slavering, capitalist hyenas'. Their every action was prefaced with, 'In a last desperate effort to avoid the inevitable fate predicted for them by scientific Marxism ...' or 'In defiance of universal justice and the interests of the people ...' As a good ally of the Soviet Union, I raged against the fearful, old men who thought they could talk the Dutch into independence with endless conferences instead of bowing to 'the irresistible force of class struggle as revealed by Marxist-Leninist thought.' It was clear that by now the Brits just wanted a piece of paper – any piece of paper – to cover their modesty as they ran away from 'the ultimate dictatorship of the proletariat.' And Soekarno and Hatta became 'the guilty, elitist collaborators with the Japanese fascist, occupation regime, their hands stained with the blood of a million of our brothers and sisters'. By the stringing-together of such expressions, my broadcasts became almost content-free and the Colonel was absolutely delighted with them.

And then salvation finally came. One evening, I had wandered down the track away from the main studio to enjoy a cigarette and a little precious solitude. I found an occasional cigarette added welcome city flavour to the pure mountain air and in war everybody smokes, just as a way of proving to themselves that they are still alive. Suddenly, two figures stepped out of the mosquito-buzzing shadows.

'Don't be afraid, K'etut. It is only us.' Reza and little Uki! Their grins lit up the darkness. 'We've heard your broadcasts, comrade K'tut. We've been waiting for two days for you to come out. We've got the jeep hidden down the road. We've come to liberate you and take you home as booty.'

Home! The word brought tears to my eyes. I was shaking with a rush of repressed emotions. We all hugged, then I hitched up my sarong in a most unladylike fashion and started running for my life. Whatever people may say, smoking is good for your health.

The next day I went back on the air for Rebel Radio. In my captivity, I had fallen foul of all manner of minor infections and skin diseases. I had not realised how much we depended on Reza and his ground-up herbs and simples to stay healthy. The skin was flaking off my soles, leaving great, bleeding sores and the toes were turning black so that I was scarcely mobile and had to be virtually carried to the microphone. And yesterday's cross-country race had done my feet no good at all. But Reza prepared an ointment of ground seaslugs that stank like a week-old corpse, driving everyone else from the broadcasting booth and soon my toes were back on their feet. And then the silent, old lady from the Surabaya cement factory shuffled in with a cup of weak tea. Somehow she had found us like a homing pigeon and simply resumed doing what she did. We still had no idea who she was but the biscuits seemed to have disappeared as a casualty of war. Home! In any war a sense of belonging becomes even more precious.

A while later, the Red Colonel was one of thousands killed by the national army as they snuffed out the independent Indonesian Soviet Republic declared by communist rebels around Madiun. I wrote a piece for a leftie Australian newspaper about it, all about these 'snarling traitors to the glorious people's revolution'. Somehow I couldn't stop those old words and expressions from the past creeping back into it. Apparently the Americans picked it up and – mysteriously – liked it. President Soekarno was no longer a dangerous collaborator. Now he was a valiant anti-communist and a bulwark against the new foe.

* * *

The revolutionary struggle had already lasted too long for Bung Tomo. By now his vow to eschew barbers had turned him into a little fuzzball with so much hair and beard that he resembled nothing so much as the stern Old Testament prophets of the Wee Free Kirk that still lurked in the nooks of my memory from childhood and Sunday school. The Dutch had put a price on his head – rather more than on mine – and were said to have dedicated squads seeking to track him down and kill him. So, people said, he had numerous suicidally hairy lookalikes leading them a merry dance over all of east Java. Come to think of it, anyone could be lurking under all that smelly fluff. I wondered whether anyone had checked recently. Then I saw the blazing eyes and there could be no doubt it was still him. He was sitting in one corner – a little huffily I thought – at a big meeting of leaders of the revolutionary struggle in the fair city of Yogyakarta and he kept dragging his fingers through his lion's mane and checking his knees furtively for dislodged fleas. The government had moved there from Jakarta after an attempt by Dutch gunmen to assassinate Prime Minister Sjahrir. Oddly, the republicans left Sjahrir behind in Jakarta when they moved.

At the front were the dapper 'old men' that Bung Tomo so despised, Soekarno and Hatta, delivering a smooth and well-manicured account of the Indonesian struggle to the world's press. Bung Karno was, of course, not old at all, being in his early forties and devilishly handsome in his gleaming, white uniform and *peci* hat. The sudden sprouting of those little black hats to replace batik headcloths had been the first visible sign of the Republic coming into being. As a public relations exercise, it was important that Indonesia be seen as modern, progressive, forward-looking, which is why I had been summoned to Yogya and abandoned my sarong for a fancy frock and high heels and had my newly blonde hair all shooshed up and my bosom jacked up to Sumatra but Bung Tomo seemed to take our immaculate grooming as both a form of betrayal of the revolution and a personal affront and stonily ignored my discreet, little waves of the hand. Thus do people end up foolishly bickering more over symbols of things than the reality of the things themselves. Or perhaps he simply no longer recognised *me* in my new disguise as an international vamp. I had been summoned to the new republican capital when it moved and helped out in everything from writing Bung Karno's English speeches – like the present one – to acting as interpreter for the various ministers and broadcasting on the new Radio Free Indonesia.

We were in the *Merdeka* room of the Merdeka Hotel, very probably on *Merdeka* Street that led off *Merdeka* Square and holding copies of the *Merdeka* newspaper. The boys busy renaming Indonesia and purging it of Dutch hadn't really got into their stride yet and only death would lend enough granitic solidity to names like Soekarno, Hatta and Soedirman to make them available for topographical use all over the archipelago. They had spread crisply handsome, young officers around the place to show Indonesia had clean linen and good teeth but their old Japanese-style uniforms were a PR disaster with the Westerners, summoning up all sorts of unhelpful associations. I must have another word with Bung K. I had written his speech by pasting together bits of Abraham Lincoln and Thomas Paine because it was vital to stop all the communist jargon and give them something that appealed to the liberal democracies. And after the usual applause, it was my job to circulate, guide and deftly direct the journalists' assessments as the wasp-waisted waiters dispensed drink and smiles. Bung Tomo, I noted, had slipped away, taking his easily outraged modesty with him, like the priest who leaves before the wake really gets going and he becomes an embarrassment. Apparently he had made some injudicious remarks about the politicians who were talking to the Dutch, struggling to give away again the gains made by the Indonesian armed forces – or in Bung Tomo's own terms, 'The young men fight like wild bulls. The old men talk like castrated goats.' When the Japanese had decided to take back Bandung to meet the terms of their agreement with the Allies, Bung Tomo had sent the Bandung boys a crate of lipstick as a sneering comment on their lack of manliness. God knows how much makeup they got when the British moved in to replace the Japanese and the 'old men' urged them to co-operate to avoid bloodshed and simply evacuate the southern sector. They had replied by complying but setting fire to it first. Nasty yes, but Indonesians are practical people. I was sure that makeup hadn't been wasted and gifts from it were now making terrible inroads into the virtue of the Bandung ladies. I wondered how Lukman, Reza and Uki were getting on. I missed them like a mother hen her chicks.

I was dutifully lecturing some brittle bimbo from *The Washington Times* or the *Wichita Gazette* or some such rag on the parallels between the American and Indonesian struggles for liberty and she seemed to be taking to it like a hangman to rope and scribbling away happily. Out of the corner of my eye, I could see the bosses glad-handing their way round the room, taking care of the business interests with clasped hands and big smiles. Bung Karno was offering cigarettes, the odd whispered joke, the occasional declaration of sincere affection that went straight to the solar plexus. He was master of all that. Were they *Merdeka* brand cigarettes in those days or have I invented that? I cannot be expected to remember everything. The Republic was desperately, almost comically, short of money. Its entire gold reserves were kept in a shoe box under a bed upstairs and the booze at the party was from a huge Japanese cache unearthed by chance the previous month. Otherwise we would have been drinking water. The Japanese had smashed everything before they withdrew so we were living like barbarians building campfires in abandoned Roman villas. Even the glasses for the reception had been borrowed from local, Chinese restaurants. None of them matched.

'Say honey. Ain't you that guerrilla lady that lives out in the jungle with all those half-naked boys?' She fluttered fake lashes with fake modesty and licked her pencil eloquently. 'Even if there are certain ... compensations out there, you sure must miss the comforts of home.'

'Look it's not a matter of ...'

I tried, as always, to redirect the conversation back to the outrageousness of the colonial system, the Atlantic Charter, universal human rights, but it was hopeless. Some pools are too shallow to register the impact when even the biggest rock is heaved in. A colleague appeared over her shoulder.

'Miss Tantri?' He drained his glass, immediately grabbed another from a passing tray and indicated my own. 'Gin and tonic, huh? Must make a nice change from those endless Molotov cocktails you're so used to lobbing around.'

'Well, as a matter of fact I have never been involved in any act of overt violence.'

A third appeared, rubber-necking between the other two.

'Did you say Tantri? You Surabaya Sue? Wow! The wild woman of Indonesia? Gee, can I get your autograph for my folks?' He shoved a notepad and pencil in my face. 'Could you maybe draw that dagger thing dripping with blood you see on the walls and something about death to all whites? And then sign "with love to Wayne".'

Others started gathering round, pushing and shoving, plucking at me like I was a pile of pullovers in a sale. One of those horsey, over-finished New England sorority sisters who wear tweed skirts and blazers elbowed her way through and started asking about where my family were from, as if I was the sort that got hung up in family trees. I felt like a lone, triggering crystal in a super-saturated solution of boredom. I saw Bung Karno look over at the noisy mob and frown in mid-oration, upstaged, downwinded, losing his thread and his audience. He wouldn't like that. People joked that the most dangerous place to be in Indonesia was standing between Bung Karno and a camera.

A few weeks later we saw the result of the conference when a bundle of American magazines flopped limply onto the press office floor. How many lives had been risked to get them to us? Very little about liberty or death but lots about me. Added to that, the bimbo reporter had managed to get my name wrong so that I appeared mysteriously not as Tantri but as someone pretending to be Miss Daventry. Perhaps that was just as well since the article was rife with Nudge! Nudge! insinuations that I was having hot, steamy jungle sex with the entire Diponegoro Division and possibly Wink! Wink! occasional underage orang utangs. I would have preferred it had they simply put it in Ma's raw Glaswegian and said that I 'banged like a shithouse door'. Why do women play men's game by snarling at each other in terms of their sexual availability? Even worse, she got Bung Karno's name wrong –

artists. But I have always regarded the gossip about his rampant sexuality as overstated. That story that the KGB filmed him in at an orgy in Moscow and showed him the film in a blackmail attempt only to be asked by him for more copies to show around – that never seemed to me to ring true. The proof is that in all out time together, he never showed the slightest sign of sexual interest in *me*.

But then sharp-eyed Mrs. Soekarno, Fatmawati, herself a third wife after all, saw to it that, when together, we painted nothing but bunches of chastely plucked, native, Indonesian flowers arranged in tall Chinese vases and some saw in this a metaphor of her influence on foreign policy. In those days every detail was overinterpreted and while the Dutch viewed everything in terms of the sinister and calculated chess moves of *Realpolitik*, the palace was thick with mystical augurers, wafting numerologists, necromancers, astrologers and scruters of entrails and portents of all kinds who looked back to the ancient Hindu myths and prophecies so that the president's every action was as closely studied and soothsaid by his own supporters as the bowel movements of Louis XIV. And the principal requirement of government reports was to have auspicious numbers of sections and paragraphs and so on which explains why so many of them were full of nothing. Even our painting got involved and was closely observed by a squad of pencil-licking bookies' runners. If Bung Karno chose a green background in a picture, that was a reference to Loro Kidul, the Goddess of the South Seas, and so the Sultan of Yogya – our host and one of her mystical husbands. A dab of red from the hand of one of Balinese ancestry, meant that he had doubts about the loyalty of the army. Too much white meant he thought palace treachery was afoot. Or maybe it was the other way round and what deep meaning lay behind his decision to paint only five flowers when there were actually six in that vase?

The British army had finally forced the Dutch to the negotiating table by the simple expedient of threatening to pick up their ball and go home in a sulk if they didn't. The result was the Linggadjati agreement, a recognition by the Dutch of Indonesian sovereignty over Java, Madura and Sumatra in return for some vague agreement to form some sort of joint realm under the Dutch crown.

I mercilessly painted in a bilious frangipani on my canvas and nagged. 'The problem, Bung, is that all the terms of Linggadjati remain undefined. It can be twisted to mean anything the Dutch like.'

He touched in a sinuous stem with flickering brush on his own. 'Maybe so, K'tut, but therein lies its advantage for us too. Now *we* can twist it to mean exactly what *we* want. The Dutch will try to nibble away at it from their side, we from ours. It moves the conflict away from pitched battles where we can never win and every time they protest to us, they are admitting that we exist. That's why I stacked the National Committee to get it through.' He pointed a paintbrush at me. 'It is the sleep of reason that produces war.' That line would be coming up in a speech soon. I had written it.

'But it will also lead to internal disputes as the different local groups twist it for *their* own ends.' I reached over to his canvas and straightened the flower stem by diminishing the highlights.

He sighed and compromised by shading in a pale offshoot that concealed the stem entirely, creating a façade of consensus. 'Then I act the great statesman, above factional quarrels, and speak as the voice of the people. The more they fight, the more they need Soekarno. The people know where Soekarno's heart is. Ducks flock together but eagles fly alone.' Bung Karno always managed to swim in the lethal currents and tides of Asian politics without quite getting his hair wet. 'You know that thing I always do in speeches when I play with the crowd? I ask ...' He lay down brush and palette, puffed out his chest and intoned like a priest, his hand creeping up unconsciously into the grandiloquent gestures of the demagogue. '"Shall I settle for ninety percent *merdeka*?" And they all shout "Nooo!" And then I do, "Ninety-two percent *merdeka*, then?" And they all howl "Nooo!" And then I look puzzled and go, "Well, what about ninety-five percent *merdeka*?" And so on up, teasing them with "ninety-nine and a haaalf percent merdeka?" Negotiating as if I am buying mangoes in the market and then – when I get to a hundred – only then do they all shout "Yes!"' Then I say, "How much? I can't hear you – louder." And they roar, "A hundred percent!!" and I say, "What? I still can't hear you – louder." And they scream, "A hundred percent!!!"'

It was true. The big cheeses all had very different oratorical styles. Bung Karno liked to joke and play. Bung Hatta loved his abstract nouns. Bung Tomo referred to the shedding of bodily fluids rather more than was strictly necessary.

'Yes, Bung, but you know that's an old trick from Western pantomime. Usually, it's the hero who is stalked by some great danger that the crowd can see but he can't. And they scream "Behind you! Behind you!" but he can't see it because he's looking the wrong way. The more he looks, the more they scream and stamp, the less he sees. Maybe that's how it is with you.'

He chuckled and took up his brush again. 'Thank you, K'tut.' He waggled a finger at me. 'I will remember that. But things are getting better. Today I saw a sign – a rat in the palace.'

'A rat? A sign? You mean a sign from above? Or do you mean in a dream?'

He shook his head. 'A sign from above? A dream? What are you on about? No a real rat, all fat and glossy and running down the hall. Up till now the people were so hungry they were forced to catch and eat the rats and they had all but disappeared. I don't know how we held on to the deer in the palace park. If rats are coming back, then it shows there is food about and that means things are getting better.'

It was true. And rats were not the half of it. There had been all sorts of rumours about gangs of starving children and packs of savage dogs that had been seen stalking and preying on each other in the ruins, dogs eating children, children eating dogs. 'Now tell me some Hollywood gossip. You know I love gossip. Tell me that story again about the star, Lupe Velez, trying to have a fancy suicide and being found with her bare arse sticking up in the air and her head down the toilet after she killed herself in such a complicated and beautiful way. That makes me laugh. A lot of people have planned my funeral and being a president doesn't make you laugh a lot. One day I should like to visit Hollywood. Perhaps they will make a film of my life but who can play Soekarno?'

I realise it is totally futile to try to talk facts with someone who is a hopeless fantasist like Bung Karno. He loves my stories of Hollywood scandal. Naturally, I invent freely.

Chapter Eight

The Buginese sailing vessel had dropped anchor halfway between the island of Karimun Besar and Singapore. The water was calm, delivering just the odd, lazy splash against the hull and the wind was a mere gentle, ruffling zephyr. If the Dutch navy turned up, we would run northwest to British waters, if the British we would turn east towards Indonesian. At the moment there was just a greasy Singapore tug out there but what they were doing was quite interesting. From afar, it looked as if they were tipping shoal after shoal of silvery fish back into the water from great buckets. They glistened and gleamed and caught the sun as they tumbled in with a fat splash. Only through the glasses could I see it was not fish at all but guns and that there was a Brit in a khaki uniform worrying over some sort of list with a pencil. There were too many guns in Asia, too may shells, too many mines. Now the big war was over, governments were dumping them by the hundred thousand and the cheapest and easiest thing to do was chuck them in the sea.

'You see, Ketut,' said Ah Beng. 'The water here very shallow because of the shoals. Soon as the Brits are gone, we send in the divers and the arms be deliver to your – ah – specification – all clean and grease and ready for use – good like new.' Ah Beng was a very handsome and plausible Chinese with a ceramic complexion and pencil-straight black hair and no emotional expressions at all.

'When?' I asked.

'We have to sell your opium first. I keep tell you. At the moment it drug on the market. Because it opium you think I talk poppycock?' People say the Chinese have no sense of humour. Don't believe it. It's just that they have a very bad sense of humour if Ah Beng's was anything to go by. We had to use agents like this all over the world. Because Holland was still the recognised authority and had imposed a blockade, they were often, legally speaking, engaged in smuggling. Sometimes this meant they were men of the highest, ideological commitment, sometimes they were crooks and the Republic must have lost a fortune in thefts and doublecrossings. The revolutionary government had had some difficulty in finding an honest agent in the US. There, I had been able to help with my American contacts and they were now represented – bizarrely, I admit, but efficiently – by Matty Fox, the producer who turned Universal Pictures around. Bung Karno loved the Hollywood connection. Joe Kennedy had already burnt his fingers and his bridges in diplomatic service otherwise I might have dropped him a line. I wondered if he had forgiven me for the Louella indiscretions.

This trip was a total nightmare. The Minister of Defence had sent me on a terrifying blockade-busting flight via Sumatra where the stockpile of government opium was hidden deep in caves. Opium was a government monopoly in Indonesia in those days and had only been banned in Singapore by the Japanese, so it was a moot point whether that regulation was still valid. Other Indonesian envoys were trading sugar, vanilla, quinine and birds' nests all over the East, anything to keep the Republic's finances afloat. We had to dodge Dutch fighters and a terrible, tropical storm in a wobbly old Dakota run by air pirates and short of fuel, load up the plane and land across the causeway in Malaya, truck the cargo into the city to Ah Beng's warehouse and it would be sold and ultimately converted into guns and an unused British field hospital to be shipped back via a small port in

Thailand. The hidden costs, the bribes, storage charges, transport, the commissions, took massive bites out of my dwindling budget while delay followed delay. The price of the guns was always going up, the value of the opium down. The particular guns I wanted were suddenly in short supply while it was now the wrong season for opium, the wrong kind of opium, the wrong trademark that people did not trust. I knew absolutely nothing of either commodity. Of course, no one gave receipts or proper documents. It was painfully obvious that I would never talk my way out of allegations of stealing when I got back to Yogya – if I got back – with what would almost certainly be the wrong guns. And always there were more delays. Much of my purchased stock was sold off by British quartermasters who then had to arrange for fires in the stores to cover up the losses. There had already been fires all over Singapore and the military police were getting suspicious, not having received a cut.

Its task finished, the tug started its engine, coughed, gobbed out dirty water, belched smoke, pirouetted and headed back for Singapore. One of the coolies gave us a cheery wave with a length of rope.

'Do they know what we're doing?'

Ah Beng turned and laughed. 'Of course they know. They our men. Why else you think they kindly dumping them in such shallow water so they so easily recover? You almost can reach down and pull them out from here.'

They slipped me ashore near Changi Point. I waded to the beach with my frock tucked up in my drawers like a little girl paddling in the Clyde and memsahibed my way back to Scotts Road, bullying myself aboard an army truck of returning nurses who chattered with medical boldness about their boyfriends. I was staying in the bland villa of a Javanese sympathiser who was keeping his head down. There had been fighting between Javanese – *romushas* stranded by the war – and Malays out in Geylang around the Happy World Amusement Park and I was hardly living high on the hog myself, being dependent on Ah Beng and the unsold opium for money but determined not to borrow more than absolutely essential at his usurious rates.

That evening there was a phone call. I had a mysterious visitor. He entered somewhat unusually for a senior diplomat of advancing years – over the back wall of the garden and landed on a banana tree – and arrived puffing and sweaty, with torn trousers but giggling. It was Abdul Monem, Egyptian special emissary of the Arab League. We settled him in with a glass of cool lemonade and he straightened his tie and drew himself up to his full height on the overstuffed sofa and bowed over his paunch.

'Madam K'tut. I am Mohamed Abdul Monem, here as the special envoy of King Farouk and the Arab League to extend official recognition to the Republic of Indonesia and offer the establishment of full, diplomatic relations.' Then he collapsed miserably down into the cushions. 'Unfortunately the Dutch refuse to let me in so I am stuck. Any ideas?' We gave him more lemonade.

This was a major diplomatic coup. It could be the unblocking of the logjam that would bring dozens of other countries to recognise the Indonesian Republic and influence the UN in its attempts to bring pressure on the Dutch. It was the same old dilemma, diplomacy or guns? This time it had to be diplomacy. The next day I set to with Ah Beng, touring the harbour, investigating the cost of finding a boat to dodge the blockade or maybe sailing to Yogyakarta via the Philippines. Everything was locked down tight by the Brits. Then we discovered that the British and Dutch authorities had granted special permission for a Dakota that would carry some of the starving and stranded Javanese back through Dutch airspace to Yogya and hatched a plan to hide Monem amongst them. That fell through for fear the British would find out and stop the rest of the mercy flights. Depressed, I went out to a street stall and dug through my pockets for a few, last cents to buy a bowl of noodles. I had been scrounging lunch money from Mr. Monem for days and now I was so poor I had to haggle the price of noodles down.

In such a situation, there was only one thing to do. I went back to the villa, dressed myself up to the nines, painted my face and drove out to the airfield in the biggest, shiniest car I could borrow. There, I grandly chartered a spanking, new plane from a Philippines operation, disdainfully signed a phony cheque on behalf of the Indonesian Republic for $10,000 and Mr. Monem and I did a Glaswegian, moonlit flit from Kalang under the very noses of the authorities, our illegal plane taxiing to the end of the runway with its propellers still turning as we ran from the bushes and scrambled aboard. In a trice, we had turned and were barrelling back along the airstrip, as all hell broke loose around the airfield, and flying far out beyond Sumatra at full speed so as to be out of range of Dutch fighters.

At Maguwo, in Yogya, the airstrip was covered with parked trucks to prevent any unannounced Dutch visits and we had an anxious ten minutes of circling in God-given cloud as the strip was cleared for our unannounced landing, while scanning the horizon for forewarned fighters that might be lurking at our only possible destination. I have to say they did Mr. Monem proud with bands and pomp and salutes and a big bunfight at the palace. His chubby, little face glowed with unalloyed joy at the speeches of mutual love and support. The two American pilots were the life and soul of the party, relieved, no doubt, to have made it alive. I wonder if they ever got paid. I sure as hell didn't.

Chapter Nine

One day I was summoned to the office of the Minister of Defence, Amir Sjarifuddin. The minister's quarters had just been moved to a new building from the ground floor of the Merdeka Hotel where I also lived and my courier was a stern, young officer called Suharto who arrived in a long-nosed Chrysler and clearly missed the days of Japanese, gratuitous face-slapping. From his glowering, silent intimidation, I feared I was being arrested for some capital crime and past horrors flooded back so that I arrived at the defence building a quivering wreck.

As we drew up the officer turned to me. 'Sister K'tut. This is not a taxi service. Petrol is short and expensive. As a foreigner, I hope you will be willing to demonstrate your loyalty to the Republic by making a donation towards your transport costs.' I looked up and saw the driver rolling his eyes and grinning at me in the rear-view mirror. He had seen all this before then. Having dressed in haste, I only had a few, scruffy Japanese notes with me. I handed them over in a bunched fist. He looked down on them in sneering disbelief but pocketed them anyway. It was the first time I had ever been mugged. It is strange to think that this same Suharto would be one of the executioners of Bung Amir but a short while afterwards.

Several cups of water inhaled in the waiting room and a few gulped-down cigarettes somewhat revived me, even though hungering and thirsting Muslims frowned on my blatant disregard of religion for it was the arid fasting month and they would take nothing till dusk. The building was buzzing with stiff-legged military and secretaries running in and out, jeeps screeching to a halt every few minutes and people shouting in the stairwells. It was unlike any ministry I had ever seen, tingling with an excitement that was near-panic. Normally they are places of slow time.

I already knew Amir as a gentle communist – in fact both a Christian convert and a tolerant communist – with the face of a benevolent owl. Bung Karno believed there were only two forms of religion – the differences between Muslim, Christian, Hindu etc. were irrelevant – those forms of belief hostile to life and those supportive of it. It was one his sacred Five Principles of Indonesian nationhood that we had all learned to chant back at him together with a lot of other pieties whose feet barely touched the ground. This was probably at the height of leftist party power when half the ministries seemed to be occupied by openly communist PKI members. Like all men who smoke pipes, Amir always had a need of jackets with pockets full of accessories, matches, pipe-cleaners, poking implements, tobacco pouches that gave him a permanent look of being weighed down and harassed. I had visited his office before and it was exactly what you would expect of an Oxbridge don, all scribbled notes and stacks of periodicals menacing a terminal bookslide. Propped in one corner was the violin that he played beautifully. At any moment I could be offered a glass of sherry and a mildly reproving but helpful comment on my last essay.

I was shown into it, a weird still centre of peace and calm. The door closed and we were back to the slow, ministerial time of a man who was being blatantly by-passed and kept out of the loop. Amir swivelled in his chair, plumed fragrant smoke like a volcano and smiled impishly. The room was stiflingly hot, the furniture careworn and heavily Dutch, the sort that seemed to disapprove of you. His Dutch diplomas were carefully framed on the wall behind his chair – if you wanted to insult someone in their own language you had better be fluent in it – and beside them was the mounted analysis of his urine sample from a fashionable Amsterdam clinic. There were, it seemed, many paths to distinction. The scars from his encounter with the Japanese he still bore on his body. 'Do sit down K'tut. Would you care for a glass of … water?'

'Water? No thank you Bung Amir. It would be unkind to ask a fasting person to bring me water.' Of course, he was a Christian and I would be assumed to be the same. In Indonesia, only the criminally insane have no religion and Bung Karno was careful to doff his *peci* equally to all faiths though not everyone, even in Yogya, practised what Bung Karno preached. Even the mystical goddess of the South Sea was to be included. Since all the rulers of Java had some sort of relationship with her – father, husband, lover – Bung Karno let it be known that he rendezvoused with her in a hotel room on the coast every Wednesday afternoon as a modern business man would his mistress.

Amir looked thoughtfully at his pipe and laid it down, cupped in a Javanese tourist ashtray that swarmed with curlicued flowers. He was a very trim smoker. The stem was never wet with saliva or sticky residue as when other men smoked pipes. 'I really should give this thing up, a habit I acquired as a student in Holland. Pipe tobacco is the whole problem of Indonesia in one small tin. The Dutch grow it for nothing here using child labour. The children become addicted to nicotine from touching the leaves while their parents starve to death. They export it, blend it, package it, charge import duty and sell it back to us for a fortune. We make cigarettes and cigars in Sumatra and Semarang. Why not pipe tobacco that tastes like this?' He looked crestfallen. 'Of course, the factories would now be in Dutch hands again.'

'Dutch hands? Has something happened?'

He ran his unDutch hands through tired hair and gestured at the outer door. 'Reports are coming in that the Dutch have attacked again, claiming violation of the Linggadjati agreement. It started at dawn. Yesterday. They've seized the principal ports in Sumatra and are advancing on all fronts in Java and pushing down from the north with heavy armour and non-stop airstrikes. They will be bombing us here any time now. Clearly this has been planned for months.' He shook his head in frustration. 'The mistake was allowing the Japanese to disband their local defence forces after the surrender so we had to build an army from scratch instead of just taking one over. Oh, I warned Soekarno and Hatta but you know you could take them to a restaurant and the only way you could get those two to stop just talking about the menu and actually decide what they wanted to eat was to get a Pemuda to hold a knife to their throats. Bung Karno likes to see himself as a thinker but he is really just a dreamer. I once wrote...' He pointed vaguely to some article, printed somewhere, lying in that heap there and shut his mouth. It was not the moment for disloyalty. 'Our forces are heavily out-gunned as usual but they are striking back and slowing down the Dutch, attacking stretched lines of supply but we have to spare them from suicidal acts. The army must be saved for total guerrilla warfare if that is what it comes to. It is all in the hands of the soldiers now.' He pointed at his stacked desk. 'At least we are still churning out papers and not yet burning them.' For an intellectual the ultimate cry of hope and despair.

'But what am I doing here? Do you want me to go back on the radio? Is that it?' I was already editing the text in my head. 'Treachery', 'Stab in the back' – or, 'Gallant, barefoot patriots crushed under the iron heel of tyranny'. Yes, that was better, classier.

'No. No. We have others for that, white people like Coast and Bondan who are useless at anything else. Some people don't help to carry luggage. They *are* luggage. No, what we have in mind for you is rather special as far as luggage goes.'

* * *

'Wim, darling! How lovely to see you. What a super surprise!' He was in the bar of the Hotel des Indes in Jakarta, where I was told he would be and clutching a beer to his bosom like it was a long-lost friend. Being a real long-lost friend, however, I went unclutched. The hotel was struggling back into civilian business after its various wartime requisitionings though a little understaffed owing to Pemuda reprisals against any Indonesian working there. Recently a pastry sous-chef had been fricasseed alive. I remembered that, during their occupation, Hatta had been installed in the hotel by the Japanese and found it hard to get served by the local staff who became deaf and blind to his every need. Around us all white faces again now, of course, a shock after Yogya, and a battered-looking palm court Eurasian orchestra, shiny at cuff and collar, sawing away at a syrupy version of the old hit 'Terang Bulan,' 'moonlight.' And on every table it was the raw white gleam of old-fashioned but serviceable linen. What I could have done with a few modern textiles! It was clear Wim had been in the bar for hours. 'You're drunk,' I said, sliding into a chair at his table and picking up our conversation pretty much where we had left off in Surabaya.

'Manxi? What the hell are you doing here? I hardly recognised you. Thought you were dead as a matter of fact. I sort of assumed you'd been gang-raped and your head cut off in the usual way. Maybe not in that order. 'Course I'm drunk. What else is there to do in a shithole like Batavia? Except maybe sex. And you can only do that so many times a day and I've done it but I find I can drink steadily from dawn till dusk, pace myself right. You can't do that with sex.' He swatted away a fat fly that was circling his beer. Two barflies, one glass then.

I was as nervous as a dog in a Chinese restaurant. In theory, no one knew that Manxi was Surabaya Sue. But after those pictures they had published from Yogya ... I had dyed my hair again – gone back to red and pulled it back into a bun of disapproval – wore a blind woman's dark glasses and was dressed as a Dutch housewife in some sort of dreadful, flowery housecoat thing. Most cunning, I was clumping around in a pair of ghastly flat shoes, almost clogs really, that changed my height and the way I walked and on my head I had the sort of sunhat bonnet affair one of the Voortrekkers might have worn to goad an ox-cart across the *veldt*. Just to be on the safe side I had even turned up the American accent a notch or two. To think I had risked my life in the mountains for years – for this. In my bag nestled some fake identity papers the ministry had given me but who knew how long they would withstand proper scrutiny. My real security lay in a white face. The Javanese barman, too young and intelligent-looking, was hovering with ears apout and showing far too much attention to our conversation for someone not supposed to speak English. Obviously a Pemuda spy. He should be more careful. I ordered a beer and shooed him away.

'I see the uniform's Dutch now, Wim.' He also had one of those pseudo-American haircuts that are just one step short of a scalping, perhaps the revenge of Red Indian barbers.

He shrugged down at the shoulder flashes. 'Now all the Brits have run away again – just like they did in Malaya – it makes me less obvious.' Yes, I thought, and when they left they waved their fists in the air and shouted '*Merdeka*!' to the dock workers and that was the Seaforth Highlanders, the same regiment that began the first British occupation of Java under Stamford Raffles in the previous century. 'You don't want to stand out in a crowd these days.'

I certainly didn't. I took off the dark glasses.

'So did you come here straight from Surabaya?'

He glugged more beer and gave a soft, ladylike belch. 'Like hell I did. Semarang first. Another mess, another shithole. The Brits had disarmed the Japs and then realised they couldn't deal with the extremists on their own, so they rearmed them and they really got stuck in. Tough, little buggers as you've every reason to know. Nasty business, each side massacring the other, Eurasians crucified and chucked in the river, little Chinese girls raped to death. But the Japs came through and, in the end, the Brits tried to give the Jap commander the DSO for services to the British Empire! When something like that sounds reasonable, it's the world that's gone crazy. Perhaps you think this is not a joking matter but the Indies has taught me that people are never more ridiculous than when they are being totally serious.' He narrowed his eyes and nodded, trying to look as wise as an owl and ending up just looking as tight as one – ridiculous. 'The politicians back home wouldn't have it of course – the medal I mean. Now The Hague is trying to give away all the gains just made by the Dutch army in the last "police action". They've stopped our advance before we could finish the job – frightened of America and the UN. Gutless bastards! Another week and we'd have swept the extremists into the sea. There's a difference between pouring oil on troubled waters and pouring it on raging flames. All that vicious fighting in Surabaya may have come as a bit of a shock to some of *us* but you can be sure it scared Soekarno to death, showed him he wasn't in control of anything. Now we have the Van Mook line with Java split into a leaky sandwich between us and the republicans but that won't hold. You'll see. It's only a matter of time. So where were you?'

I was in mid-gulp and started coughing. When it had stopped, 'Oh here, there. It was all confused after the fighting in Surabaya. I just kept my head down. Then I was up in Bandung for a bit. Oddly, I thought I'd try Semarang. I always liked it there but I'm having trouble with my stuff. A friend looked after my house here during the war and the extremists burned half of Bandung down so there's nothing left up there. They won't let me take everything I need back to Semarang – something to do with keeping the roads clear for military transport. I can't get through the road blocks. They tell me I need some sort of a priority pass. Can you help, darling?'

He shrugged. 'Sure, why not? I can give you a chit. No need for clear roads now that those windy sods have caved in ...' He was off on a rant again. I tuned out and studied the bar. This was a dangerous place. You never knew who you might meet. A man had come in, wearing some sort of shiny, green uniform, hawkish but smugly handsome, late twenties, looking somehow newly minted and heading towards us with a worrying fixity of purpose. As his shadow fell over the table, Wim looked up, lit up, stood up.

'Turk!' He stretched out his hand and they did one of those firm, manly double-grip things. 'Manxi, this is my friend Turk Westerling!' said with pride, almost infatuation. The man smiled a languorous lounge lizard smile and bestowed a handshake. Nasty piggy eyes. Cold hands. Who had hands that cold in the Indies – Indonesia? 'Sit down, Turk. Join us.'

The lizard smile turned into a shark's. 'No time, I'm afraid. I have to go to HQ. The enquiry. Why else would I be dressed like this? I came to pick up my lawyer.' A point across the room followed by a martyred look. 'I just wanted to wish you luck with the new project. I gather it's … proceeding. Keep me informed. See you around.' He nodded and shot me a look that lingered just long enough to seem threatening, telling me I had been filed away somewhere, then walked across to a table of civilians who all leapt to their feet and began pounding him eagerly on the back and contesting with each other the right to stand him a drink. They looked the sort of crew who made a lot of money doing something very boring.

'Marvellous man,' breathed Wim. 'Marvellous! Do you know Mountbatten picked him as his personal bodyguard and the rebels have put a price of 20,000 English pounds on his head? They call him Turk because he was raised in Istanbul. They know how to treat rebels there. Do you know, in a few short months he saved South Celebes from the extremists they sent over from Java.' He lowered his voice. 'And he always says his chief weapon was a golf club.' He tittered.

I frowned. 'A golf club?'

Wim nodded and whispered. 'Interrogation. Getting the terrorists to betray each other with a few well-applied golfing shots without using the *usual* golf balls – if you get my meaning – and then mowing them down like dogs. Apparently, in any village, after a demonstration drive or two, even the toughest nut would crack as our Turk carefully teed him up. So – one way or another – they all ended up spilling their guts.' A snigger. Then, bitterly, 'But are the government grateful? Do you know what they've done? They've started a secret inquiry into what went on while he was out there, set the bloody, blood-sucking lawyers on him. They're trying to pretend they didn't know and they'll hang him out to dry. That man's a hero! Think how many lives he saved in Celebes, think how many innocent villagers he protected from those Javanese thugs in the Pemuda.'

I felt dizzy and revolted but stuck to my main clause as they taught me at school. 'What's your new project, Wim darling? Your friend said you had one.'

He tapped the side of his nose with an unsteady finger. 'Ah, can't talk about that one. Very hush-hush.'

I pouted. 'You can tell me all about your brave friend but you won't tell me how clever you are? But darling that's just not fair. You have the right to be proud of yourself too.'

He brightened. 'I do, don't I? All right. Hey, here's an idea. Instead of telling you, I'll show you.' He grabbed his beret from the spare chair and drained his beer. 'Come on. I've got a jeep outside.'

I hesitated and looked across the room. One man was standing, demonstrating golfing swings, with lots of elephantine bum-wiggling, to the hysterical laughter of the rest. Westerling was simpering and blushing like a girl being paid her first compliment.

Then suddenly, a man I knew walked in and sidled over to the bar, laying out big braggadocio gestures on every side like a round of drinks. He was more rotund, more confident-looking and in an American colonel's uniform but there could be no mistaking him with that clenched-buttock, shake-your-sticking-balls-loose–with-gravity walk. It was Bob Koke, my old enemy from the Bali hotel trade. I slipped my dark glasses back on and crushed my bonnet down hastily over my face.

'Let's go,' I said.

* * *

I was expecting the ride from Hell. With all the beer he had drunk, Wim shouldn't have been driving a jeep at all. Close up his breath smelled like that of a cat I once had. But I was wrong. He drove like a little, old lady on her way to church, respecting others' rights of way, slowing at every intersection, courteously allowing pedestrians to step out in front of him. He even stopped for two heavily laden Indonesians to cross with a pig slung between them on poles.

The city had changed since my last visit. Everything had a makeshift, unshaven, wartime look and there was khaki everywhere. The only relief lay in the Jakarta trams that were daubed with paint patches in all kinds of cheerful colours to cover up the *Merdeka* slogans. The Pemuda no longer rode free of charge and, most striking of all, the conductors had resumed bowing to every Dutch passenger. And even white people wore the oddest combinations of clothes, anything to maintain basic decency – evening jackets over nightdresses, dress shirts over pyjamas so that the whole city looked on its way to a weird ball of bacchanalian disorder. Yogya was a different world where colonialism was already but a dim memory, a brief interlude blown away by a great wind of change. Here, it still lay on every hand. But then here the mutilated and injured of war had been filed neatly away whereas in Yogya, you saw them on every corner, young men with torn bodies and missing arms and legs or shattered faces, reduced to begging on the streets. What both shared was that every road was gap-toothed with fire-scorched buildings. But here alone there was business on every empty lot, bustling trade, life reasserting itself at the imperial trot, vigorous weeds pushing up through the broken concrete.

Much has been written about the plight of the Chinese after the Dutch surrender of WWII, subjected to every form of terror and despoliation, first by the Japanese and then by the revolutionaries. Even families that had been in Java for centuries were still not regarded as properly Indonesian. Lukman had once shrugged the whole thing off. 'A mongrel can give birth in a stable, that doesn't make mutts into horses' and snorted with fine, equine disdain through flared nostrils. But business is business and some Chinese played an essential part in the battle for the young Republic. In Surabaya, an important part in the supply chain had been the Chinese dealer who had negotiated to buy the steady supply of empty beer bottles from the British barracks. It was a nice, little earner for the quartermaster-sergeant and went straight into his back pocket. Only during the fighting did the Brits realise that the bottles were being shipped into the countryside to be sold to the Pemuda and made into Molotov cocktails to be thrown back at the British camps. Empty bottles were strategic military equipment and Karl and Ma would have made a killing in Surabaya. The trade was more important than it might seem. There was one particular little Indian officer, a tank commander called Zia ul-Haq, who stirred up endless trouble for the Brits. It was not that he particularly objected to Molotov cocktails being thrown at his tanks but non-halal Molotov cocktails were just not on, especially from fellow Muslims. It was exactly the sort of thing that had triggered the Indian Mutiny and its ghost put the wind up the British generals.

We were in Kota, Chinatown, and ideograms snarled up the sides of every building. Goods were stacked out on the pavements, hung from walls, strung up in doorways, everything from tin baths to fighting cocks. We pulled up in front of an old Chinese godown surrounded on all sides by a modern chainlink fence and with armed sentries outside, black Ambonese of the colonial army, many still bearing the marks of the Japanese camps where they had been treated even worse than the Dutch. Wim flashed a pass and was saluted in through the gate and parked against one wall. We walked down a gloomy corridor whose walls and floor were stained with a hundred past sins of incontinence. Wim's boots made odd sucking sounds on the lino paint. I couldn't help wondering if this was another place where Westerling had so cheerily practised his golfing shots. Then, into a cavernously shuttered space full of hot, still air and the smell of mildew with dust dancing in the slashed sunlight. Crates of military hardware lay stacked everywhere, stamped with long serial numbers, and other machines of death draped with tarpaulins with just their steel snouts protruding, great green and yellow drums embossed with stencilled skulls and crossbones and – suddenly – rows and rows of smiling Balinese carvings, laid out on shelves. I recognised the form, of course, the standard pair of male bust with teased-up headcloth and female with flared dance headdress, staples of the tourist trade. I had seen a thousand in my time on Bali. Gathered together like this they looked like a headhunter's hoard. I thought of Westerling again and shuddered.

Wim stopped and pointed with pride. 'Mine,' he said simply. 'Fresh in from Singers.'

I didn't quite know what to say. 'Yours? Are you a collector, Wim? Or do you mean you made them yourself? And why would anyone import Balinese carvings from Singapore? Are you going into the tourist trade?'

He shook his head unwisely and staggered under the impact. 'No. I mean I invented them, my idea. Look closer.'

I picked one up, looked at the top, the bottom, could see nothing out of the ordinary. A tourist carving like so many others. Junk.

Wim sniggered. 'Can't tell, can you? What do you think they

are made of?'

I shrugged. 'Some sort of softwood. They use anything these days.'

'Composition C-3, the latest plastic explosive.'

I nearly dropped it. Laid it hastily back on the shelf.

'No need to worry. It's totally inert until you set it off with a fuse. You can play football with it till then. I shouldn't eat it though if I were you or put it too near an open fire. It's raw explosive mixed with sawdust as a phlegmatizer.'

A what?'

He preened in insider knowledge. 'A phlegmatizer – a technical term of the trade. It makes the explosive phlegmatic, stable ... and painted down so you can't tell the difference from wood. Clever eh? You can carry these all over the shop and no one would ever suspect, stand them on the sideboard, let the maid dust them if you want to. Then, when you need to use one, you just drill a small hole, pop in a pencil fuse and boom! Up goes a railway bridge!'

I suddenly remembered the man astride the jeep bonnet on the road from Surabaya, clutching his two carvings in the mist and rain like they were very life to him. A saboteur?

'How lovely, Wim. What other toys have you got?'

He reached in another box, drew out a bottle of extra-hot chilli sauce. 'Make any meal go with a bang.' I raised quizzical eyebrows. He waggled it at me. 'Try to twist the top off here – see – and you start a five second fuse before it explodes. The idea is that blokes would bend down, trying to get the stiff top off, hold it against their laps to get more grip and boom! They become Westerling-proof! Only problem is most of the Javanese I know would think that chilli that actually blew your balls off was just the sign of a good batch!' He laughed. 'But you could be sure no

Dutchman would be fooling around with it.'

'Oh my God!' I manged to hang a smile on my face. 'I mean – how clever, darling. Did you really invent these all by yourself?'

He doodled coyly with his left foot in the dust and fluttered his eyelashes bashfully. 'Oh, it's been an uphill struggle,' he sighed. 'One shipment of our mango hand grenades went astray and ended up issued to native troops as rations. That ended rather badly. Very badly in fact.'

'Never mind, Wim dear. You'll come through. You're a very dogged sort of chap.'

'Dogeared?' He pouted. 'Why would you say that – call me dogeared?'

'Not dogeared. I said "dogged".'

'Dog*head*? ... What?' He looked confused, crestfallen and hung over. 'Oh Hell, forget it. Let's go and get a drink.' He brightened. 'Hair of the dog and all that.'

* * *

In the whole Nakamura affair, the only person whose relative honesty seemed beyond question was Thio Wie Koen, the Chinese 'fence' and professional criminal who handled the stolen goods, and he was banged up in jail. The Americans and the British, of course, were ultimately to blame for the whole mess or maybe the Japanese for the suddenness of their surrender which brings us full circle. After they dropped the atom bombs the Americans dumped the whole problem of the Jap forces in Indonesia in the laps of the Brits who were in no position to do much about them. Even the local surrender in Singapore had to be policed by Japanese troops like turkeys mixing their own stuffing. So the Jap army in the Indies was left high and dry with no means of survival. It is not to be expected that a bunch of heavily armed and very hungry young men would allow themselves to starve to death so they hit upon a relatively benign solution. As the Indonesians were busy declaring their independence up one end of town – through the good offices of the Japanese navy – up the other end, the Japanese army commander ordered the Kempeitai to seize the contents of the government pawnshops so that they could be used to finance the maintenance of their troops. Captain Hiroshi Nakamura obligingly removed some ten steel trunks and five crates stuffed with gold and jewellery and great bundles of cash and took them to headquarters.

But then, not quite. On the way, he admitted dropping off some ten million dollars' worth at his mistress's house, a leggy, Eurasian beauty known as Carla Wolff. What happened to the bulk of the loot was not known. Some thought that maybe it was converted into rice for the troops. Others that it just disappeared into kitbags and melted away back to Japan. Of course rumours about the treasure took on a life of their own for Indonesians love gossip. Occasionally someone would claim to know it was buried in Menteng and a wild crowd would suddenly appear in a flash with hoes on their shoulders and dig up all the gardens, heedless of the owners' protests. Or maybe it was in Bandung where harmless squatters would have their shacks knocked down by rampaging treasure-seekers. I know where it was. It never got to HQ at all.

Miss Wolff was not the sharpest blade on the penknife. She immediately started wearing diamonds to do the shopping and talking to the neighbours about eating her breakfast off gold plates and sleeping on a gold bed. Ears were pricked. Local snitches grassed to the Dutch who laughed at the whole idea of chests of gold and jewels. The Brits, who had been raised on

Treasure Island, paid more attention and soon poor Carla found her house ransacked by excited military police reliving their boyhood fantasies. Western men are prone to that in the tropics, as I know all too well. Perhaps it's something to do with going back into short trousers. After all, the process of male maturation is best seen as growing up in mastery of a peashooter only to have – at adolescence – a scary bazooka thrust into your hands without a revised manual. No wonder men are prey to constant anxiety. A few hours of being slapped around in a chair back at HQ prompted Carla to draw the boys a treasure map – of her own free will – and they romped off through the city with it, on a no-girls-allowed adventure, yodelling with joy. Thio Wie Koen whose house lay in the crosshairs of the X on the map was infinitely obliging, handing over bundles of worthless Dutch guilders that, as an honest and innocent banker, he had been asked to sit on and had stashed in an enormous, antique, iron safe. The Brits brought in a crane and carried the whole thing off – safe and all – for the photographers and dramatic courtroom display as a symbol of evil. Various people were convicted of miscellaneous deeds of ungodliness, Nakamura got a sentence of ten years and served hardly any of it and a long bicker began about how much more of what was by now known as 'Nakamura's gold' had disappeared into Dutch and British pockets along the long, judicial pathway. The newspapers adored the story. It had sex, gold, corruption, a little judicious, judicial violence, even a huge diamond hidden inside the hollow heel of a crashing, British army boot. Carla loved all the publicity and was much photographed – sheathed in silk but still leggily provocative – and managed to make the world's oldest profession once more exotic and mysterious though she had to swop her gold bed for a prison straw paliasse for a while. The Brits were shown in the newspapers handing over the remnant of the treasure to the Dutch – absurdly regarded as the legal owners. The real legal owners were of course ignored. Carla found a new rich friend and got herself a smart, new hairdo. Many hands dipped into many pies and many years later, one of Carla's frequent daughters would be married to an Indonesian Foreign Minister. Everything died down nicely. Business as usual. Then the Black Fan moved in.

Towards the end of the war, Nakamura had been involved with this secret organisation which is why the Brits had first been interested in him – that and the fact that he was the interpreter between the Japanese and the Indonesians throughout the Proclamation of Independence affair. The Black Fan were set up to fight the Allies, under Japanese leadership, if the shit ever hit the other metaphorical fan and the West attacked Java. It had never been activated but still existed because trying to officially dissolve something that did not officially exist was like trying to shoot a ghost but – like everything else – it had shivered into a thousand factions as different groups reinterpreted its purpose. In Surabaya, it had been hijacked by the Eurasians – now calling themselves 'Dutch' again – and been a particular focus of Bung Tomo's rage. It was likely they were behind the flag incident at the Oranje Hotel. In Jakarta, the Black Fan stood by the Republic yet regarded themselves as rightful heirs to Nakamura's golden inheritance. A short visit to Thio Wie Koen's house and Westerling-type interviews with his domestics established that the garden of the abandoned house next door was the place to dig. They dug – or rather the servants did. The Black Fan found the rest of the treasure and seized it. Not wanting to waste perfectly good holes, they then shot the servants and pushed them in and fired the house out of sheer bad habit. The treasure was clearly unsafe and useless in Jakarta. It had to be got to the republican capital, Yogya, to be used to keep the war going. That was now to be my job.

* * *

The bar of the Hotel des Indes was not the brightest place to hold a secret rendezvous. I had no idea who I was supposed to be meeting. It was evening and the servants were pattering around, preparing for the dinner rush. The *rijstaffel* here was justly famous, dozens of small but delicious Indonesian dishes – served with an aristocratic disregard for the washing-up involved – that you mixed and matched to your own taste. Looking around, I could see no one who was an obvious contact. Perhaps that was the point. They were the sort of burghers for whom the hardships of the Indies once more amounted to having to keep the liqueur chocolates in the fridge. Even Wim was not around, probably neglecting his drinking to keep up his sexual quota for the day.

Parched air was blowing in from the veranda carrying sounds of the city with it and rustling the potted palms and the dogged, old orchestra were back on with – oh no! – 'Terang Bulan'. The singer was a very pretty, kohl-eyed Eurasian girl in a black *cheongsam*. At one stage in her act, she sashayed around the room among the indifferent patrons like Fanlight Fanny. Their minds were wholly on their stomachs and they swatted her away, bending over their plates of asparagus soup that looked and smelled uncannily like the product of an elephant's hot ejaculation. She paused by my table, fixed me very firmly in the eye and sang the first verse again – out of place:

The full moon is shining on the edge of the river.
A crocodile is floating and people think it's dead.

Don't believe what people say.
They are brave enough to swear an oath but are afraid
    of death.

I realised for the first time what a thoroughly weird song it was. She ran her fan coquettishly across my face, a fan made of ostrich feathers dyed black – a black fan. Very subtle.

The band took a break in a clatter of musical instruments and thin applause. The singer gave me another significant look over her shoulder and walked off, swinging her hips the way Charlie Chaplin did his cane. Somehow, it came out all wrong and, in that sheath dress, she ended up looking like a penguin. Still, I had seen *Casablanca* and knew how these nightclub vamps worked. I followed.

The dressing room was really a poky cupboard. I pushed through the door behind her and she turned and stared back at me, gimlet-eyed – the inevitable cocked cigarette wafting smoke, heat melting the makeup on her face and making her look like a failed waxwork. It was a place where – apart from allegedly beautiful singing stars – they also stored unwanted parasols for the veranda. Somehow they had squeezed a dressing table in too. Queen Wilhelmina looked doubtfully down at us from a cheap print on the wall.

'Password,' she said.

That pulled me up short. 'Password? No one told me anything about a bloody password. What's the point? We both know what's what. Let's get on with it.'

'Password. Listen sister, it's a dog-eat-dog world out there. No tickee, no washee. Password.' She had seen *Casablanca* too and let her lip curl Bogartishly.

I thought desperately. '*Merdeka*,' I said.

She laughed. 'You see. You knew it all the time.' Oh my God! She reached back and took a derisively small handbag from the dressing table, fished in it and pulled out a piece of paper. 'Here's the address. Make sure you're not followed. Go there now. They're waiting. Memorise the address and eat it.' They were treating me to dinner of a sort then. She sucked on her lip nastily. 'Christ, they said you were a plain-looking woman but in that frock you look like the bride of Frankenstein.' A veritable film buff. 'And the shoes, darling. The shoooes!'

* * *

The rickshaw driver was not happy. 'You should not be out alone at night, madam. It is not safe for you. It is not safe for me either to have you in my rickshaw. There is madness about.' He was the usual wisp of a man with incredible power in his legs, a sort of human praying mantis.

It did not seem unsafe. Nowhere in Indonesia ever seemed unsafe to me. We had left behind the thronged streets, teeming with the roadside stalls of sunset and lit by a thousand smoky lamps and were in one of the well-heeled areas of Jakarta, though he barefoot, me in clogs and the tyres hushed by deep, soft dust underfoot. Bungalows set back in lush grounds, curving, country roads like in the American deep south but brightly lit, big shade trees, the odd smart Dutch sentry patrolling and no lights on inside with everyone tucked up safely in bed by 9 o'clock at night. It was the sort of well-ordered place where you used to find a dozen convicted murderers from the jail shaving the grass with huge, razor-sharp machetes while guarded by one small man with a stick. They probably still had night watchmen here who pottered about signalling 'All's Well' by the tinkling of bamboo gongs. Security is never a fact but an assumption. Most of these houses had been requisitioned by Japanese – now gone – and their current ownership would be a matter of some confusion, since much of the seized Dutch property had been hastily sold on by the Japanese to the Chinese. And now everyone had ended up feeling entitled but dangerously outraged. We pulled up outside a white building looking like a child's drawing of a house, complete with bay windows and a chimney that can never have been used except by Santa. It was much further than I had thought. I had negotiated hard with the rickshaw driver and I paid him double what I had promised to slake my guilt. He stared down at it in incredulity. No one had ever done that before. '*Merdeka*,' I said in explanation.

I walked down a concrete path, a faint but grateful wind hissing through the palms overhead, my pseudo-clogs echoing off into darkness. Some great insect of the night whirred past like a clockwork toy and made me duck. No sign of life inside. I stood on the step and hesitated. I could stand there all night. Taking my courage and the doorknocker in both hands, I rapped loudly and heard it ricochet through the house. Something about the sound said it was empty. Nothing stirred. There was a poem somewhere about this – travellers knocking on moonlit doors. Tell them I came and no one answered. I felt relief and turned to go but old notions of duty and loyalty flooded back, not so easily dismissed. I knocked again, then tried the door. Bugger! It was unlocked. That meant I had to go in. Of course – as in every horror movie – the light switch did not work, mere futile clicking, but there seemed to be a sort of dull glow under a door at the end of the passage. Every instinct was to creep, holding my breath – perhaps there was a huge hole in the floor just waiting for me to fall through – but if there was anyone intent on doing me harm, they knew

I was here and were well prepared so that mere creeping would not save me. So instead I clogged heartily down the corridor and threw open the door.

'*Merdeka*!' It was truly a word for all occasions.

Three astonished, brown faces looked up at me. One paused in the act of bringing a cigarette to his lips. They were sitting round a table, playing cards in an otherwise bare room. Curtains whose hideous pattern was an offence against Nature were tightly drawn over the windows. The players must have been there some time since the cigarette fug would have smoked kippers. On the table lay two huge revolvers that you could have beaten a buffalo to death with but no one moved a hand towards them. Then the furthest figure leapt up, sending his chair crashing to the ground and his face broke into a ravishing smile.

'Sister K'tut!'

'Uki! How? When? What are you doing here?' At first I had not recognised him dressed in a sarong and *peci* hat.

He laughed. 'Let me look at you, K'tut. Wah! In that outfit, with those shoes … you look like a miniature Dutch housewife – except you don't look angry.'

'But how did you …?'

'I grew up in Jakarta until I was sent to the Koranic school in Surabaya. I got a message that my mother was ill so I came back here. Here too there is fighting to be done.' He looked older, thinner, wearier. In Bali, a mark of maturity is to file down your teeth. The world seemed to have taken a file to Uki's whole body and spirit.

'What of Lukman and Reza?'

His face fell. 'Lukman went north to Madiun, to the communists. Reza is still in Malang. He married a girl there and left the army. I think she was a nice girl. He always wanted to be a farmer and make things grow. Oh, sorry. Let me introduce my Uncle Wirno and Pak Dion, they are in charge of the operation.'

We shook hands, muttered greetings, the usual Asian wet fish handshake and hands pressed to hearts. Two older men, quieter, reflective types. Dion looked at me hard, got straight down to business. Only Uki offered me a seat. 'We needed Uki to make sure you were who you claimed to be. Otherwise we wouldn't have bothered with a silly boy like him.' He sneered at Uki who seemed to shrivel in his gaze. Not a nice man. 'Now we've done that, this is the plan. We have to move fast. Here, too many people are getting interested, especially that commie queer Tan Melaka and his nancy boys.' His lip curled in contempt. To avoid wasting the tail end of the look he threw it at Uki. I could tell that Pak Dion and I would not be chums.

Uncle Wirno chimed in. 'As we told them in Yogya, the Nakamura loot is hidden in four big jerrycans. We filled them up with the gold and jewellery and poured hot wax over them, leaving just a few inches at the top for a separate compartment that is filled with petrol. If anyone looks inside all they will see is petrol. The weight is right. If they slosh it around all they will hear is petrol. We hang the cans on the outside of the truck. Inside, the truck's filled with Dutch furniture which is all anyone will search if we are stopped. You unload the stuff in Semarang and then you have to slip across the Van Mook line into republican territory and on to Yogya, on horse and on foot. It won't be easy.'

'You could do that yourselves. And what do *I* have to do?'

'The whole of North Java is locked up tight as a drum. We expect *you* to get the travel permit from your Dutch friend – without that we can do nothing – and you sit up front and show your big, ugly, white face, slap the stupid natives around if they dare come near and scream at the troops at the roadblocks if they

city, the roadblocks were manned by pink conscripts straight from Holland and a little more finicky and very, very jumpy. It would have been better if I had spoken Dutch but I did my snotty American act and I did it well, trumping their Dutch snottiness with my transatlantic own. I complained loudly at being stopped at all, at being made to get out of the truck, at being made to stand in the hot sun, at having my goods turned over. I dropped Wim's name and the nickname of the governor and – God help me – Turk Westerling's for good measure. Right on top of the pile of my worldy goods I flaunted the two fake Balinese carvings Wim had given me as a disconcerting, last-minute present. You never knew, someone might recognise them as a *laissez-passer*. I had suggested flying a Dutch flag but my companions balked at that. Still, our little act left the troops grinning like Cheshire cats and rolling their eyes in our dust, glad to see the back of us. The jerrycans, lashed to the outside and clanging at every pothole, were mercifully ignored. There were, I suddenly realised, five of them not four. Of course, one of them really was for petrol.

Then we were out on the open road, taking the southern, less-militarised route, and we all felt the atmosphere lift just to be out of Jakarta in a cool sunny day that got even cooler as we headed for the heights of Puncak. A short while ago, this would have been too dangerous a route, since the area swarmed with militia who delighted in shooting up the road and burning down the houses when there was no traffic to occupy their minds but, in accordance with the latest ceasefire, republican forces had withdrawn to the other side of the Van Mook line and now once more mist clustered and curdled peacefully in the hollows of the tea plantations as it had for a hundred years. Andrew was not a great conversationalist, it was true, but he liked to sing. Unfortunately, all he knew was hymns. The first slopes prompted

'Rock of Ages' in a fine, ebony, baritone voice that made the hair on your neck stand up. His rendition of 'Abide with Me' in Dutch was completely unironic and as we ground down the escarpment he embarked on a tune that – in English – would have urged the hills of the north to rejoice. It was infectious. Shrugging off my Wee Free constraint, I joined in. Then I treated him to a solo rendition of 'Oh God Our Help in Ages Past' and he replied with an unseasonal but spirited version of 'We Three Kings of Orient Are' with horn accompaniment. Poor Uki can never have been subjected so intensively to the sounds of the Christian faith.

It was a day of easy travelling. We even stopped off along the way to bathe in the hot springs and eat our leaf bundles of fried rice with our fingers. It began to feel like a holiday but then another lorry pulled up with excess of macho panache and out spilled a bunch of new Dutch recruits, knees unbrowned and overly boisterous with too much blood and sperm in them. They looked sneeringly at us as we ate together in unsegregated harmony and without benefit of cutlery, made monkey gestures and pissed impudently against the trees as if in our faces, while we stared back at them blankly. I could see Uki beginning to heat up. Luckily we were completely unarmed but that just made us feel more vulnerable. We could not afford any trouble. We packed up and left to hoots and jeers. We had not gone fifty yards when we heard the rat-a-tat-tat of automatic fire behind us. At first, I thought it was more boyish exuberance, then I looked back and saw green-clad figures bursting out of the tree cover and spraying bullets at the screaming boys who had stupidly posted no guards like real amateurs. Then came the sharp bang of a grenade and their lorry went up in a sheet of flame that sent a gust of hot air and a stench of roasting flesh over us. Andrew started braking and peering in the mirror – not the thing to do when people were shooting.

'Go!' I screamed. 'Go!'

He stamped on the accelerator and we fish-tailed away. After some hours of silent rumination Andrew reached a conclusion. 'The outer islands do not want to fight for *Merdeka*,' he said. 'Maybe they would like it but they lack the anger. Only the Javanese have the anger and, when the Dutch have gone, we fear to be ruled by them in their anger.' He nodded glumly but soon revived us somewhat by singing a Dutch version of 'Onward Christian Soldiers' in a voice that merged into the bass growl of the engine. Even little Uki joined in, bravely lah-lahing the chorus from the back of the truck.

* * * *

Bandung had been blasted apart by peacekeeping. The whole south of the city was a windblown desert since the withdrawing militia had fired it in patriotic pique. Admittedly that was where most of the Chinese had lived so the act was double-edged. I spent the night in a filthy hotel room that still smelled of smoke while the boys had a better time of it on the cool veranda and kept me awake with snores that sounded like a herd of foraging bush elephants. The hotel staff counted it a mark of my nasty American meanness and suspicious nature that I insisted on the jerrycans being stored inside my room. We actresses must suffer such things for our art.

We set off before dawn, the truck still stinking of human barbeque, determined to make it to Semarang the same day. It was hopeless. Much of the road surface had been ripped up by manoeuvring tanks and heavy rains had completed the work of destruction. Aircraft circled threateningly overhead. We spent hours grinding through the mud, in the midst of heavy traffic, both military and civilian, our souls unuplifted by Andrew's hymns. At several points we got stuck. The tyres were old and worn and would not grip despite our pushing and throwing branches under the spinning wheels that covered us in slurry from top to toe. We finally decided to head north to join up with the coastal road and it was night before we reached Pekalongan. Perhaps that was just as well. By dawn's early light the devastation caused by recent events was clear – the ousting of the feudal regents who had sent the people's sons off to die in Japanese labour camps and the massacre of the Chinese and the collaborating government officials. Fresh, new graves sprouted everywhere. Some of them were local boys the Japanese had tested new and untried vaccines on. This bloodsoaked interregnum was referred to in smooth bureaucratese as the 'Three Regions Movement'. The Indonesian army had put it down after a vicious battle only to now have the Dutch move back in, Shiva's weary wheel going full circle with divinely gripping tyres. There was another reason we stayed the night. Having only one functioning jerrycan for fuel, we now ran out of petrol.

Ironically, as we should have learned from our cargo, petrol was worth its weight in gold here. The next morning, after a stale breakfast of mildewed rice porridge, we scoured the market and sidled up to the hotel staff with heavy hints of still heavier tips. Petrol? No chance, they sneered. It was not like that first time, back in Bali, where the gods led me to run out of fuel outside Nura's palace. Here we were just stranded in Hell and without hope of redemption. Finally, Andrew discovered a platoon of fellow-Ambonese colonial troops camping on the beach. Two windblown hymns later our problem was solved in the idiom of armies everywhere. 'It fell off the back of a truck,' he grinned, tying the petrol securely onto the back of our own.

The endless fields changed from sugar cane to tobacco and back again as we bowled along a well-maintained road. Brightly dressed workers teemed between the rows of crops, indistinguishable from the flowers, as in a romantic Dutch 'Beautiful Indies' painting, while the light glinted off the nearby sea that freshened both the earth and the air with its neatly marcelled waves. It did not look like a country at war with itself. From afar, sunlight gleamed on the roofs of the well-proportioned city buildings and monuments, a fine example of colonial town-planning. Only when seen from much nearer would it all prove as raddled by time and neglect as poor, dear Gloria Swanson had in close-up.

The roadblocks were tighter here. The Dutch were enforcing a blockade of republican areas, cutting them off from imports of food and stifling exports with their warships cruising just over the horizon in angry vigilance. At the entry to the city was a guard post where my goods were thoroughly rifled, the hideous sofa turned upside down and prodded forensically and Wim's travel permit treated with extreme suspicion by the officer in charge – to the point of telephone calls to HQ. It had been a mistake to have the signature of someone with too high a rank on it. I must have underestimated Wim. A young lieutenant returned and gave a smart salute. Wim must have done his stuff. 'Proceed. You are lucky there have been no attacks on this road all week. Otherwise we would not let you through. Why does your truck smell so bad? Have you been transporting rotten meat?' A sad truth, nowadays human flesh was just meat. We said nothing but shrugged and smiled politely. They stamped our passes. It was no longer the moment for stamping my feet.

We had been given an address out in the cool garden suburb of Candi Baru – duly decoded, memorised and the paper it was written on eaten. The Indonesians had an obsession with sending us coded messages, communicating in great chains of z's, k's and w's that looked like the world's longest Polish surnames. It could take hours to translate the simplest, trivial note. Old Joe Kennedy had a better approach, 'put nothing in writing' but then he had secret names for everything and everyone. He was always and everywhere 'The Big Boss' – in capitals – while Gloria was 'the vehicle.' Architect Karsten's original, non-racial principle for Candi Baru had somewhat crumbled under pressure of war and the Chinese had flocked together here in a vain search for security. They were happy to see a new, white face apparently moving in, a hopeful sign that their troubles were finally over. No one seemed to know exactly what was to happen now so we settled down to wait in our fine villa with its Balinese carvings on the sideboard and listened to the slow ticking of the hall clock. God knows we had enough furniture. The truck was parked as far away as security allowed and downwind, as its sweet stench of human flesh steadily ripened in the sun. Only after three days did we find the severed human hand trapped in the folds of the canvas roof, blueish-black and swollen up like a curry puff, with the shrivelled tendons pulling the fingers into an obscene gesture – I suppose that's what you call having the last word like Ma with her unpaid gas bill all those years ago – after which the stink finally began to dissipate on the wind. It should be easy enough to slip through the line and make our way home to Yogya. Home? Yes it was home now.

To pass the time, I began to tame the garden, cutting back the intrusive weeds, weighing in on the side of aromatic frangipani and bougainvillea. No matter how much it was insulted, the world of plants always came back. A beacon of hope for the new republic. But somehow the weeds always sprouted far more vigorously than the cultivars. Not so hopeful then. Or perhaps it was just proletarian plants triumphing over useless aristocrats, native plants over outsiders. Politics was everywhere and there was no escape even in the rustling flower borders any more than on the strikebound plantations and estates. Of course, it was only a matter of days before the gossip started amongst the neighbours. It was the usual sexual tittle-tattle, all whispers and sniggers, the nonsense chatter that a single woman suffers in a house full of men whenever undergarments of both sexes appear mingled on the washing line – what you might call 'oral' sex in its truest sense. I cared not a hoot but it was bad for us to be noticed so I got in an ancient, female maid whose busybody pottering guaranteed the chastity and due hierarchy of sleeping arrangements and kept the knickers unentangled. And as soon as she left every afternoon I took Andrew to bed with me.

Ladies, a hard man is good to find and – as the white folks back in America used to say – it's true what they say about Dixie! That young man had been greatly blessed and was happy to share that blessing with me, a body that was a *smorgasbord* of unknown tastes and textures. The kinky hair not at all like a doormat but wonderfully soft and silky. There were no passionate avowals between us, they were not needed. It was not exactly romantic love but simply a matter of nature reasserting itself inside the house as it was outside and it was a time of honeyed madness, friendly, uncomplicated, even funny – a time of musky nighttime warmth and the comfort of waking to the sound of another human heartbeat caught in the morning flutter of the windblown curtains and I astonished myself by behaving like a schoolgirl – baking cakes, giggling, putting bright flowers in jamjars. I remembered fondly my joking about my womanly needs with the boys in Malang the night of our 'victory' broadcast when they were feeling their oats and off tom-catting. Those needs had finally come home to roost. One dawn, I woke up at cockcrow laughing from my sleep at an old joke that had popped into my head from girls' school. 'Q: Why should you always ask for boy jelly babies in the sweet shop? A: Because with boy jelly babies you always get that delicious, little bit extra!' But I wonder, was it even about sex? After all, for generations women have been having sex with men for the much realer comfort of sleeping with them.

Initially, little Uki was shocked by the new arrangement, like a teenager whose mother still shows green shoots of sexual life but after a few days he came to me, took a deep breath and made a resolute and manly declaration. 'Big sister,' he blushed. 'You are not a beautiful woman, so you cannot hope for a real Indonesian man who is Sundanese or Javanese. It is natural that you and Andrew are together. It is like the humping of buffalo.'

* * *

We set off at dawn, five of us, ourselves and two others come over from Yogya, slipping across the demarcation line and meeting up with a gnarled dwarf who was tending six tough and sceptical little horses tethered under a tamarind tree. We took the jerrycans and each a bundle containing a change of clothing and, for some reason, the Balinese carvings and abandoned ourselves to the embrace of fortune. Its first gift was two battered tommy guns and a cumbersome, Japanese rifle with only three bullets that we had to carry.

'Sister, you will ride. The rest of us will walk.' Andrew being the gentleman. The jerrycans were hitched onto the horses' backs, the guns slung over the men's shoulders.

'Nonsense,' I snapped. 'I'm not some frail, little china doll. I'll walk like the rest.'

He sighed. 'You walk too slowly. You will hold us back. It is better you ride. We must move fast. We may be followed.' I rode – on a saddle that was like sitting astride a bundle of chopped firewood. We were led along little, zigzagging mice trails that circled the villages and ducked under the trees and were obviously made for the use of smugglers. We travelled for days, camping at night under tarpaulins, avoiding roads and clattering across rivers on stony fords. The dwarf looked after the horses and navigation, while the two other Javanese did the cooking and spoke their own local language so that they could only reliably communicate via Uki. For me they had set aside some precious cans of British bully beef that I insisted we all share. We ate them with rice and chilli and hardly talked at all but lived surrounded by a cloud of iridescent, twittering birdsong. It was the mating season for them but not for us. Andrew and I kept our distance by unspoken agreement. Time and place are everything. We both knew that ours had passed.

It is no great way from Semarang to Yogya and there is a fine, main road that the Dutch always used, preferring to sail from Batavia to Semarang rather than taking the land route but we avoided it, heading out far to the east to make sure we were in secure, republican territory and skirting round Mount Merapi, a great, lowering, smoking, volcanic presence. Every time I asked how far we had to go there would be a long process of passing the message from Uki to the Javanese to the dwarf and the answer would come back – always the same. 'A little bit far still.' I had looked at Merapi from so many sides now I began to suspect that we were simply circling it endlessly but who can remember the silhouette of a conical volcano? It is like trying to remember the different sides of an orange.

We were coming down a slope, ricefields on one side, scrubby forest on the other – our steps softly tree-muffled and drowned in a skirl of rasping cicadas – when a series of sharp, metallic clicks told us we were no longer alone. We were surrounded and a dozen pairs of young, expressionless eyes were peering at us down a dozen gun barrels. It was like an uprising against the teachers by the third form.

'Hands up!'

Boys of that age have no experience of life and so no pity. The whole of Java was awash with starving, feral children, some acting as guerrillas, others as criminal gangs with no one sure any more where the line lay between the two. Perhaps there was no line any more. It is at such points that you become abruptly aware of how you must appear to others. A white woman – to villagers we are all 'Dutch' – and an Ambonese – both defined as 'the enemy' with their Javanese lackeys. They were as unconvincingly dressed as ourselves, some with British army blouses – complete with bullet holes and bloodstains worn like medals – one or two with Australian bush hats, some with overlarge Dutch boots and others barefoot – but all painfully skinny and underfed with great, soulful eyes that had seen too much. Some looked angry but others about to cry, as if a single, kind word would make them burst into tears. Gathered together they looked like the urchins' chorus from *Carmen*. I let Uki do the talking. A woman should not appear to be too pushy, too 'Dutch'.

I could see that Uki was not making much of an impression. There were language difficulties. He was disconnected and confused, lying of course about us and our mission, but had not had the sense to prepare something in advance to which he would stick, come hell or high water, which is always the secret of plausibility. Ask any politician. It was time to intervene.

I spoke in my very best Indonesian and smiled, smiled, smiled as I climbed very slowly off the horse. 'Excuse me.' They all turned and lowered their guns at the sound of a woman's voice. A very good sign. I put my hand gently around the shoulders of the smallest and gestured at the bundle of possessions tied in front of the saddle. He leant against me, starving for motherly love. Give me a bag of sweets and I'd have them all eating out of my hand in minutes. But, of course, I had no sweets. My voice choked. 'I have something here that may help. May I …?' I dumped it on the ground so they could all see what was inside. No hidden guns or grenades. Nothing nasty. I dug out the letter from General Soedirman, carefully preserved and presented it to the young man who seemed to be the leader. He looked at the envelope and turned it over and returned it politely. Of course, they were local village boys. He could not read. None of them could. Now, they asserted, we would have to go and find a man of learning. In a village around here, I knew, that probably meant some illiterate and opinionated old imam who had mastered a few verses of the Koran off by heart and would have our infidel throats slit on a whim. Not a good idea.

'Wait!' I crouched and dug further. I pulled out a photograph of myself and Bung Karno smiling together at the conference in Yogya and held it out proudly. They gathered round and uttered 'Wah!' and burst into loud chatter, by now completely forgetting to point their lethal weapons at us. Alas it did not solve our problem. It was now clear we were people of such enormous eminence that we could not possibly be allowed to just pass quietly by. We must go off and meet the man of learning as an absolute necessity, perhaps we should be taken even further afield to meet a man of even greater learning. It was obvious we must either fight or go with them. We went, half guests, half prisoners, all keeping a sharp eye on each other.

It was a trek of several hours through patchy landscape and then yapping dogs announced a settlement of some sort through the rustling trees. We walked out into a clearing of beaten earth hedged in by simple, thatched huts. People tumbled out in various states of undress and stared at us. Only men. No women to be seen. And all armed. A bad sign. Everyone started talking at once and pointing in different directions. A curtain twitched back across the door of a hut and a big man emerged looking annoyed, wondering what all the noise was about. He straightened up. It was the man of learning. It was Lukman.

He had done well for himself, filled out, put on weight – no *taken* on weight – assumed an air of substance and sported a beard. He looked astonished.

'K'tut! Little brother Uki! How did you know where to find me?'

'Well ...'

* * *

'After Surabaya I began to think. I began to read.' His eyes were sore and watery from constant exposure to cookhouse woodsmoke, not from reading. 'I read the story, "Surabaya", written by that writer, Idrus, the one who came to see us at the cement factory. I think I would have shot him dead if he had still been around, I was so angry, but later I came to see that his sarcasm about things was right. The old men just want to put themselves in the place of the Dutch. They don't want things to really change. We must immediately nationalise all Dutch property and deport every last Eurasian, repudiate the national debt, redistribute the land to the peasants, throw off the Dutch queen, ban the use of the Dutch language, trams should be free but here there are no trams so we should have new trams in every village ...' Lukman went off on a rant, gathering up the loose threads of a whole lifetime's resentments, rattling over the points like one of his imaginary trams. We should have been sitting round a jolly camp fire, sharing confidences and memories in the flickering firelight but the night was too hot for a camp fire so we just sat in a circle and stared blankly at the empty centre as if we were looking at a pie with no filling.

'... and forbid the serving of potatoes in schools ... So why are you going to Yogya?'

Uki grinned and dropped his voice to a whisper. 'We have had an adventure. We are taking back ...'

'Vital information,' I interrupted and glared at Uki. 'We have been collecting information about the Dutch stance in the next round of negotiations, stuff our delegates need to know to strengthen their hand in The Hague. We must get it back to them as quickly as possible.' The fewer people who knew what we were up to the better. They might well decide they could find a better use for our cargo.

Lukman grinned and shook his head. 'You remember how Bung Tomo used to talk about the fiery Pemuda versus the old men and their endless conferences – wild, bull buffaloes versus bleating, castrated goats. Nothing has changed. Nothing. The politicians cannot be trusted. They are not the solution but part of the problem. Only the army can act as the guardians of the people's liberty. Only the army is honest.' He looked at the outer darkness where our horses were tethered and the jerrycans were stacked. 'You have much petrol there, sister, and this route belongs to us. Perhaps you will give me some? About half should do.'

Uki and I froze and looked at each other. 'It is not mine to give. It is urgent to get it to Yogya. They have tanks there that are desperate for fuel. They need it for the tanks to defend the city.'

'They also need it for the big, fancy saloons the old men drive around in, waving at everybody and smiling to themselves. What if I were just to take it? How would that be?'

'Tanks,' I urged. 'They need it for the tanks. You do not have tanks here.'

'No.' Sadly. Bitterly. 'Here we do not have tanks. Keep your petrol.' He got up and went huffily to bed, leaving us in a backwash of petrol-fuelled guilt.

The next morning when we got up, Lukman had already stalked off on patrol but one of his men was sent to accompany us to join up with the Yogya road that followed the southern coast in from the east. We clanked on with our jerrycans intact, sounding for all the world like medieval knights in armour.

'It is no trouble,' our escort smiled away our thanks when we reached the tarmac. 'No trouble is too great for friends of Pak Lukman. Did you know he is a hero of the Battle of Surabaya? There he led an attack that killed over a hundred Indians. Some he killed with his bare hands, others by just looking at them.' He raked us with his own blazing eyes in demonstration. 'Those boys are so brave – real men – not just talkers. We all live in their shadow. Wah!'

So Lukman had become a basilisk. Our lingering guilt evaporated like the mist in the sun and the absurdity of his words kept us smiling as far as the first roadblocks around the city. Even in those early days the Revolution was already being eaten alive by its own cancerous myths and I could feel myself being squeezed to fit into the narrow mould of official history till I came out like one of those identical jelly babies of my childhood. And, of course, all jelly babies had to be boy jelly babies with that little bit extra.

* * *

'K'tut, we owe you an enormous debt of gratitude. The contents of those three jerrycans will make a tremendous contribution to the war effort. It is a pity that Amir cannot be here to welcome you.' We were back in Yogya after a relatively easy final stretch on horseback, in the palace – Bung Karno in one of his spotless, white uniforms, sitting on an old, collapsing, rattan chair and flicking disdainful cigarette ash onto the red carpet. I remembered what Bung Amir had said about his inability to make choices. Maybe the uniform was a response to that. It was either on or off. Simple.

'Three? There were four. What happened …?'

He shrugged and smiled – as ever – waving the inconvenience of precise accounting away as beneath his dignity. 'Three, four … what's the difference? You will notice that half the cabinet have gone. Amir for instance. After he signed the Renville agreement with the Dutch, accepting the Van Mook line, there was no saving him politically. He knew that of course but he had to sign it so the international community would bring pressure on the Dutch and stop the attack. He sacrificed himself for the nation. So now he is no more.'

'Yes but if one of the jerrycans has gone missing …' I sounded like someone singing that horrible roundel about green bottles hanging on walls they made us learn at school.

'I have a present for you, from the Indonesian people.' He reached elegantly into a jacket side pocket with the sort of smooth-handed gesture a dandy would use to slide out a slim, gold cigarette case. It was a slim, gold cigarette case with alternating bands of white, red and yellow metal. 'For you. We would wish you to have it as a memento.' He looked at me unblinkingly and smiled.

It was a bribe of course, to keep my mouth shut, to look the other way. Impossible to refuse without giving offence, a flattering sign that I was now an accepted insider, one of the family, one who spoke the language of give and take and due deference – the *real* language of Java. Once I took it, any shortfall in the accounting would be on my head as much as anyone else's. But surely it was too big to go through the mouth of a petrol can? It couldn't be part of the loot. I tried to remember the exact dimensions of the battered, old jerrycans but I couldn't be sure. The whole point about the jerrycan business is that you don't notice them. Prudence, good manners, covetousness – it was a breathtakingly beautiful object – all pushed me in the same direction. Anyway, wasn't President Soekarno in some sense the very incarnation of the Republic? No line could be drawn between him and it, as the Dutch had found out to their cost. There are times when too much thinking can be dangerous and ungracious and anyway, wasn't I due a little payback? In all the time I had been at the Republic's beck and call I had never received a penny in proper pay, just food and lodging and scraps like the palace dog.

'Thank you, Bung.' I received it with demurely lowered head and in both hands as a gift of consequence. It slipped ever so willingly and without friction into my bag – to be seen as the true authentication of my change of nationality. This was the way things were done here.

The tension disappeared. 'So who should I make my new Minister of Defence? Soedirman would have been the obvious choice and it was grotesque for a fighting soldier like him to die of tuberculosis, an old man's disease.' He sucked smoke into still-healthy lungs. It was an important decision since Bung Karno had the good sense to leave military decisions to military men and never interfered in them. 'It must be someone who listens to his men. I used to tell Soedirman that the most important thing an officer ever learns is how to say, "Carry on sergeant." Tell me who you would choose. Ah, wait, here is my wife.'

Fatmawati was a nice, down-to-earth woman and a good mother. You could imagine that story about her hand-stitching together the first flag of the Republic for the Proclamation of Independence might actually be true – as it clearly wasn't for poor, old Betsy Ross and Martha Washington. But then it seems it's everywhere a woman's job to sit and patiently sew things together while men strut around and rip them apart. And she scrubbed up nicely as the mother of Indonesia. As she walked towards us and turned her head, I noticed she was wearing a sumptuous, new pair of ruby earrings that literally glowed about her face. I tactfully forbore to admire them. Then badness overtook me. Perhaps it was some sort of a mental short-circuit between Bung Karno, Jane Russel and exploding busts.

'Actually, Bung, *I* have a present for *you*, two fine Balinese carvings that I picked up in Jakarta – very phlegmatic. One even looks like you. I'll send them over.'

I wonder if they are still there in the palace. It never occurred to me that someone might decide they were so ghastly that they should be used as kitchen fuel, which would have had interesting results. As curiosities, they are probably objects of some value now. Poor Wim's plans came to nothing again. No thousands of ready agents, eager to blow up railway bridges for the Dutch, ever existed across Indonesia and the military planners soon realised that they depended almost entirely on the reliable transport of supplies – much more so than the guerrillas. It wasn't like a rerun of their time in Holland under the Germans but the exact opposite. It should really have been Bung Tomo's boys blowing up the bridges. Had they realised this, they would have turned around and gone home in shame. Poor Wim, a sheep in wolf's clothing and a man for whom every silver lining had a hidden cloud.

Chapter Ten

There were two of them, one tall and thin, the other short and plump and they took it in turns like those Japanese slaps delivered first to the left, then the right of my face. Now, the tall one came back in, threw a limp, brown dossier down on the table and himself into a chair. He let his whole face sag and sighed. I had pushed my luck once too often, slipping into Singapore and sliding round the normal controls, only to be picked up by a shore patrol in Little India – convinced they had caught a dangerous spy – and dragged off in mid-samosa. I should never have lit up that clove cigarette in public.

'It won't do, Mrs. Pearson. You can't expect us to allow you to come and go from Singapore like this, just wandering in and out illegally and simply get away with it. Don't you see that the fact that you don't have a passport is not an excuse? It makes it worse. We already have enough on you to put you away for years then give you back to the Dutch since their territory is where you admit you came from. I think you need to co-operate with us.' The accent was Brit-ish but with White Commonwealth tonalities.

He let that one sink in and, when I made no response, hauled open the cover and stabbed at the page with a forefinger. A very neat forefinger that. Nice, clean nails, no smoker's patina of tar, unsullied by toil. Men's hands are always interesting, something of an obsession with me. They tell you a lot. Maybe he was higher up than he seemed on first view. 'When you were picked up in the city, in fact, you were bearing a passport of the Indonesian

Republic which we do not recognise.' He took out a fresh sheet of paper. 'Passport number one.' That made him smile. 'What is the reason for your visit to Singapore?'

'I am a refugee of British nationality. I am here precisely because I need to sort out this business of passports. Second, I wish to recuperate from the injuries I sustained in a Japanese prisoner-of-war camp. Third, I wish to write a book concerning my experiences. Fourth, I don't want to stay in Singapore. I want to go to Australia.' I watched as he wrote that down. Four points on four, tidy lines, he liked that.

He raised his eyebrows and drummed his fingers on the dossier. 'A book? Not political activity then? No guns? No opium or aeroplanes? No smuggled diplomats? Have you any evidence of that?'

'You will also have found in my luggage a manuscript that I wish to work on. In Australia, that is.'

He frowned and dug back in the file. 'Ah yes. Well, we'll have to take a look at that won't we? I'm afraid you have something of a notorious reputation, Mrs. Pearson, and it may take some time for us to...'

'Don't call me that. My name is K'tut Tantri.'

He smirked back at me and slipped his pen in his inside pocket. 'Well that's rather what we have to decide isn't it? The matter at issue. Who exactly you are and exactly what you've been up to.' He closed the file, stood up and whisked away, the door slamming and locking behind him. Being locked in alone made me feel like a child, shut in the coalhole back in Glasgow and I shivered despite the heat.

* * *

'Number one. James Hay Stuart Walker was your father. You lived at 30, Moss Street, Garston and he was a commercial traveller not a boilermaker or an archaeologist as you claim in your memoir. You didn't live in dire poverty in a tenement. Your circumstances were actually quite comfortable. You weren't an only child. Walker had kids by a previous. Don't you think we consult public records? A lot of security services have been interested in you.'

'Number one,' I said. 'James Walker was *not* my father. You will see from my birth certificate that Ma was three months pregnant at the time of the wedding. He may have been a commercial traveller at one stage. Mostly he just drank. When I was ten, he walked out on us and I took the train to Glasgow Central with the intention of looking for him, was overwhelmed by the crowds and stood there crying. A big policeman came up and was kind to me and they put out a search bulletin for him. When they found him in a bar he was so ashamed he came home and stayed off the booze for three months. Of course, that didn't stop him giving me a belting. As for poverty, what is the point of growing up in Glasgow if you can't sing a song of starvation, violence and rats. It would be like growing up in Paris and not living in the Eiffel Tower. In fact, we had to move frequently and ended up living in some nasty back alley full of dustbins. Like Queen Victoria, we were not a mews. Do you have a number two?'

He sighed again. 'Did you type this manuscript yourself or did someone write it for you? It's shopgirl fiction isn't it?'

'I did, though I prefer dictation. It frees one's mind from the concern with process.'

He frowned. 'So why do you write so much in the present tense? All this happened – if it happened – years ago.'

Now it was my turn to sigh. 'This is not a creative writing course. The present is the only reality. To be remembered at all, things have to be recalled into the present. Moreover, I have worked in the movies as a scriptwriter. Movies are the art form of our age and they exist only in the fleeting present. Attempts at any other tense on the silver screen are always cumbersome and affected and unconvincing. I am thinking of you and your friends in the past tense right now.'

He had to stop and think about that. 'All police reports are in the past tense because they're supposed to be real. I think that tells us something about the truth of your so-called memoir.'

'Police? Is that who you are? I confess I am a trifle disappointed. I imagined you were something much more glamorous.'

He glared. 'Okay, we'll come to the script-writing later. We've checked with the British records. There is no evidence of any Walker being involved in the Glasgow labour movement, as you claim.'

'Impossible!' I sneered. 'Sheer invention. Walker is a very common name. Why there were two other Walkers in the same class as me at school. Mere statistics dictate that there would be a Walker somewhere. If not, that would indicate that the records are incomplete or have been deliberately tampered with.'

He closed the folder irritably. 'Come off it. Who the hell would go to the trouble of changing your records, Mrs. Pearson?'

I smiled. 'As you yourself remarked, a lot of security services have been interested in me at one time or another. Now, do you think I might have a cup of tea? I'm afraid I have lost track of the passage of time in here, being, as we are, without windows and trapped in the present tense.'

* * *

'Why would you even admit to something like that business with

Ambassador Kennedy – conspiracy, perjury, Christ knows what else?' The short, fat one was back, Tweeledum. He was sweating as though he had been the person accused of all that. The beige dossier had grown a little thicker. He wore a ratty, old jacket with elbow patches, not a suit, so was presumably lower down the pecking order than Tweedledee. They had at least brought me tea today though with measly amounts of sugar and in one of those ghastly Works Department blue cups. In Java we take lots of sugar even in savoury dishes. But the tea came with a proper matching saucer and with two dry biscuits, no doilie. Unexpected.

'Isn't one of you supposed to be nice and the other one nasty. If you're both nasty to me, it isn't going to cut any ice. Anyway, it's all long ago and far away. Statute of limitations. I'm only a little, old lady. Quite harmless. Maybe I don't remember so well and it's just an *aide-memoire*. Remembering requires forgetting ninety percent of what actually occurred and it's hard to write a life without turning it into a story or even a morality tale. And you've decided in advance that my manuscript's all lies. Perhaps it is. How would you ever be able to tell?' I smirked. I was messing with him. If he couldn't be sure about something like this how could he be sure about anything?

'That's the trouble with lies, Mrs. Pearson. They're hard to remember unlike the truth. You tend to wander and contradict yourself.' He sipped his own tea delicately but his hand was shaking and he had one of those inexplicable spasms of the arm that hit you from time to time and sloshed it on his trousers. 'Jesus Christ! Would it surprise you to learn that there is no trace of anyone called Walker associated either with Senator Kennedy or the RKO studios?' The bureaucrat's answer to everything. Only believe the paper. He rubbed at his inside thigh sourly, saw me looking and blushed.

I remained demure. 'Who says I was using the name Walker? I was, after all, married.'

He frowned and looked down at the dossier. 'Ah yes, Mr. Pearson. Tell me about Mr. Pearson. This mysterious Mr. Pearson who allegedly gave you an American passport. Was it love at first sight? Did you perhaps meet on a tram?'

I smiled and set the smirky expression irritatingly on my face like a mask. That tactic had served me well at school. The headmistress had termed it 'subaltern insolence' in more than one school report. 'But I don't want to lapse into – what was it now your friend said? – "shopgirl fiction".' I waited until he tried for the cup again, then said. 'Mr. Pearson was a shortarse.' He coughed gratifyingly and got the dossier point blank with a mouthful of tea, hastily wiped it off with his handkerchief. 'Shortarses are frequently a little pushy. I speak as a shortarse myself. And,' I continued, 'he was of Swedish origin. People always imagine Swedes as walking, blond treetrunks. Well he wasn't. Yet his shoe size was still bigger than his IQ and he was fourteen years older than me.'

He pouted and pencilled a note.

'But he had a nice house and car and a flourishing, little furniture restoration business and he got on well with Ma.'

'Sounds as if Dr. Freud would have enjoyed your family.' The pencil circled, closed in for the kill, hit paper. 'Hmm. It is on record that you once claimed to have had two children by him, both tragically lost in a road accident while he was driving under the influence. As usual, no trace of any of this can be documented. What were their names?'

'Who?'

'The children. What were their names? You may be – as you yourself say – a "shortarse" but you tell tales that are tall enough for anyone.'

I'd had enough. My patience, as Herr Hitler used to say … It was time to do 'little-old-lady'.

The lace hankie is an indispensable prop to a woman on the make. I had tutored Eunice Pringle in the strategic use of it, to great effect, for her courtroom scene and, at the crucial moment, the silly girl had just chucked it down like a tarpaulin. Now, I fumbled mine blindly down from my sleeve, indicating scattiness and senile helplessness and pressed it hopelessly to my eyes. A lace hankie is non-absorbent – full of holes – nastily sharp-edged as a thing to wipe around sensitive membranes – and totally impractical – which is the message it carries about its owner. It just shouldn't be out there in a rough world to be sullied and torn. When you let it fall gently, it flutters like a pair of see-through panties. A lace hankie is fancy knickers for the nose and men respond accordingly. They can't help it. They have been trained that way. I dropped mine with great professionalism and clutched at my heart, the fluttering of the one reflected in the other. 'I can't … talk about that. It is just too painfuuul,' I wailed. 'My babies! My poor, poor babies!'

In a flash he was dithering up on his feet, looking as confused as the ninth leg of an octopus, ringing for a female wardress to tidy away the mess of tea and spilled emotions he had made. Anything to get away from the spectacle of this ghastly, womanish sentimentality that now made me fling myself across the desk in a state of collapse. I thought of going for the teacup but that too had been drained. No point in knocking it over now. I struggled to my feet, clasped my breasts, hooting out my grief for my lost sucklings, let my knees buckle and was led away clutching at the big, strapping girl who answered the call and took me away down the corridor. She was called Janice. Interviews for today were over.

It was a small and charmless room they took me to, not exactly a cell but not far short of it, the way a kept mistress is not quite a whore. Given my own biography, perhaps I should have avoided that thought. There was a small, hard bed, the sheets worn but clean – unmade from this morning. Clearly maid service was not included in the tariff. In one corner a washbasin with fly-blown mirror – probably a real one, unlike that in the interview room that no doubt concealed a camera and recording apparatus. The window incorporated three closely spaced, vertical mullions with glass in between, disguising bars as an architectural quirk. Through them lay a scrap of grass and a flagpole with the Union Jack run up and going a little ragged in one corner like the sheets. All those damned flags. I had slept in grass huts and on the backs of trucks, even leaning against a field gun or in a genuine prison cell with seething vermin and snarling guards. Yes, I had seen worse. It was a place designed not yet to humiliate and break you but – for the moment – to contain and observe. There was a barely concealed threat in the chipped plaster and the hole worn in the linoleum. I lay down on the bed and closed my eyes, turned my senses off and retreated back into my own head.

* * *

'It won't do I'm afraid, Mrs. Pearson.'

Today, it was the tall one, Tweedledee. He had a shaving cut under his chin and was wearing cufflinks not buttoned cuffs. Did he have a job interview? Or perhaps it was for me. No. I could see now he had a button missing on one cuff. He was wearing a plain, gold wedding ring. A neglected husband.

'Your wife,' I said, 'what's her name?'

He looked surprised. 'That is hardly to the point.'

'Then let me tell you about her.' He looked tired. I pictured his wearisome home life with the faded, resentful wife announced by his ring finger, as dry as a Javanese lawn in the hot season. 'English-born, a graduate, maybe in Eng. Lit. She will be resentful about being cleverer than you. Resentful about having to look after your two noisy kids. Resentful about the unfulfilling job she has had to take teaching in some down-at-heel secondary school to help pay the rent and the maid's wages. She'll be called something like Sarah. You see how easy it is to do your job.'

A shadow passed across his face, then surprise. Then it closed down again as he bit his tongue. 'We're not here to talk about me but you.' He blushed and raised the dossier in authority. It had got bigger since yesterday, probably with the transcripts hammered out by busy, little typists overnight. How many family dinners around Singapore had that ruined? 'Talking of names, why have *you* got so many?' He opened the dossier. 'Muriel Walker, Muriel Pearson, Manxi, Manx, Miss Tenchery, Mrs. Daventry, Miss Oestermann, Sally van de As – I like that one – Molly Rosenberg, Vannen, Vanine, Vanessa Modjokerto, Surabaya Sue and K'tut Tantri. Rather more than the average woman would need, I think.'

'I am not the average woman. Those are not all me and there are others you don't mention. I worked in Hollywood where names are a fluid medium. We are quite different people at different times. Don't you find yourself thinking back and being quite amazed at some of the things you have done in the past under different circumstances? Don't you find yourself thinking, "Can that really have been me?"' Clearly not. 'Why not have a different name for each of the different people you have been? I am under no obligation to maintain continuity of identity for the convenience of the Singaporean authorities. A lot of those names were made necessary by the prying of people just like you.'

'Except,' said the fat one, Tweedledum, 'it didn't happen like that at all.' He sighed and reached into the dossier. He had the sort of smug world-weariness at the sins of lesser beings that suggested he might grow up to be a Conservative candidate. 'Do you think intelligence services don't talk to each other? We have a report here from the Dutch NEFIS.' He had those half-moon reading glasses that make you look down your nose, a pose that also fitted him. 'They checked into your background in Bali most carefully. The family of the Rajah of Bangli confirm here that they scarcely knew you, that you bullied your way in, brought by a tourist tout and that they rented you an old garage round the back of the palace enclosure, as they thought for your car, but then found you actually living there in fearful squalour. There was a suggestion of some sordid, sexual liaison with one of the family, if not both father and son – possibly overlapping as it were – that shame prevented their confirming. According to the Dutch the Balinese are big on shame.' He laid it down and looked at me with distaste. 'Unlike some.'

'Look,' I said, 'even you must realise that it is all a matter of interpretation. Of course my family in Bangli downplayed my connection with them. I was a freedom-fighter, an enemy of the Dutch. They weren't going to admit to something that could land them in jail or worse. And the Dutch have always been happy to smear me. As an insider, I'm sure you know how easily that's done. The Dutch always tried to stop any contact between outsiders and locals, lest it bring down the empire that was founded on separation and discrimination. In their own fevered imaginings, any woman who sat in a car beside her driver must be an adulteress about to be carried off to the harem and you can't imagine what a tight, smug, little community it was. Or perhaps you can. I don't think Singapore is so different. I can't tell you how often I had to suffer browbeatings by absurd, lecherous, little men of the colonial service, ogling me as they threatened to deport me as "undesirable". They all hated me because I saw right through them and they couldn't take that. The whole colonialist enterprise is founded upon a huge bluff, a terror that someone will point out that the Emperor isn't wearing any clothes and that the natives will laugh.' I was becoming a little heated.

'But *you* did more than laugh though, didn't you Mrs. Pearson? Very much more.'

'I've never denied it. I'm proud of what I did after the war.'

He scanned down the page again. 'We are talking about *before* the war and then *during* the war. It says here that Bangli is where the Dutch built their big lunatic asylum and that to say that someone is from Bangli is to imply that they are just plain mad. That must have been very tiresome for you. But that of course is just a joke and the Dutch aren't really known for their jokes are they? But maybe the Balinese are. I believe Tantri is a girl in the local version of the Arabian Nights who has to make up fairy stories to keep a nasty rajah amused and he only spares her life to find out what outrageous tale she will come up with next.'

We looked at each other and both laughed, our first moment of real, human contact. 'A little like us?' I suggested.

* * *

'Oh for Christ's sake, Mrs. Pearson. Boo bloody hoo! Give it a rest.' He threw the transcript down on the desk and rubbed his eyes, loosened his tie and yawned. 'There was no mortgaging of the ricefields in Bali by noble peasants so you could build your bloody hotel. There was no cornucopia of ancient coins laid at your feet. Moneylenders don't lend in ancient, silver dollars. Pull the other one.' Tweedledee is back and in a snotty mood. 'Do you really expect me to believe that a bunch of rice-farmers are going to sell their children into slavery for the crazy ambition of a foreigner which they could never even begin to understand?' He slurped at his morning coffee. Then made a face. I had been offered none.

'I ask you to believe nothing. I am simply telling you what happened. Is it so hard to believe that they saw me as their friend and helped me as I had helped them?'

'Frankly yes. For the Balinese to be as you describe them they would have had to have wings and a halo. I find no mention in your account of the island of the epidemics of smallpox, diphtheria and endemic starvation that were also part of the scene.'

'I see that you have never travelled in Indonesia. If you had, you would be far less ready to dismiss out of hand the possibility that other people might be kinder, less selfish and more open-minded than ourselves in the West, even in the midst of the greatest difficulties. If you travel far enough you get to a point where you are willing to believe almost anything. That is why it broadens the mind.'

He tutted and dealt out piles of stapled documents on the table top like a man setting up a game of patience. He teased one out.

'Right. Here is a statement that the Dutch acquired from the American OSS.' He passed it over. 'It's from a Mr. Bob Koke, an American from Hollywood, who invested in a hotel in Kuta just before the war. Apparently, his female business partner proved unreliable. His wife said that she tried to get her hooks into him but she was more a vampire than a vamp.' He looked up. 'I suppose that must be an American joke. There was a question of funds removed from a joint account, funds subsequently used to construct a rival establishment across the road. I believe that partner was you.'

'Bob was always jealous of me as was his ball-breaking wife. He was a tennis gigolo, all forehand smash and capped teeth – at least he put his money where his mouth was. He thought all he had to do was flash those china teeth and flutter his eyelashes and any woman would swoon. Well I didn't. His wife was a silly lobsick goose who thought she could paint – though certainly no oil painting herself. I had been a highly successful scriptwriter and journalist whereas he had merely "designed movie sets" and introduced Bali to the surf board. His idea for a hotel was limited to that ramshackle beach set he claimed to have created for *Mutiny on the Bounty*! I ask you. Who needs anyone to design a beach! In fact, I was never convinced that he had any genuine link with Hollywood at all. He was a sad fantasist who took colourful events from my own life to adorn his own rather dull biography. Why, I once heard him repeat a cruel wisecrack Joe Kennedy made to me about Gloria Swanson, as his own experience. In those days, when shooting the stars in close up, they would sometimes smear the lens with Vaseline or take them through gossamer tissue to hide any lines. "When we were filming *Queen Kelly*," Joe cracked, "we tried shooting poor, old Gloria through gauze but it was still no use. In the end, we had to use a Witney blanket!" Joe never wasted any time on Irish gallantry. Oh, I don't want to talk about it. It is all still too …'

'"Painful?" I think, is the word you use.' He dealt out another wodge of papers with croupier coolness. 'Hmm! People who stayed in your own bungalows seem to have experienced something quite different from the fairyland, Balinese palace of your memoir. How about "a set of dirty native huts". I have here copies of reports from the Dutch secret service into the activities at

Manxi's bungalows just before the Japanese invasion – apparently a place of ill repute on the beach much used by hot-blooded, young Dutch flyers from the airbase right next door. There was some question of possible security leaks, found to be without substance and the report recommended turning a blind eye to the prostitution on the grounds of containment of an unavoidable evil.' He sat back, folded his arms, raised an eyebrow quizzically, tried not to look smug. 'So it seems that in the official view you were not just "undesirable" but "an unavoidable evil", Mrs. Pearson. Quite a compliment. And as for your fellow artists, they are also less than complimentary – regarding you and your work as something of a joke.' He scrabbled in another pile like a cat covering its excrement, pulled out more muck-raking vilification and pushed it across.

I refused to read it. I was unmoved. 'You are confusing the first hotel with the second. As for art, all great artists have been regarded as a joke, especially by their fellows, Picasso, Chagall, Henri Rousseau ... You don't know them? No I thought not. As it is, yapping reviewers do not interest me.'

'And yet ... And yet not a single one of your wonderful paintings has survived to speak out for you as an artist and explain what you were doing in Bali. How very odd.'

'There was so much confusion during the war. Wars and tropical climates are not kind to paintings. An artist is not be judged by quantity but quality. A single painting can change the world. Some of my pictures, I confess, I destroyed myself. I have always been my own fiercest critic.'

* * *

'I liked that bit about the wild sea releasing your innermost emotions,' said Tweedledee, briskly tapping his teeth with the edge of the transcript till it turned soggy, 'a sort of reverse pathetic fallacy. A touch of quality that. But look, you must stop going on about this great, romantic figure Prince Nura. You're not doing yourself any good with it. We know all about him. He was no great shakes, not even a little Valentino sheikh. He's reliably described as "short, dumpy, usefully unimaginative to the Dutch". He was never engaged in the rebellion, only had the most rudimentary education – oh and you *did* habitually sleep with him. Many witnesses confirm it.'

'Did I ever deny that? Why would I? Why all these questions?' I questioned. 'Is this a matter of just meeting immigration requirements or are you trying to psychoanalyse me? What is the interest to you of my prewar sleeping arrangements? God knows, they barely interest *me*. Or are your big brothers, America, Holland, pulling your strings? What's it all for?'

'It goes to the question of your reliability. The Dutch would like to get their hands on you. We must protect our citizens from dangerous elements. You are a notorious person.'

'Why thank you dear. That's exactly what the Dutch always used to say in my youth but you know, after a certain age people go glum and get respectable. I don't know why. It's nice to be still thought of that way at my time of life. It makes me feel like dear, old Mae West in her glory days. I expect the Japanese said much the same too when they tortured me but they were harder to understand.'

'You surely would not compare the Japanese methods with our own?' He blinked. It had actually hit home. He took a breath and shook his head. 'Would you care for some coffee? Sugar?'

Whatever he might say, Tweedledee was clearly troubled almost to the point of humanitarianism. I had got under his skin.

He nodded at Janice who lumbered to her feet and headed off down the corridor, a dreamy expression on her face. Had he just called her 'Sugar'? We women are such fools, building crystal castles on the basis of some man's long eyelashes and a suggestion of weightiness around the crotch.

'I merely meant that it brought it all back, that it was deeply upsetting. It took me years to forget and now you are demanding that I remember. The memory is a dangerous thing. If you look back at good times, you realise what you have lost. If you look back at bad times, it brings the horror back anew. In Indonesia at that time it was often dangerous to remember too much and you taught yourself to get out of the habit.'

'Not "painful" this time? That is what you usually say, isn't it, when you want to dodge a question?'

I felt anger well up inside up. I resisted it, knowing he was provoking me deliberately. 'Your methods may be different from the Japanese, the aims are the same. Interrogation has nothing to do with the elicitation of useful information. It's all about proving your own petty power. As you well know.'

'I had hoped that you might find it therapeutic, that it might strike a chord that would lead you to unburden yourself of the rest of the truth. And yet, Mrs. Pearson, we find, as usual, all sorts of odd gaps in what you choose to tell us. Why, for example, did you stay in Bali in the face of the Japanese invasion? Most Westerners found it prudent to leave – except the neutrals.'

'Who left and who stayed was a lottery. We used to talk a lot about the Dutch officers who had flown their mistresses out to Australia and left their wives behind. Where else was I to go? I had no means except for my hotel which – as it happened – the Japanese immediately destroyed. I had made Bali my home. I considered myself Balinese, so a sort of neutral.'

'Hmm. Bob Koke says here that, once he'd gone, your first thought was to march across the road and throw your weight about, grab his bit of the hotel and his car and scare his staff into submission by threatening to have them shot when your friends, the Japanese, arrived.'

'I told you Bob Koke and I weren't friends. He made that up.'

'Yet you held a British passport at that time? An American passport? Both?'

'I also have an Indonesian passport, as you know. In a world full of power-mad bureaucrats, you can never have too many passports.' Janice returned with the coffee and put it down on the desk in front of me with a wan smile. Most of it was in the saucer. She was a clumsy girl.

'Yes, I have that passport here before me. But not – crucially – from that time. How would it have been possible? There was no such thing as Indonesia for you to be a citizen of. So you were necessarily – as I said – British or American or both and any act of collaboration with the invading Japanese would have been an act of treason. And it seems there may well have been such acts.' He sighed and reached into the file again. The voice dropped to a machine gun rat-a-tat. 'Did you, or did you not, run the Bali hotel as a facility for Japanese military personnel?'

I laughed in his face. 'I did not – though it would have been a wonderful revenge. Apart from all their attempts to undermine my business, the Bali Hotel actually banned me from the grounds.'

'Yes. You said that. And did you, or did you not become the mistress of a Japanese naval officer, highly placed in the Balinese administration and subsequently found guilty of war crimes? You were seen frequently as a passenger in his car – a rather ostentatious and distinctive vehicle. There can be no mistake about it.'

'I most certainly did not. Major war crimes are seldom committed on the back seats of staff cars. I don't think you realise the position of women under a foreign occupation. As a man how could you? It was necessary for my work with the resistance to cultivate good relations with powerful people who could be used by us for our own ends. Propositions were often made that could not be flatly refused. In such circumstances a woman has to develop delaying tactics that might avoid confrontation and turn a situation suddenly dangerous. The world is not as straightforward as simple men may think – be they Western or Japanese.'

'Is that a yes or a no?'

'Women at that time were often forced into arrangements that they neither sought nor relished. Each side may well have had entirely different ideas of how voluntary a relationship might be.' I looked at Janice and she offered a furtive smile of encouragement. I sipped my coffee. Hang on. What was this? Somehow Janice had slipped a tot of whisky into it. Good girl! 'Lovely coffee, dear. Thank you.'

'So is that a yes or …?'

'No. Absolutely no. The fact that I had to escape from Bali to Java hidden under the seat of a Chinese bus rather proves the point. I can only speak of any such relationship as seen from my own side, of course.' I balanced the coffee on my lap. I didn't want it getting too close to Tweedledee's flaring nostrils.

'Hmm. And then, after all this unpleasantness in prison of which you speak in such detail, the Japanese suddenly let you go. Now why do you imagine that was?'

I shrugged elaborately, nearly lost the coffee, caught it just in time. 'I imagine they had had their fun with me and saw no point in detaining me any more. Haven't you got a note about it there in all that stuff?'

'Well, oddly ...' He smirked and pulled out another sheet of paper and scanned it sceptically. 'It seems that you were not simply flung out into the street as one might have expected – or shot for real – but seen being politely escorted back to Surabaya on the train by a Japanese officer where you were admitted to a private room in the Simpang hospital. It doesn't say here what class of carriage you travelled in. The other details we have. And shortly afterwards, the Japanese radio started new, shortwave broadcasts of particularly offensive propaganda to Australia using the voice of a young woman with a marked Scots accent. Several people, including Bob Koke, identified that voice as yours.'

I smiled sourly. 'Enough of bloody Bob. He had every reason to bear me a grudge. We ended up in court over the hotel business. There was bad blood between us. And, as you can hear for yourself, I haven't got a Scottish accent.'

'Not now perhaps. But then ...? Some people can turn it on and off at will, you know – speak with forked tongue and all that. I think you mentioned earlier in your script that you had deliberately learned to imitate BBC English just for office use. A bit of a linguistic chamaeleon then. Let me play you a little to jog your memory.'

He went over to a table set up against the wall and twiddled with some knobs on an extraordinary gadget that recorded sound on a spool of tape instead of a shellac disc. A loud hiss, followed by thumping, martial music. Then a very young voice emerged, alternately swelling and shrinking through the fog and crosscut by moans as of some deep-sea creature. 'I want to talk to you about our Australian prisoners. You know we have thousands of them all over the East. You know how they were abandoned by the British in Singapore and Hong Kong and Batavia. They all ran away and left them. Many of the men who ran away are there with you, relying on your protection, claiming to be heroes. There is a saying here, "To survive the angry tiger you do not need to run faster than the tiger, only faster than the friend who stands beside you." This is not the war of our Australian prisoners and we look after them until we can send them home to you after the final Japanese victory. This is not your war either. It is a war made by your leaders for their own ends and it is an unjust war. There is no dishonour in you ending it right now so that we can all live in peace. You remember how good peace was? You remember what it was like to have your husbands and sons about you. The only people preventing that happy state are your own generals and politicians who have betrayed you. This a painful truth but a truth nonetheless ...'

'Nasty that – very. Oh, and there's your favourite word, "painful", again. Do you deny that that is your voice?'

'I think you don't know very much about Scottish accents,' I gulped. I would not cry. 'That one sounds rather Edinburgh to me.'

'Really? Yet all our experts say most definitely Glasgow.' He sat down, made a little steeple with his fingers and looked at me through it, blew a little gale across the roof ridge, huffing and puffing but not yet blowing my house down. 'Of course, perhaps I should mention that my elder brother was one of those Brits who ran away on the last troopship out – badly wounded of course. He lost a leg. Limped away rather than ran, then.' He slapped the cover of his folder shut, stood up and flounced out like a dancehall girl who has just had her bum pinched.

Just my luck to find one of those rare creatures that actually liked their siblings. What were the odds? Janice looked at me reproachfully and bit her nails, always a nasty habit. Now he was angry, her face said. All my fault.

Tweedledum sucked in his bottom lip and laid down the piece of paper he had been reading. 'But again it can't have been quite like that, can it?'

No Janice today. Perhaps she does not bother to sit in on dumpy, little Tweedledum. Perhaps unsexy Tweedledum with the currant bun face is thought not to need a chaperone to reign in his stallion sexuality in my presence.

'For once you have made the mistake of being specific, Mrs. Pearson, given us dates and places. There was no joyful liberation of Western women by smiling rebel forces, no *feu de joie* at the Ambarawa camp. Far from it. What really happened was that British soldiers arrived first and fought for their lives alongside Japanese troops against the mob of attacking Islamist Pemuda. There is a full report in the archives by Wing Commander Tull who was in charge of supplying the camp by airdrops from Dakotas, a necessary expedient since road supply was made impossible by hostile, local forces. Before thousands of witnesses, on 22nd November 1945, the rebel fighters broke through the defensive perimeter of the camp and drove the mainly Dutch civilians – starving women and children – into a compound where they mowed them down with machine gun fire and threw hand grenades among survivors before they could be driven off. They then maintained a steady bombardment of mortar fire on the undefended prisoners' compounds over the next few weeks, killing and wounding many more. Are you now admitting to being complicit in that horrendous war crime or were you not there at all, or were you just looking the other way?'

Hot and strong today. I spoke carefully. 'The revolution was not a single force. There were all sorts of groups with all sorts of different aims. Some were political extremists, others religious. You cannot imagine the confusion. Occasionally they fought with each other, sometimes they submerged their differences or switched allegiances. Yet behind it all was the belief that the world had been offered a final opportunity to begin afresh, that it was possible to keep an idea pure and realise it in all its virtue. I can only tell you that the young men who broke me out of Ambarawa were the finest kind of idealists who would never have been involved in any such atrocity – and there *were* Indonesian atrocities just as there were many Dutch. Surely you already know this or are you the innocent victim of British propaganda?'

Tweedledum smiled then blushed, ashamed of himself for his levity. 'Me, an innocent victim of propaganda? You will pardon me but, coming from you Mrs. Pearson, I really find that rather funny.'

* * *

Tweedledee looked down at the dossier like my old headmistress looking at a report on a recalcitrant pupil. 'A minor point. There was no radio broadcast of the Independence Proclamation. That was just PR – another word for lies. The famous, "authentic" recording was mocked up in a studio after the event. The picture of the actual Proclamation shows just a standard microphone not a radio mike and don't you think it's nice the way the declarers of independence stand around in Japanese poses of respect and submission with their hands in front of their balls?'

'The Japanese may have been midwives to the birth of independence, but the child is purely Indonesian.'

He snorted. 'But that's just by the way. So now we get to it. You have avoided the question. At the time of your own Proclamation broadcast what passport did you hold?' He paused, pen poised in mid-air, as if to administer the fatal blow.

'American, of course. I've already told you.'

'The marriage to Karl Pearson, yes. But had you formally renounced British nationality? That's the issue here.'

'I forget what it said on the form. In those days having more than one nationality was treated a bit like bigamy but I had abandoned it and it me, a bit like Karl. Surely you have your own records?'

'You see, if you hadn't, then any actions in support of the Indonesian fighters, in time of war, might be held to be treasonable and subject to the most severe penalties.'

'But the British and the Indonesians weren't at war. They never had been – "formally" as you say. The Second World War was over, all the neat pieces of paper had been signed and the bills were being sent out. And after the Oranje Hotel incident, the Brits and the Indonesians had come to terms and "formally" signed an agreement so that they were "formally" allies of some sort. I believe the agreement was that the two sides would keep out of each other's way and that the Brits would make no moves to disarm the patriots, an agreement they promptly broke. I was there, you see. I saw. I was at the Red Bridge that day, the day the real fighting began.'

'So you say. But you continued your activities *after* the fighting with the British had started, didn't you? This much-vaunted Indonesian patriotism of yours, I wonder if you didn't just think, "After all my acts of treason, the British and Americans will want to hang me and the Dutch shoot me, I'd better become an Indonesian nationalist since there's nowhere else to go." That's really what happened isn't it?'

'You mean I should have become even more loyal to the Brits *after* they started raining bombs down on my head, deliberately

collection point for whites and Eurasians where they were then dragged out, killed and their corpses piled up on the club's outside dance floor. Perhaps you did not notice that during your nice tea? I quote. "Before each execution Soetomo mockingly asked the crowd what should be done with this enemy of the people. The crowd yelled "Kill!" after which the executioner named Rustam came forward and decapitated the victim with one stroke of his samurai sword. The victim was then left to the bloodthirstiness of boys 10, 11 and 12 years old who further mutilated the body. I can't say how many people were dispatched this way but it was certainly in the hundreds. From my position, I could see into the back of the garden where there was a tree on the riverbank. One by one, women were tied to the tree. According to the shouts of the executioners and spectators they had lived with Japanese. Peeping through the lashes of my downcast eyes, I saw a spectacle so shocking, repulsive and gruesome in its reality that it may never have been equalled in history. Completely absorbed in their grisly business, the executioners – the champions of liberty! – then thrust their bamboo spears into the genitals of their helpless victims with all their might. The heartrending screams and the collapsing and shaking of the body of the poor woman only drove the bloodlust of the executioners still higher. They drilled through a certain point in the abdomen with the bamboo spears just long enough so that the unfortunate woman gave up the ghost from her wounds and blood loss. Then the bodies were thrown in the Mas river round the back of the Simpang Club." So it wasn't used just for jolly bathtime fun between the romping boys as you suggest.'

He lay down the paper and put his hands together like a judge summing up. 'Later, it seems, your chum Soetomo ordered them to pile up the severed heads and corpses from the dancefloor and throw them in the sea. You are right, Mrs. Pearson. Japanese habits did die hard among the people they had trained and armed. But sometimes there is a little poetic justice. Admiration is a two-edged sword – no pun intended.' He scanned another piece of paper. 'Other witnesses swear they caught other Pemuda literally drinking the blood of murdered Japanese prisoners inside the Babutan jail, apparently as an expression of their regard for the military virtues they had imparted to them in training.' Janice had begun to sniffle into a handkerchief. He shot her a frown.

The meat pie rose up in a belch. I struggled to talk through it. Tweedledee would see it as weak, womanish nausea induced by his penny dreadful tales. 'All lies. Propaganda from the Allies. Typical, incredible falsehoods. I saw no such thing. They would do anything to discredit the movement. I don't believe a word of it. But you must remember there was very little reason left in the world at that time. There was no normality any more. Everyone had gone a little mad. The Dutch did very much worse.'

He shook his head irritably. 'I don't think that's the point. We are talking about your own complicity in war crimes here.'

'War crimes?' I boomed, Lady Bracknell's 'Handbag?' echoing in my head. 'War crimes? In that case what about the bombing of Surabaya?'

* * *

There was something in the wind – something judgemental. Both Tweedledum and Tweedledee were here, sitting to attention. A third chair stood empty in between. Unlike their own, that chair had arms, a boss's chair, then.

'Please sit down, Mrs, Pearson. We shan't keep you long. We are just waiting for our colleague.'

I sat as primly as possible. We stared at each other. The air became strained. Who were we waiting for, Churchill? I tapped my fingers and sighed, opened my mouth to say something. Then the door opened – we all turned – and in waltzed Janice. I giggled at the anti-climax and then she went and sat at the head of the table, put down the folder and looked up at me with a firm, businesslike expression I had never seen before. That wiped the smirk off my face.

'My staff and I have had a final discussion of your case Mrs. Pearson and feel it is time to make a recommendation to the minister based upon the evidence laid before us.' She tossed the fake blond hair back behind her ears and grinned at me. The little hussy! The two Tweedles chuckled at my obvious discomfort. I had been taken for a ride. Just what had I said to her in those moments of girl-girl intimacy over the meat pies and the cups of tea when I thought *I* was pumping *her*? I realised for the first time how insidiously I had been drawn back into an institutional sense of Britishness by the resonating memory of school dinners – seduced by the romance of stodge and boiled cabbage in the canteen. 'I'm afraid that everything you have presented to this panel is both mendacious and meretricious. We find that there is *prima facie* evidence of smuggling, infringement of immigration and foreign exchange regulations and arms and drug dealing. Further, we have proof of irregular, financial transactions of all sorts that would be of great concern to your Indonesian sponsors. Oh and perhaps we should not forget high treason and participation in war crimes.'

'So what are you going to do – hand me over to the Dutch, the Americans? Send me back to Blighty?' I found it hard to suppress a tremble in my voice.

'No, Mrs. Pearson. That would be a great waste of your talents. Such a record suggests to us that you are more than qualified to be a recruit for our own intelligence services. You have an excellent, inside knowledge of the current Indonesian leadership which is something that interests us greatly. I would suggest you come and work for us. We can arrange for that visit of yours to Australia to be made possible and for this file to find rest in a safe place away from the public eye.'

'Out of the question! The freedom of Indonesia is a noble cause to which I have dedicated years of loyal service, a cause for which I would lay down my very life. I couldn't possibly do anything that would harm my friends!'

Janice gave an I-told-you-so look to either side and clasped her hands together in her lap. She leaned forward and dropped her voice and spoke slowly and with emphasis as if to a dull-witted child. 'Nor would we ask you to. All we want is information. Surely, it would be of benefit to both nations to understand each other better and to avoid misunderstandings. Your Indonesian friends, as we see from your luggage, have left you high and dry and virtually penniless. We would be prepared to pay you, of course.'

'You insult me further by suggesting my loyalty is for sale? You think I would sell my honour to keep my comfort?' I stuck out my lower lip and flashed hostile outrage around the room. 'How much?'

* * *

The stateroom aboard the sleek SS *Marella* offered a rare interval of peace and prelaxation. It was the first time in years I had been cossetted with proper food and a luxurious bathroom with real, flowing, hot water and the effects on my physical and mental wellbeing were almost immediate but it also made me aware of how very tired and fragile I had let myself become. After all, I had come to the Indies in search of paradise and found war, revolution and death. I discovered a hidden passion for fancy cream cakes and the first time I ate high tea – the only truly civilised meal in the Western canon – I burst into tears in the china-tinkling saloon – as overwhelmed by a sense of loss and futility in the face of a rum baba as I had been by the nostalgia of a NAAFI meat-slime pie. After that, I kept mostly to my cabin, taking exercise on the deserted, nocturnal decks – letting the wind snatch away my terrors and enjoying anonymity, secure in the knowledge that no one knew who or where Surabaya Sue was. Left on my own in my cabin, I cried a lot.

There are few places better than Australia to bring you rapidly down to earth, for the Australians have always been the awkward squad of the British Empire with a permanently truculent set to their shoulders. It is as if the force of gravity is stronger there, keeping your feet more firmly on the ground, and the coarse Australian sun bleaches the flow and colour out of unctuous, British bullshit. Or perhaps it is just that it's a country full of red meat, thick and solid as common sense. As we tied up at Fremantle, I became aware of a strange rumbling outside and, peering through the porthole, saw a great crowd gathered round the gangplank. The dockers had turned out to welcome me, waving gay banners as vigorously and happily as the Jakartans of Van Mook's return. 'Good on ya, Sue!' 'Hands off Indonesia!' Alas no 'Death to Van Mook.' At the end of the world war, the 'wharfies' had blacked all Dutch vessels in support of the revolution and even rubbishing their own, treasured 'White Australia' policy to allow Indonesian dissidents to stay. The Dutch had been up to no good in Australia, imprisoning Indonesian sailors there who refused to work on their ships or serve in their army and trying to spirit 'troublemakers' away to prisons that were virtual death camps in New Guinea. There had been trouble at a Dutch military base. People had been shot. Attempts had been made to deport aboriginal wives. My wobbly travel documents did not permit me to descend the gangplank so I turned out on deck dutifully and strutted and waved to them in my best batik. I wasn't sure about that clenched fist *merdeka* salute and how it might go down here. Didn't Italian fascists do that?

Melbourne was a whirl of frustrated press attention, baying at me from the dockside. In Singapore, I had promised to refrain from all political activity but the government was tying itself into knots over whether it supported the Indonesians or not and whether they would even allow me to land in Sydney when the ship got there. As it was, I just flounced down the gangplank with six pieces of luggage and no passport and told the press to let the government know that my address would be the Australia Hotel if they wanted to see me. People were dying for accurate information about the Indonesian situation. How could I refuse them? Instead of peace and quiet it was noise and confusion. Questions were asked in parliament, ministers were hounded by press and opposition and I was grilled – fair barbied – by the media, giving talks, interviews, denying rumours about me circulated by the Dutch. I was a communist, a fascist, I had run a brothel in Bali, all that rubbish dredged up again. Being hard up, I arranged for most of this press attention to take place at restaurants and stuck them with the bill. God how I ate!

After a while, it was clear my moon was beginning to wane, coverage was slipping down from the quality press to the redtops and I was reduced to singing for my supper at one of the less fashionable Sydney yacht clubs in front of the starched shirts of the most conservative bunch in the city. They looked like a convention of bank branch managers and failed estate agents. Hardly any reporters had turned up, being by now familiar with my song. My audience was dozing, fuddled by drink. Then

I had a bright idea.

'I should like to announce ...' I said at the end, over the ruins of the salmon Wellington – the meal had been unfilling but I could get something better on the way home. I'd noticed a proper fish and chip place just down the road. '... that I have been touched by the sympathetic response of the Australian people to the plight of innocent Indonesians who ask for nothing more than to be left alone and in peace. However, some of your newspapers have been less than fair to me. All sorts of outrageous allegations have been made. I have therefore instructed my solicitors to begin proceedings for libel against some of the muck-raking Sydney press. I wish to let it be known here and now that I will not settle for less than a million US dollars in damages.'

That woke them up. There is something about the phrase 'a million dollars' that resonates like a teaspoon thrown into an empty teacup. One old buffer with a neatly regimented line of pens in his blazer badge pocket sat bolt upright and shouted, 'Why a million?'

'Because a girl has to live. I'm Surabaya Sue though I haven't got a Surabaya sou to my name so I'm suin'.'

It brought the house down. They laughed till their dentures dropped out. That little joke got me back on all the front pages even if I couldn't really raise enough cash even to pay for the stamp on a summons.

The news from Indonesia wasn't good. I scanned the newspapers compulsively. The Dutch were consolidating the Van Mook line. The communists were restive as the new government under Hatta tried to disband some of the wilder militia groups, stripped Bung Tomo of his armed support and reformed the national army under firmer, central government control. Civil war bristled and threatened on every island. At the turn of the year, there would be the menace of an Islamic secession under the Darul Islam movement and a full communist uprising in Madiun, put down by the army, with great bloodshed and hundreds if not thousands executed after the fighting. More people died there than in the Battle of Surabaya but censors would ensure Indonesia was not told about that. I feared for Lukman. In the midst of all this, the Australians decided that in the last three months I had tarred my own feathers enough with my communist supporters in the country to justify my deportation back on the SS *Marella* to Singapore. I went with regret. This time there were no flags and no banners and still no British passport.

Singapore was as keen to pass the parcel, or perhaps fling the hot potato, as Australia, and I was met off the ship by a blank-faced immigration officer from Sutton Coldfield with a terrible cold who hustled me immediately to the airport. Tweedledum and –dee and Janice made themselves scarce. They must have got a rocket for unloading so much trouble on Australia. At the airport, I was signed for by another blank-faced man from Dayton, Ohio, with a bad cough who handed me the flimsy ghost of an American passport stamped 'Valid for single re-entry into USA only' and escorted me to the very steps of a waiting aircraft that throbbed with impatience to be off. So I arrived 'home' and stood alone in the dark, windswept snow of New York, shivering in my thin, tropical frock and with my luggage ranged around me, coughing and sneezing and with my own coagulating snot sticking in my throat like an iced oyster – symptoms that were doubtless parting gifts from my Anglo-American, Singapore nannies. This time the word 'home' had a bitter aftertaste. Time for some home truths, then. I was ill, penniless and a certified leftie in a country floundering in a tidal backwash of anti-communist hysteria. It was Christmas. I was hungry.

Chapter Eleven

'I saw you that time in the Hotel des Indes. Don't think you got away with it. I recognised you right enough. But Christ! You've really piled on the pounds since Bali.' Bob Koke, CIA agent, in a white seersucker suit with a Panama hat on the hatstand. Clearly maintaining his tropical credentials although the leisurewear look and the Hawaiian shirts of Bali had now gone for good. We were sitting in a bland Washington office with a great, grey, steel desk, just down from the Capitol. A wall calendar showed a busty girl with deranged eyes sprawling on the wing of a bomber labelled 'Big Boy'. In post-war America everyone seemed to be working for the government and enslaved by phallic imagery in cars, architecture, even those great, shiny ashtrays like bombs they stood erect outside the elevators. The sign on the door said that this was where an accountant conducted his business but that was an awfully ambitious mirror for a legitimate accountant to have on his wall. Someone in the outer office was hammering away at a typewriter – the olive green, government-issue Corona they all use – another dead giveaway.

'I figured it was no business of the United States to get you shot for collaborating even if you deserved it. It would be a pretty shitty world where we only got what we deserved, wouldn't it? It was amnesty time anyway. Of course I *was* still a little ticked about the Bali deal but every little thing I did had to involve the Dutch and the Brits and Christ knows who else in triplicate and you would have made a helluva lot of paperwork. *You* always do.

In those days, if we'd wanted to, someone could have dropped the colonial army a couple of bucks to take you out one night with a machete in a dark street. Simpler times, Manxi.'

The typewriter went oddly silent when he stopped talking.

'Thank you for that.'

The typewriter clacked briefly again and stopped. They were clearly typing up our conversation live as it happened. I was an outside broadcast. There must be a bug somewhere. It was the straight version of that scene from *The Great Dictator* where Charlie Chaplin is dictating to a typist and there is a total but comical lack of fit between the length of his speech and the length of her typing. I had met Charlie when he came to Bali, a nice but unhappy man, uncomfortable in his own skin. I abruptly started up again, deliberately talking at breakneck speed.

'How long have you worked for the agency. In Bali? No? Later? Yes? Of course the CIA didn't exist then, did it? Like Indonesia. You were in an airforce uniform. The last time I saw you. Was that just a front? Maybe you can be both airforce and agency, I don't know. I don't know anything about spying or collaborating. As you saw, I'm just a simple girl who ran a hotel.'

The typewriter rattled along. The bell tinged like a streetcar careering out of control. Someone swore in a man's voice. Bob held up his hand.

'Whoa! Slow down, Manxi. Cool your engines. I was recruited after we left Bali for the States. They needed people who spoke Malay and only the Brits had them. I tried to get hold of you discreetly after that sighting in Jakarta but you'd left and nobody knew where you'd gone. That guy Wim you were with told me you'd talked about Semarang which was off the map to us. Nice guy. Smart as a whip too. Original thinker. Do you know he told me he ran this network of spies back in the Surabaya days?

He collected together this bunch of sweet, little old ladies who were just invisible to the Indonesians. They wandered in and out of everywhere with these little cups of tea they'd made. People thought just because they didn't have any teeth they couldn't speak Dutch and Javanese and Madurese and didn't have any ears. You wouldn't believe the stuff he picked up through them.' He swivelled forward in his chair and opened a brown dossier. Another of those damned dossiers. I wondered how much of the Singapore stuff had found its way in there. Not a lot by the look of it since it was quite slim.

'It says here you recently applied for an American passport that was refused?'

I nodded.

He made the rictus of a man afflicted with wind. 'Now that's kinda a double bind. If we give you one now, it means you were entitled to one during the war which makes some of the things you did treasonable. On the other hand we'd rather have you over there than over here. Those talks you give, those articles you write, they stir things up in a way we don't find helpful. We're very interested in Indonesia. Sure, since the republicans took out the commies in Madiun, we don't see any immediate danger. Of course the factory workers went on strike too and they caved in to them. But I guess you don't know how nasty industrial strikes can be like we do. But we'd like to know more about the current leadership. Fact is, up at the White House, they're screaming for gen so they can find a way out. Who's in? Who's out? Bung Karno. Who advises him these days? Is he stable? Can he be bought? What colour socks does he wear? Who's he sleeping with? We're real interested in his health. Do you figure you could get us a stool sample?'

I looked puzzled. 'A stool sample? He doesn't sit on a stool.'

'Oh come on Manxi, don't play dumb with me. Stool. Shit. Doody. Yeah. I assume the toilet arrangements are pretty informal.' He shrugged. 'OK, well maybe some blood, then. Throw a fit, punch him on the nose and make sure you get plenty of blood on your frock, whatever. Use some initiative. Sperm would be good too. Maybe you ain't got the tools for collecting that one, Manxi, looking more like a sperm whale yourself these days, though I hear he throws it around generously enough.'

'Look,' I said. 'I quite literally won't do shit for you.' Then, of course, the idea popped into my head that I might do just that. Mine or Bung K's, how could they tell the difference between two turds? Or maybe some thrusting young palace guard's or a wobbly, old gardener's? What would be the implications of a substitution and how could I best use it to knock the crap out of US foreign policy? I would have to think about that. 'If you're so keen on controlling things why don't you act a little smart yourself, do something useful and just threaten to cut off Marshall Aid till the Dutch return to the conference table. Sabre-rattling's no good. They know you're not dumb enough to get bogged down in any hopeless colonial war like the Brits did. I say, let your big bucks do the fighting. I'd rather be over there too but if you think I'm going to spy on my friends for you, you're badly mistaken. If I go, I go as a free agent. You should know that my love of Indonesia is so strong that I am almost to be seen as a victim of it.'

He smirked and flicked the dossier cover back and forth between his hands. 'That so? Really? A victim of it? I like that. Oh my! You know why Soekarno likes you? It's not a meeting of minds. It's because you're short. He's got this thing about tall people, anti-Dutch and all that. Intimidated. You may be short but I understood you'd always been … flexible.' He looked down. 'That would let us be a little flexible too. Talking of big bucks,

I see you don't have a whole lot in your bank account at the moment and you're running up a lot of bills – taxes, utilities, telephone – my but you make some interesting phone calls, Manxi!' He looked back up. 'I guess the film industry ain't too kind to those of your particular political colour at the moment. Says here you've been scratching a living peddling cheap Balinese carvings around the souvenir stores. Your friend Wim gave me a pair. The Dutch were having some sort of a fire sale on 'em. Louise loves 'em. We didn't have time to take much when we had to get out of Kuta to avoid the Japs.'

'That hammy prick Ronald Reagan got me blacklisted after I bent his ear at Grauman's Chinese Theatre one night about Indonesia and he got on his high cowboy horse about sacred capitalism.'

'"The Gipper"? One of our loyalest Americans. A true patriot. But let me tell you a story, honey. Maybe you've been a little out of touch with developments in the Indies. You will know that the US managed to persuade the Dutch to stop their nonsense by pushing them into that ceasefire conference with the republicans on board the USS *Renville*. But now the Dutch've gone and done it again! A coupla days ago, they attacked the Indonesian positions all along the Van Mook line and dropped paratroops into Yogya. They've rounded up the republican government and shoved them off into exile on some godforsaken island called Bangka. The aim was to draw the national army into a fight and wipe them out but, instead of defending Yogya, they just withdrew and faded away into the jungle and the government was switched over to Sumatra. So the Dutch are left looking stupid and holding their own dicks – and the entire, republican government which is much the same thing. Now, what's interesting is they were able to pull it off so easily because they'd been monitoring Indonesian military traffic all year, knew just where everyone was. It seems somehow their men in Singapore got hold of a bunch of old communications with translations from Semarang via the Brits so they managed to crack the code. Security agencies are leaky sieves, Manxi. It's even just possible some of the stuff *they* got to know could get back to the Indonesians, together with how *they* got to know it. I suggest you should think about that. I don't think I ever mentioned ... Back in the day, when you were a hot property and Soekarno was still trying to do a deal with the Dutch, he offered to throw in your extradition to them as a sweetener. You never were a good friend, Manxi, and you never inspired real friendship. You're not going to convince me your farts smell of mouthwash and, say what you like, I never saw you as the sort of person who would get herself between a good cause and a firing squad.'

'Is that all?'

'Talking of friends ... one more thing. I think you know Amir Sjarifuddin?'

'Bung Amir? Yes. A dear man. What's happened? Have the Dutch got him? Have they hurt him?'

'Before they evacuated Yogya, your friends in the republican army took the prisoners left over from the communist uprising in Madiun and shot the lot. Amir was one of them. He was some sort of a commie right? I thought you'd like to know.'

'Thank you.' I swallowed hard and blinked back tears. I wouldn't give him the satisfaction. 'By the way, Bob, those Balinese carvings of yours. Make sure you keep them somewhere nice and warm. If you have a mantlepiece over a fire perhaps that would be a good spot or maybe even arrange them around the hearth itself so they catch the firelight. Coming from the tropics, if they get too cold, they'll split you see and you wouldn't want that.'

He was surprised at my goodwill. 'Gee thanks for the tip,

Manxi. I'll do that. So what'll it be? Do you go back and work for us – nothing too nasty just keep your eyes and ears open – or not at all?'

* * *

'The war is over. You missed it, K'tut. We all thought you had run away and deserted us. Of course, everyone said you were a spy, which was absurd. But it wasn't so bad in Bangka,' said Bung Karno, waving a Merdeka cigarette. 'They could have chosen somewhere much worse.' Soldiers – Indonesian soldiers – in neatly matching pairs stamped up and down outside the tall windows. 'There was a joke that we ended up in Bangka because they gave the pilot an envelope telling him what his destination was but marked "Not to be opened until arrival". I know that fool Sjahrir said I was happy there because my room had seven mirrors, which wasn't true, but there were other compensations. One way and another, the Dutch have arranged for me to tour the whole of our glorious Indonesia in my various exiles. It is they that have convinced me of its fundamental unity across our 20,000 islands. He may claim to be a great thinker now but during the Japanese occupation, Sjahrir just sat cosily at home and read nice books while I was out there wrestling with the real issues.' We all die a little with each success of our rivals. He flared his nostrils and tapped off ash with the gesture of an orchestral conductor bringing in the flute section, letting it fall on the carpet. Perhaps he hated those chemical, blood-red carpets as much as I did. They seemed to be made to soak up the bloodshed of palace coups. 'I thought it was clever of the Dutch to drop dummies on parachutes over Yogya so that our troops opened fire and gave their positions away. They seemed to know everything about our dispositions. I stood in the palace yard and thought how beautiful the silky parachutes looked in the sunshine – like floating jellyfish drifting in the current of the sea. Even when the parachutes were Japanese you used to think of cherry blossom. When I was a boy we all flew kites and you always imagined yourself soaring up there in the clouds with your kite. Sjahrir never had any imagination. There was no poetry in his soul.'

'Yes,' I said. 'The dummies. That would be it. That's how they knew. Though I doubt those poor air cadets they strafed at Moguwo were thinking about their kites even if they were still just young boys.'

He sipped sweet, cold tea, 'I was most embarrassed for the Indians. It was nice of Nehru to send that plane to whisk us away to the UN but a little silly to send it via Jakarta. Of course, the Dutch just sat on it.' He shuffled his own backside, looked around and sighed with the satisfaction that comes to a man from arriving home after a long trip and settling his rump firmly on a familiar chair. I felt much the same. 'But anyway, it all turned out for the best. The Dutch military victory in the second "Police Action" set the whole world and the UN against them. The turning point was when the US suddenly switched their negotiating position and threatened to cut off Marshall Aid. There was some sort of a presidential order from Washington. That was it. Why didn't they think of that before? Where did they suddenly get the idea? Then the Dutch finally knew they had to make peace. So winning the battle for Yogya lost the Dutch the war and now it's just the haggling.' He looked through the window at the peaceful garden and sighed again, tapping his fingers on the arm of the chair. He always had the same perfect manicure and compulsively clean hands. Other, lesser people with dirt under their fingernails would be doing that haggling now in The Hague. 'There's no doubt any more about the outcome – not that there ever was really. Then comes the hard part – what do we do with this freedom we've won? No one has wanted to think too much about that for fear of taking their eye off the immediate problem. And at least we kept the army intact.'

I thought about my own release from the Japanese camp and the sense of sheer emptiness that overwhelmed me when freedom, my dearest hope, became – incredibly – true. To just sit in the sun and feel the wind had been enough, all that I had been capable of. Then I heard myself say quietly, 'But Pak Amir is dead.'

He shot me a warning look like I was a fly in his soup. 'Yes he is dead. It is a pity. He was a friend from the early days. I sent Lieutenant Colonel Suharto to try to negotiate a peaceful resolution with the communist rebels but they wouldn't have it. Then, in all the confusion of the Dutch attack ... well ... but Suharto did a sterling job retaking the city of Yogya and holding it, as he did for a while, to strengthen our position at the peace talks.' He bent forward and dropped his voice. 'Now, something more interesting. Tell me about this new girl called Jane Russel with the very big breasts and her special bra gripping from underneath designed by the aircraft man. I have been reading something and I knew you would know all about it. I asked the head of the air force but he couldn't explain. He just muttered something about the attachment of the wings of B-36s. And no one else in the cabinet knew. I suppose I could set the Bandung Technical College onto it.'

I gave him the most sensational version lifted from the gossip rags, spicing them up even more with innuendo-stuffed lines about 'fittings' but forbore to mention another sterling job Suharto had done. For Bung Karno's principled refusal to join the guerrillas in the mountains had not been seen by everyone as a mark of courage. He was, after all, a city boy known to like his city comforts. While he argued that the Dutch Governor General had not run away from the Japanese so he could not do less and run away now from the Dutch, perhaps the two cases were not strictly similar. There had been an embarrassing film of Bung Karno grinning and posing chummily with the enemy, being saluted up and down by them – he trim and unruffled as always – so that it appeared as if he was a man on a relaxed holiday rather than an oppressed prisoner and there was a part of the outraged republican army that had wanted to take over and squeeze the civilians out. It had been touch and go. Fortunately, a loyal, young officer had made an impassioned speech to the vacillating Yogya garrison on the evils of military coups. That officer had been Lieutenant Colonel Suharto.

* * *

27th December 1949. It was the day everyone had dreamed of and the day no one could quite believe had finally come yet, like everything that had been so long aspired to and fought for, it carried the seed of threatened disappointment within it, for every dream fulfilled is a dream lost. Bung Karno had been right about that. And what was peace but just an absence of war, a mere minus quantity with no attributes of its own? All round the world the newspapers would run the pictures of Queen Juliana stoutly signing some document with Hatta – in fact the Dutch surrender but given some more fancy and sweeter-smelling name – and people would be puzzled and a little upset that she wasn't wearing her crown, just some silly feather in her hair. The radio had been stoking up anticipation and now the first rays of the sun began to stab through the trees on what seemed, at first, just another hot day in Jakarta. But at dawn, sniffing a major event, the food sellers had already set up their stalls around the Koenigsplein, now renamed – guess what? – Merdeka Square and great, silent crowds had settled in front of the old Governor General's Gambir Palace, now renamed Merdeka Palace. Smoke from their fires began to blow and billow across the grass and the sprawling bodies, appropriately, as if in the still aftermath of some great Napoleonic battle. The silence was extraordinary. Crowds in Indonesia are never silent but today I floated through them like a ghostly vision in my best white tule and showed my pass to the smart, young guards on the gate, themselves shivering with wordless excitement. Overhead on the portico roof, fluttered the biggest red and white flag I had ever seen. Fatmawati must have been up all night, mouth full of pins, sewing it.

Inside it was like an ants' nest when the aardvark drops by, with servants rushing around glowing with self-importance and bumping into each other on more of those hideous blood-red carpets. They were downright dangerous. Why, only the other day, I had tripped over one in the Bogor palace and accidentally whacked Bung Karno in the face, giving him a nasty nosebleed, just like poor, dead Lukman at the Oranje Hotel. Luckily, he had forgiven me at once as I tended him and sponged off the gore into my blood-soaked hankie and tucked it away in my bag. A buffet was laid out on the side tables with silver serving dishes and the Indonesian dignitaries, hungry men in best bib and tucker, were already spooning away joyfully at the fruits of victory. Over against the other wall stood a clutch of Dutch military, themselves clutching hats and sourly not eating so I dived into the sumptuous fried rice, not out of appetite but to show to which camp I belonged. Anyway, once you have known real hunger you don't lightly say no to any fuel stop.

'Hallo, K'tut.' It was Bung Tomo at my elbow, still windblown as tumbleweed, as if he had just wandered in from the mountains all fluffy. That he spoke to me at all showed how alone and out of things he must feel. And those coal-black eyes still gleamed with unquenched fire. Also not eating, a man made for fasting, flagellation and self-denial. Nevertheless, politeness required me to gesture at the food before I could return to my own.

'Come and eat.'

He shook his head, locks flying everywhere. 'Already.'

'You don't look very happy, Bung. What a face to make on the day the president returns from Yogya and the new government of a free Indonesia is finally installed! Now at least, according to the terms of your oath, you can get your hair cut.'

He blinked, not used to being joked with. I didn't care. It was a day for happiness not sulking. 'You may be right, K'tut. But do you think that if a man comes back from years at the war and is presented with a baby and told it is his, he should just smile and say it is lovely and accept it even if it is an ugly, deformed, bastard child like this our new Indonesia?' He stalked over to the food table and began to rip savagely at a stick of satay with his teeth as his boys had once attacked Dutch flags with theirs.

A mass susurration, as of bees, washed in from outside. As I looked out across the pillared terrace, the crowd that stretched to the horizon seemed to rise and suddenly part in two waves like the Red Sea in Cecil B. DeMille's epic and there, like Moses, was Bung Karno standing up in the rear of a lush convertible, hand outstretched and gliding smoothly forward – dry-shod as always – leading his people to the Promised Land – slowly, slowly. War had changed from a thing of spilled guts and the stench of death to ballyhoo and silver trumpets.

'He should have come on a tank,' says a military man, headshaking.

A great agonised howl tore from a million throats, a mass oral orgasm compounded of lust, frustration and inexpressible desire rippled across the crowd. '*Merdeka*! *Merdeka*!' The very ground shook under our feet, fear quivered in the eyes of the Dutch delegates, Bung Tomo still tore at the grilled meat and crushed it with uncompromising teeth. Time slowed. The world shifted out of focus as Bung Karno entered the pall of smoke and dust haze and finally emerged again, the car turning so the sun was a golden halo behind him, at the gate. The guards gave up all attempts to hold back the crowd, stood back and they surged forward, flag-waving, dancing, screaming and for a second I found myself again in a tram in Glasgow, a young girl with my whole life before me, as its windows smashed and tinkled to the ground around my feet. Tears began to stream down my face. Most of the Indonesians seemed to be crying too.

Bung Karno stepped out of the car and tripped lightly up the stone steps and turned, a tiny, dapper figure dwarfed by the significance of what was happening and the massive, Doric pillars looming behind him like the shade of history. He raised both arms and, for a second, it looked for all the world as if he would break into a tap dance routine or simply ascend straight into the air, twirling up like Elijah in a picture I remembered from the Sunday school wall. Then it was just him and the people. The rest of us faded into nothing.

'*Diam*!' He called for silence. '*Diiiam*!' and began to speak, the high, clear voice floating out over the crowd and echoing back, shimmering, from across the square. I don't remember what he said. It really didn't matter. Something about his years of wandering in the desert and how it was everybody's freedom that we were marking and how we should all be friends. At the end it was washed away with a million roared '*Merdeka*'s, a million flags in red and white and Bung Tomo still stood behind him in shadow and tore at the impaled, burnt flesh with sharp, gleaming teeth, stick after stick after stick, his other hand full of the greasy, little spears that he had no place left to thrust.

* * *

I came out of the Information Ministry into stark, midday sun and stopped dead in my tracks. It was weeks since the transfer of power but some of my colleagues had still not quite made it back to work from the celebrations. Yet I liked to tell myself that the people in the street were subtly changed, more upright, taller, walking with more self-respect as citizens of a free country. At the bottom of the steps, across the road, a grey truck was parked with the passenger door open and a tall European in shorts and sports shirt was reaching inside for his bag as his local driver was climbing out the other side. There was something about him – even from that odd angle – that was familiar. As he turned, I recognised him at once. It was the man Wim had called Turk Westerling. The golfer. He might be dressed as a civilian but he still walked like a soldier as he made his way to the back and flipped up the canvas hood. What the hell was he doing still in Indonesia? Why wasn't he in jail or in Holland or, better still, burning in Hell? Then his driver stepped out from behind the vehicle into the road and I recognised him too. It was Uki.

I ducked behind a kerbside food stall selling the horribly sweet and sticky, moon-shaped pancakes they also called terang bulan, my blood and the boiling oil both thundering in my ears, and watched as Westerling gave orders, counting off points on the palm of his hand with his index finger. Little Uki nodded, just stopped himself in time from saluting and they set off in opposite directions along the pavement. The stallholder intruded into my view trying to sell me a pancake, waving it in my face. It looked about as appetising as an old man's ankles. At least there would be no Westerling-type chilli sauce on it. I pushed him aside and, after a moment's hesitation over the neighbouring satay stall, followed Uki.

It was hard keeping up. I had been putting on a little weight. Sedentary city life rapidly takes the edge off any imagined fitness and Uki was setting a brisk pace in the hot sun. Shadows lay across the street like iron bars. He dodged down a side passage, crossed over and plunged into an alleyway clogged with stalls. By the time I reached the end of it he had disappeared. I moved forward cautiously, looking in the shops to right and left, people dodging around me like fish around a cruising crocodile. Many of the doors stood open, disclosing glimpses of little, domestic hells. Here, a group of five-year-olds were sharing a quick fag in a doorway. There, in another, a woman was wiping diarrhoea off the legs of a toddler with her hand. I was more than halfway down when I saw him come out of one and set off again with a package under his arm. He criss-crossed several more streets with me in tow and disappeared again into a garage. I hovered uncertainly, eyes fixed on the open double doors. Mostly, it was bicycles, not cars, being repaired in there with loud sounds of Wagnerian metal-bashing. I walked up and down, undecided. I pretended to look at some cloth on a stall, watched a man grinding ice on a toothed steel barrel that would have made a great instrument of torture for Turk Westerling. Suddenly, someone touched my elbow. I turned. Uki.

'Let's get out of here,' he hissed. 'You shouldn't be here. The others wanted to shoot you. Follow me.' He raised a placatory hand to the open garage door where another man stood in dramatically ripped overalls, looking out grimly with something hidden behind his back and we set off again to a nearby coffee stand shaded under a tarpaulin. We ordered two coffees – black, full of grains, stultified with sugar. I never understood how the Javanese could not know how to make a decent cup of Java. But those vegetable rolls there looked good.

Uki smiled. 'Fat,' he said, pointing at me. When Indonesians say you are fat, they mean you are looking well, a compliment. 'Did you really think you could follow me and not be seen? How many white women with red hair and in batik dresses are there on the streets of Jakarta these days? How are you, sister?'

'I saw you,' I puffed. 'I saw you with Westerling. What the hell's going on? Let me have a couple of those lumpiah rolls there.'

He blushed. 'You saw me?' He looked away. 'You don't understand, K'tut.'

'Damn right I don't. You know who he is? What he did?' The rolls were delicious.

Uki nodded and sipped the grainy brew, like sand with caffeine in it. 'It's not what you think. Times have changed. There are different enemies now. It's not simple like back in Surabaya. You know the government troops shot Lukman when they retook Madiun? The republicans. He was one of the prisoners taken to the jail there after the communists surrendered. They stood him against a wall and shot him in cold blood. A friend of mine saw it with his own eyes and he was lucky to hang on to his eyes.'

'Oh my god! Poor Lukman.' I saw him again in my own mind's eye back in 'simple' Surabaya, grinning, proudly wearing his own hot blood on his young face like a trophy, so very much alive. We all smiled so much more then. Now it was a lost art for me.

'We used the Japanese to defeat the Dutch but now we are free of direct Dutch rule, we Sundanese have to use them against the Javanese. The agreement is for a federal United States of Indonesia under the Dutch queen but the republicans want a single, united Indonesia under the Javanese. They will gobble up the lesser states like our own, Pasundan, one by one. Westerling has managed to bring together all the forces in Sunda into APRA, the Legion of the Just Ruler – Muslims, communists, colonial troops and Sunda nationalists – to hang on to our independence.' Their meetings must be something to see. 'They have sent an ultimatum to the republicans to respect the federal constitution. Pak Dion and Uncle Wirno have explained it all to me. And we have leaders with magical powers – much stronger than Bung Karno's. They are wise men who have seen much. Even the Dutch respect them.' His eyes glowed with passion.

I groaned and held my head. 'Independence under the Dutch? Magical powers? They're trying to play you off against each other to stay in charge. How do you think the Dutch conquered the Indies in the first place? They set one group against another. Don't you see that?' I took an outraged swig of gravelly coffee and choked. I had grounds. Perhaps another roll would clear them.

'Of course that is what the Dutch will think but they are stupid and we can use them for our own ends.' He drew himself up proudly. 'We have a plan.' He thumped me on the back until my coughing fit subsided.

'What's the plan?' I gasped. People were staring. I hoped it wasn't one of Wim's dogeared plans.

'Ooh, I can't tell you that but it's a very good plan. We have supplies and equipment and it's already here in Jakarta, ready to go. Turk says we can't lose. After all, he says he is the Just Ruler of the Joyoboyo prophecies. You know the prediction that there would come a time when carriages would move without horses, when wires were stretched round the earth and then the Japanese would come and chase away the Dutch …'

'Yes, yes, and be replaced by the Just Ruler after one maize harvest … Bung Karno is always going on about it too. I've heard it all a thousand times.'

'Well, there you are then. It is destined to be.' He waggled his head in self-satisfaction. Then, shyly. 'Can I ask you something, sister? Why did you never go back to Bali? You were always telling us how it was paradise, but you never went back. Perhaps you should go back now. You would be safer there.'

I sipped more coffee and choked again. 'It wasn't that I didn't want to but the Bali I knew has gone. I couldn't bear to go back and see it all smashed and broken. You know how, in the West, some couples go back to the place where they spent their honeymoon – the holiday just after they have got married. It is always a mistake. It invites comparisons. I know when I was in Bali, now so many years ago, people were already saying, "Ah you should have been here twenty years ago. *Then* it was really paradise." But now? I think it would break my heart.' It was true. But the world also has a cruel way of making us no longer want something once it is attainable. When I was a little girl I lived in the absolute certainty that no cake would ever be baked in my house when I grew up. Instead, I would sit at a table and lick bowl after bowl of delicious, uncooked cake mix, all thick and spicy, from a wooden spoon even if it gave me worms as Ma warned me it would. It never happened. As soon as it became possible, the idea was loathsome, the flavour sickly. Perhaps it was the same with the taste of freedom.

I took a rickshaw back to the house and told the driver to ride past Wim's godown. Sure enough, there was the same grey truck I had seen parked outside the ministry and crates were being manhandled onto the back. Westerling, it seemed, had taken over Wim's warehouse – lock, stock and gun barrels – so maybe some of the hundreds of explosive Balinese busts were still lodged in there somewhere, waiting to burst upon an art-hungry world. In theory, the old colonial army was supposed to be absorbed into the new national force but huge mutual distrust and lack of money meant that fragments of all sorts of war-surplus military had been left to moulder in every corner and backwater of the archipelago. By the front gate, the Ambonese guards were still in place as if they just went with the building. They must have been wondering just who it was they were working for and who they were guarding it against but out of long habit they simply saluted any Dutch uniform or face that came their way. As people who had waited for nearly four centuries for independence, maybe they weren't the pushy kind.

* * *

'Don't go to the office tomorrow. It will be dangerous for you. Uki.'

I stared down at the note, effortfully scrawled on the back of an old envelope, one of those pinky-brown ones the post office uses. Could Uki read and write? I wasn't sure. Maybe someone had had to write it for him. He had been at a Koranic school where chanting off by heart is the main activity. A small boy had slid the note under my door at dawn and pedalled away furiously on a bike far too big for him. I saw him as he skittered round the corner at the end of the street, skidding in the dust. I turned the note over. There was an address in the Menteng area left printed on the other side in a precise, official hand.

'Oh, Uki, Uki.'

I wondered whether the note had been written last night in which case 'tomorrow' meant today or whether it was still tomorrow. I looked at the clock. The gado-gado salad seller would be round soon and I had to be ready to run down the path before the neighbours snapped it all up. Either way, I padded into the bathroom and tentatively splashed chill morning water from the big jar over my feet. People swore that way it didn't come as a shock to the body. Yet it made me gasp and shudder as I spooned coldness over my head and shoulders and my heart raced and the blood roared in my ears. Through a curtain of hair and water I scanned the chipped, old floor tiles for wisdom as I tried to worry the cheap, harsh soap into foam and fought for breath against rising panic. What should I do? Which way did duty lie? If I did nothing people dear to me would be killed. If I acted, Uki was at terrible risk. I groaned. Mildew-smelling water swirled down the plughole in which, as if conjured by magic, Westerling's smirking face appeared. That decided it. Perhaps Lukman had been right, it was who you hated that ultimately defined you, not what you believed or who you loved. A *cicak* lizard slalomed around the walls and nodded vigorous agreement. I slipped a sarong over my wet body and tottered carefully back to the living room – the floor tiles were lethal when wet – and picked up the great Bakelite sledgehammer of the telephone, a perk of Information Ministry employees. Would it work today? Often it didn't but even a broken telephone was still a valuable asset, an addition to a state employee's list of excuses for not going in to the office. It had never felt heavier in my hand.

* * *

The news started trickling in as I sat at my table in the Ministry of Information. It began as a slight ruffling of feathers among the journalists as we sat in the usual fog of cigarettes and stale coffee stink and exploded into a real cat among the pigeons. At dawn, colonial troops had seized Bandung and driven the Siliwangi Division out of their own headquarters. There was still a Dutch military unit up there and some of the Siliwangi troops had sought safety in their barracks and asked for their big brother's protection against their big brother's other army. The world was still making crazy alliances. Trucks from Bandung had been stopped as they headed for the capital and were now ablaze, cutting off the road link. Maybe they contained military supplies but no one was sure. There had been sporadic firefights around Jakarta. A warehouse in the Chinese quarter had been seized and found to contain arms and ammunition, road blocks had been doubled and groups of men in stolen National Army uniforms had been discovered moving into the centre and been either captured or shot. Following a tip-off a private address in Menteng had been raided. Of course, none of this had officially happened until the editor of the day decided what version of all this was the government line and that would take hours, in which time rumours would have flashed around the city at the speed of light. I gathered up my possessions and left. The Ministry of Information was always the last place to find out what was really going on.

I knew what I must do. I retraced my steps of a few weeks ago, threading my way through empty streets and closed stalls back to the garage. People here had already smelled something on the wind, kept away or battened down the hatches as they had so often before in recent history. The garage looked deserted with the double doors firmly locked against the world. I knocked. It sounded obscenely loud, like a fart in a cathedral. An eye at a crack in the door and then the sound of a bolt being drawn. A gap opened an inch or two. Uki. I pushed my way in and Uki rebolted the door and turned. It was dark inside with just a little light filtering in from high windows at the back. He was wearing an army uniform and looked terrified and suddenly about twelve years old.

'It's all over,' I said. 'The coup has failed. You have to run for it. You can't stay here. They will come for you. Once you saved me from that terrible communist colonel who kidnapped me. Now I can help you.'

'I was supposed to shoot the cabinet today but nobody came for me like they promised.' He sounded peeved, like a little boy who had been denied an ice cream he had been led to expect. Ice cream. There was a new place round the corner that sold ice cream. It was pricey but they did a great chocolate sauce. I shook the idea away.

'There's no time for that now. I mean, it's all over. You have to ditch the uniform and run. Go west into the mountains. They are still fighting in Bandung but it's only a matter of time.' I dug in my bag and handed over a wodge of old notes. 'Here's some money, enough to get you out of the city and back to your village. The men with magic can protect you there.'

He took it reluctantly and stood looking at me, unconvinced. 'What about Turk Westerling? I can't just abandon him.'

I was exasperated. 'You can be sure he will take good care of himself. People like that always do. He's probably already on a plane to Singapore with his pockets stuffed with gold. You have to understand you are fighting for your own life. Go!'

He looked as if he was going to cry, raw fear in his eyes. 'No, not Singapore. If this fails Turk has a plan to start again in West Irian. They will found a new Dutch colony in West Irian, begin all over again in the jungle.' His mouth squared again for crying. 'I don't want to go to West Irian. They eat people there and I haven't got anything else to wear.'

I swore under my breath, looked around, grabbed the ripped overalls off a nail, ripping them more. 'Get rid of the army shirt, wear these.' He obeyed as if in a daze. It didn't look right. I seized a hunk of metal, some car part – a big end, a small end, some sort of bloody end – and shoved it into his hands as a prop. 'Carry that.' I opened the door and pushed him out into the dusty street and he wandered off slowly like a zombie, a caged bird suddenly released into the frightening wild, the money still clutched in his bewildered hand. At the corner he turned and waved sadly, like a lost child. I never saw Uki again.

the perfect, translucent cubes, rare as diamonds but flowing like water tonight. On the top floor, the presidential suite had sexy, bulletproof glass but guards had been posted there to prevent the swarms of curious children from riding the lifts above the second floor. And outside, the new Welcome Monument was lit up by blazing spotlamps, a superhuman male and female Indonesian couple in bronze, leaping like dolphins and waving. Bung Karno had rampaged through central Jakarta leaving a trail of construction behind him. The woman clutched a bouquet that looked like a Molotov cocktail she was about to swing round and hurl through the plate glass windows. But it was time to forget all that. The revolution was over and life had become an everyday thing. War had dissolved into mere political pageantry. But the sense of satire lurks deep within the Indonesian soul. It might be outlawed but it could never be snuffed out and was never fooled. All the pretentious statuary of the new Jakarta had nicknames that deflated their public pomposity. Bung Karno was enormously pleased that the huge, towering pinnacle of the national monument, gushing flames at its tip, was known as 'Soekarno's last erection' – though perhaps the word 'last' aroused in him some small anxiety.

There was still a lot of talk about the hotel, even a whole year after its opening. Why was the president of a currency-poor nation squandering money on prestige projects when millions lived in destitution? Didn't people want rice not monuments? The cash was said to come from war reparations squeezed out of the Japanese so why was it not going to those who had suffered under them? Each brick was cemented with the blood of the martyrs of the revolutionary struggle! Actually, of course, there weren't that many bricks – it was far too modern a building for that – but journalese clichés die hard. Bung Karno always said we had to feed minds as well as bodies and I had quoted that and written all the other, predictable answers – waffling on about the generation of foreign exchange and modernisation, neo-colonialism and development – in a dozen press releases until I myself was irked by them and their pathetic fictions. The hotel was there as just another stage for Bung Karno since he was an addicted, hambone performer hooked on limelight and needed to star on it.

The ladies had now discovered the deodorized American toilets with their built-in cisterns and hushed flush and they were flocking for the experience of not pulling a chain but pressing a button like the one that launched the atom bomb. But Allah! It was true then that these people wiped their uncircumcised backsides with paper not washed them clean with water! They gagged in horror.

The band switched to 'Terang Bulan'. They seemed much more comfortable playing that. Perhaps it was Bung Karno's deliberate snub to Malaysia who had grabbed the corny, old song as their national anthem and outlawed its public performance except in their own service. They had tricked it out with new words full of patriotic mush but to me it would always be about sneaky crocodiles lying doggo in forgiving moonlight and just waiting to bite your legs off. Confrontation of the new, neo-colonial federation even in music. The slogan 'Crush Malaysia' was now the new '*Merdeka*', the best Bung K could do by way of a new storyline to revive interest and jack up the ratings. He had just delivered it in a speech I had written. The music suited the jerky, cocky strut that was his version of dancing.

I was covering the reception for the international press but I was deathly bored. I had lived this life too long. Over the course of more than ten years, journalism had become a weary treadmill in a hamster's cage. A sudden, American homesickness gripped me. Not to miss American luxuries when they were over the other side of the world was one thing but now here they were in the middle of my own city, tempting me, making me abruptly tired of what was suddenly pointless poverty and discomfort. For me they didn't mean novelty but nostalgia. I wandered across to the reception desk where a very dark, very handsome young clerk in a very dark, very handsome new suit was standing, nervously gripping the counter with both hands and lobbing perfect grins at the world. It is wonderful the way that each generation sloughs off the sins and stains and disappointments of the last to emerge bright, shiny and hopeful. The thought struck me that he could have been Uki's son – no, nephew. I wondered how Uki was. *Where* he was. In the west of Java, the embers of Westerling's uprising were still glowing and smoking underground but the flame was long snuffed out – like Westerling himself, smuggled back to Holland by the Dutch. Someone told me he had become a very bad opera singer there. So much for the new homeland he planned to hack out of the jungle in West Irian with his bare hands. Enough of the past.

'How much is a suite per night?'

The clerk grinned again and bowed and wrote down a figure on a piece of paper, turned it round and slid it across the counter-top back to me with both his beautifully maintained hands and the light gesture of a concert pianist. They almost put Bung Karno's to shame in that the nails of the little fingers were kept extra long and polished. Bung K's hands had long fascinated me and he would occasionally fling out some throwaway, personal revelation that took your breath away like a medicine ball to the stomach. One day we had been discussing my views on Dutch foreign policy when he suddenly began talking about a girl he knew as a schoolboy.

'*She* was Dutch. I was crazy about her, insane with love. Can you believe it? Oh, I would have made any sacrifice. Just before we had sex, when I knew it was coming, I even cut the fingernails on my left hand and filed them smooth on the brick wall of the school till they bled, so as to be ready! Women don't like sharp fingernails in certain places, do they K'tut?'

One glance at the paper told me why this soft-handed clerk didn't dare put the price into words. It was outrageous. I gasped, half at the price, but also half in memory of Bung Karno's blithe declaration.

'Breakfast is included,' he mollified. His breath smelt of peppermint. He had been stealing the after-dinner mints. 'With choice of tea or coffee.'

'With choice of tea or coffee? And free milk and sugar as well? And use of a teaspoon? Wah! Very well then,' I said, radiating stunned admiration. 'In that case, I can hesitate no longer. Reserve it for me at once. I'll send for my luggage tomorrow.'

He clapped his hands together in glee. 'And how will madam be paying. American dollars?'

'You will send the bill to my friend Bung Karno,' I instructed and waved across the floor at him. Bung Karno still looked very suave in his brushed *peci* that concealed the bald spot and jazzy, military ribbons but perhaps a little heavier in the thigh and with a suggestion of jowls – still surrounded as always by the prettiest women. But nowadays, there was an air of one of those cunningly mummified Hollywood stars who had got typecast too young and ended up endlessly reprising the same undemanding rôle in a soap opera that he had once played in a Cecil B. de Mille epic of the wide screen. Of course, neither soap opera leads nor dictators often have great endings do they? Their chief virtue is just to go on and on in a dull and comforting familiarity till they are written out of the script in an abrupt cataclysm. He was a little surprised at my uncouth gesture but smiled and flicked back an acknowledgement to the greeting. The light caught his fingernails. He was always a gentleman.

The clerk took in the acknowledgement and stood abruptly to attention. 'Yes, madam. Of course. And how long will madam be staying?'

'Indefinitely.'

I had given my life to Indonesia and now that Indonesia had become an American hotel it seemed only proper that I should live in it. After all, as midwife and godmother, I had helped a hundred million people to freedom, hadn't I? I headed back across the room to the buffet and grabbed a fresh plate. Some of the chafing dishes were starting to run low and you could never be absolutely sure they were going to refill them again.

* * *

Although everything was in theory closed for the night, the sleepy watchman saluted and waved me up with an extended, courtly arm contained within a ragged sleeve, scruples soothed by my Ministry of Information pass – which it was too dark to read anyway – and a few coins. The light of the full moon – *terang bulan* – washed the upper layers of mellow stone in golden light and trickled down the terraces though they still radiated the heat of the contesting sun. In silhouette, the ancient temple of Borobodur sprawled contentedly over the hillside as it had for more than a thousand years and looked like a souvenir drawing in Indian ink, or a fat Buddha about to let fly a sated belch or maybe a stack of giant Chelsea buns. On the lowest level, someone had repeatedly daubed '*Merdeka*' in red paint but it was already weathering and flaking away beneath the tooth of time, just as the structure's original fairground colours had been bleached like those of Greek statuary and medieval cathedrals to the classic white of antiquity. History strips things down to the bare essentials. I mounted the steps slowly – one by one – bringing my feet together at each step and squeezed through the narrow passageways, each uniquely carved with panels that marked the upward trajectory of the slim, Buddhist aspirant towards nirvana. I panted a little, having reached the age where our bodies start to take their revenge on us. Creatures of the night, indifferent to the sacredness around them, scuttled about on their mundane business. In the distance an owl hooted – to Javanese a scary 'ghost bird' – to me a comforting sound of enduring Nature.

The massive building had withstood indifferently fire and earthquake for more than a thousand years, the succession of religions and dynasties, the convulsions of history, the fulfilment of the Joyoboyo prophecies, the Indians who brought cloth, the Portuguese who brought custard tarts, the Dutch, the Japanese, the British and the new, political faiths they dragged along with them and still it stood unmoved and implacable, having shrugged off centuries of volcanic ash and risen again. It had even survived the vandalisation of the Christian Department of Works that had tried to bodge it back together with cheap cement and the Muslim Javanese fanatics who had sought to blow it apart with expensive explosives.

These days, I blanched a little at the endless demands to climb ever higher, drawing comfort and strength from the rootedness of the towering rock of ages, smooth beneath my hands as beneath those of the millions of pilgrims who had trod this path before me. It was as if their faith had soaked into the stonework and consolidated it into some new and immutable substance. We spiralled up from the world of desire, up through the world of forms and out into heavenly formlessness and dissolution.

I felt the need to come here beneath the forgiving stars from time to time just to reassure myself that, through so much history, so much revolution and war and blood, the unfaltering rhythm of the great heart that is unchanging Indonesia beat steadily across the millennia. It beat through my blood too. After all, I was equally a creation of many times and places yet bound by none. My father was a famous archaeologist lost in the jungle or – I forget – was it an explorer? – who determinedly pushed beyond the boundaries of the known. I slid a worn, gold case from my pocket and selected a clove cigarette, lit it and puffed until my racing heartbeat steadied and slowed. When they come to make a movie of my life, Borobodur will be an essential backdrop. Perhaps there will be a big scene where I stride across its summit with Bung Karno and we look out over the world with pointing fingers to map out the course of the free Indonesia that we have jointly sired.

I walked up to one of the Buddha figures, trapped in its latticework cloche of stone – so like the baskets put over Balinese fighting cocks when they are given an outside airing – and stretched through to touch the cold, raised hand like Adam reaching out to God in the Sistine Chapel, transient clay reaching out to permanent stone in a gesture that was purely human and – I suppose – the very opposite of the intended, Buddhist message. I stared out over the arid plain where pale oil lamps glowed in simple huts with woven walls and people lived unchallenged by such neighbouring monumentality. I liked the speculation that Borobudur had once been erected here in the centre of a vast, primordial lake, layer after layer, a giant lotus blossom reaching up from the dark, primeval mud towards heavenly enlightenment. Perhaps one day I would paint it in exactly that way. Probably it wasn't true. But then, as I often have to insist in a literalist world, why stick to an ugly truth when there is always something so much more lovely to say?

French Politics, Society and Culture

General Editor: **Jocelyn Evans**, Professor of Politics, University of Leeds, UK.

France has always fascinated outside observers. Now, the country is undergoing a period of profound transformation. France is faced with a rapidly changing international and European environment and it is having to rethink some of its most basic social, political and economic orthodoxies. As elsewhere, there is pressure to conform. And yet, while France is responding in ways that are no doubt familiar to people in other European countries, it is also managing to maintain elements of its long-standing distinctiveness. Overall, it remains a place that is not exactly *comme les autres*.

This new series examines all aspects of French politics, society and culture. In so doing it focuses on the changing nature of the French system as well as the established patterns of political, social and cultural life. Contributors to the series are encouraged to present new and innovative arguments so that the informed reader can learn and understand more about one of the most beguiling and compelling of all European countries.

Titles include:

Gill Allwood and Khursheed Wadia
GENDER AND POLICY IN FRANCE

David S. Bell and John Gaffney (*editors*)
THE PRESIDENTS OF THE FRENCH FIFTH REPUBLIC

Sylvain Brouard, Andrew M. Appleton and Amy G. Mazur (*editors*)
THE FRENCH FIFTH REPUBLIC AT FIFTY
Beyond Stereotypes

June Burnham
POLITICIANS, BUREAUCRATS AND LEADERSHIP IN ORGANIZATIONS
Lessons from Regional Planning in France

Tony Chafer and Emmanuel Godin (*editors*)
THE END OF THE FRENCH EXCEPTION?
Decline and Revival of the 'French Model'

Jean K. Chalaby
THE DE GAULLE PRESIDENCY AND THE MEDIA
Statism and Public Communications

Pepper D. Culpepper, Bruno Palier and Peter A. Hall (*editors*)
CHANGING FRANCE
The Politics that Markets Make

Gordon D. Cumming
FRENCH NGOs IN THE GLOBAL ERA
France's International Development Role

David Drake
FRENCH INTELLECTUALS AND POLITICS FROM THE DREYFUS AFFAIR TO THE OCCUPATION

David Drake
INTELLECTUALS AND POLITICS IN POST-WAR FRANCE

Jocelyn Evans and Gilles Ivaldi
THE 2012 FRENCH PRESIDENTIAL ELECTIONS
The Inevitable Alternation

John Gaffney
POLITICAL LEADERSHIP IN FRANCE
From Charles de Gaulle to Nicolas Sarkozy

Graeme Hayes
ENVIRONMENTAL PROTEST AND THE STATE IN FRANCE

French Politics, Society and Culture
Series Standing Order ISBN 978–0–333–80440–7 hardcover
Series Standing Order ISBN 978–0–333–80441–4 paperback
(*outside North America only*)

You can receive future titles in this series as they are published by placing a standing order. Please contact your bookseller or, in case of difficulty, write to us at the address below with your name and address, the title of the series and the ISBNs quoted above.

Customer Services Department, Macmillan Distribution Ltd, Houndmills, Basingstoke, Hampshire RG21 6XS, England

---

The 2012 French Presidential Elections

The Inevitable Alternation

Jocelyn Evans
Professor of Politics, University of Leeds, UK

and

Gilles Ivaldi
Researcher in Politics, Université de Nice Sophia-Antipolis, France

First published 2013 by
PALGRAVE MACMILLAN

Palgrave Macmillan in the UK is an imprint of Macmillan Publishers Limited, registered in England, company number 785998, of Houndmills, Basingstoke, Hampshire RG21 6XS.

Palgrave Macmillan in the US is a division of St Martin's Press LLC, 175 Fifth Avenue, New York, NY 10010.

Palgrave Macmillan is the global academic imprint of the above companies and has companies and representatives throughout the world.

Palgrave® and Macmillan® are registered trademarks in the United States, the United Kingdom, Europe and other countries.

ISBN 978–1–137–01163–3

This book is printed on paper suitable for recycling and made from fully managed and sustained forest sources. Logging, pulping and manufacturing processes are expected to conform to the environmental regulations of the country of origin.

A catalogue record for this book is available from the British Library.

A catalog record for this book is available from the Library of Congress.

To Gayle, Cosmo and Georgia
To Gina and Chiara

Contents

Tables, Figures and Maps

Tables

Figures

Maps

Acknowledgements

This book grew from an informal project we began to cover the 2012 presidential race, partly as academics interested in French politics and partly as academics wanting to take part in a more public-facing commentary on the lead-up, campaign and outcomes to the elections. Much of the material in the book started life, and in very different shape, on our election blog, 500signatures.net. We are very grateful to those who liked the blog, and even more to those who Liked it, and fed back on it. From the blog, a number of individuals and organisations asked us to comment further for their own outlets. We are very grateful to Policy Network, *Renewal*, Nottingham University's Ballot and Bullets blog and EUROPP at LSE for the opportunity to expand on our ideas under their banners.

Given our respective interests in the extreme right portion of the election, and in particular forecasting it, we should acknowledge the 57 anonymised political scientists who took part in our experimental survey and answered the question, 'What is your own estimate, today, of Marine Le Pen's score in the first round of the presidential election in April 2012?' With a mean of 17.06 per cent, collective guesstimating outperformed many polls (even if, somewhat worryingly, those that thought about the answer longer than a day did worse than those who didn't...). We do not use this experiment in the text, but it at least gave us some encouragement that our own forecast, which we do use, was realistic – even when some polls suggested it wasn't.

We are grateful to Prof. Kai Arzheimer for the completeness of his replication dataverse, which allowed one of us to remember and thereby replicate their legislative forecast model in Chapter 7. Without it, we may have been none the wiser how multiparty forecasts performed in the France of 2012.

We are also grateful to the support and patience of Liz Holwell, Amber Stone-Galilee and Andrew Baird, all at Palgrave, in the delivery and production of the manuscript, and publication of the book.

Finally, we are grateful to our respective (and in one case erstwhile) institutions, the University of Salford, UK, and Université de Nice Sophia-Antipolis, France, for providing the infrastructure and time to complete the book.

1
Introduction

The victory of François Hollande on 5 May 2012 in the presidential run-off came as little surprise to observers of French elections. Since the first opinion polls published in June of the previous year, Hollande's candidacy appeared guaranteed to remove the incumbent, Nicolas Sarkozy, from the Elysée. Throughout the long pre-campaign period, and the campaign itself, the likelihood of Hollande's victory hardly wavered. Certain events gave Sarkozy a chance to rebuild a reputation at best tarnished, at worst shattered, by a singularly negative *quinquennat*. The euro crisis and the Toulouse shootings presented an opportunity for the President to act as statesman, in a timely reminder of what a French President is elected to do. But, with the exception of one brief overlap in polling scores during the campaign, Hollande's consistent trend throughout the entire campaign was towards electoral success.

Of course, 'obvious' election outcomes are only confirmed as such once they have occurred. Until the declaration of the second-round result, a potentially surprise result through a Sarkozy victory could have come to characterise the 2012 race. To claim a victory foretold, then, requires a level of consistent evidence pointing to an inevitable result. More prosaically, even for an election seemingly settled in advance as the titular 'inevitable alternation', we need to ask precisely which elements of the French political landscape, campaign sequence and voter priorities underpinned Hollande's success. Beyond the details of electoral victory, how can the Socialist candidate's victory be interpreted *grosso modo*? We would suggest three possibilities that existed for characterising 2012 before the election – alternation, stability or protest. By definition, the stability hypothesis can be ruled out – the surprise outcome, featuring a Sarkozy victory, would have been the stable option. Alternation, after the fact, is of course a given. Nevertheless, we examine

1

the extent to which the institutional set-up, party system and campaign led to that outcome.

However, the extent to which protest characterised the presidential and legislative outcomes also needs to be examined carefully. An interpretation of the grounding for Hollande's victory is important to inform our understanding of the performance of other candidates, in particular the third-, fourth- and fifth-placed Marine Le Pen, Jean-Luc Mélenchon and François Bayrou. As we shall see, of these, Le Pen and Mélenchon's performances, garnering over a quarter of the vote, clearly point to a high degree of dissatisfaction with mainstream politics, particularly in the focal point for expressive voting, the first round of the presidential race.

The interplay between alternation and protest also presents the possibility of a more nuanced interpretation of Hollande's victory. To what extent was the election of the Socialist candidate a *de facto* vote of confidence in the capacity of the Left to offer a successful alternative to the Union pour un Mouvement Populaire (UMP) incumbents? And, conversely, to what extent was it a vote of no confidence in the incumbents, to be replaced by the only governing alternative available in a bipolarised system such as France? These are the overarching questions which we endeavour to answer throughout this book.

To coin a phrase, elections of whatever predictability and hue do not take place 'in a vacuum'. It is a constant of most analyses of national French elections to place the most recent ballot at the end of a seemingly smooth and discernible evolutionary trend in party system dynamics beginning in the early years of the Fifth Republic (Brouard et al., 2009). With a few notable exceptions, the literature analysing this evolution has agreed on the shape and direction of change. In 2012, the new challenge for mainstream parties within the system was to maintain the two-bloc dominance re-established in 2007, and to which the new *quinquennat* and electoral calendar are conducive. For radical parties and possible splinter candidates within the UMP, it was to disrupt this bipolar dynamic (characteristic of the party system type) and to return to the more polarised and fragmented model of 2002, with a shift in the balance of forces on the extreme left in favour of Mélenchon's Front de Gauche (FDG) and the electoral revival of the extreme right under Marine Le Pen's leadership.

The conceptual root of these analyses, drawing implicitly upon the party system framework developed by Sartori (1976), always regards the evolution of the party system in four phases. First, the Fifth Republic imposes an institutional structure which requires a strategic reorientation of the multiple sub-national and *notable*-oriented party structures of the Fourth Republic. With two national movements pitched against each other, the Parti Communiste Français (PCF) and the Union pour la Nouvelle République (UNR), both of which under the Fourth Republic had acted as anti-system parties (Bartolini, 1984), competitive space was to be found principally amongst fluxes of PCF voters to the moderate-facing Section Française de l'Internationale Ouvrière (SFIO), and amongst the remaining cadre parties of the Right to de Gaulle's presidential party.

The second phase witnesses the construction of coherent bloc competition on both the Left and Right in the lead-up to the relatively short-lived but influential singularity of the bipolar quadrille, through the construction of two moderate parties of government flanking the centre. To link the construction of the Union pour la Démocratie Française (UDF) on the centre-right and the nationalisation of the Parti Socialiste (PS) on the centre-left may seem to conflate two very different phenomena in French political history, but in party system terms their effect is very similar. The creation of the PS from the SFIO in 1969 prior to the absorption of François Mitterrand's Convention des Institutions Républicaines (CIR) at the Epinay Congress of 1971 looked to coalesce what in reality were a series of regionally controlled factions into a single national-level party which could compete across France on an equal footing with the predominant Gaullist party, as well as with its radical PCF neighbour, and thus enable a leftist party to become truly *présidentiable*. On the Right, there was no issue of an absence of a presidential party, given the presence of the seemingly infinitely renewable and rebrandable UNR. However, since the departure of de Gaulle and the death of his successor Pompidou, continued factionalisation of *notables* key to the Right's hold on the Elysée could not be sustained to the left of the Gaullist party, and particularly in supporting the modernising social liberal agenda of Giscard d'Estaing.

The third phase, beginning in the mid-1980s and lasting until 1997, saw a continuation of alternation between the now balanced Left and Right blocs in governmental terms (if not in the presidential equivalent), but precisely through this alternation of weakened governmental executives, either through the deadlock of cohabitation or through minority governments from legislative weakness, there appeared not only strong anti-establishment forces on the extreme right, but also alternatives to the ailing PCF on the extreme left.

The party system which formed the bedrock to the electoral competition of 2012 is directly linked to and a reaction against the end of that third phase. Granted, there have been developments within the system and the party structures since 1997, but the competitive array of the moderate left, the presence of a fragmented set of extreme left parties and the continued 'pathology' of an anti-system far right party in the form of the Front National (FN) are constant. The one competitive change of importance which, simultaneously with the constitutional reform of the presidency to last five years rather than seven, can legitimately be said to herald the beginning of a fourth phase was the formation, some 20 years after the Socialist example, of a hegemonically oriented party of the Right, in the shape of the UMP. Yet it is only in the results of 2012, and the relative disappearance of the centre-right force that was the vestiges of the UDF, that this phase attains any clarity. From a consolidation of democratic opponents (Phase 1) to the balancing of Left and Right blocs (Phase 2) through electoral instability by institutional artefact (Phase 3), Phase 4 represents the stabilisation of an essentially bipartisan system with competitive tensions in the centre-right and far right.

In both cases, however, these tensions look to be resolved through a further consolidation of the UMP hegemony. As we will explore throughout this book, the Mouvement Démocrate's (MODEM) continuation as a relevant force was enabled by its security in endorsing the UMP's power. As the UMP fell to the Socialists, so the MODEM's edifice crumbled in challenging for influence on the losing bloc. On the right flank of the UMP, the FN's once immutable isolation has declined to the extent that the 'republican front' strategy – Left and Right versus extreme right in any electoral run-off – has been abandoned, and the FN plus influential hard right wings in the UMP, increasingly at the sub-national level, now talk of collaboration if not coalition.

Of course, more nuanced analyses of party system developments are possible, going beyond a simple four-phase approach (Cole, 2003). But across these, the logic of a consolidation to *bipartisme* is incontestable. Moreover, the reason for this development is clear. The presidentialisation of the system to ensure that parties act as presidential support groups, at whatever point of the electoral cycle, aiming for a two-candidate run-off, means that, in the long term, those groups must move towards a bipartisan logic. The simplicity of this premise is confounded by sub-national elections, non-rational decisions by candidates acting outside institutional dynamics and other political 'shocks', which may, in the short term, multiply candidates or even parties. However, in the long term, other things being equal, the domination of two principal parties in conflict over the presidential position must dominate.

Historically, Charles de Gaulle and the UNR fulfilled this premise early in the Fifth Republic's lifetime. The anti-system positioning of the PCF meant that it was unable to provide a balanced opposition to draw votes from other left-wing and centrist parties. Paradoxically, the symmetrisation of competition meant that the logic of the *septennat* and majority government was thwarted by cohabitation – voters felt able to support a government at odds with the presidential position. It is only since the enforced coincidence of the presidential and legislative terms that the role of party as presidential driver has returned.

Overlaying the party system dynamic are of course precisely the confounding factors such as personality effects of minor candidates, regional considerations and political shocks, which render an election to some extent difficult to predict in a deterministic manner.[1] Chapter 2 looks precisely at the knowns and unknowns of this election in terms of the aspects of the election which correspond to the long term in French elections, and those elements which constitute shorter-term confounding factors. To use a horse-racing analogy,[2] knowing the form of the main candidates, and specifically the two likely front runners, where would the smart money lie? As we shall see from polls of intended vote and popularity, as well as a number of exogenous factors known to influence elections – the state of the economy and involvement in military campaigns, for example – François Hollande emerged favourite. But to extend the analogy just briefly, where would the other candidates place? Or, at least, what would one expect from their performance, even if precision is not possible?

At the electoral level, the ruling UMP had been delivered a number of successive blows by French voters during Sarkozy's presidency. The UMP had experienced a first notable setback in the 2008 local elections, handing a number of their municipality strongholds – for example Reims, Metz, Caen or Saint-Etienne – to the Left. Following the municipal elections, the latter controlled 29 out of the 40 largest cities with 100,000 inhabitants or more. Simultaneously, in the cantonals, the Left had captured an additional eight departments, totaling 58 out of 102 general councils. Despite a bright spell in the 2009 European elections in which the presidential party and its allies of the NC had taken the lead with 27.9 per cent of the national vote, the UMP faced another severe defeat in the 2010 regional contest, polling a mere 26 per cent in the first round, as opposed to 32.1 per cent for the PS and their allies – with some of the Socialist contenders winning over 60 per cent of the second-round vote – picking up a net total of 21 out of 22 metropolitan regional councils. The 2011 cantonal elections resulted in the highest losses for the mainstream Right since 1958, with the Left taking an additional four departments from the UMP. In September 2011, due in part to the series of electoral setbacks in local ballots since 2004, the Right lost control of the Senate for the first time in the history of the Fifth Republic.

Given the bipolar dynamic present in the system since 2002, the inevitable conclusion for the elections was an Hollande–Sarkozy second-round run-off and ultimately an Hollande victory. Under the Fifth Republic, only two presidential elections have seen a run-off between candidates other than of the mainstream Left and Right, and each is regarded as an aberration caused by a specific constellation of political factors. In 1969, Georges Pompidou and Alain Poher faced each other, placing Right against Centre-Right. Unable to form any Left unity with the communists, a large proportion of the Socialist Party opted to support the Senate president Poher to garner anti-Gaullist votes unavailable to Gaston Defferre. Poher's defeat in the second round from the marginalised senatorial position ended the 'experiment' with centrism (Pierce, 1998: 25).

In 2002, Jacques Chirac and Jean-Marie Le Pen made the second round – a Right candidate against an extreme right candidate. In this case, a lack of Left unity was again to blame, not in terms of voters supporting a centrist candidate, but rather the self-proclaimed pluralist Left falling prey to its own logic and dividing the vote sufficiently to drop the expected victor, Lionel Jospin, into third place. As we will examine throughout this book, none of these issues applied to the Left entering the race in 2012. If anything, the principal concern in the months leading up to the election was the possibility of an incumbent President being beaten into third place by his extremist rival. Although this rapidly proved to be an unfounded fear when the campaign proper began, even this would have resulted in a Left/Right run-off.

Table 1.1 provides the outcome for the presidential elections of 2012. The surge in popularity for the PS was corroborated by the outcome of the first round of the presidential election, in which Hollande took the lead over Sarkozy with 28.6 per cent of the valid vote cast, besting Mitterrand's performance of 1981 (25.8 per cent), and a significant improvement on Royal's score five years earlier (25.9 per cent). The performance by the Socialist candidate was accompanied by a substantial increase in the total for the Left at 44 per cent of the vote, up from 36.4 per cent in 2007. Voter backlash against the government's austerity policies and Sarkozy's presidency resulted in a significant drop in support for the UMP runner, down to 27.2 per cent of the vote from 32.4 per cent five years earlier – adding the votes for the

Table 1.1 Results of first and second rounds of presidential elections (2012)

	Percentage in first round	Percentage in second round
Registered (n)	46 028 542	46 066 307
Abstention	20.52	19.65
Voters	**79.48**	**80.35**
Spoilt and blank	1.52	4.68
Valid	77.96	75.68

Candidate	Percentage of first-round vote	Percentage of second-round vote
François Hollande	28.63	51.64
Nicolas Sarkozy	27.18	48.36
Marine Le Pen	17.90	
Jean-Luc Mélenchon	11.10	
François Bayrou	9.13	
Eva Joly	2.31	
Nicolas Dupont-Aignan	1.79	
Philippe Poutou	1.15	
Nathalie Arthaud	0.56	
Jacques Cheminade	0.25	

Source: Ministry of the Interior.

Chasse Pêche Nature Traditions (CPNT) candidate Frédéric Nihous, who had competed independently in 2007 before endorsing Sarkozy in 2012. The outgoing UMP president was defeated by his Socialist challenger in the second-round run-off, polling only 48.4 per cent of the vote compared with 51.6 per cent for Hollande.

With 17.9 per cent of the vote and just under 6.5 million votes in the first round of the 2012 presidentials, Marine Le Pen achieved her party's best performance ever, which confirmed the electoral resuscitation of the far right after the FN had navigated shallow electoral waters in 2007. When compared with the historic 2002 benchmark, this score was remarkable insofar as it occurred in a context of higher turnout: expressed as a percentage of registered voters, the 2012 result by Marine Le Pen outperformed the total vote by the two far right candidates – Le Pen and Mégret – ten years earlier (13.9 and 13.2 per cent, respectively).

In the first round of the 2012 presidentials, Joly polled a mere 2.3 per cent of the vote, showing only negligible gains on Voynet's catastrophic result of 2007. Numerically, this was to be in stark contrast with the legislative scores, where there has been continuous improvement in parliamentary representation since 1993, and where the institutionalisation and thereby expected legitimation of the Greens has walked hand in hand with enhanced electoral cooperation with the Socialists.

Bayrou's score in the first round of the presidentials certainly came as great disappointment to the MODEM. The centrist candidate polled 9.1 per cent of the vote, representing a loss of over 3.5 million votes on his 2007 performance. Exit polls were remarkably consistent in showing the magnitude of the swings that had occurred in the electorate of the centre: on average, about six in ten former Bayrou supporters had changed allegiance between the two elections. The MODEM runner had lost a third of his former electoral support to the candidates of the Left – a quarter had gone to Hollande – while another 15 and 8 per cent had travelled rightwards to Sarkozy and Le Pen, respectively. In 2012, Bayrou failed to reassemble his 2007 heterogeneous constituency. Electoral losses were particularly notable amongst the younger tranches of the electorate, which had joined Bayrou's bid in greater numbers five years earlier; simultaneously, the more traditional centre-right electorate consisting of older Catholic voters seemed to have shifted further to the right to support Sarkozy in the first round of the presidentials.

This summary of the presidential elections has presented some of the standard 'take-home' messages commentators provided in their analyses in the immediate aftermath of the election. In this book, what we aim to provide is a more structured analysis of where this result came from, in terms of standard themes we would expect to find in any political science analysis of an election, in particular from an institutional and party system perspective. One guiding premise is that the election result of Hollande's victory was, more than many other elections, largely foreseeable as a result of a series of political and socio-economic factors, and therefore the information we present, and the order in which we present it, is structured largely in terms of the background and lead-up which determined this outcome, followed by more conjunctural and therefore unpredictable events, and finally the aftermath of the presidentials – the legislative elections in June, and first period of Socialist government for a decade.

In that vein, Chapter 2 assesses the knowns and unknowns of the election, and sets out the key areas to be developed in the book as thematic analyses. It considers the context of the 2012 election in terms of the position of unpopularity Nicolas Sarkozy and the UMP government found themselves in, alongside an economy experiencing a significant downturn, and how this framed the election as a vote of no confidence in the President. It then looks at the competitive position of the other major players in the first round of the presidentials, to establish the likely competitive pressure points where the Left challenger needed to gather electoral support, either for the first round or in anticipation of the second, and the Right incumbent conversely needed to establish primacy by himself. It then moves on to look at those elements of the election which were significant because of their unpredictability – turnout, the eventual size of the radical vote and the vote choice of the pivotal *couche populaire* section of the electorate.

Chapters 3 and 4 then provide further detail on how this competitive array came to be, considering party dynamics and the candidate selection processes in turn. Since the previous presidentials of 2007, party performances in sub-national and European elections had laid down a relatively coherent set of markers as to the likely line-up and outcome for the 2012 race in an increasingly bipartisan system, but one still fractured by a mosaic of radical Left parties on one side, a collection of centrist movements in the middle and a still deep rift between moderate and extreme right on the other. How these tensions resolved themselves across the previous *quinquennat* was to shape presidential competition significantly.

With the party actors established, the identification of the 'best' presidential candidate then preoccupied the majority of parties in the immediate pre-campaign period. How parties chose to pick these candidates, and the role played by personality and policy in this process, was important not so much for the identities of the individual candidates themselves, but for the varying levels of associated ideological compromises and intra-party tensions which the selections revealed. With perhaps the exception of Marine Le Pen, the strategies and programmes of the top five candidates emerged as a direct result of their supporting parties' own dynamics, rather than the candidates' own profiles. In short, as we argue in Chapter 4, the identity of the candidates themselves, perhaps most obviously for the eventual winner, was of lesser importance.

Chapter 5 then moves to look at the policies and issues which defined the ideological content of the election campaign. Since 2007, there had unsurprisingly been a shift towards economic and social issues in public opinion, against which candidates and parties were forced to adapt their programmes to portray economic management credibility, within the confines of European fiscal discipline, as well as identifying realistic solutions to the dual problem of unemployment and pensions. Candidates of the mainstream all had incentives to suppress the European issue given its intra-party divisiveness which had caused so many problems in the 2005 ECT referendum. Consequently, much greater emphasis was given to micro-economic issues in the presidential campaign. Moreover, the renewed threat of the FN to the mainstream right led to a return to polarised positions on the cultural dimension, with Sarkozy looking to rerun his 2007 strategy of a hard right stance to pull support away from the far right flank. Five years and one incumbency later, the strategy had little success.

These three chapters set out, then, the standard dynamics of any candidate-centred election – party dynamics, candidate selection and policy positions. Common to all elections, particularly high-profile candidate-centred ones, are also the campaign events which punctuate the race, exogenously – as external events which may or may not independently influence the outcome. Campaign events may act as shocks to the election – changes in voting behaviour may result. Alternatively, the events may simply highlight specific aspects of policy or issue debate, or frame the election more broadly, without altering significantly the general outcome. For 2012, the five events discussed in Chapter 6 stand out in particular as worthy of analysis, precisely because they framed significant issues within the election, rather than because they changed the direction of the vote. Indeed, even those events with an ostensibly 'political earthquake' quality to them, for example Dominique Strauss-Kahn's elimination from the race before it had begun, were remarkable in the way the institutional and party system dynamics apparently suppressed any such shock to the election.

From the unpredictable to the potential for prediction, Chapter 7 reviews the election forecasts made prior to the presidentials, and considers what insights into the race such simplified models provide, as well as the accuracy of their forecasts. The chapter also looks at the use of polling as a rolling estimate of likely election outcome, and the issues associated with this in the French case. It also provides a specific, now *ex post* forecast of the legislative elections, again to look at how this model helps us to understand the 2012 elections in the *longue durée* of French legislative races, particularly in how the new electoral calendar has stripped National Assembly elections of much of their idiosyncratic character now that they act as a presidential follow-on.

Finally, Chapter 8 looks at the key outcomes of this follow-on, considering how party performances led logically from their presidential candidates' own result. Once again, the prior 'unknown' of turnout proved vital in shaping the outcomes, not least in the detrimental effect it had on the FN's chances of capitalising on Marine Le Pen's success at the presidential race. For the two main blocks, the Left found the cooperation amongst most of its constituent parts in the presidential run-off continuing to work to its advantage in the legislative first round, although the radical Left's continued fragmentation hindered that wing's ability to make an impact. On the Right, the inimical neighbours on either side of the UMP ensured that the presidential isolation of Sarkozy equally left his former party alone – and its abandoning the ideal of the *front républicain* in the face of even a reduced FN challenge won it few admirers from any part of the spectrum.

Our aim, then, is to provide a thematic analysis of the background and mechanics to the elections, as part of the evolution of the Fifth Republic, and its institutional resilience in the face of political tensions caused by parties and personalities, as well as by its own internal dynamics. We do not pretend that the analysis which follows covers every last detail of the machinations and motivations of French presidential candidates and their supporters. We provide instead what we believe to be the elements which allow us to understand why the system delivered what it did to govern France in 2012.

2
Knowns and Unknowns: Identifying the Critical Spaces of the 2012 Elections

The parameters of electoral performance are broadly known well in advance of an election. Relative party size (in terms of the vote share); poll ratings close to the election date; safe constituency outcomes; mutual stand-down (*désistement*) pacts in advance of legislative run-offs – all narrow the bounds of variation to the final electoral outcome. Subsequent chapters will explore each of these in detail, but using examples from previous French elections, this chapter studies the extent to which foundations to election outcomes were stable, and what these indicated the bases to the 2012 result would be. In particular, this chapter discusses theoretically the incorporation of increasingly salient macro socio-economic issues relating to the economic and debt crisis. These created a new set of external constraints on the formulation of credible presidential platforms by the major parties, but also affected the way voters assessed the state of the national economy and the extent to which the incumbent President should be held responsible for it.

Three alternative scenarios were presented to voters by political actors during the 2012 campaigns, depending on party position. The PS and its allies referred repeatedly to the historic 1981 victory and first alternation in power by the Left (alternation). On the Right, there were hopes that, albeit profoundly dissatisfied with Sarkozy's presidency, voters would eventually choose what they knew in times of deep economic crisis and growing uncertainty regarding the future of France and Europe (stability). Finally, radical parties on the fringe called for voters to deliver a knockout blow to the mainstream that would shake the whole political system (protest). To a large extent, the lead-up to the 2012 elections gave no indication of being anything out of the ordinary in terms of an electoral race. In the presidential elections, the two main candidates could reasonably claim to represent the majority of the Left and Right blocs respectively. By March 2012, three other candidates – Marine Le Pen, Jean-Luc Mélenchon and François Bayrou – were performing well in the polls, representing the centrist and the more radical sections of the electorate. A range of minor candidates added to the competitive mix, claiming to articulate something other than policies arrayed along the classical axis of competition. Similarly, the legislative elections followed the presidential outcome as night follows day: a resounding victory for the presidential party and its allies; a robust parliamentary majority; and both vote and seat share differentials over the defeated Right camp precisely inflated due to a fall in support for the losing side, the presidential race having once again bestowed the status of *fait accompli* upon the legislative elections.

In the sections which follow, we divide between the 'knowns' of the elections – which aspects of the race were broadly defined during the longer-term lead-in to the campaign – and the areas of competition, where uncertainty around their size and outcome (e.g. turnout or extent of radical vote) maintained a level of potential variability in the final result.

1. The 'knowns' of the 2012 French elections

Some aspects of the 2012 elections were foreseeable and established months, if not years, before the election. Together with the impact of the economic crisis, the growing dissatisfaction with Sarkozy's policies and style of presidency were crucial elements of the elections which would have a decisive impact on the outcome. At the institutional level, the design of the five-year term with the presidential election preceding the legislatives was also likely to shape voter choice and regime preferences, preventing the return of another period of divided government (*cohabitation*) while accentuating presidential electoral swings in the legislatives (Gschwend and Leuffen, 2005; Dolez and Laurent, 2010; Dupoirier and Sauger, 2010). Finally, the electoral rise of the Left across all mid-term elections after 2007 was a preliminary indication of significant shifts in allegiances in the French electorate, which would likely herald a victory for the opposition in 2012.

1.1. Economic crisis, incumbent popularity and the anti-Sarkozy referendum

Following one of the core assumptions of classical economic voting theory, which posits that voters tend to blame the incumbent for bad economic times retrospectively (Lewis-Beck, 1988), a defeat of the ruling right-wing majority could be anticipated as the most likely outcome of the 2012 presidential. The victory of the Left certainly supports the classic 'reward–punishment' model: the faltering of the economy led a majority of voters to support the candidate of the opposition, and to vote Sarkozy out of office. Times of economic hardship together with an exceptionally low popularity in the lead-up to the presidential election fostered the conditions for a grievance referendum against the UMP incumbent.

The 2012 elections took place against a backdrop of financial and economic downturn amidst turmoil in the Eurozone and political uncertainty. Following the outbreak of the 2008 financial crisis, France had entered a period of profound economic instability which had cast doubts on the sustainability of the French social model. In the lead-up to the 2012 presidential election, the country was confronted with a deterioration of its economic situation, accompanied by an abyssal external trade deficit and sluggish near-zero GDP growth. Unemployment peaked at 10.0 per cent of the active population in the first quarter of 2012, reaching its highest level since the late 1990s and drawing close to the symbolic 3 million job seekers (see Figure 2.1). The rise of fixed

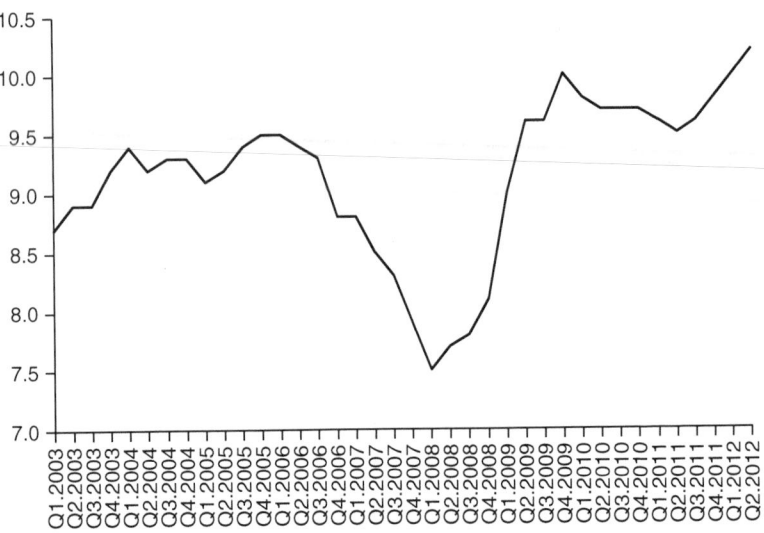

Figure 2.1   INSEE quarterly unemployment rate (2003–2012)
Note: ILO definition, seasonally adjusted, average over quarter.
Source: http://www.insee.fr/fr/themes/info-rapide.asp?id=14.

consumer expenditure – for example, housing, energy and transportation – had led to a stagnation in household purchasing power. Poverty had risen consistently since 2007, with 13.5 per cent of the population below the poverty line.

As we will examine more closely in Chapter 5, economic issues topped the presidential agenda, with polls showing that voters were increasingly concerned with social insecurity, unemployment and the rising cost of living. The year preceding the election was rife with workers' strikes and social conflicts stemming from the multiplication of lay-off plans in the declining industrial sector. The closing of the ArcelorMittal steel plant in Florange was the most emblematic of these, and crystallised the many fears and social anger with Sarkozy's failure to deliver on his 2007 promise of increased purchasing power for all of France's 'hard-working classes'.

Together with the aggravation of the economic crisis and rise in unemployment, the highly unpopular budgetary austerity policies conducted by the Fillon government weighed down Sarkozy's re-election prospects. In August 2011, the French Prime Minister had unveiled a first set of austerity measures amounting to €11 billion in new taxes, cuts in public spending and the closing of tax loopholes, all with a view to trimming the country's deficit down to 4.5 per cent. Following the loss of its triple-A credit rating in January 2012, the government was forced to put forward a second painful debt reduction package – including a rise in VAT – increasing the financial pressure on voters already severely hit by the recession. The UMP government implemented measures that eliminated tax credits and froze most government spending in a further effort to reduce the budget deficit and commit to fiscal discipline.

Sarkozy entered the presidential race in February with the lowest popularity ever achieved by a French President, at 68 per cent of negative ratings (TNS-SOFRES), which revealed the depth of political discontent with both the policies and personal style of the incumbent. Since the very beginning of his presidency, Sarkozy had alienated a large tranche of the electorate by his *bling-bling* presidency, eschewing the modesty – publicly, at least – of previous incumbents and instead apparently using the position to enjoy its trappings to almost monarchical heights. Let us note here that Sarkozy's popularity began to plunge during the first year of his presidential term, at a time when the unemployment rate had fallen below 8 per cent, indicating that Sarkozy was most likely being held accountable for his style of presidency rather than the state of the French economy *per se*.

In 2007, Sarkozy's presidential victory party was notoriously held in Fouquet's, the exclusive restaurant in Paris, with a guest list including a large number of society 'hangers-on' from outside the political world who had supported his campaign. In the summer, he enjoyed holidays first on an acquaintance's yacht, and then in the US resort of Wolfeboro, apparently paid for by the Cromback and Agostinelli families.[1] Similarly, presidential favour seemed to fall clearly on his family: in 2009, Jean Sarkozy, his second-eldest son, was nominated at the age of 23 to head the Établissement public pour l'aménagement de la région de la Défense (EPAD) agency responsible for running La Défense business district, although the backlash resulted in his relinquishing the nomination. His attitude to opponents, particularly of the vocal grass-roots variety, betrayed a contempt for mass opinion. Most notoriously, at the Salon de l'Agriculture in 2008, a member of the crowd refusing to shake his hand met with the response 'Eh bien casse-toi alors, pauv'con' – whatever the perceived snub, hardly a presidential riposte.

Most damagingly, Sarkozy was perceived as a President who saw nothing wrong in compromising the independence of the statesman to ensure his own support and re-election, as well as shoring up the fortunes of his presidential majority party. Indeed, two names continued to pursue the ex-President well after the election, in relation to funding his campaigns for the presidency: Bettencourt and Gaddafi. Both are alleged to have provided illegal campaign funds for Sarkozy in 2007. Similarly, even in the second presidential debate, his opponent could legitimately raise the issue of his presence at Hotel Bristol for a UMP fund-raiser,[2] tarnishing the image of a presidency which, since de Gaulle, was meant to be 'above' party politics, at least the grubbier elements of finance and patronage.

When compared with his predecessors, Sarkozy's exceptionally low average approval rating two months prior to his re-election bid was at the very low end of the spectrum, with no less than 68 per cent of negative opinions. In 1981, Giscard had received 51 per cent, Mitterrand 34 per cent in 1988 – in part due to cohabitation with the Right – and Chirac had a 51 per cent negative reading a few weeks ahead of the 2002 presidential earthquake. Support for Sarkozy had been at its highest in the first few months of the presidential term in the second half of 2007, a short-lived honeymoon period during which he received an average 65 per cent of positive ratings, besting all his predecessors (see Figures 2.2 and 2.3). His popularity plunged by no less than 30 percentage points during 2008 before stabilising at an average 35 per cent in the course of 2009 due to his high-profile management of the financial

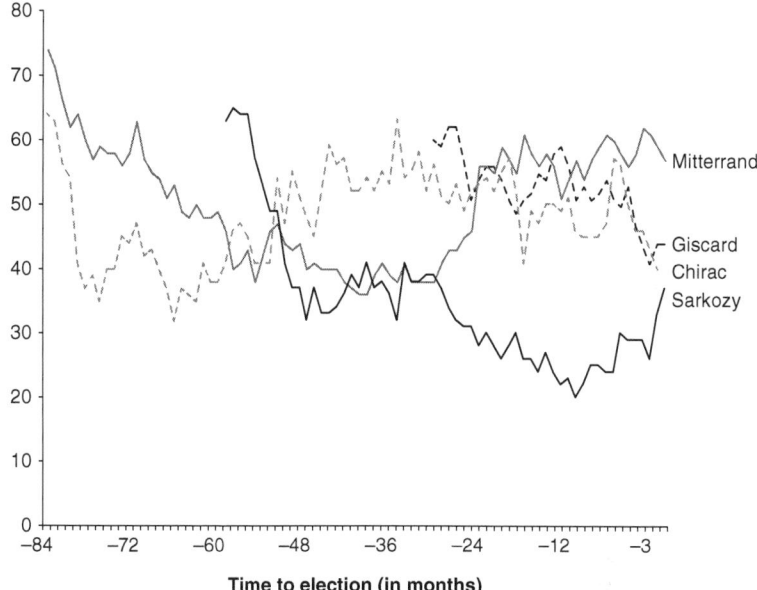

Figure 2.2 Comparative pre-election presidential popularities (1981–2012)
Note: TNS-SOFRES monthly presidential popularity data; % of respondents who say they 'trust the President to solve the problems of the country' (1981–2012); seven-year presidential term in 1981, 1988 and 2002; Giscard 1981: series beginning in October 1978.
Source: http://www.tns-sofres.com/popularites/cote2/

crisis and Eurozone tumult. The last 30 months of Sarkozy's presidency saw a steady decline in popular support from late 2009 to early 2012, with his ratings sliding further down into the lowest range in the final year. Sarkozy's lowest point of 20 per cent of approval was reached in May 2011 in the aftermath of the very unpopular pension reform and the unfolding of the Woerth–Bettencourt scandal.

As we have seen in the previous chapter, the Left in opposition had made significant gains across all second-order elections from 2008 onwards. That consistency of performance was reflected both in terms of the convening effect of the Socialist candidate, and in poll ratings heading in the diametrically opposite direction to Sarkozy and the Right's. Within the Left bloc, Hollande appeared capable of unifying the entirety of the electorate, with the partial exception of some radical Left supporters of Arthaud's LO, examined in Chapter 3. That positive support existed at party level in favour of the Socialists was evident in popularity data (see Figure 2.4). In 2012, the pre-election measures for the PS

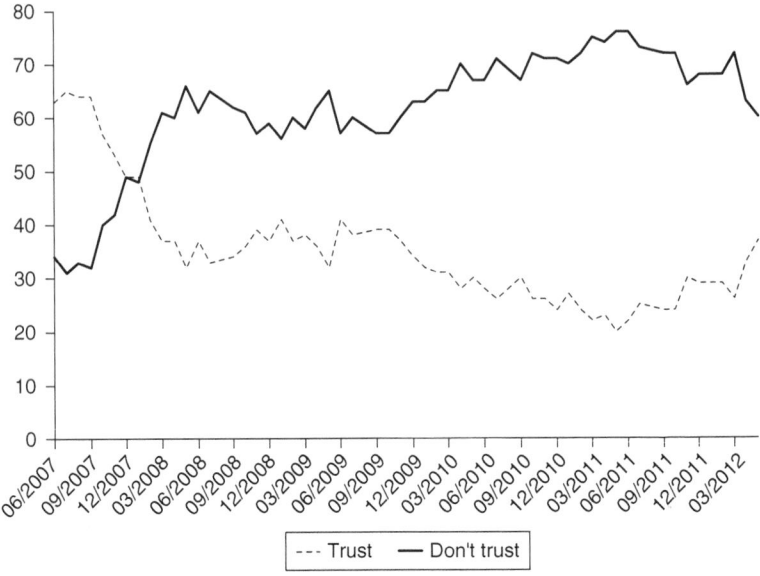

Figure 2.3   Sarkozy's presidential popularity (2007–2012)
Note: TNS-SOFRES monthly presidential popularity data; % of respondents who say they 'trust/don't trust the President to solve the problems of the country' (2007–2012).
Source: http://www.tns-sofres.com/popularites/cote2/choixdate.php?perso=sarkozy.

displayed a clear improvement in favourable ratings over the 12 months preceding the election, an upward trend partly attributable to the success of the open primaries, looked at in Chapter 4, and resembling that of the victorious presidential bid of the Socialists under Mitterrand in 1981. In contrast, views of the PS in the lead-up to the 2007 election had almost remained unchanged going into the presidential. Five years earlier, in 2002, positive ratings for the Socialists had even sloped *downwards* in the final 12 months before the election.

Thus, whilst the consistent performance of Hollande in the campaign undoubtedly accounts for some element of the eventual presidential success, his party's performance prior to his nomination as candidate – and, as we will examine in Chapter 6, when it was perhaps the nomination of another Socialist grandee, Dominique Strauss-Kahn, which many anticipated being of presidential relevance – would already have set *any* Socialist candidate on the way to a strong electoral return.

Of course, the popularity ratings of neither the Left nor Right candidates or their parties operate independently of each other. The sheer level of discontent against the UMP incumbent meant that the Left

45 per cent of those who had voted for Hollande 'wanted him to be President', as opposed to 55 per cent who said they mostly wanted to 'stop Sarkozy' (IPSOS–*Le Monde*, May 2012).

As we will explore in Chapter 8, the legislative outcome becomes plebiscitary in following the presidentials, to the extent that the French electorate would be issuing a vote of no confidence in their executive leader a month after having given a majority mandate (Elgie, 2003, 2006). In 2012, the presidentials themselves were a vote of no confidence in their executive after five years, as much as they were a vote of confidence in the alternative.

1.2. A strong performance by Marine Le Pen

Marine Le Pen's assumption of the FN presidency in January 2011 was widely regarded as an inevitable succession which promised both to reinvigorate a radical party which had to date peaked electorally in 2002, as well as providing a less divisive face to lead a party regarded as a pariah not just by the Left bloc but also by many on the moderate right. These two expectations were not independent. Jean-Marie Le Pen's success *en trompe l'oeil* in facing off against Jacques Chirac ten years previously simultaneously revealed an electoral ceiling through which an FN with him at the helm seemed powerless to break. The stability in the first- and second-round votes (less than 1 per cent difference), and indeed in absolute vote numbers between 1995 and 2002 (Shields, 2006: 124), identified the extent of far-right electoral appeal at this time. The significant fall-off in the legislatives which followed constituted a contingency of Le Pen's inability to push his first-round success further, while revealing the party's patent lack of economic and governing credibility. France's evident embarrassment at the FN's continued presence in the *ballottage* mobilised a vigorous anti-Le Pen campaign to return the otherwise unfavoured Chirac with a record majority of 82.2 per cent.

Marine Le Pen, therefore, was identified by many as a successor who, whilst inevitably open to accusations of nepotism, could go beyond the elderly white male appeal of much of the FN's politburo, to appeal to other demographics previously of limited presence in the FN's electorate – women and younger voters in particular. Her role within the party was to promote its *dédiabolisation* – essentially, to render it acceptable to a broader segment of the population to vote for the FN, and thereby to lower the *cordon sanitaire* erected by the moderate right. To some extent, this barrier had already been raised ideologically, if not electorally, by the move to the Right of the UMP in 2007 in a bid to capture the FN's electorate, as well as increasingly vocal local and regional politicians looking to shore up support against a renewed Left by cooperating with the far right. However, no national-level agreement had been put forward, nor looked likely to be in the near future.

That successor role proved in the long lead-up to the election to be well founded. In the 2010 regional and 2011 cantonal elections, the party won 11.4 and 15.1 per cent of the vote, respectively; 2011 in particular was seen as the result of rejuvenation of the party by Marine Le Pen. The cantonal elections took place in a propitious context marked by fears of new waves of immigration arising from the Arab Spring, combined with growing anxieties about the economic downturn and the Eurozone crisis. Admittedly, the high percentage was based upon a record high abstention rate (55.7 per cent), therefore questioning the usefulness of the cantonal ballot as a proxy for the next presidential election. Nevertheless, in the same period, Le Pen's own voting intentions had peaked at 24 per cent, with popularity scores regularly in excess of 30 per cent and substantially above her father's ratings at comparable points in time in the past (Evans and Ivaldi, 2012a: 48).

The expectation entering the campaign for 2012 was of a strong performance for Marine Le Pen, at least equivalent to her father's score in 2002 (16.9 per cent), if not that of the combined Le Pen–Mégret vote at 19.2 per cent. In the context of an unpopular incumbent and a placid Socialist challenger, the prospect of perhaps record abstention at a presidential race raised the possibility of an even higher percentage share. Higher turnout would be expected *not* to favour the extreme right candidate.[3] One other obstacle remained to a powerful performance, namely the 500 signatures needed to stand. As usual, the expectation was that the FN candidate would struggle – at least, appear to do so – to secure the requisite names, due to the conspiracy (in the FN's opinion) of mainstream parties to convince sympathetic local officials not to give her their backing, as well as dissident right-wingers such as Carl Lang announcing a poaching of almost 400 signatures himself. The inevitable court challenges to make the *parrainages* anonymous failed, and perhaps just as inevitably she did receive the 500 signatures, with a couple of days to spare. The lead-in to the first round was thus predictable in its drama and in the threat which the Le Pen family candidate posed to the mainstream Right, the political establishment and, for many commentators, to liberal democracy.

1.3. The presidential marginalisation of the Greens

The Green party (Les Verts) has become an established actor on the mainstream Left since its inclusion in the *gauche plurielle* government of 1997–2002. Since the friction between Waechter progressives and Voynet pragmatists in the late 1980s and early 1990s (Villalba, 2008: 45), a decision to focus on electoral success by acting as an environmental foil to the Socialists has led to a series of more or less successful electoral pacts designed to ensure Green representation in the National Assembly, as well as appropriate government participation.

Following their electoral returns in the 2009 European and 2010 regional elections, the French Greens could justifiably enter the presidential race with high expectations of a strong performance. In 2009, the new Europe Écologie coalition led by Daniel Cohn-Bendit had polled 16.3 per cent of the vote in the European ballot, the best electoral performance ever by the Green movement, trailing the Socialists by just 0.2 percentage points. Going into the 2010 regionals, the EE coalition had incorporated Antoine Waechter's Mouvement écologiste indépendant (MEI) and had run autonomously in all the regional constituencies, winning 12.2 per cent of the vote. Moreover, since these elections, the Fukushima disaster in March 2011 had further raised the saliency of environmental issues, and principally the continuation of nuclear power in France. From a party competitive perspective as well, the landscape appeared auspicious. The Greens' coalition agreement with Europe Écologie, to unite in the EELV party, allowed them to run a single primary to identify a *candidate unique*. Moreover, unlike Voynet's candidacy in 2007, and Noël Mamère's five years before that, the EELV candidate, Eva Joly, was not confronted by a regressive ruralist opponent in the shape of CPNT candidates Saint-Josse or Nihous.

However, two sets of factors suggested that Joly might not necessarily build upon this propitious electoral context. First, the aggravation of unemployment evidently limited the saliency of environmental issues in a debate already strongly oriented around materialist concerns around the economy. Post-materialist, growth-averse policies would not easily resonate with the electorate. Moreover, the mainstream parties, particularly the Socialists, had long since integrated an environmental strand to their programmes. In 2007, Nicolas Hulot – unexpectedly defeated in the EELV primaries – had pushed a non-partisan environmentalist platform to the forefront of the presidential agenda. His 'ecology pact' had been endorsed by nearly all presidential contenders and had since diffused into mainstream policy-making – for example, Sarkozy's 'Grenelle de l'environnement' or Hollande loudly proclaiming the rollback of nuclear power through the closure of France's oldest nuclear plant in Fessenheim. In that respect, the 'Fukushima effect' gave the Greens no additional leverage in the campaign.

More importantly, the 2012 presidential campaign epitomized the growing cartelisation paradox facing the Greens since their strategic incorporation into the Left pole of French politics in the mid-1990s. Perhaps a Green party of old, in its role as post-materialist protest movement, could have pushed a presidential candidate into upping the environmental ante for the Socialist candidate. However, Mamère's performance in 2002 illustrated the potential of a coalition which actively supported minority Left-associated candidates (see Table 2.1). Since the *gauche plurielle* and the decision to collude with the Socialists at the legislative stage, both to ensure seats in the National Assembly and ministerial weight in the government, the capacity of EELV to make a nuisance of itself to win more presidential support was limited. By 2007, Voynet was hampered by a left-wing electorate that wished to *voter utile* and ensure Ségolène Royal's safe passage to the second round. Then, 2012 was similar from the elite perspective. By mid-November 2011, party leaders had accepted substantial policy trade-offs in order to negotiate a beneficial legislative agreement with the PS, a tactical U-turn which put an abrupt end to the strategy of autonomy pursued by the coalition in 2009 and 2010.

Eva Joly therefore faced the unenviable task of campaigning as an independent candidate whilst bound by the terms of the strategic compromise reached by EELV and their Socialist partners. The

Table 2.1 Green/EELV voting trends in national elections (1974–2012)

Year	Election*	% valid	Note
1974	P	1.4	René Dumont
1978	L	2.2	
1981	P	3.9	Brice Lalonde
1981	L	1.1	
1986	L	1.2	
1988	P	3.8	Antoine Waechter
1988	L	0.3	
1993	L	7.8	Alliance of Verts (4.0) & Génération Écologie (3.7)
1995	P	3.3	Dominique Voynet
1997	L	4.1	PS–Green pact in 29 constituencies, 7 deputies
2002	P	5.3	Noël Mamère
2002	L	4.4	PS–Green pact in 57 constituencies, 3 deputies
2007	P	1.6	Dominique Voynet
2007	L	3.2	4 deputies
2012	P	2.3	Eva Joly (EELV)
2012	L	5.5	PS–EELV agreement in 63 constituencies, 18 deputies

Note: *P = Presidential; L = Legislative.
Source: Ministry of Interior, National Assembly.

conciliatory tone of the EELV *porte-parole*, Cécile Duflot, over the agreement on nuclear power clearly flagged an unwillingness to fight the Socialists on policy in the campaign, and, above all, a marked loss in credibility on the one 'defining' issue of the environmental movement in France. As Table 2.1 confirms, the progressive implantation of a party with coalition potential had not been accompanied by similar presidential improvement.

1.4. Fragmentation of the centre

Since its role as the presidential party of Valéry Giscard d'Estaing in the 1970s, and the *quadrille bipolaire*, the centre-right party in the French party system has seen erosion and decline define its contemporary position until 2012. In 2007, François Bayrou had given an unexpected third-place performance, with 18.6 per cent of the vote (see Table 2.2). Facing the hard Right campaign of Nicolas Sarkozy appealing to the authoritarian-conservative and xenophobic wing of the French electorate, Bayrou's offer had focused on socially supportive, even liberal policies, accompanied by budgetary discipline and an

Table 2.2   UDF/MODEM voting trends in national elections (1974–2012)

Year	Election*	% valid	Note
1974	P	32.6	Valéry Giscard d'Estaing
1978	L	21.5	
1981	P	28.3	Valéry Giscard d'Estaing
1981	L	19.2	
1986	L	Unitary lists with the RPR	Proportional representation
1988	P	16.5	Raymond Barre
1988	L	18.5	
1993	L	18.6	
1995	P	–	UDF support to Gaullist candidate É. Balladur (18.6%)
1997	L	14.7	
2002	P	6.8	François Bayrou
2002	L	4.8	
2007	P	18.6	François Bayrou
2007	L	7.6	UDF–Mouvement Démocrate
2012	P	9.1	François Bayrou (MODEM)
2012	L	1.8	Centre pour la France

Note: *P = Presidential; L = Legislative.
Source: Ministry of Interior, National Assembly.

economic realpolitik underpinned by an emphasis on small state laissez-faire combined with a welfare safety net. In trying to assert his party's distinctiveness and status as a 'new' political force, Bayrou had also strategically adopted a more confrontational style embedded in a 'soft' anti-system position calling for a 'constructive protest vote' against what was deemed the old established order dominated by the PS and the UMP.

In the first round of the 2007 presidentials, Bayrou had undoubtedly benefited from a protest dynamic to his vote, particularly in towns and wealthier suburbs (Bréchon, 2008: 189), where his performance had also built upon the contrasted personal valence of the Socialist runner Ségolène Royal to attract a more leftist electorate (Sauger, 2007). Whilst a classic candidate of the centre-right in 2002, in terms of the social profile of his supporters, by 2007 the older religious female with higher education had been joined by a younger male tranche of the electorate (Lewis-Beck et al., 2012: 30–31), allowing him to almost triple his score between the two elections.

Past the 2007 presidential success, however, the newly founded MODEM suffered the organisational and political costs of emancipating itself from the mainstream Right after Bayrou had refused to endorse Sarkozy against Royal in the presidential run-off. The vast majority of the members of the former UDF parliamentary party defected to the UMP before the legislatives, and joined with Hervé Morin in forming the Nouveau Centre (NC), a new satellite centrist organisation of the UMP. This internal schism accentuated Bayrou's isolation within the party system, progressively forcing the MODEM into the role of a Scandinavian type of pivotal party at the centre of the political spectrum, which would balance towards either the Left or the Right as political circumstances dictated. At the organisational level, the history of the centre-right has seen an atrophied cadre-party model rely upon a small group of *notables* to form strategic alliances amongst themselves and with the more mass-party Gaullists. In a modern political system offering social media, issue campaigning amongst heterogeneous electoral pools and declining party membership for traditional movements, a cadre party ought to represent a viable model once more. Yet, the MODEM's experience indicates how this can equally lead to marginalisation and electoral irrelevance.

Historically, the organisational weakening of the UDF had been accompanied by a steady electoral marginalisation since the end of the 1980s, notwithstanding the 'magical parenthesis' of 2007. The set of intermediary elections which took place during the five years of Sarkozy's presidential term confirmed the continuing decline of the

MODEM on its way to becoming an irrelevant political force in the shadow of the monolithic UMP. In the 2007 legislatives, the share of the UDF–Mouvement Démocrate vote had already gone down to 7.6 per cent, allowing Bayrou's party to secure only five parliamentary seats, as opposed to 19 for the dissident NC in the bosom of the UMP. In the 2008 municipals, the MODEM won less than 4 per cent of the vote across cities with more than 3,500 inhabitants and Bayrou was defeated in Pau, where he was symbolically denied the mayorship by an implacable three-way contest against both the PS and the UMP. This setback was immediately followed by the loss of two senators in September 2008, which altered the balance of power to the detriment of Bayrou's supporters within the centrist group in the Senate. In the 2009 European elections, the party received only 8.5 per cent of the vote, down from 12 per cent five years earlier. The steady decrease in electoral support for the centre was even more marked in the 2010 regional and 2011 cantonal elections. In the former, the MODEM won 4.2 per cent of the national vote and could only progress to the second round in the Aquitaine region. Bayrou's party was further marginalised in the 2011 cantonals where the MODEM ran in 238 cantons totalling a mere 1.2 per cent nationally, up to 10.1 per cent on average in the cantons where the party was present.

This succession of electoral setbacks cast major doubts on the viability of yet another independent centrist strategy in 2012. Going into the 2012 first round, then, the likelihood of a repeat third place seemed very unlikely. First, Bayrou's presence still remained very much that of a 'one-man band', with no discernible construction of a strong militant base to support the candidate. Furthermore, rather than entering the competition as an aspiring bronze medallist from 2007, Bayrou looked to be a man isolated by the withdrawal of other centrists. In the months preceding the 2012 presidential election, he had failed to unite the whole of the centre-right, at a time when the centrists of the UMP were still progressively distancing themselves from Sarkozy's rightist strategies. In particular, the MODEM proved incapable of pre-empting the newly created Alliance républicaine, écologique et sociale (ARES), which had brought together Jean-Louis Borloo's PR, the NC and other minor dissident centrist groups from the UMP (see Chapter 3).

Second, not only had the novelty effect of 2007 faded, but the choice of issues which Bayrou prioritised in his campaign also gave little hope for distinctiveness or policy renewal. His promise to continue spending in 2013 and 2014 at the level of 2012 would be an attractive alternative to the UMP austerity package, had it not already been adopted by a

Socialist candidate with stronger Keynesian credentials. Commitments to higher-rate tax rises and VAT increases could not appeal to right-wing voters concerned by this in a left-wing programme. The emphasis on institutional revolution, with relatively esoteric commitments to restricting government size and adding a dose of proportionality to the legislative electoral system, would simply not chime with an electorate focused on economic issues. Finally, the polarised nature of competition had drawn support away from both flanks of his electorate, leaving only the core of educated social liberals which had characterised the MODEM electorate. Two polar candidates 'blackmailed' to a greater or lesser extent by their extreme flanks meant the overwhelming likelihood of centrifugal dynamics away from the centre for voter transfers. By mid-April, as expected, the vote intentions clearly put Bayrou back in fifth position with just over 10 per cent of the vote.

2. Spaces of electoral uncertainty

The key areas of uncertainty lie principally in the eventual distribution of votes across the candidates in the first round of the presidential election. By the second round of the election, the competitive dynamics of the race are principally determined by the agreements of the losing candidates on whom their voters should support. In some cases, the prompt from a candidate is not followed deterministically – for example, Bayrou's revelation that he would vote Hollande – but in general, the winner of the second round is the candidate who has his/her bloc most completely secure. In the first round, who turns out, the type of party they vote for and then the profile of electorate for each candidate is the key to the overall placings, and the possible variation in this, however predictable the other elements, constitutes one direct influence on the variability of outcome. For the purposes of this book, then, it is important to identify early on (a) how this variation related to the concrete reality of *les présidentielles en France 2012* and (b) what an analysis of the eventual voter dynamics tells us of how the race panned out. Whilst an entire body of literature on French elections, let alone elections worldwide, has focused on the individual vote motivations of individuals (Lewis-Beck et al., 2012), taking voter arrays by candidate as an *outcome* of the electoral black box – parties and candidates mobilising voters – rather than an explanatory mechanism, we can dispense with this element relatively quickly, before moving in subsequent chapters to the key events of the pre-campaign and campaign period which in part resulted in these patterns of individual behaviour.

Uncertainty about the final shape of the competitive arena stemmed mostly from the state of French public opinion amidst times of economic hardship, with polls showing unprecedented levels of social and economic pessimism. With respect to the latter, trends in public perceptions of economic prosperity, as revealed in Gallup's end-of-the-year barometers, showed a marked increase in pessimism, with a record high negative net score contracting to −79 in December 2011, making France the most pessimistic of all 51 countries included in the survey worldwide (see Figure 2.5). According also to the yearly barometer polls by the Department of Health, highly negative perceptions of the French society as 'unfair' were stable at a high average of 72 per cent of the population since the early 2000s, reaching 75 per cent in November 2011. The same surveys showed that feelings of growing socio-economic inequalities had become pervasive for nearly nine out of ten (89 per cent) respondents in 2011.[4]

The months leading to the 2012 campaign apparently favoured the mainstream parties over radical alternatives. In a period of economic

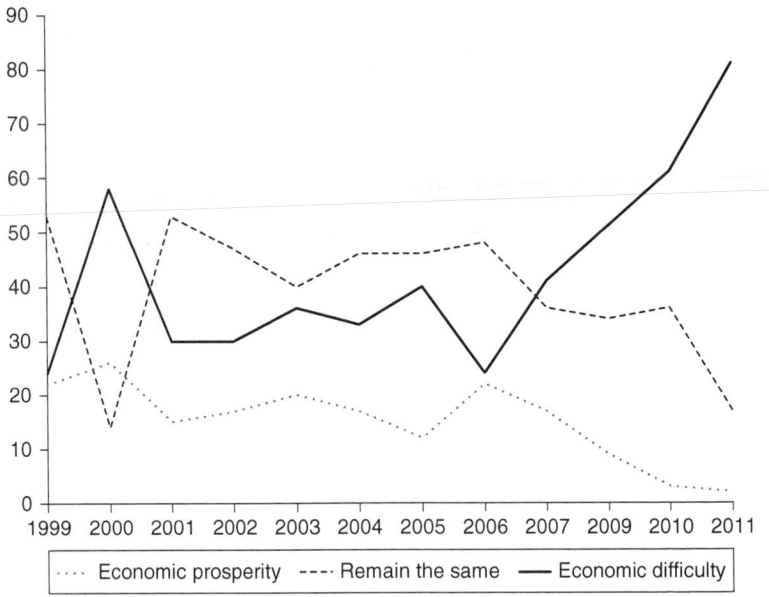

Figure 2.5 Trends in public perceptions of economic prosperity in France (1999–2011)

Source: GIA Annual Global End of the Year Barometer on Hope and Despair conducted by affiliates of WIN–Gallup International Association (www.gallup.com.pk).

crisis, strong credible economic policies, with well-devised plans for recovery, would be a *sine qua non* of successful presidential campaigning. Economic credibility and candidate valence do not favour small party endorsement of even populist measures: public debt crisis is of a scale to require governing credibility and a need for realistic debt reduction policies of the type the UMP and PS could offer. By the end of 2011, however, the relative easing of the Eurozone crisis significantly lessened the likelihood for the materialisation of the 'stability vote' scenario scripted by the UMP's spin doctors. With the French public now turning their attention to domestic issues of unemployment and purchasing power, Sarkozy lost in part the ability to play upon his position as incumbent head of state to demonstrate his international presence and credibility as a statesman. As fears of a major financial meltdown dissipated, so the stability scenario fell away.

There were questions, however, over whether voters' anger would translate into a mechanical re-balancing towards the mainstream Left or, on the other hand, could result in another replication of the more fragmented, centrifugal and volatile protest elections of the past, in particular 2002. Voter turnout was a first crucial factor that was likely to shape presidential competition and the balance of forces between established actors and their peripheral challengers. Other important issues included the magnitude of possible electoral swings among the *couches populaires*, whose electoral support had been paramount to Sarkozy's successful presidential bid in 2007. Finally, there was speculation about the size of radical support for both Mélenchon and Le Pen, in what began to crystallise as the 'battle of the extremes' in the lower tier of presidential competition.

2.1. Turnout

Looking at the series of second-order elections that had taken place since 2007, the possibility that voter turnout in 2012 would match the high level of political enthusiasm manifested five years earlier was anything but a given. The wave of political mobilisation that had materialised in the 2007 presidential contest, where abstention had gone down to 16.2 per cent from a record high 28.4 per cent in the 2002 ballot, had proved ephemeral: in the first round of the legislatives which immediately followed Sarkozy's election, the proportion of non-voters rose back to 39.6 per cent, a drop of 4 percentage points on the preceding election of 2002 and more than twice the levels of the late 1970s.[5] Sarkozy's presidency was disquieted by a marked trend of decreasing voter turnout, beginning with the 2008 municipal election where abstention rose to a dramatic 33.5 per cent in the first round, the highest since 1947. Abstention peaked in all subsequent elections, reaching 58.7 per cent in the 2009 European ballot, 53.6 per cent in the 2010 regionals and 55.7 per cent in the cantonals of March 2011.

Together with the electoral recovery of fringe actors – most notably the FN and the extreme left through the newly formed FG – public opinion polls pointed to the continuing wariness of national politicians by French voters (Perrineau, 2011). Declining turnout rates in mid-term elections reflected growing popular estrangement from the ruling UMP and, to some extent, the absence of a perceived credible alternative on the Left of the political spectrum. These cast doubts about the final shape of political competition in the 2012 presidential election, potentially reviving fears of yet another systemic shock. Disaffection with party politics and negative attitudes towards political elites were widespread in the French public throughout Sarkozy's presidential term. As revealed for instance in the CEVIPOF barometer

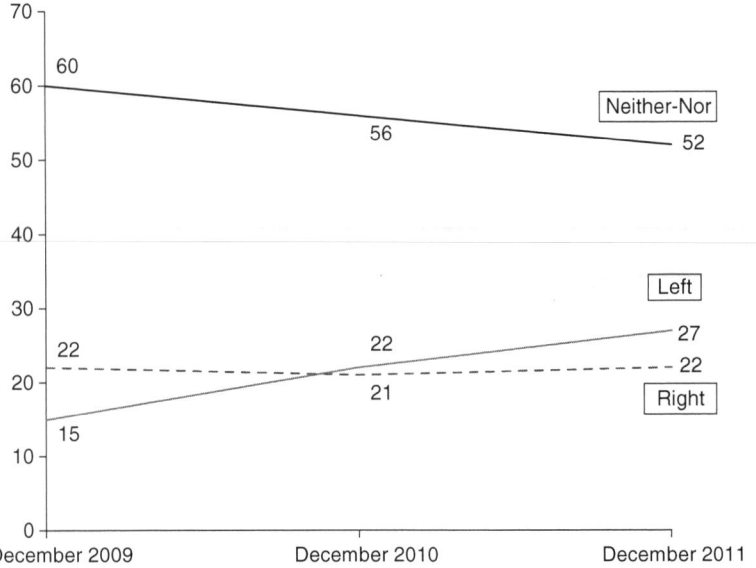

Figure 2.6   Public opinion trust of the Left and the Right (2009–2011)
Note: CEVIPOF *Baromètre de la confiance politique 2009–2011* (end-of-the-year surveys conducted in December); % respondents who said that 'they trust neither the Left nor the Right to govern the country'.
Source: http://www.cevipof.com/fr/le-barometre-de-la-confiance-politique-du-cevipof/presentation/

end-of-the-year surveys conducted between 2009 and 2011, an overall majority of voters continued to express their distrust of both the Left and the Right's ability to govern the country, leaving therefore more space potentially available to radical fringe parties or abstention (see Figure 2.6). Compared with 2007, voters turned out at a lower rate in the first round of the 2012 presidential, with a 79.5 per cent participation down from the 83.8 per cent who had taken to the polls five years earlier (see Figure 2.7). Despite some alarming pre-election polls anticipating a major rise in abstention, turnout in 2012 was similar to that observed in presidential elections during the 1980s and 1990s, in which 80 per cent of French voters on average would cast a vote.

By contrast with the steady downward trend in voter turnout in all other elections, this confirmed that the presidential ballot remained one essential mainstay of the institutional architecture and electoral politics of the Fifth Republic. Albeit limited in size, the decrease in turnout showed that both the Left and the Right had failed somehow to create a political momentum similar to that of 2007, in particular amongst lower socio-economic status voters traditionally less inclined to cast a ballot. By deserting their former presidential champion, the latter had already caused the UMP severe losses across all intermediary elections

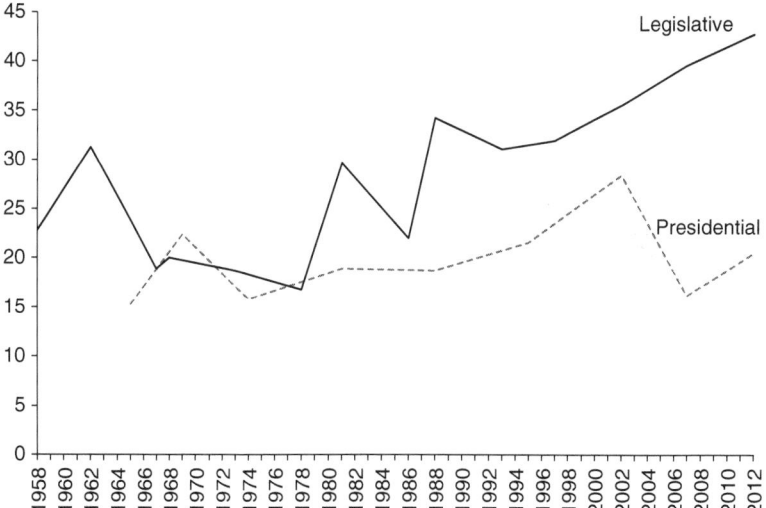

Figure 2.7 Abstention in presidential and legislative elections in France (1958–2012)
Source: Ministry of Interior, National Assembly.

after 2007. As we discuss below, significant sections of this electorate defected to radical parties, or stayed at home, instead of supporting the mainstream candidate of the Left in April 2012. In the run-off, participation flatlined at 80.4 per cent, showing no significant rise in voter turnout between the two rounds. Another important nuance is visible in non-valid voting. That voters were also increasingly dissatisfied with the strict bipolar framing of party competition in the decisive round was revealed in the substantial increase in blank and spoiled ballots from 1.9 per cent in the first round up to 5.8 per cent in the second. This was particularly true of Le Pen's first-round voters, who seem to have followed the lead of their candidate in casting a blank vote in the Hollande–Sarkozy duel.[6]

2.2. Size of the radical vote and the return of party system complexity

The second aspect of uncertainty was the magnitude of a possible wave of discontent that would foster electoral support for radical fringe parties, and could potentially lead to a significant reshaping of the more stable party system that had materialised in 2007. Such an outcome would be reminiscent of the 2002 presidentials, where voter disgruntlement had translated into party system fragmentation, voter disengagement and the rise of peripheral anti-establishment actors. In 2007, focus was principally on François Bayrou, with Jean-Marie Le Pen slumping in the polls compared with his performance five years earlier. In 2012, Marine Le Pen returned the extreme right to a position seen to be potentially challenging Sarkozy, although for a period in February and March, Jean-Luc Mélenchon appeared to be challenging her for third place from polling figures.

In reality, the chances of either Le Pen or Mélenchon overtaking either the UMP or the Socialist candidate to take second place were vanishingly small within what increasingly looked like a 'two-tier' structure of party competition – the upper tier opposing the principal mainstream candidates for the Left and Right, the second battle involving the two leading radical candidates, Le Pen and Mélenchon. Yet there were important issues regarding the size of the radical vote *in toto*. On both sides of the political spectrum, the magnitude of this vote would increase blackmail power for peripheral anti-system actors. A surge in presidential support would allow Mélenchon to exert greater polarising pressure on the more timid economic agenda of the Socialists. It would also determine to what extent the PS would be able to generate the political momentum needed first to return it to presidential office, but more importantly to uphold political legitimacy and conserve future public support for the inevitably unpopular austerity reforms which would result from the its pledge to reduce France's national debt and budget deficit. Similarly, a strong performance by Le Pen would certainly force Sarkozy to shift his campaign further to the Right, while ultimately weighing on the President's chances of winning re-election.

Decline in extreme left performance in French elections has been steady since the early days of the Fifth Republic. Equally, since the apparent death knell of communism in 1990, the constituent parts of the French extreme left, if not the PCF itself, have been able to rein-vent themselves to offer a social egalitarian alternative and foil to the mainstream Socialists. In 2012, however, mobilisation on the radical Left came not from one of the established revolutionary candidates or parties, but rather from the previously Socialist interloper, Jean-Luc Mélenchon. The overtly populist appeal enshrined in his *Place au peuple* campaign slogan, and a focus on relentless opposition to Marine Le Pen's campaign (see below) finished by drowning out the traditional standard bearers of the extreme left – Philippe Poutou (NPA) and Nathalie Arthaud (LO) – and mobilising a score close to that achieved by the entire extreme left in 2002, an election often characterised as a 'mainstream minority' outcome.

At party system level, the size of the radical vote would provide an indication of the polarisation and possibly a revived complexity of the French presidential arena and waning of the post–21 April 2002 legacy of *voter utile*. The 2002 election had shown the culmination of 'proportionalist' behaviours, whose development has been regarded as a by-product of the strong incentives for electoral mobility provided to voters by the array of second-order elections held under proportional rules, and how the latter have progressively contaminated the classic two-ballot majoritarian system in the first order of France's electoral politics (Parodi, 1997). By contrast, the 2007 election had exhibited a substantial decrease in party fragmentation and the diminishing strength of those 'proportionalist' trends observed in earlier presidential contests since the late 1980s (Cautrès and Muxel, 2009).

In 2012, widespread uncertainty provoked by the deteriorating economic conditions benefited protest parties on both sides of the political axis, revealing the breadth and depth of political discontent directed at Sarkozy's presidency. The rise of anti-system actors on both extremes of the spectrum, concomitant with the decline in centrist vote, changed the contours of the party system and resulted in a centrifugal shift in the distribution of votes, resembling the more polarised pattern of competition that had occurred in the 2002 presidential election.

Taking the proportionate strength of the parties located at the extremes of the system as a relatively crude indicator of party system polarisation – an approach used for instance by Pelizzo and Babones (2007) – the 2012 presidentials displayed a significant centrifugal re-balancing with the total share of the radical vote rising to about a third (31 per cent) of the votes cast (see Figure 2.8). This pointed to the persistence of the underlying fragmented and *contestataire* pattern of party support which has developed since the late 1980s (Cole, 2003). In 2007, the dominant parties of the moderate left (PS), the centre (UDF) and the mainstream Right (UMP) had secured over 75 per cent of the first-round vote whilst fringe parties on the extremes of the political spectrum had lost a substantial proportion of their previous presidential support, down to 20.6 from 37.2 per cent in 2002.

2.3. The *couches populaires* vote

Having taken into account the actual electoral pool provided by turnout, and the aggregate vote destinations by type of party (mainstream/protest), the final symptom of the electoral profile is the voter array by candidate. Voter dissatisfaction and the spectre of a strong protest vote in 2012 were a central feature of the anticipated vote among

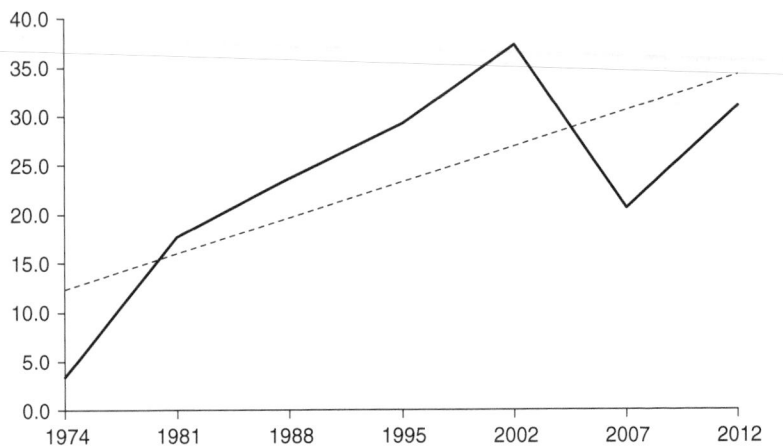

Figure 2.8 Polarisation as the total size of the radical vote in presidential elections (1974–2012)
Source: Ministry of Interior, in % of the valid vote cast; authors' calculations.

the lower social strata and France's crisis-ridden electorate. In a period of economic crisis, the downturn in employment and financial stability is a greater threat to social groups with modest incomes and reliant upon state support, particular when this selfsame support is identified by the government as requiring substantial cuts to ensure a reduction in national deficits. In the context of a UMP government evoking, in the lead-up to the election, austerity – tax rises, pension reform, below-inflation benefit increases – as a solution to the Eurozone crisis, a considerable degree of electoral instability would be expected amongst these *couches populaires* in their support for a candidate and government likely to improve their lot – and by what means. For Sarkozy, Hollande, Le Pen and Mélenchon, these voters would therefore be a focus of their campaigns, to convince a numerically large tranche either to stay with or to move to them.

Sarkozy's reputation as a President of the rich and his government's open acceptance of the need for economic downsizing hardly placed him in a strong position to appeal to lower socio-economic status voters. Moreover, the campaign promises of 2007 which had led to significant support amongst *employés* and *ouvriers* moving to his first candidacy (Strudel, 2007; Perrineau, 2009), thereby substantially increasing his cross-class appeal, had for the most part not materialised – unlike five years previously, voters were not voting for an unknown quantity (at least, at the executive level). Campaign pledges that only austerity could solve France's crisis would not be expected to be sufficiently convincing to attract by themselves lower-income voters in any numbers. Sarkozy's first election manifesto in the form of his interview to the *Figaro Magazine* in February 2012[7] clearly showed that he would once again play the 'hard Right society' card, focusing instead on broader social issues, including law and order and immigration, to attempt to appeal to the same voters from 2007 who had moved inwards from Le Pen to support the UMP candidate.

Inevitably, the FN's own strategy would be to dissuade voters from repeating their 'mistake' of 2007, and supporting the *tribune populaire* that the far right party sees itself as constituting. The presentation of a more complete economic policy by Marine Le Pen aimed to establish the FN's credibility as a future party of government, but in reality the credibility battle between her party and the UMP would be based on negative credibility – disenchantment with non-delivery of promises by the ruling coalition, leading to protest voting, rather than positive credibility for the FN. In particular, the disconnect felt by voters in the *zones périurbaines* – at the periphery of major towns – from the urban centres dominated by the Left and the rural areas owned by the main-stream Right would likely lead, as in 2002 and 2007 (Ravenel et al., 2003; Bussi and Fourquet, 2007), to a geographically peripheral profile to the extreme right vote amongst the *couches populaires* (Fourquet, 2012: 62).

Looking at Sarkozy's polling figures amongst routine non-manual and blue-collar workers in the lead-up to the 2012 campaign, as reported by Mergier and Fourquet (2011:10) from pooling successive waves of IFOP cross-sectional pre-election polls, it is clear that these groups had already deserted the President and that a significant proportion of former Sarkozy supporters in those lower social strata (*CSP–*) were prepared to travel rightwards to the FN (28 per cent) or simply abstain (26 per cent) in the first round of the 2012 presidentials.

Granted, the conservative UMP would not be the natural party for many of these voters, who would be predisposed more to the Left or indeed increasingly the FN. However, the comparison with the 2007 breakdown for self-reported presidential votes across the various occupational strata is instructive (see Table 2.3). There was much greater equity amongst the proportions of different occupational strata for Sarkozy in 2007, due in particular to his ability to pull a larger share of the

Table 2.3   First-round presidential vote by occupational strata in 2012

% 2012	Mélenchon	Hollande	Bayrou	Sarkozy	Le Pen
All	11 *(+9)*	29 *(+3)*	9 *(−10)*	27 *(−4)*	18 *(+7)*
Craftsmen, shopkeepers	9 *(+9)*	18 *(0)*	10 *(−12)*	40 *(−1)*	17 *(+4)*
Professionals, higher salariat	9 *(+8)*	34 *(+6)*	12 *(−13)*	29 *(−4)*	9 *(+5)*
Middle salariat	14 *(+12)*	34 *(+5)*	9 *(−11)*	21 *(−9)*	15 *(+8)*
Routine non-manual	13 *(+11)*	28 *(+3)*	8 *(−11)*	20 *(−7)*	24 *(+11)*
Workers	14 *(+12)*	24 *(+1)*	8 *(−9)*	17 *(−6)*	32 *(+12)*
Retired	10 *(+8)*	29 *(+4)*	9 *(−6)*	34 *(−5)*	14 *(+5)*
Other inactive	11 *(+9)*	27 *(+3)*	8 *(−8)*	29 *(0)*	19 *(+9)*

Note: Polling averages, rounded figures. Change on 2007 between brackets (Mélenchon/Buffet, Hollande/Royal, Marine Le Pen/Jean-Marie Le Pen). **2007 presidential election** (*N* = 5 surveys), first round (22 April 2007): CSA-*Le Parisien*, exit poll (*N* = 5,009); IFOP-CEVIPOF–Panel Electoral Français (V2), post-election poll (*N* = 2,208); IPSOS–*Le Point*, exit poll (*N* = 3,397); LH2–*Libération*, exit poll (*N* = 1,537); TNS-SOFRES–*Le Figaro*, exit poll (*N* = 1,500). **2012 presidential election** (*N* = 5 **surveys**), first round (22 April 2012): Viavoice–*Libération*, exit poll (*N* = 1,511); OpinionWay–*Le Figaro*, exit poll (*N* = 10,418); TNS-SOFRES–*TriElec*, exit poll (*N* = 1,515); IFOP–*Paris Match*, exit poll (*N* = 3,509); IPSOS–*Le Monde*, pre-election poll (*N* = 3,152).

working class and routine non-manual vote in the direction of the mainstream Right. In 2012, his electorate realigned to that of a classic conservative party – stronger amongst the self-employed, professionals and upper *salariat*, weaker in the middle *salariat*, routine non-manual and blue-collar workers. Particularly in a period of economic malaise, other things being equal, the middle classes prefer right-wing policies to those of a redistributive Socialist, or even Social Democrat. Conversely, the *couches populaires*, especially blue collar, start to move elsewhere – not necessarily to the Left however.

Between 2007 and 2012, Sarkozy's most substantial losses were found amongst those occupational groups as well as in the lower middle class, with shares of the vote dropping by 6–9 percentage points on average across polls. In contrast, the UMP candidate secured his hold on the economically inactive population, particularly retirees, in social groups (women, religious, elderly, higher economic assets) which traditionally support the conservative Right in France (Evans and Mayer, 2005). Retirees voted 34 per cent for Sarkozy in the first round of the 2012 presidentials, down from an average of 39 per cent five years earlier. In the run-off, polls estimates show that Sarkozy achieved an overwhelming 56 per cent majority of the vote among pensioners, down 4 percentage points according to comparable surveys conducted in the second round of the 2007 presidentials. The persistence of differential electoral support for the UMP amongst retirees is of course corroborated by the distribution of the right-wing vote across age bands, with the over-65 group being solidly over-represented in the UMP electorate.

Both the Socialist and Front de Gauche appeal during the campaign looked to offer an alternative to austerity and hard-line illiberal social policies promoted by the Right. The Left's offer was an ideological shift away from the spending cuts of the UMP towards a sustainable growth-driven rescue plan. The credibility of the offer here was predicated not on 'we can manage this economy better' but rather 'there is a different economy to manage' – a return to a positional approach over assumed valence. Summed up in Hollande's campaign slogan, *Le changement, c'est maintenant*, the notion of a change in direction to French society and economy was designed to appeal in concrete terms to those sections of society for whom the status quo appeared to offer nothing but material atrophy, at best, and a significant decline in living standards at worst.

The data in Table 2.3 show, however, that Hollande achieved his best performances and made substantial gains amongst upper and middle *salariat* voters, winning the support of an estimated 34 per cent of the vote in both categories, particularly those employed in the public sector.

He appeared less able on the other hand to extend Socialist support amongst routine non-manual voters and, above all, blue-collar workers, a deficit which was only partly compensated for by Mélenchon's forming a successful coalition on the PS's Left flank. Mélenchon's promotion of feel-good, but essentially unsustainable, interventionist policies certainly served to mobilise anti-austerity support amongst sections of the electorate unconvinced by Hollande's more moderate but similarly growth-inspired policies. In 2012, the *couches populaires* leaned in even greater proportion towards the new radical redistributive agenda of the FN. Marine Le Pen expanded her party's support among manual low-skilled workers as well as non-manual routine employees in the lower *salariat*, whilst being still less popular among the upper social strata with higher education and economic assets. The intensification of the FN's working-class appeal, together with a relative drop in petty-bourgeois support, amplified the well-established trend towards 'proletarisation' in the political support for the far right (Perrineau, 1995; Mayer, 2002). In 2012, Marine Le Pen achieved her best scores in the lower occupational groups, with an estimated 32 per cent of the blue-collar vote, outperforming both the Socialist and neo-communist candidates. Additionally, the FN candidate won about a quarter of the routine non-manual vote, which reflected the growing appeal of the far right to what has been recently conceptualised as the 'unskilled proletariat' in the routine service sector (Oesch, 2006).

Whilste the *couches populaires* had been keen to express their preference for more radical policies in the first round, their fierce anti-*Sarkozysme* helped them travel towards the candidate of the mainstream Left in the run-off, albeit not giving Hollande's social-reformist bid wholehearted support. Polling figures[8] for the demographic breakdown of the Socialist vote in the second round show that blue-collar workers voted 57 to 43 per cent for Hollande in 2012, up from 53 per cent for Royal five years earlier. Comparable figures for the lower *salariat* exhibited a 54 to 46 per cent split of the *employés* vote in favour of the Socialist finalist. Simultaneously Hollande made substantial gains amongst middle-class voters, with an estimated 59 per cent of the vote in the presidential run-off. In the end, the competitive array determined by the elites, rather than the masses, marshalled the respective electorates to their final destinations.

∗   ∗   ∗

Establishing the principal areas of competition in the elections provides a backdrop to our subsequent analyses of the various elements of the electoral race, from the pre-campaign to the post-presidential legislatives. Of course, the reason that the competitive array of the presidential race is clear in advance is due to the years leading up to this key election. The presidential election does not take place in a vacuum. Political parties campaign and compete in sub-national elections, which gradually define the coalitions and cooperation, as well as the divisions, which structures the number and political location of the likely *présidentiables*, even before these organisations get around to running their candidate selection processes (if they have one). Once parties have established broadly who is talking to whom, and whom they will back, the presentation of specific programmatic and issue positions of the eventual candidates serves to cue voters to assess political supply, either through the proxy of party support or by direct evaluation of these issues. We use this (albeit simplified) chain to structure the next three chapters of the book, considering in turn party cooperation and competition, candidate selection and policy issues, again to identify the main influences of these pre-election stages on the eventual outcome.

3
Party Cooperation and Conflict: Actors' Competitive Positioning

In the wake of the excessive party system fragmentation and associated plethora of presidential candidates from the mid-1990s to 2002, a reversion towards bipolarisation had been clearly visible in 2007. In 2012 the fragmentation of the presidential supply was at levels similar to 2007 (Table 3.1). The ideological and competitive dynamics of this fragmentation were the source of some debate with some complexity in the relationship between the moderate and extreme right vote's relationship in the *longue durée* (Grunberg and Schweisguth, 1997, 2003; Andersen and Evans, 2002, 2005). By the 2007 election, however, it was evident that France's politics was reverting once more not just to the *quadrille bipolaire* of the 1970s, but a two-pole system oriented around the PS and the UMP (Grunberg and Haegel, 2007, 2008).

Following the 2002 'earthquake' presidentials, a significant reconfiguration of the party system occurred as mainstream parties on either side of the spectrum progressed towards greater intra-bloc cohesion both strategically and organisationally. Systemically, the *quinquennat* and fixing of the electoral calendar had worked in achieving one of their objectives. On the Right, the principal rationale for the formation of the UMP in 2002 was to provide a single mainstream Right party behind which voters could rally to provide a majority for Jacques Chirac and eventual successors, even if politicians and commentators alike were sceptical of its ability to form a cohesive party (Knapp, 2003; Cordell, 2005: 197). By 2007, the political hegemony of the UMP over the French Right, and most evidently its potential 'strike force' in the legislatives, provided Sarkozy with the resources to deter dissident presidential candidacies from within his own political family, and to cluster in due course most of the former UDF troops in the legislatives. On

Table 3.1 Effective number of first-round presidential candidates (1995–2012)

	1995	2002	2007	2012
Effective number of candidates*	5.97	8.75	4.70	4.77

Note: * The effective number of candidates or parties (Laakso and Taagepera, 1979) is formally defined as the inverse of the sum of squared individual candidate/party proportions of the vote.

the Left, the realisation of the political cost of party fragmentation and the disruptive nuisance of splinter candidates from the former 'plural Left' cartel on 21 April 2002 underlined the need for cooperation during the preparatory stage of the 2007 elections, resulting in formal electoral agreements between the Socialists and both their PRG and MDC allies, the latter throwing their support behind Royal's presidential bid.

The clear centripetal and bipolarising tendencies that were demonstrated in the 2007 elections significantly damaged the fringe parties. The decline of the PC had only been partly offset by reasonable sums of votes across a multiplicity of radical Left candidates. Similarly, the FN successes of 1995 and 2002 had been replaced by almost single-digit failure by Jean-Marie Le Pen. Even the Green *gauche plurielle* partners of 1997–2002, who had proved remarkably disruptive in power, now linked to the PS as self-confessed junior partners. Overall, the electoral outcome of both the presidentials and the legislatives saw the collapse of the communist party, the Trotskyite organisations and, most dramatically, the FN. With the UMP domination and partial absorption of the UDF, there appeared to be no significant competition on their immediate flanks. The FN in particular met with severe electoral losses in the June legislative ballot, which paved the way for the modernisation and change in party leadership that would take place in 2011. On the extreme left, one crucial issue was the fractionalisation of the anti-capitalist and anti-globalisation vote, with no fewer than five candidates running individually in the 2007 presidentials. Finally, in spite of his relatively good showing as the 'third man' in the presidential race, Bayrou failed to prevent the implosion of the UDF and the subsequent political marginalisation of the MODEM in the 2007 legislatives.

Beginning with the post-2007 reshuffle in the party system, the first section of this chapter looks at the changes that have taken place in the structure of competition and how parties and candidates have navigated the successive periods leading to the 2012 elections. We consider the ideological positions and intersections of the political parties, both as presidential support groups and as independent electoral competitors, in terms of inter-party cooperation, especially on the post-*gauche plurielle* Left, as well as the potential for inter-party competition as mapped by the social and attitudinal distribution of the electorate. The second section looks more specifically at relationships between parties and blocks across the two rounds of the presidential, and how cooperative strategies may have enhanced the dynamics of mobilisation by the mainstream Left in the second round, while constraining voters' opportunity for expressive voting. In particular, we consider the continuation of the relatively closed structure of competition that had emerged in 2007, the absence of presidential rivalry dividing potentially 'compatible' parties of the mainstream and the repositioning of political actors on the periphery of the party system.

1. The post-2007 party system

The centripetal and bipolarising dynamics in the 2007 elections resulted in the consolidation of UMP–PS dominance and a change in the structure of competition in the form of a model of 'imperfect bipartism' (Grunberg and Haegel, 2007). Because of their marginalisation, the other political forces in the party system had to reconsider their strategic positioning and potential for inter-party cooperation within an increasingly closed structure of competition dominated by the two larger mainstream parties. Looking at the reconfiguration of the party system in the post-2007 period, it is clear that a number of parties – mostly on the Left of the political spectrum – made significant efforts to form more competitive electoral coalitions that would enable them to dislodge, to some extent at least, the existing UMP–PS duopoly and alter the balance of power within each political camp.

The succession of local and second-order elections that took place between 2008 and 2011 certainly provided parties with cues on how to forge such alliances, with concrete KPIs of their electoral appeal to voters. To a large extent, those elections telegraphed the outcome of the 2012 elections and laid the foundations for the model of asymmetric intra-bloc cooperation that would dominate both the presidential and the legislative ballots. Prefiguring the union of all left-wing forces against Sarkozy in 2012, parties of the Left displayed a good deal of republican discipline throughout the period, akin to *la concentration républicaine* in Goguel's formulation of the Third Republic (1946). But there was growing evidence that the UMP on the other hand would suffer from the opposition of both the MODEM and the FN on its Left and Right flanks, respectively.

1.1. Challenges to the UMP–PS duopoly

In the post-2007 period, the two dominant parties of the mainstream confronted a number of internal and external challenges as they strove to maintain their political supremacy over their respective camps. In terms of party cooperation, and to begin here with the PS, the party faced strategic issues regarding its somewhat paradoxical hegemony, with the imperative to build new alliances to its right while upholding the more traditional system of cooperation with the other actors of the Left. Immediately after the 2007 defeat, Hollande had for instance clearly indicated that the Socialists would seek to lead a broad coalition ranging from the PCF to the MODEM, which acknowledged both the diminishing strength of all non-Socialist partners, and conversely Bayrou's personal success in that presidential race.

The reconfiguration of the Socialist collaborative strategies was manifest in the 2008 local elections, where the Socialists' dominant position allowed them to impose variable geometry alliances, building predominantly upon a classic 'union of the Left' with their natural allies (PCF, PRG, Greens) nationally, while simultaneously entering *ad hoc* electoral pacts with the MODEM or even the far left (LO) at the local level. The PS encouraged common lists with Laguiller's organisation in 65 cities.[1] Concurrently, the Socialists ran together with the MODEM and other parties of the Left in a number of municipalities (such as Dijon, Montpellier, Grenoble and Roubaix), which demonstrated a dose of political pragmatism in achieving electoral competitiveness.

The 2009 European elections, which saw the PS significantly damaged electorally while the other parties of the Left gained political momentum through the shaping of new coalitions (see below), altered the overall balance of power amongst opposition parties, a change in the *rapport de forces* which progressed into the 2010 regional election campaign. Intra-bloc fragmentation materialised on that occasion, preventing the Socialists from aggregating their allies in the first round, particularly because of the success of EELV and the shift to the Left by the PCF as part of the newly created FG. The second round, on the other hand, displayed a high degree of partisan discipline with all minor political forces of the Left lending their support to the PS in all but one region (Bretagne, where the EELV list did not step down in the second round).

In the case of the UMP, the early stages of Sarkozy's presidency were remarkable for the 'opening' of the presidential majority to personalities originating on the Left such as Bernard Kouchner, Éric Besson, former Socialist Minister for Commerce Jean-Marie Bockel, Socialist councillor and feminist activist Fadela Amara and Martin Hirsch, former head of Emmaüs France. Evidently, the dual purpose of this tactic was first to deflect the accusation of having moved too far to the Right during the 2007 campaign in appropriating FN-branded issues, and second to embarrass the Socialist opposition by accommodating a number of their peers. To some extent, this *ouverture* mirrored Sarkozy's tactic of triangulating his political message, a communication strategy which he had used in the past to distance himself from his public image of right-wing hardliner (e.g. his advocating voting rights for foreigners) or that of a zealous advocate of neoliberal Reaganomics.

Looking at the internal array of the UMP, the first three years of the *quinquennat* also displayed a notable re-balancing towards the centre of the party after the clear shift to the Right in the campaign. This was demonstrated by the representation of the liberals, Christian democrats and radicals of the UMP in the first two Fillon governments (including some potential *présidentiables*) such as Jean-Louis Borloo, Hervé Morin, Christine Boutin and Jean-Pierre Jouyet (Fillon I), followed by Valérie Létard, Rama Yade, Nathalie Kosciusko-Morizet, André Santini, Alain Joyandet and Chantal Jouanno in Fillon II. With Villepin under threat from the Clearstream political scandal, Sarkozy was able to maintain a reasonably high level of party unity at a time when the UMP and the government would begin to encounter political obstacles, while experiencing a significant drop in popularity and their first major electoral losses in the 2008 local elections. The organisational cohesion and electoral resources of the majority party were well in evidence in the 2009 European elections when the UMP met with little competition from either side – with the exception of DLR and the MPF – and took the lead, polling 27.9 per cent of the national vote, well ahead of the Socialist opposition. In the 2010 regionals, the UMP ran unitary lists with the NC, La gauche moderne, MPF, CPNT and Alliance Centriste across most regions.

Significant strategic shifts occurred in 2010 in the aftermath of the UMP's electoral debacle in the regional elections, and were exposed in the now (in)famous 'Grenoble speech', which marked a return to the general discourse of immigration and crime that had dominated the 2007 presidential campaign. The presidential revival of the authoritarian and anti-immigration repertoire stemmed from the necessity of addressing the electoral rebirth of the FN and rise of Marine Le Pen in the regionals, and as such antagonised the moderates within the party, most notably Prime Minister Fillon himself. Internally, Sarkozy's endorsement of what came to be referred to as the 'Buisson' strategy – in reference to the role played by Patrick Buisson as political advisor on the shift rightwards in 2007 – resulted in a significant alteration of the balance of power between the various party factions, seeing a rise in influence of the hardliners of the Droite Populaire alongside centrist marginalisation, as revealed by the third reshuffling of Fillon's government in November 2010. In particular, the clanging departure of key representatives of the moderate wing, such as Borloo and Morin, would echo well into the 2012 presidential campaign, with Borloo and other centrist leaders eventually withdrawing in the interests of Right unity.

The UMP veering to the Right and the domination exerted by the former RPR over the moderates had important organisational consequences, as the centrists began to distance themselves from the presidential party, a move which foretold the secession by the UDI which would occur after the 2012 elections. Borloo's PR ceased official cooperation with the UMP in May 2011, instead joining the newly founded Confederation of the Centres under the umbrella of the Republican, Ecologist and Social Alliance (Alliance républicaine, écologique et sociale, ARES). The new centrist coalition comprised Morin's NC, Bockel's Gauche moderne as well as the small Democratic Convention (Convention démocrate, CD) led by Hervé de Charette, and was intended to lay the ground for an independent centrist candidate in the 2012 presidentials.

In competitive terms, the impact of the electoral revival of the far right became even more noticeable in the 2011 cantonals, where the UMP came to question the effectiveness of the tactics of the republican front before eventually abandoning it. This official adjustment to a 'neither PS, nor FN' strategy by the party proved a divisive issue revealing antagonistic positions among national leaders, most strikingly the public disagreement between Sarkozy and his Prime Minister. Internal conflicts in the cantonals heralded the debates that would later take place in the UMP during the 2012 legislative campaign and the continuation of the 'neither nor' code of conduct in cases where the FN would be in a position to progress to decisive second-round run-offs.

On the Right of the political spectrum, the 2010 and 2011 election provided voters with important cues as to which strategies parties were likely to push forward in the 2012 ballots. Opposition to both the PS and the UMP, on the one hand, and the waning of the republican front on the other were central to the shaping by the FN of inter-party competition into three-bloc contests, giving a clear indication of Marine Le Pen's intention to ride the wave of political discontent with the outgoing President, come the life-size electoral tests of 2012. In the 2010 regionals, the FN was in a position to progress to the second round in 12 regions where the party ran in three-way contests and, more importantly, made significant gains on its first-round scores (+2.5 points on average). The nuisance power of the far right was partially restored in the subsequent cantonals in which Le Pen's party won 15.1 per cent of the first-round vote – up to 19.2 per cent in the 1,440 cantons where the FN was running candidates – and progressed to the run-off across a total of 403 cantons. That voters in the new 'Marine' electoral constituency were also less keen to lean back towards the UMP in the decisive round was revealed in the vote swing on the Right: across all run-off cantons where the mainstream Right faced a two-way contest against the Left, the former fell short by an average 4.5 percentage points of the combined first-round score of the Right and the FN, which barred the UMP from achieving an absolute majority in an estimated third of the cases.[2]

The electoral resuscitation of the FN coincided with the progressive emancipation of the MODEM from the mainstream Right, under way since Bayrou's refusal to endorse Sarkozy against Royal in the 2007 presidential election. An organisational schism in the former UDF had preceded the legislative campaign, leading to the forming and attachment of the NC to the UMP by the vast majority of centre-right MPs. That strategic divergences persisted after the 2007 sequence was revealed in the oscillatory movement by the MODEM in the 2008 local elections, where the party's grass roots distributed themselves across both sides of the political spectrum by negotiating electoral pacts with the PS and the UMP alternately. The MODEM's journey left brought the paradoxical situation of the UMP as a dominant yet relatively isolated force to the Right of the French party system further into focus. Simultaneously, the blurring of its political identity as a force traditionally anchored to the centre-right resulted in severe electoral losses in both the 2010 regional and 2011 cantonal elections, casting doubts on the viability of its own independent centrist strategy in 2012.

1.2. Reconfiguration of the extreme left

The disparate elements of the French extreme left experienced severe electoral setbacks in 2007, which not only contrasted with their exceptionally high level of presidential support five years earlier, but also revealed their inability to fully exploit the political momentum created by their victory as key actors in the 2005 European referendum 'No' campaign. Whilst the *vote utile* and re-balancing of the party system towards the centre, stemming from the spectre of 21 April 2002, undoubtedly accounted to a significant degree for the electoral defeat of the far left in the 2007 ballots, the fragmentation and inflation in the number of parties were equally crucial factors in their electoral misfortune.

In the immediate aftermath of the 2007 elections, both the anti-capitalist and anti-liberal components of the Left underwent substantial organisational transformation, leading to the forming of two new coalitions, namely the NPA and the FG, and a change in their respective strength. The former originated in the LCR and was created in February 2009 as an attempt to unify the multitude of small groups within the anti-capitalist Left. Central to the new party's strategic positioning was maintaining both the revolutionary political identity of the former LCR and a strict demarcation from the PS, while opening itself to civil society political activists. The newly formed NPA proved more ambivalent however about coalescing with the anti-liberal components of the French Left, in particular the FG. The LCR party congress of January 2008 gave an 83 per cent majority to the 'political autonomy' motion, leading to the marginalisation of the sections of the party which had supported a more conciliatory approach to potential partners on their Right flank. As a consequence, the NPA underwent a schism in March 2009 with the departure of its less radical wing embodied by Christian Piquet's Gauche Unitaire, which eventually joined Mélenchon's FG in the lead-up to the European elections. Four months earlier, the unitary project had been rejected by LO's party congress of December 2008 on account of the NPA's aim of aggregating a growing array of political groups beyond the tight nodes of Trotskyism, which would dilute the core identity of revolutionary socialism by incorporating anti-globalisation, trade unions, NGOs and even environmentalist movements.

The persistence of the NPA as a fractionalised minor political force was manifest over the 2009–2012 period. In the 2009 European elections, the party ran individually across all metropolitan regional constituencies, receiving only 4.9 per cent of the national vote, with its isolation being reinforced by the simultaneous decision by LO to run their own lists. Intra-party fragmentation resurfaced in December 2009 after a membership vote on the party's strategy in the forthcoming regional elections had revealed profound divergences in the party's rank and file, with about a third (31.5 per cent) of the membership supporting the minority motion put forward by the proponents of electoral cooperation with the FG. In the 2010 regionals, the NPA competed alone in 15 regions but nevertheless formed pragmatic electoral pacts with the FG or PG in a total of six regions, while LO ran independently in all cases. More importantly, however, the decision by the NPA's national political council to support 'technical fusions' with all other parties of the Left in the second round marked a significant departure from the anti-system positioning of the old LCR, which prefigured the implicit endorsement by the NPA of the Socialist candidate as 'the lesser of two evils' in the 2012 presidential run-off.

The transformation of the Trotskyite movement occurred in the context of a larger reconfiguration of the party sub-system of the Left, which saw the strategic repositioning of the PCF and a change in the balance of power between the anti-capitalist and anti-liberal wings. Following the demise of the *gauche plurielle* in 2002, the communists had distanced themselves from their former Socialist partners. The participation by the PCF in the Jospin government between 1997 and 2002 had significantly undermined the ability of the party to sustain its traditional tribune function in the competitive space – in party system terms, its blackmail potential over the moderate PS, whereby the PCF had traditionally articulated strong redistributive economic policy preferences with political protest. In 2007, the communists had failed to establish their leadership over the anti-liberal camp, and Buffet's independent presidential bid had resulted in yet another harmful electoral debacle. Taking its cue from the cooperative strategies developed during the 2008 campaign against the Lisbon Treaty, the PC entered a formal agreement with Mélenchon's PG ahead of the 2009 European ballot. The PG had been created in February 2009 after Mélenchon and Dolez had left the PS a few months earlier, with the objective of mimicking Die Linke in Germany.

The FG was publicly launched in March 2009 and consisted of the PCF, the PG, the Gauche Unitaire (former NPA members) as well as a myriad of smaller leftist organisations. In the 2009 European elections, the FG received 6.5 per cent of the national vote and won five MEP seats, outperforming the NPA. The successful bid was replicated in the 2010 regional elections, where the FG totalled 5.8 per cent of the vote and 97 seats nationally, but achieved double-digit scores in some of the PC's traditional strongholds such as Auvergne, Limousin and Nord-Pas-de-Calais. In terms of inter-party competition, the FG moved further to the Left in the regionals by establishing links with more radical forces such as the NPA in the vast majority of the regions (17 out of 22), whilst the PC maintained joint lists with the PS in only five constituencies (Bourgogne, Champagne-Ardenne, Lorraine, Basse-Normandie and

Bretagne). In the 2011 cantonals, the coalition was extended to include Chevènement's MRC and received 8.9 per cent of the vote, which represented a significant improvement on the PC's score in 2004 and, more importantly, placed the FG ahead of EELV as the second party of the Left.

1.3. The Greens' dual strategy

Together with the reshuffling of the extreme left, the pre-2012 period saw the emergence of a new ecologist movement originating in the 2009 European election campaign, which prolonged the process of institutionalisation of the Green party. In 2007, Les Verts had experienced a severe electoral setback in the presidential election. In the legislatives that followed, the Greens had failed to come to a formal agreement with the PS and as a consequence had competed independently, winning 3.3 per cent of the vote.

The 2007 elections revealed the precariousness of the Greens' position in the party system and the need to maintain cooperation with the PS to ensure political relevance. That the party had managed to capture four legislative seats was largely due to the benevolence of their former Socialist allies in the field. While showing a new lease of life for the Greens, the 2008 municipal elections fostered political collaboration with the Socialists across some of the country's largest cities, prefacing the pre-campaign tactical agreement of 2012. The new generation of leaders – Duflot, Placé – that took over the party engaged in the process of professionalisation which was deemed necessary to progress towards greater institutionalisation, and to enhance the overall political weight of the party both nationally and locally. Over recent years, the cartelisation of the Green party had intensified, enhancing its political prospects and limiting somewhat the impact of the party's electoral weaknesses in the first-order arena of French politics. This is revealed for example in the significant increase in the number of Green officials elected at both the local and national level (over 2000), the forming of an independent group in the Senate and, as a consequence of this, and most importantly, growing access to public resources and state funds.

After 2007, the Greens also confronted the need to bring together the increasingly fractionalised and ideologically heterogeneous ecologist movement that had seen the development of new political groups and the emergence of highly popular leaders such as José Bové, Nicolas Hulot or Daniel Cohn-Bendit since the late 1990s. The building of the EE coalition in 2009 can therefore be regarded as the organisational response by the Greens to the above imperative of unifying the ecology camp, a response which was approved by 71 per cent of the party congress and embedded in the election of Duflot as national secretary in December 2008.

In the European elections, the newly created EE platform won an impressive 16.3 per cent of the vote and 14 MEPs, coming in neck and neck with a Socialist party in electoral freefall after its Reims congress. The 2009 political momentum enhanced the attractiveness of EE for political leaders and activists both within and outside the ecologist family (e.g. Antoine Waechter's MEI, Stéphane Hessel and Bruno Rebelle, former director of Greenpeace in France), which allowed for the diversification of its political personnel and candidates in the 2010 regionals. In the latter, EE ran independent lists across all constituencies and received 12.2 per cent of vote and about 260 regional seats. The regional success accelerated the organisational merging of EE with the Greens, which took place in November 2010. EELV won 8.8 per cent in the 2011 cantonals, in which the party competed individually against either the Right or the Left across 88 of the second-round run-offs.

All the above developments are an indication of the Greens' dual strategy of combining party professionalisation and governmental credibility, on the one hand, with continuing *ouverture* to civil society, on the other. In 2010, the coalition's *Manifeste pour une politique écologique* officially endorsed the main strategic objective of establishing electoral alliances which would allow the party to assume power at all levels of France's governance. The preparation for the 2012 presidential programme also demonstrated substantial efforts to formulate more realistic economic and budgetary policies, breaking away from the utopian environmentalist agenda of the past. Simultaneously, the organisational flexibility of the new EELV structure was conceived as a means of preserving the party's traditional links with the myriad small activist groups in the ecology constellation as well as in its thriving *alter-mondialiste* neighbourhood.

2. Parties and blocks in the 2012 presidential election

As we have noted, on the supply side of electoral politics, the political landscape of the 2012 presidential election campaign bore a great deal of resemblance to the structure of competition unveiled in the series of successive intermediary elections that had taken place since 2007. A simple glance at the final array of presidential hopefuls shows the elevation of the political threshold for candidacy and the continuous decrease in absolute number of presidential runners on both sides of the spectrum since 2002 (see Figure 3.1). The partisan supply for the 2012

Figure 3.1 Presidential candidates in France (1965–2012)
Note: Other marginal non-partisan candidates excluded from Left and Right subtotals: 1974, $n = 3$; 1995–2012, $n = 1$.

presidentials was also very similar in shape to that of 2007, pointing first and foremost to the persistence of weak competition and strong aggregative tendencies in parties or coalitions of the mainstream, most evidently in the UMP, which maintained its ascendancy over the whole of the parliamentary Right. On the Left, the 2012 presidential contest was characterised by a slightly lesser degree of party fragmentation resulting mostly from the re-composition of the ecologist movement, while the PS continued to secure political support from its immediate flanking partners.

2.1. Continuing fragmentation on the extreme left

Strategic disagreements persisted on the extreme left of the political spectrum in the lead-up to the 2012 presidential election. The core divisive issue was again that of political cooperation with the PS and whether parties should pursue mutually beneficial coalition-building in the presidentials and, more importantly, in the legislatives. Each of the two main actors – that is, the NPA and the FG – were characterised by the unstable balance of forces that existed between their radical wings and 'intersectional' factions which would consider entering electoral pacts with their more centrist counterparts. This was true for instance of the NPA 'unitary' tendency's advocating an alliance with Mélenchon against the majority line of partisan identity, or of the divergent views that were found within the FG between the provocative claim of political independence by the PG, on the one hand, and the more accommodating strategy by the PC inside the FG coalition, on the other.

Electoral cooperation was certainly encouraged in 2012 by the memory of the blatant failure by the radical Left to preclude party fragmentation in the 2007 presidentials. Despite long-standing historical and ideological disputes, the NPA sought without much success an alliance with LO to build a more competitive anti-capitalist pole against the PS, a partnership which could possibly be extended to incorporate the FG after the presidentials. With regards to collaborating with the FG, internal disagreement over party strategies manifested itself in the first NPA party congress in early February 2011, with the majority motion defended by Besancenot winning only 40.8 per cent of the membership vote, against 27.2 per cent for the supporters of an NPA/FG pact. The strategy of presidential autonomy that was eventually pushed forward by the NPA on account of the FG's continuing ambivalence towards the Socialists was strongly resisted by the 'unitary' current (Gauche anticapitaliste) in the party, with a number of national leaders such as Myriam Martin, Pierre-François Grond and Hélène Adam calling explicitly for a Mélenchon vote in the first round of the presidential ballot.

Internal divisions in the NPA mirrored the important strategic dilemma confronted by the FG over issues of future legislative cooperation with the PS, possible governmental participation and, in the longer term, the perpetuation of local agreements in the 2014 municipal elections. These were accentuated by the uneven balance of organisational strength within the FG coalition, which remained largely favourable to the PC. As we will discuss in Chapter 4, the FG's entering the 2012 presidential campaign resulted in a trade-off between its two main partners whereby Mélenchon was selected as presidential candidate in exchange for an allocation of legislative seats more beneficial to the PC. Beginning with the 2011 cantonals, the communists had maintained their advantage in running 1,396 candidates as opposed to only 242 originating in the PG.

The development of the presidential campaign revealed the strategic disagreements that had emerged earlier. In his position as presidential runner, Mélenchon embarked on a clear anti-PS first-round strategy, which contrasted with the more moderate position by the PC. In competitive terms, this shift to the Left was intended to weigh on the PS and preclude a centripetal move by the Socialists towards an alliance with Bayrou and the MODEM. The radicalisation by Mélenchon increased the ideological distance with the PS and took the FG further to the Left on economic and fiscal policies. It also led him to reject both the alleged austerity plan of the Socialists – witness for instance his attacks on a possible 'Hollandreou' government in reference to the austerity package voted by the PASOK government in Greece – and cabinet participation by the FG after the legislatives. Overall, the 'Left of the Left' entered the presidential campaign with a lesser degree of fragmentation, due in fact to the reshaping of the ecologist pole and the inclusion of Bové's leftist anti-globalisation groups in the EELV coalition as early as 2009.

2.2. Aggregation around mainstream candidates

As had already been the case in 2007, strategies of bloc unification persisted in 2012. In the first round of the presidentials, the larger parties of the mainstream were successful in securing electoral coalitions by absorbing their smaller flanking allies, which enhanced their level of competitiveness and diminished in return the likelihood of yet another disruption of the traditional bipolar format of presidential competition similar to the 2002 election. The latter had undoubtedly served as a powerful catalyst for party transformation, resulting in the acceleration and accentuation of existing strategies of polar concatenation by both the PS and the parliamentary Right, which were already well under way in the 2002 legislatives.

2.2.1. *The hegemony of the Socialist lead*

On the Left, Hollande advocated a strategy of maximising his vote in the first round, which in his view would give him crucial political momentum ahead of the run-off against Sarkozy. Consistent with the theory of 'concentric circles' that he had expounded ten years earlier immediately after the 2002 debacle, the Socialist candidate certainly benefited in 2012 from a higher level of intra-party discipline, avoiding disgruntlement by his former primary rivals, and was simultaneously able to exploit the organisational and electoral resources of the PS to negotiate stable electoral deals with the smaller parties of the centre-left. Moreover, because of the crystallisation of negative attitudes towards Sarkozy, a wide range of personalities, trade unions and interest groups manifested their more or less explicit support for the Socialist runner, most unequivocally the CGT, which publicly called for a vote against the outgoing President.

At party level, the fragmentation which had diluted the Left bloc vote in 2002, removing sufficient slivers of votes for Jospin to fall behind Le Pen, was not present. Hollande's presidential bid received support from both Chevènement and the PRG. The former stepped down from the presidential race in early February 2012 and reached an electoral agreement with the PS over about ten reserved legislative constituencies before publicly announcing his support for Hollande in March. After Baylet had endorsed Hollande in the Socialist primary of 2011, the PRG had logically maintained close links with the PS candidate, and finalised a similar deal in January 2012, whereby left-wing radicals were allocated 30 legislative constituencies. In 2012, inter-party cooperation on the Left was extended to include EELV, which contrasted with the failure by the PS to coalesce with the Greens five years earlier. In 2007, substantial divergences regarding some of the Greens' core policies, most significantly nuclear power, and the reluctance by the PS to abandon what was deemed a sufficient number of seats for the ecologists to aspire to forming their own parliamentary group after the legislatives had precluded the signing of a joint platform.

In the lead-up to the 2012 elections, however, the two parties partly overcame their differences and secured a contract for the legislative term. As we will examine further in Chapter 5, whilst revealing policy convergence on a number of cultural and institutional issues (e.g. gay marriage, minimum pension age at 60 or a dose of proportional representation), the joint programme hardly concealed the persistence of more profound disagreements over environmental issues, despite the PS endorsing a progressive albeit very limited phasing out of nuclear energy. Central to the arrangement was the Socialists' willingness to provide their partners with a parliamentary group through the allocation of 'safe-seat' constituencies. That the latter were able to broker such a beneficial deal with their dominant Socialist partners cast doubt in return on the political opportunity for EELV's strategy of presidential autonomy as some leading personalities within the coalition – for example, Mamère or Cochet – questioned the viability of Joly's independent candidacy at a time when she was polling on average a mere 2.5 per cent of the presidential vote.

The various electoral pacts forged by the PS in 2011–2012 revealed the uneven balance of power within the French Left, resulting from uncontested Socialist supremacy and the realisation that most left-wing parties, including those on the fringes of the party system, would eventually convene to defeat Sarkozy and the UMP. This was certainly the case with the implicit yet unconditional support lent to Hollande by PCF leader Pierre Laurent in the lead-up to the first round, Laurent indicating that 'the FG would call to vote for the leading candidate of the Left' in the presidential run-off (*Europe 1*, 3 April 2012). Not only did this provide Hollande with the opportunity to articulate conflicting policy preferences – for example, the traditionally pro-nuclear power stance of the PC or the MRC in opposition to the Greens, or the varying positions of the PS' partners on European integration – but the Socialist candidate also made clear during the campaign that his future government would only be accountable for his own 60 campaign promises, thereby significantly diminishing the significance of the PS–EELV or PS–MRC electoral platforms.

On the other hand, there appeared to be few chances of a similar formal presidential agreement being reached with Mélenchon, although the Socialists were careful not to close the door on possible arrangements in the legislatives. On the presidential campaign trail, representatives of the Left wing of the party – such as Marie-Noëlle Lienemann and Arnaud Montebourg – advocated cooperation with the FG, while Martine Aubry admitted to the possibility of communist ministers entering a future Socialist government. One reason for Hollande ruling out presidential collaboration with the FG was that there seemed to be no immediate electoral threat to Socialist hegemony in the first round. As was clear from the polls, Mélenchon would mostly draw his support from the extreme left and potential abstainers, together with the more traditional electorate of the PCF, rather than substantially encroaching on Socialist territory. As Figure 3.2 shows, the FG dynamic would also result in an increase of the Left's total in the first round. The 'step' to Hollande in the run-off was that much smaller. EELV's integration *de facto* into the future majority also ensured support for the PS candidate – and, as seen from Joly's scores, at the expense of their own candidate in the first round.

2.2.2. The isolation of the UMP incumbent

These dynamics of electoral mobilisation on the Left contrasted with the paradoxical situation of the UMP we have already described as a dominant yet relatively isolated political force on the Right of the political spectrum, notwithstanding Sarkozy's ability to amalgamate the whole array of the UMP's constitutive parties in the lead-up to the first round, replicating the 2007 formula of inter-party cooperation. In the early stages of the presidency, the unpopularity of Nicolas Sarkozy and specifically a number of Right *notables* focusing on challenging a right-wing President who had, either ideologically or personally, become

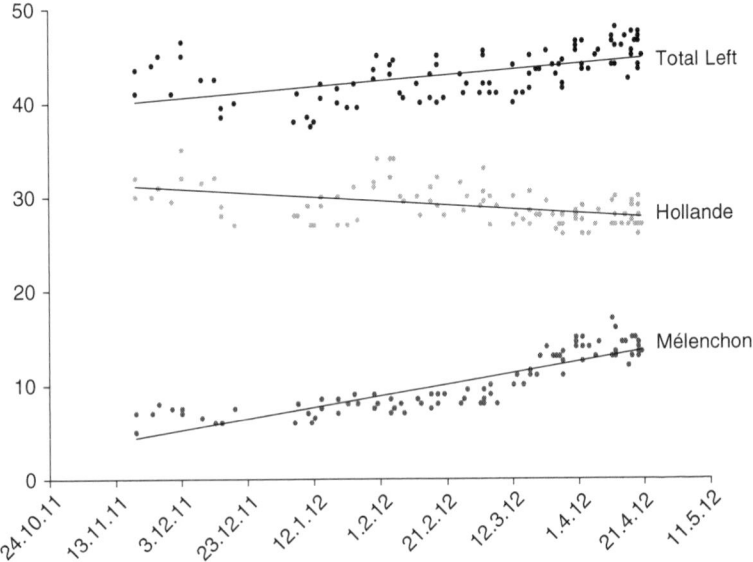

Figure 3.2   First-round presidential voting intentions for Hollande, Mélenchon and the Left: November 2011–April 2012

Note: Total Left = Hollande (PS) + Mélenchon (FG) + Joly (EELV) + Arthaud (LO) + Poutou (NPA).

Source: All pollsters (*N* = 94 national polls).

a target indicated a possible return to the 2002 situation where six moderate-right candidates contested the race.

The magnitude of public discontent with the incumbent President together with the electoral rebirth of the FN and the progression of the Left in the polls narrowed the political space available to dissident candidates on the Right, as there were growing fears that an increase in right-wing party fragmentation could possibly place Sarkozy behind Le Pen, resulting in a 'reverse' 21 April 2002 in the form of a PS–FN run-off. Borloo, Morin and Boutin all withdrew to ensure not splitting the Right vote. Additionally, the organisational strengths of the UMP allowed Sarkozy once again to exert political pressure on his centre-right allies, discouraging potentially disruptive presidential hopefuls with almost explicit threats of retaliation in the legislatives. The impact of the above public opinion and partisan factors was perceptible in both the decision by Frédéric Nihous' CPNT to rally behind the UMP in late February, and the utter failure of de Villepin to dispute Sarkozy's leadership of the Right camp. Throughout the pre-campaign, despite the progressive collapse of the Clearstream political scandal, polling support for the RS president trailed at less than 2 per cent nationally, showing that only a very modest pool of voters were leaning towards Villepin's cross-cleavage 'national unity' platform. De Villepin was less inclined to follow the example of his right-wing *confrères*, given the undoubted grudge element to his candidature against Sarkozy, but was forced to withdraw from the presidential race in mid-March 2012 when faced with insurmountable difficulties in collecting the 500 endorsement signatures.

Within the UMP, Sarkozy received the support of two minor parties, the PCD and Jean-Marie Bockel's Gauche moderne. Despite her threat to unleash *'une bombe atomique'* should politicking prevent her from collecting the requisite signatures, Christine Boutin withdrew from the presidential race in mid-February 2012 after Sarkozy endorsed some of the traditional religious and socially conservative agenda of the PCD, most notably by reaffirming his opposition to gay marriage and to euthanasia. On the other hand, the issue of presidential nomination revealed internal division and diverging strategies in the NC, where participation in the UMP presidential bid was challenged both by the proponents of political independence as well as by those supporting Bayrou's candidacy and joint legislative ventures on the centre-right. The Nogent-sur-Marne party congress of February 2012 endorsed Sarkozy by an 83.5 per cent majority vote as opposed to 16.5 per cent for the pro-Bayrou motion put forward by Jeremy Coste, leader of the NC youth organisation. Yet the principle of an autonomous centre-right candidacy reminiscent of the old UDF, which had originally been advocated by Morin before he renounced the presidential race, received the support from about two-thirds (67.6 per cent) of the party's delegates, showing that the NC integration into the UMP had become more problematic over the years.

Internal division in the NC reflected more general disagreements and positional conflicts amongst the UMP's centre-right allies over Sarkozy's shift to the Right in the opening of the presidential campaign. As early as 2010, a number of centrist leaders had expressed criticism and disapproval of the so-called 'Grenoble' strategy of radicalisation, revealing the growing ideological heterogeneity within the presidential majority. In 2012, the right-wing liberals continued to distance themselves from the hard line taken by the outgoing President on immigration and European issues. This led for instance Jean Arthuis' Alliance centriste to endorse Bayrou in the first round of the presidentials while calling for the reunification of the centre-right in the legislatives independently from the UMP. The diminishing appeal of Sarkozy's unitary candidacy to the centre ground of his party manifested more evidently in the PR after Borloo had withdrawn from the presidential race in October 2011. In March 2012, 76 per cent of the PR party congress voted what was deemed 'watchful support' (*soutien vigilant*) for the outgoing President, with national leaders such as Borloo and Rama Yade publicly expressing reservations towards Sarkozy's moving rightwards in the campaign. This resulted in the decision by the latter not to participate in the launch of the UMP presidential bid in Villepinte on 11 March, and heralded the formation of the splinter UDI after the legislatives.

The deterioration in intra-party cohesion mirrored the strategic grid-lock faced by the UMP externally, as the presidential party confronted competition on both its Left and Right flanks by the MODEM and the FN, respectively, and consequently lacking any potential allies and elec-toral reserves for a successful bid in the run-off against the Left. The fight for the centre ground of French politics remained key to the 2012 presidential race, concerning predominantly the UMP, which tactically attempted to secure Bayrou's support for the run-off on several occa-sions. These attempts were most explicit from Jean-Pierre Raffarin, Alain Juppé and Valérie Pécresse, who all openly posited a presidential ticket with the MODEM before the first round, whereby Bayrou would lead Sarkozy's government after the legislatives.

The experience of Bayrou's candidacy in 2007 had shown that a dis-tinct political space could exist for a 'third-way' candidate independent of both the Left and the Right based upon an aggressive stance against the UMP and PS duopoly. The political marginalisation of the MODEM across all intermediary elections since 2008 had, however, significantly lessened Bayrou's political weight and overshadowed his ability to repli-cate in full his previous presidential performance. In competitive terms, Bayrou's confrontational positioning within the party sub-system of the Right had also progressively taken the MODEM further away from the UMP and certainly closer to the Left on a number of cultural and insti-tutional issues, in clear opposition to Sarkozy's style of presidency and his reactivating the 'Buisson' line after 2010.

The isolation of the MODEM in the 2012 presidential election corrob-orated the narrowness of the political space available to parties outside traditional two-bloc politics, but most importantly it was the result of the failure by Bayrou to build coherent and stable electoral alliances over the 2007–2012 period, during which vast sections of the former UDF electorate had become disoriented. Whilst showing a significant rise in support for his candidacy from about 7 up to 14 per cent of voting intentions over the few weeks immediately following his official entry in the presidential race in November 2011, national polls displayed a reverse trend from mid-January onwards down to a steady 10.3 per cent average first-round vote in the final three weeks of the campaign – a signpost indicating that Bayrou could well be moving from third in 2007 down to only fifth place in April 2012.

At party level, Bayrou did not succeed in dislocating the centre pole of the UMP nor in attracting high-profile personalities – for example, his unsuccessful call upon Villepin to join his campaign – who could have bestowed credibility upon his presidential bid through independence, equidistant from both the Right and the Left, with the exception of the marginal support received from 18 former UDF senators. Moreover, unlike Royal in 2007, Hollande showed very little interest in collaborating with the MODEM. Whilst acknowledging ideological proximity with Bayrou and a common dislike of Sarkozy's policies – which would eventually materialise in Bayrou's support for the PS in the run-off – and occasionally pronouncing in delphic utterances on the extent of convergence between the two, Hollande ruled out political cooperation with the MODEM, reaffirming both his Socialist identity and primary ambition to unify the whole of the Left.

Lastly, the campaign battle over right-wing territory confirmed the pattern of competition that had been observed in 2010 and 2011. In the 2012 presidentials, the FN perpetuated the 'neither Left, nor Right' approach of positioning itself as a third competitive bloc against the so-called 'UMPS nomenklatura'. In this sense, Marine Le Pen did not deviate from the strong populist posture that historically had allowed the FN to channel political alienation and disaffection into the polls. In practice, this anti-system line translated predominantly into an 'anti-Right' position, which had been epitomised in the 1997 legislative elections, where the FN caused severe electoral losses for the UDF/RPR coalition in the second round. Beginning with the 2010 regional campaign, the FN increasingly targeted the outgoing President and majority in order to win back voters who had defected to Sarkozy in 2007 and dislodge the UMP coalition – possibly by attracting the Right pole of the party – with a view to ultimately replacing it as the main political actor of the Right.

2.3. The politics of blocks in the second round

The cooperative and competitive strategies that had prevailed in the lead-up to the first round continued over into the run-off, which displayed similar dynamics in terms of how the presidential parties and candidates effectively clustered together in support of the two finalists.

The outcome of the first round confirmed the persistence of a clustered multiparty system dominated by the UMP and PS, while exhibiting a 'two-tier' structure of competition whereby neither the FN nor the FG were in an actual position to challenge mainstream party electoral supremacy. As had already been the case in 2007, system stability was enhanced by the institutional features characteristic of the two-ballot majoritarian system, which continued to shape the expression of voter preferences, reinforcing the existing bipolarising trends. The volatility in Bayrou's first-round support in the centre ground of French politics certainly revealed the *vote utile* and the swing by significant sectors of his former 2007 supporters back to the Left and Right poles of the party system.

Asymmetric party competition across the two sides of the political spectrum endured in the presidential run-off, revealing first and foremost the strong mobilisatory appeal of Hollande to the whole of the Left and the concomitant effect of Bayrou travelling a leftward path since 2008. All left-wing presidential runners, with the notable exception of Nathalie Arthaud's LO, endorsed Hollande immediately after the first round. EELV candidate Joly called explicitly for her voters to support the Socialist candidate in the run-off while indicating that the Greens would participate in the latter's second-round campaign and would consider entering a Socialist-led cabinet. The building of the coalition of the Left was bolstered further by Cohn-Bendit's initiative for a joint 'appeal to all ecologists' to rally around Hollande in the second round, which was signed by a range of pro-environment personalities such as Bové, Lepage, Alain Lipietz as well as by PRG deputy (at that time) Christiane Taubira. On the far left, both leaders of the FG Mélenchon and Laurent urged their supporters to oppose Sarkozy unconditionally in the run-off – a notable semantic difference from endorsing Hollande himself, thereby avoiding vouching for his policies – an appeal which was also echoed by CGT leader Bernard Thibault, Jacques Cheminade and NPA presidential candidate Poutou, who asked voters to simply 'kick Sarkozy out' (*dégager Sarkozy*).

The above array of presidential endorsements demonstrated the persistence of the spirit of the well-established political tradition of *désistement républicain* – that is, the mutual dropping out between ballots in favour of the strongest first-round candidate of each camp – as well as the magnitude of 'negative support' for the PS already discussed in Chapter 2. Left-wing cooperation and strategic anti-incumbent convergence undoubtedly lessened the political challenges to Hollande by the rest of the Left, and to a large extent freed him from the tactical imperative of having to accommodate the potentially conflicting policy preferences of the parties in his heterogeneous *ad hoc* second-round coalition.

Simultaneously, the positioning of the FN by Le Pen reduced somewhat the distance between the Left and the extreme right both strategically and ideologically. Such proximity had been partly illustrated by the FN's showings in the 2011 cantonals: in the second round, the far right had won an additional 10.7 percentage points on average across the 127 cantons where the FN was contesting two-way run-offs against the mainstream Right – a progression similar in size to that observed in duels with the Left (+10.6 points in 266 cantons), which indicated that a substantial proportion of left-wing voters had in fact turned to Le Pen's party to defeat the UMP and its allies. In 2012, the more leftist agenda of redistribution, welfare expansion and state intervention pushed by the FN into the presidential arena to address the preferences of working and lower middle-class voters took the far right closer to the Left on the economic axis, thereby allowing Hollande to expand his second-round appeal to a proportion of the disenchanted and crisis-ridden electorate that had supported the FN in the first round. In strategic terms, the accentuation of the anti-Sarkozy discourse by Le Pen in the final stage of the campaign contributed to uniting left-wing voters and some of their far right counterparts behind the common goal of voting the outgoing President out of office.

Lastly, the building by Hollande of a broad run-off electoral coalition was facilitated by the MODEM's move towards the Left in reaction to the more centrifugal shift by the UMP candidate courting the votes of the FN during the presidential campaign. This was evidenced for instance by Bayrou's harsh criticism of 'the humiliation of Sarkozy's running on the double behind the FN's ideas' (*Le Monde*, 2 April 2012) and his officially backing Hollande personally on 3 May 2012. The marked deterioration in support for the independent centre resulted in a significant weakening of Bayrou's ability to weigh on the direction or polarisation of party competition in the run-off. That the MODEM leant towards Hollande can be accounted for by two sets of factors. First, the 2007 strategy of disconnection from the centre-right had allowed the party to recruit former members of the Left or ecologists, such as Jean-Luc Bennahmias, Yann Wehrling or Jean-François Kahn to cite but a few, who would naturally lean back towards the Left in classic bipolar races. Second, the political relocation of the party was also a by-product of the development of coalescent strategies with the PS and the Greens at the sub-national level, the significance of experiences of joint municipal administration being for instance revealed in the mobilisation in favour of Hollande by local leaders of the MODEM across a number of cities where they were collaborating with PS executives (Lille, Montpellier, Lyon and Grenoble, for example).

Hollande's broad mobilisatory appeal in the second round contrasted with the political isolation confronted by Sarkozy, as none of the first-round candidates would back the outgoing President. One first difficulty was the need for Sarkozy to reformulate his presidential bid in a manner that would appeal to the deeply antagonistic values, sociological profile and policy preferences distributed across Bayrou's and Le Pen's voters. This translated into a clear organisational division of labour during the run-off campaign, with the centrists of the UMP (e.g. Morin, Raffarin, Giscard and Arthuis) courting Bayrou over issues of budgetary discipline, while Sarkozy would receive the support of the hardliners of the Droite Populaire to send unambiguous messages to the FN electorate, at the evident cost of increasing intra-party fragmentation and factional competition within the right-wing majority. That the UMP candidate was however predominantly budging to the Right became manifest in the lead-up to the second round as Sarkozy continued to mimic the far right on a number of FN's proprietary issues such as immigration, crime, Islam or slamming the press and the French elites. A significant departure from the politics of ostracisation that had prevailed during the Chirac era, Sarkozy clearly took the UMP one step further to the Right by bestowing democratic and Republican legitimacy upon Le Pen's party.

While crucially alienating both centrist leaders and voters, this final campaign move by Sarkozy lacked the ability to convince those who had supported Le Pen's presidential platform in the first round. Nor did he manage to gain support from Dupont-Aignan, who had endorsed his candidacy five years earlier. The game-changing performance by the FN leader and her capacity to win back presidential support from the UMP gave the far right yet another opportunity to play its traditional role of nuisance within the party system. In the aftermath of the first round, FN leaders ruled out political cooperation with the mainstream Right, spinning out the party's 'neither Left, nor Right' doctrine and portraying Hollande and Sarkozy as 'interchangeable candidates of the establishment'. Whilst she refused to endorse either of the two run-off candidates and called for a 'blank vote', Le Pen clearly concentrated her fiercest attacks on the incumbent President between the two rounds with a view to precipitating his electoral fall to damage the unity of the majority party in the subsequent legislatives – a potential gold mine for National Assembly seats, even if it did not turn out that way, as we shall see in Chapter 8.

Table 3.2 Average voting transfers between the first and second rounds of the 2012 presidential in pre- and post-election polls

	Hollande	Sarkozy	Abst. Blank DK
Pre-election polls ($N = 8$)			
Mélenchon	84	5	11
Bayrou	34	37	29
Le Pen	18	54	28
Post-election polls ($N = 3$)			
Mélenchon	81	6	13
Bayrou	32	41	27
Le Pen	17	54	29

Source: All eight pre-election polls conducted between 2 and 4 May 2012; three post-election polls conducted by TNS-SOFRES, IPSOS and IFOP on 6 May 2012.

Polling data on electoral transfers between the two rounds of the 2012 presidential largely corroborate the above pattern of inter-party competition, with a higher degree of intra-bloc discipline on the Left, the distribution of Bayrou's voters across both sides of the spectrum and FN voters moving away from Sarkozy in the run-off (see Table 3.2).

Looking first at the series of eight national pre-election polls conducted in the final week before the second round, an average of 84 per cent of Mélenchon votes declared they would support Hollande, as well as about a third (34 per cent) amongst those who had backed Bayrou in the first round and were prepared to cross the ideological line. On the Right, there was some evidence of about half (46 per cent) of the FN electorate defecting either to the Left or to abstention/blank. The few post-election polls conducted immediately after the run-off largely confirmed the above figures: 81 per cent of Mélenchon's supporters said they had shifted to Hollande. According to those polls, 32 and 41 per cent of Bayrou's votes went to Hollande and Sarkozy, respectively. Most importantly, only 54 per cent of the far right electorate lent their support to the outgoing President in the run-off, a swing that ultimately played a critical role in determining the final outcome in favour of the Left.

* * *

The competitive dynamics of the first round present a relatively clear picture of asymmetric cohesion between the two blocs. The ability of Hollande to rely upon support built across a number of years of electoral cooperation between elements of the radical Left, the mainstream and even uneasy collaboration with centre-right forces ensured the long-term availability of a stable vote which was simply not on offer for Sarkozy. In the end, the incumbent President's only chance in the run-off was to attempt to secure as high a proportion of the mainstream Right vote from the first round (insufficient by itself) as well as convincing enough of the far-right support to turn out for him to total more than the left-bloc benchmark.

Part of Sarkozy's plan in this respect was to trade on his own reputation as a hard-nosed accomplished statesman who would deliver, even if other aspects of his personality had done him absolutely no favours for almost the entirety of his presidency. That the eventual run-off differential was relatively close, at least in comparison to the polling scores of a few months earlier, is a testament to the energy and no small degree of success he had in mobilising a respectable, if not winning, share of the vote. In that respect, the individual (rather than the programme or the political affiliation) mattered. In similar vein, however propitious the array of reliable allies a presidential candidate has in the first round, and whatever the implications polling leads suggest at various junctures of the race, party machines need to be certain that, as well as putting forward the candidate who will represent the party's ideals and aspirations, they have also ensured that the face put to such ideals 'fits' as a *présidentiable*. Whether there is one or a few potential choices to do this depends very much on the state of the party in the pre-campaign period. Whether the personality of the candidate and their ability to mobilise valence-related support will be decisive depends very much on how the competitive dynamics play out in the campaign. But that parties need to take the selection process seriously in order to signpost their commitment to democratic accountability and, in France, the primacy of the Republican ideal is undeniable. We turn in the next chapter to precisely that selection process, and its impact on the eventual roster of candidates.

4
Candidate Selection Processes and Effects

The process of selecting candidates is a key function both administered by and shaping political parties (Katz, 2001). Over time, it has become a crucial aspect of the political process in France, imbuing an increasingly personalised and candidate-centred structure to competition, with direct consequences for the way politics operates and ultimately for the quality of democracy. In 2007, the strong focus on leadership and charisma in both Sarkozy and Royal's campaigns epitomised the existing trend towards the presidentialisation and personalisation of politics (Clift, 2005). The personification of executive dominance was amplified further during the five years of Sarkozy's 'hyper-presidency', which saw a significant sidelining of both the Prime Minister and the centre-right parliamentary majority, as well as excessive mediatisation of the President's personal life.

Going into the 2012 elections, one crucial challenge confronted by parties was therefore that of picking 'optimum' presidential champions with strong campaigning skills and an immediate appeal to the mass public, but who could also evade the shortcomings of the exacerbated style of personalised politics that prevailed during Sarkozy's reign. Such objectives were key for instance to Hollande's attempt to portray himself as a 'normal candidate' in the campaign. During his presidential term, Sarkozy's wielding of nearly all levers of power also substantially reduced the role of well-established political buffers (*fusibles*) – most evidently the Prime Minister and his government – while weakening his own party on the ground. Unlike 2007, Sarkozy entered the presidential arena with a clearly more fragmented and somewhat demobilised party after the successive electoral blows taken by the UMP in mid-term elections, detailed in Chapter 1.

In 2012, however, parties varied considerably in the preferred mechanisms of candidate selection. Their choice of procedure was dependent upon a number of organisational factors such as the existence of a strong leadership and the balance between rival factions. Additionally, there were obviously important implications as regards to how parties would then cooperate during the election campaign, which we examined in more detail in Chapter 3. On the Left of the political spectrum, primary candidates were also faced with important policy and valence issues, a dilemma dealt with in differing ways by the different candidates and their respective parties.

This chapter looks broadly at the mechanisms of candidate selection in the 2012 presidential elections, and more specifically at how such presidential candidate screening was articulated by parties at the organisational level. In cases where a decision was made to hold primary elections, popularity and credibility data are used to assess the utility calculus and policy/valence trade-off by party members and sympathisers. A particular focus is given to the continuing move towards a plebiscitary model of party democracy in the PS's open competitive primary. We look more specifically at the 'alternate Socialist' polls to see how informative these were in identifying Hollande as the winning candidate, whether that information was reflected at all in the Socialist primaries, and the extent to which the eventual primary choice represented the optimum candidate in the presidentials.

1. Candidate selection mechanisms in the 2012 presidential elections: an overview

A range of 'selection' methods were used across the political spectrum in the 2012 pre-election period. Broadly speaking, the procedures fell under two categories of 'undemocratic' and 'democratic' mechanisms based on elite-centred nomination processes and competitive primary elections, respectively. In the latter category, some variation was observed in terms of the size of the parties' preferred selectorate (openness) and the degree of competitiveness – measured here by a standard index for the effective number of candidates. The differences are summarised in Table 4.1.

On the Right, despite record low popularity showings, Sarkozy enjoyed his incumbent's prerogative. The official declaration of his candidature in mid-February 2012 was a mere formality as the likelihood of the incumbent President not standing for re-election was vanishingly small. However, the timing of his announcement did depart from earlier

Table 4.1 Candidate selection procedures in 2012

Undemocratic		Democratic*
UMP (incumbency) LO, MODEM, DLR (party leadership nomination, no vote) NPA (party leadership nomination, with delegates' vote)	Party membership (closed)	FN (party leadership election, with party members' vote) [1.78] FG (party convention nomination, with delegates' vote and members' vote [2.05]
	General electorate (open)	EELV (mixed: party members and sympathisers' vote) [2.42] PS (left-wing sympathisers' vote) [3.53]

Note: *Effective number of candidates in square brackets, Laakso and Taagepera (1979).

indications that he would only engage with the campaign in the final stage, possibly as late as March – by mid-February, polling inertia and a call for his presence on the field from UMP cadres led to a strategic shift by the President, with a move away from strict valence – for example, competence, statesmanship – to divisive positional issues such as immigration, social welfare benefits and gay marriage (see Chapter 5). *In camera* decisions also occurred in Bayrou's MODEM and Dupont-Aignan's DLR, revealing the 'natural' overlap between presidential nomination and party leadership characteristic of personalised cadre parties whose rationale is to provide essentially for their leaders to advance their ambition in national elections. Organisational weaknesses were on the other hand well in evidence in the legislative elections, where, as we shall see in Chapter 8, both these parties failed to achieve electoral relevance at the national level. Finally, consistent with the traditional culture of internal secrecy and dismissal of presidential politics, which dominate the extreme left, inside-track elite nominations happened in the two small Trotskyite parties (LO and NPA) where nominees were first and foremost trusted insiders and relatively inexperienced loyal party activists – Nathalie Arthaud at the closed party congress in December 2010, and Philippe Poutou in a vote at the national conference in June 2011.

Turning to the competitive procedures, an internal leadership election was held by the FN in January 2011, which served practically as presidential primary for the nomination of Marine Le Pen. Marine Le Pen's election with 67.7 per cent of the members' vote in the 14th party congress in Tours showed that a large, but far from unanimous, majority of the party's grass roots were inclined towards her 'modernising' strategic line. On the Left, primary elections occurred in all three main parties. In EELV, the nomination of the presidential candidate took place in June/July 2011 after two of the most prominent leaders of the ecology movement – Cohn-Bendit and Duflot – had announced that they would not stand in 2012. The presence of a number of unaffiliated groups led EELV to consider a mixed system of nomination including a vote both by the Verts' party members and Europe Écologie's '*collaborateurs*', and sympathisers in the general electorate. A former anti-corruption magistrate and MEP since 2009, Eva Joly entered the EELV primary race against popular TV host Nicolas Hulot.

The very few primary polls that were conducted between January and June 2011 indicated that Hulot was the preferred candidate for about two-thirds of the EELV/Green supporters, with no significant variation across time. As Table 4.2 shows, Hulot was also showing a strong lead over his opponent across all popularity polls. In the first round, however, Joly captured an unanticipated 49.7 per cent of the vote (from around 25,000 voters out of 33,000 registered members and 'collaborators'), as opposed to 40.2 per cent for Hulot, 5 per cent for Henri Stoll (a Green councillor in Haut-Rhin) and 4.6 per cent for Stéphane Lhomme (an anti-nuclear activist). In the second round, she was able to rally the anti-Hulot coalition and won a total 58.2 per cent of the vote cast.

In the Front de Gauche (FG), the nomination race of June 2011 followed a two-step procedure, beginning with a vote by the delegates in the PCF's national conference in Montreuil, which endorsed PG leader Mélenchon with no less than 63.6 per cent of the vote cast. Notwithstanding the strong resistance by the traditionalist wing within the PCF, party members confirmed the delegates' vote: Mélenchon received 59.1 per cent of the membership vote (from 49,000 out of 69,000

Table 4.2   Summary of EELV candidates' popularities as of June 2011*

Pollster	Joly	Hulot	Item
TNS-SOFRES	21	44	Should play a greater role in the future (yes)
IFOP	45	67	Very good/Good opinion of …
Viavoice	51	n.a.	Positive opinion of …
OpinionWay	43	54	Satisfied with his/her action
CSA	28	56	Fairly positive image of …
BVA	26	45	Should have more influence in French politics (yes)

Note: *National polls of registered voters.

registered members), against 36.8 per cent for the representative of the orthodox wing, André Chassaigne, and 4.1 per cent for the peripheral candidate Emmanuel Dang Tran.

The main novelty in the 2012 campaign was undoubtedly the decision by the PS to call for an open primary election outside the party's rank and file, with membership-based presidential nomination procedures having been run for the 1995 and 2007 elections (Dolez and Laurent, 2007).[1] The 2011 primary was notable for this change in the party's selectorate and the opening of the competition to all left-wing sympathisers among registered French voters. With the exception of the PRG, whose leader Jean-Michel Baylet entered the Socialist primary race, the PS clearly failed to incorporate other parties of the Left into the process of selecting a common presidential runner.

The PS election was held in October 2011 under a two-ballot majoritarian system similar to that adopted in the 2006 party membership nomination. Hollande topped the first round with 39.2 per cent of the vote, taking the lead over PS leader Martine Aubry, who received 30.4 per cent (Table 4.3). Arnaud Montebourg made an unanticipated breakthrough by taking a 'kingmaker' third-place position with 17.2 per cent of the vote, showing that the anti-globalisation and protectionist line that he had pushed into the campaign resonated with a significant section of the left-wing electorate. In spite of her personal standing amongst the French public, at least on the Left, and her status as former presidential candidate, Ségolène Royal polled a mere 6.9 per cent, which placed her well behind the front runners. A member of the future generation of leaders in the PS, Manuel Valls won a

Table 4.3 Results of the PS primary elections of 9 and 16 October 2011

	First round		Second round	
	Votes	%	Votes	%
François Hollande	1,036,767	39.16	1,607,268	56.57
Martine Aubry	805,936	30.44	1,233,899	43.43
Arnaud Montebourg	455,536	17.21		
Ségolène Royal	183,343	6.92		
Manuel Valls	149,077	5.63		
Jean-Michel Baylet	17,030	0.64		
Blank	10,978		18,990	
Total	2,658,667	100.00	2,860,157	100.00

Source: http://resultats.lesprimairescitoyennes.fr/ (accessed 14 March 2012).

core 5.6 per cent of the vote, from the Right of the party. Between the two rounds, Hollande received official support from Baylet, Royal and Valls. While refusing to endorse either of the two candidates in the run-off, Montebourg indicated that he personally would be voting for Hollande, which largely cleared the way for the latter's presidential nomination. In the second round, Hollande won the candidacy by totalling 56.6 per cent of the vote cast.

At party level, holding a primary enhanced the PS's reputation for democratic openness and transparency. Despite technical problems, confidentiality issues and criticism by the UMP, the Socialist primary proved successful in attracting over 2.6 and 2.8 million voters in the first and second rounds, respectively. This high turnout was welcomed by all aspirants and leaders of the Left as giving a strong mandate and legitimacy to Hollande. A CSA poll conducted immediately after the nomination race showed that a large majority (78 per cent) of left-wing supporters regarded the outcome of the primary as positive, and that the Socialist Party was seen as more 'unified' and 'stronger' (CSA-BFM TV/RMC/20 Minutes, 19 October 2011).[2]

At candidate level, the positive outcome of the Socialist primary augmented Hollande's popularity. Whilst voting intentions for the Socialist candidate remained stable throughout the pre-campaign, a bandwagon effect was perceptible in the candidate's ratings, across the two critical stages of the pre-campaign in March and October 2011. In the former, Hollande enjoyed a popularity surge of 12 percentage points (from 34 to 46 per cent) subsequent to his entering the PS primary. From October onwards, he rode a post-primary wave of momentum, with positive ratings climbing further to reach 57 per cent on the eve of the first round of the presidential contest (IPSOS/*Le Point*, 7 April 2012).

2. Presidential candidates and parties

The variation in mechanisms for candidate selection reflects the complex interactions that exist between presidential nominations and political parties in France. The latter have lost their monopoly in choosing their presidential champions and must adapt to an increasingly candidate-centred and mass media–dominated polity. As organisations, they are also characterised by diverging models of leadership, decision-making and membership, with notable differences in partisan cultures and the manner in which internal pluralism is addressed.

While retaining most of their idiosyncratic features as relatively weak and fragmented political organisations (Knapp, 2002), French parties have certainly become more 'open' over the past two decades to addressing the need for intra-party democracy. They have endorsed a plebiscitary model of direct membership participation to revise the party's policies, to recruit new leaders or to nominate presidential candidates. This is true for instance of the changes in leader selection procedures which have taken place in the PS and the UMP. Both parties have also enhanced internal democracy by gradually instigating referendums to consult their members on policy. Efforts at democratisation persisted in the lead-up to the 2012 presidential and legislative campaigns. The PS programme was adopted by an overwhelming majority (95.1 per cent) of the party members and officially endorsed by a national convention in May 2011, following a two-year process of internal debate through a significant number of preparatory groundwork meetings both at local and national levels. Internal debates were equally important to the formulation of the UMP's 2012 manifesto, which received 96.4 per cent of support among party members in a vote held in January 2012.

By endorsing more open and transparent mechanisms of candidate selection, the parties of the Left have also acknowledged further the presidentialisation of the French political system and the growing importance of candidates. Presidential primaries have helped these parties reduce the tension between their factionalised and proportionalist partisan cultures, on the one hand, and the highly personalised majoritarian framework that shapes competition in the presidential arena on the other. The cultural change is probably most evident in the PS, where the development of presidential primaries can be regarded as a means of adjusting the party further to the institutional logics of the Fifth Republic, a process of presidentialisation whose origins are traceable back to the Epinay congress of 1971 and the establishment of Mitterrand's presidential leadership over the whole of the Left after 1965 (Bergounioux and Grunberg, 2005).

2.1. Party leadership, presidential nomination

Besides party democratisation, however, the decision to move away from elite-centred processes of candidate selection may also reflect the absence of a 'natural' presidential runner emerging from within the pool of potential contenders in the party, and the disjuncture that may exist between party leadership and presidential nominees. Looking at French parties across the spectrum, the shift towards democratic procedures is rooted in existing political cultures and a partisan ethos of leadership.

Both in 2007 and in 2012, presidential nominations intersected almost naturally with party leadership in the parties of the Right. This was the case for instance in the MODEM, Parti radical and Nouveau Centre as well as in the FN. During the 2011 internal campaign, Le Pen took clear advantage of her position of strength in the polls by explicitly attaching the election of the new FN leader to the nomination of the future presidential candidate for the party.[3] In the UMP, despite past efforts to implement more democratic processes internally, the traditional Bonapartist culture of party unity and strong leadership has remained deeply entrenched, and the 'incarnatory' legacy of Gaullism palpable (Haegel, 2004). Albeit effectively involving direct member participation, internal leader selection procedures have been characterised by low levels of competition. In the former RPR, membership elections had been inaugurated in the late 1990s to appoint new leaders for the party, yet they had not significantly undermined the authority of Chirac over his political family. In 2007, Sarkozy had become the *de facto* presidential runner for the UMP after he had taken over the party's leadership in November 2004.

In 2012, Sarkozy's ascendancy over the French Right was clearly reinforced by his personal status as incumbent. Sarkozy's bid for 2012 had been publicly envisaged as early as July 2009 following the relatively good performance of the UMP in the European elections. Alternative hypotheses – for instance, Juppé or Fillon as candidates – were only briefly contemplated by the Right in 2011, as was the idea of 'copycatting' the PS in holding a primary election, yet there was little doubt that the President would eventually run for a second term. Sarkozy's uncontested authority allowed him to set the tone for the presidential campaign, and to free himself quite substantially from the programmatic framework defined by his party during 2011, which eclipsed the considerable amount of preparatory policy work conducted by party leader Jean-François Copé during that year.

By contrast, parties on the Left of the political spectrum have displayed a growing dissociation between party leaders and presidential nominees since the mid-1990s. In the Green movement, the disconnect between presidential candidacy and party leadership began in the 2002 presidential election and progressed into the 2007 nomination. In 2002 Noël Mamère was endorsed by the party's national apparatus. In the first internal primary election of 2006, national secretary Cécile Duflot took only the third position with 23.3 per cent of the membership vote behind former leader Dominique Voynet (35.5 per cent) and Yves Cochet (28.3 per cent).[4] The disjunctive process, which is embedded in the Greens' culture of direct democracy and collegiality, culminated in the 2012 primary campaign both in terms of the relative 'de-partyisation' of the selectorate and the profile of the main front runners. The twofold alliance with Cohn-Bendit's Europe Écologie and Antoine Waechter's MEI, together with the decision to enter formal talks with Hulot in the lead-up to the 2009 European elections, not only took the primary vote away from the Greens' membership, but also opened a political opportunity for outsiders – rather than 'born-and-bred' party activists – to enter and eventually appropriate the nomination.

A similar trend could be observed in the Communist Party, where the 2012 presidential nomination was largely dependent on the distribution of forces and political incentives within the newly built FG coalition. As we saw in Chapter 3, the preparation of the presidential campaign coincided with the partners of the FG reaching a formal agreement over the allocation of legislative constituencies. While incontestably successful in halting the steady electoral decline and bringing a new lease of life to the old PCF, the strategy of colluding with the PG led the communists to jettison their leadership, and, for the first time since 1974, they entered the presidential race without a candidate from their own ranks. Looking at patterns of cooperation with other actors of the Left, this represented a significant departure from the 2007 strategy of preserving the party's individual identity within the anti-liberal movement.[5]

In the Socialist Party, the declining relevance of party leadership and the increased prominence of candidates have profoundly altered the methods of choosing presidential nominees. A first significant shift occurred in the mid-1990s immediately after the end of the long Mitterrand era. Throughout the 1970s and 1980s, the firm authority and ascendancy exerted by Mitterrand over the Socialist Left had narrowed the scope for internal debate over the crucial issue of presidential nomination, a divisive issue which resurfaced abruptly in the notoriously catastrophic 1990 party congress in Rennes. The question was taken out of the 'smoke-filled room' in 1995 when the PS first introduced the principle of an internal primary election under a majoritarian two-ballot system in the party statutes. The gap between the party and its presidential candidate widened in the 2006 primary vote in which Royal took the nomination from her position as relative outsider, and emancipated herself from the party's 'elephants' by setting up her own political machine (Désir d'avenir).[6] Following the equally disastrous party congress in Reims in 2008, concluding with Aubry's hair's-breadth victory over Royal for leadership of the party, the official adoption in

July 2010 by the PS of open primary elections for the presidential nomination was considered part of an important effort to instigate ideological and political renewal, as well as a means to tackle unresolved issues of leadership.

A set of interrelated concerns became central in preparation for the primaries. First and foremost was of course the question of whether Dominique Strauss-Kahn (DSK) would eventually participate in the Socialist nomination race.[7] The likelihood of DSK's comeback into national politics topped the political agenda during the months that preceded his arrest in New York. In the second half of 2010, the matter was central to internal debates surrounding the primary calendar, with DSK's rivals calling for an acceleration as a strategic means to complicate his return into the nomination race. More importantly, the perspective of DSK joining the primary profoundly altered public perceptions of the purpose and ultimately the objectives of the PS holding a nomination race. In November 2010, the revelation of a secret deal dubbed the Marrakech pact between DSK, Aubry and Fabius not to run against each other – a concordat which was briefly endorsed by Royal as well – raised concerns about the impact of a possible 'invisible primary' whereby party elites would have already enthroned DSK, thereby limiting the contest to an essentially 'confirmatory' vote. In April 2011, such fears were accentuated by an OpinionWay poll showing that a DSK–Aubry ticket could garner a majority 52 per cent support among left-wing sympathisers in the first round of the primary race.[8] DSK's candidacy began to materialise in March 2011; by early May, there seemed little doubt that he would resign from his IMF position to enter the Socialist race in the summer. DSK took the lead in the PS primary polls as early as June 2009 and enjoyed an average 28 per cent of first-round support among supporters of the Left until late 2010. By December 2010, polls already showed a notable rise in DSK's ratings up to an average of 40 per cent, besting all other contenders in the first round by a significant margin.

Counterfactual hypotheses of what could have possibly happened had DSK not been arrested in New York are of course purely speculative. At the very least it is uncertain that DSK's actual return to the realm of national politics would have been as trouble-free as anticipated by the final polls published in the days leading up to the Sofitel events, discussed further in Chapter 6. Primary support for Hollande had been on the rise since January 2011. Polls conducted immediately after the arrest showed that Hollande was the main beneficiary of DSK leaving the stage, with his voting intentions almost doubling from an average 20 per cent in April up to 39.8 per cent in the second half of May. By contrast, the primary vote for Aubry only rose from 19.2 up to 26.8 per cent during the same interval, before her candidacy became more tangible, bringing her an additional support of about 8 percentage points. Strikingly, Royal did not seem to capitalise on the deposition of her former 2007 rival, as she enjoyed a mere 0.5 point increase in support in the immediate aftermath of the arrest.

In terms of party leadership, the final outcome of the 2011 Socialist primary pointed to the continuation, albeit in a more attenuated form perhaps, of the disjuncture that had been observed five years earlier. The democratisation of the internal nomination process had continued to reduce the power and legitimacy of the party leader in the presidential arena, as demonstrated by Aubry's failure to win the candidacy or even what appears to have been her initial intention to step down and endorse DSK. On the other hand, because of his former role as PS first secretary from 1997 to 2008, Hollande was certainly in a better position to reduce the party–candidate dissonance that had been significantly increased by Royal's non-partisan strategy. In 2007, the Socialists had not been able to avoid disgruntlement on the part of Royal's primary rivals, a negative carry-over which had prompted some within the party to demand that the primary be replaced by a regular party congress vote. This came in sharp contrast with Sarkozy's firm hold on the UMP after 2004, and was deeply antagonistic to one central and somehow paradoxical feature of France's polity, whereby presidential dominance invariably requires support from a strong unified party machinery and dedicated grass roots (Bell and Criddle, 2002).

In 2012, the lessons of the 2007 party malfunction had been well learned by the Socialist camp. Whilst not entirely devoid of negative campaigning and attacks, the election certainly showed a greater level of internal cohesion as all of the party's establishment rallied behind Hollande's candidacy, contributing not only to his presidential success but also, as we have seen in Chapter 2, to improving the party's public image.[9] Unlike Royal five years earlier, Hollande also took greater care not to distance himself too markedly from the official policies formulated in the 2011 programme, although he would assert his autonomy from the party's platform on a number of key issues.

Hollande's personal legacy as former PS leader was discernible in the primary polls published during the official nomination campaign, where he enjoyed a significantly higher level of popular support among Socialist sympathisers compared with those of the Left as a whole. In the former, Hollande received an average 6.1 surplus in primary voting intentions across all surveys conducted from July to October 2011, with very little variation over time. The comparable figure for Aubry was only 0.5, showing no clear difference despite her position as party leader since 2008. Turning to Montebourg, it is significant that his polling support was consistently larger among all left-wing sympathisers compared with those of the Socialist Party (8 per cent on average in the former as opposed to 4.3 per cent in the latter), which indicated that he would probably draw a substantial part of his primary vote from the immediate periphery of the PS rather than from its core.

Overall, there was evidence of a higher degree of accuracy in polls conducted on samples of left-wing sympathisers compared with those looking only at Socialist supporters. Taking the sum of absolute errors for all candidates as a measure of polling error in the final-week polls, the total figure for left-wing sympathisers amounted to 13.1 per cent across the main five contenders, halving that observed in the same polls conducted amongst self-declared PS supporters (26.1 per cent). This reflected the change that had occurred in the party's primary selectorate, as well as differences in sample size, while also showing the existing gap between the PS' rank and file and its non-partisan support. As can be seen from Table 4.4, surveys of left-wing sympathisers correctly predicted the order of the candidates. Most estimates were

Table 4.4   Final-week primary polls for the PS nomination in 2011

Pollster	Date	Hollande	Aubry	Montebourg	Royal	Valls
First round						
Harris	29/09/2011	40	28	12	6	4
IFOP	30/09/2011	42	27	8	11	5
OpinionWay	06/10/2011	43	28	11	11	6
Harris	06/10/2011	40	29	12	6	5
	Mean	**41.3**	**28.0**	**10.8**	**8.5**	**5.0**
	Final result	39.2	30.4	17.2	7.0	5.6
	Difference	2.1	−2.4	−6.4	1.6	−0.6
Second round						
OpinionWay	11/10/2011	54	46			
Harris	11/10/2011	53	47			
OpinionWay	13/10/2011	53	47			
	Mean	**53.3**	**46.7**			
	Final result	56.6	43.4			
	Difference		3.3			

Source: National polls of left-wing sympathisers.

within the margin of error, again with the exception of Montebourg, whose final score was underestimated by no less than 6.4 per cent. Interestingly, the difficulties encountered by pollsters in capturing accurately the size of Montebourg's primary support mirrored their inability to effectively measure the Fabius vote in the 2006 nomination race.[10] On both occasions pollsters confronted a similar problem of evaluating a more expressive form of protest vote by minority factions against the main policy preferences of the party's mainstream, which echoes the discussion of the 'social desirability bias' in predicting scores of extremist parties in general election polls.

2.2. Presidential nomination and party factionalism

Another rationale for the existence of primary elections is that they may mediate competition between organised factions. One important implication of a party adopting a plebiscitary model of direct democracy is to reduce the immediate salience of factional cleavages (Young and Cross, 2002). Factional competition is a central feature of political parties in France, and presidential nominations often reflect internal struggles between well-identified subgroups of elites. In a bipolar multiparty system, party factions also compete both ideologically and strategically over the definition of political alliances.

In 2012, the use of democratic procedures as a means to evade factional conflicts was found across a wide range of parties, including the more hierarchical and centralised anti-system actors. This was the case, for instance, for the FN leadership election of January 2011, which illustrated the need to arbitrate between its rival internal factions, and mediate diverging strategic lines in the post–Le Pen *père* era. Marine Le Pen's political momentum profoundly altered the internal balance of power, resulting in the decline of the heterogeneous group of elites aggregated in the orthodox church which had endorsed Gollnisch.[11] Crossing over to the NPA on the extreme left, the presidential nomination of Philippe Poutou by the party's national congress in June 2011 revealed a profound division between proponents of a radical 'identity' position and those calling for a more conciliatory approach vis-à-vis other parties of the non-Socialist Left, in particular Mélenchon's FG.

Similar issues were also visible in both the ecologist and communist primary races of 2011. In EELV, policy preferences were central to the primary campaign, in particular the issue of nuclear power, but the positions of the two front runners were also articulated with opposing views of the competitive strategies which the ecology movement should pursue in 2012. The candidacies reactivated the old political independence cleavage cross-cutting the Left/Right divide on the one hand, and the strategy of integration within the Left pole of national politics on the other. Whilst the latter strategy was defended by Joly and would subsequently be officially endorsed by the Greens' leadership, Hulot continued to advocate a position of independence vis-à-vis the two main blocks. Such a position was consistent with his more vertical approach of environmental issues forming a 'third dimension in French politics' (*Le Monde*, 12 September 2011), which had dominated in particular the non-partisan promotion of his Ecology Pact in 2007. Internally Hulot was the subject of harsh criticism from the Left of the party, primarily due to his admission that he considered seeking an alliance with Borloo's centre-right, a position which was also defended by Cohn-Bendit.

Turning briefly to the PCF, the gradual change in internal procedures for screening presidential candidates had accompanied the evolution of the party's position in political competition since the mid-1990s. In 1995, Robert Hue had won the nomination in a unanimous one-candidate election by the party's delegates in the national conference of 1994. His modernising line announced the decision by the PCF to enter the PS-led plural Left in the 1997 legislatives. In 2002, on the other hand, Hue confronted a more competitive membership vote in which both his authority and strategic choices as party leader were challenged by the orthodox wing then incarnated by Maxime Gremetz. Whilst still largely beneficial to Hue (77.4 per cent of the members' vote), the 2002 nomination race revealed conflicting strategic options amongst organised factions within the PC. By 2007, the failure of the mainstream Left in the 2002 presidentials and the concomitant rise of the extreme left altered the balance of power within the party, and caused its move away from the former plural Left Socialist allies to join forces with the vast anti-liberal movement that had materialised around the 2005 European referendum. Whilst the PC had failed then to pre-empt the political space for the radical Left, this move on the competitive axis prefigured the construction of the FG and the communists' endorsement of Mélenchon in 2012. At party level, the development of internal elections has gone hand in hand with the democratisation of the old communist apparatus since the mid-1990s, which has progressively reduced the salience of the party's pyramidal decision structure and culture of political unanimity entrenched in the principle of *centralisme démocratique*, to allow for the internal expression of dissident factions (Lavabre and Platone, 2003).

Finally, in the PS, factions have traditionally played an important role in structuring intra-party competition and providing cues and incentives for nominations. Since 1971, internal pluralism and the proportional representation of factions in the party's ruling bodies have been central to the PS's core identity, in contrast with the majoritarian domination in the post-war SFIO (Cole, 1989). In 2006, one key factor of Royal's success was her ability to appeal to a broad swathe of the party membership across existing factions and, more importantly, to navigate the European cleavage that had threatened to split the PS in 2005 (Ivaldi, 2007). The 2006 primary exhibited further the loosening of the link between organised tendencies and presidential strategies, while showing a significant fragmentation of the main subgroups of elites located to the Left of the party – that is, the Nouveau Parti Socialiste (NPS) and Arnaud Montebourg's Rénover Maintenant (RM).

In 2011, the need for presidential hopefuls to mobilise across antagonistic factions was reinforced by the much higher degree of intra-party fragmentation which had occurred in the 2008 party congress.[12] Admittedly, the opening of the nomination race to the general electorate partially reduced the salience of party factionalism, but the capacity of primary candidates to enlarge their support beyond the small circles of their close supporters was nevertheless crucial to taking the presidential nomination. The 2011 contest showed another important reshuffling of the internal balance of power among the party's national elites, which overlapped only partly with the motions that had competed against each other in 2008. At the elite level, Hollande drew most of his support from the Delanoë motion which he had personally endorsed in 2008. He also attracted a significant number of those who had supported Royal's bid in the Reims congress and, most importantly, the vast majority of *strauss-kahniens*.[13] This allowed Hollande to position himself more firmly at the centre of the party to embody the moderate social-democrat and reformist line that had been DSK's trademark since his years as Minister of the Economy in the Jospin government.

Despite Montebourg's shift towards more protectionist and anti-globalisation economics, the party's Left wing led by Benoît Hamon and Henri Emmanuelli chose to rally to Aubry's candidacy in the primary, joining forces with the core support that her personal motion had already received in the 2008 congress. Such ability by the two front runners to merge hostile subgroups of national elites contrasted with the fractionalisation that occurred in internal support for Royal,[14] as well as the absence of coalescent power in Montebourg's and Valls' primary bids. Both suffered from their lack of factional and organisational resources, and received only marginal support from party elites.

3. Candidates' positions and valence

In France as in other liberal democracies, the rise of candidate-centred politics has increased the need for parties to select candidates with a strong personal presence. Personal characteristics based on valence rather than policy or political career within the party have gained in importance. In primary elections, strategic considerations by party members and/or sympathisers of candidate viability and competitiveness in the presidential election have become critical. The proliferation of polls in the 2012 presidential campaign[15] provided voters with vast amounts of information regarding the candidates' electoral prospects as well as their policy profile and personal capabilities. We consider here the extent to which such attributes influenced choice.

3.1. The utility calculus: visibility and electability

Primary voters tend to consider first the candidates' probable appeal in the general election. This expected-utility model posits that voters 'balance their ideology or candidate preference with their interest of winning by considering competing values linked to each candidate' (Stone et al., 1995: 137). One first important aspect is the candidates' visibility in the mass media and their ability to sustain a central position within the national arena. The perception of politicians by voters is a defining element of their selectability, which, in the French case, is signalled by their inclusion in national barometers of *présidentiables* by pollsters, often translating political momentum into real presidential potential.

Looking briefly at some of the critical events that preceded the 2012 nomination races, the collapse of the UMP in the 2010 regional and 2011 cantonal elections clearly propelled a number of leaders of the opposition to the front of the political stage. Parties on the fringes of the system were among the main beneficiaries of the wave of popular discontent with the Sarkozy presidency. On the extreme right, Marine Le Pen won a personal success in the 2010 regional elections topping her father's best performance. Following two already highly publicised local campaigns in the city of Hénin-Beaumont in 2008 and 2009, this gave her a clear advantage to win the party leadership and consequently the presidential nomination. At the other end of the spectrum, Mélenchon benefited from the good electoral showings of the FG in establishing his leadership over the anti-liberal coalition. Similarly, in EELV, Joly made her first notable appearance in the political arena in the 2009 European elections, where she won her first seat as MEP on the list led by Cohn-Bendit in the Paris region.

Turning to the Socialist Party, the local elections of 2010 and 2011 certainly shaped the early stages of the nomination, providing the main presidential hopefuls with the political resources and access to the media, which were indispensable to building their credibility. Whilst significantly weakened by the outcome of the Reims congress, Aubry gained political momentum after the victory of the PS in the 2010 regionals, edging DSK's popularity in the polls and enjoying a lead of about 15 points over Hollande. The latter's popularity rose rapidly, however, following his success in the cantonal ballot in his personal stronghold of the department of Corrèze in March 2011. This allowed him to set out his candidacy to the PS primary and construct his public profile as a politician from the *'terroir'*. On that occasion, the ascendancy taken by the future finalists of the primary came in sharp contrast with the steady decline in popular support for Royal, which quite simply halved between 2007 and 2011.

This variability in political momentum and strategic timelines was mirrored in the ability of presidential hopefuls to enhance their electability – another important facet of the expected utility calculus by voters. Early in the 2012 pre-campaign, voting intention polls played a crucial role in providing cues about the candidates' respective levels of competitiveness. There is little doubt, for example, that FN members saw in Marine Le Pen a highly electable candidate with strong presidential prospects promising new electoral heights. By January, polls were showing a wide gap in the electoral potential of the two far-right contenders:[16] differences in electability were also associated with a notable variation in their level of attractiveness to the mainstream Right electorate.[17] Across the political spectrum, considerations of candidate valence and electoral appeal were of similar importance to the FG nomination: during the final stage of the process in June 2011, Mélenchon was already polling about 7–8 per cent of the presidential voting intentions, representing both a significant improvement on Buffet's catastrophic performance of 2007 and a strong incentive for PCF members to endorse the PG leader.

In the Socialist Party, candidate electability lost some of its salience in the 2011 nomination race. Five years earlier, Royal had enjoyed a substantial lead in presidential voting intentions during the primary campaign. Whilst polls were predicting that all other potential PS runners would be largely defeated by Sarkozy, Royal had emerged as the only candidate in a position not only to narrow the first-round margin, but also to secure a majority in the 2007 run-off.[18] In 2011, on the other hand, the exceptionally low popularity of Sarkozy led to a profound reshaping of presidential competition. With the exception of Royal this time, all three main potential Socialist runners – DSK, Hollande and Aubry – would take a remarkably constant, and at times clearly unrealistic, lead over the incumbent UMP President, with similar second-round polling scores between 55 and 60 per cent in many cases. In the period beginning from the arrest of DSK up until the primary contest of October 2011, Hollande and Aubry received on average 59 and 56.3 per cent of second-round voting intentions against Sarkozy in polls conducted nationwide.

3.2. Candidates' personality traits, policy positions and valences

Finally, the variation in viability amongst the main 2012 presidential runners reflected the balance that is traditionally established by voters between policy and valence components. Non-policy-related valence factors – such as the candidate's personal image, charisma, competence, empathy, integrity, personal background or their campaigning skills – are vital to the evaluation of candidates by voters (Stokes, 1963). In primary elections, the latter receive information about the skills, assets and resources revealed by the candidates, whereby they can reject low-valence presidential runners to choose the 'best' candidate based on their projected competitiveness in the general election.

Candidate valence and electoral viability also increase in salience when there is congruence in policy preferences among the various competitors (Stone and Abramowitz, 1983). In 2012, the candidates' personality profile – broadly defined as the combination of their policy preferences with their presidential credibility or capability – nuanced the political competitive and party system dynamics, and certainly influenced primary election outcomes across a number of cases. In the FG, for instance, a charismatic Mélenchon subjugated his lower-valence opponent Chassaigne in the internal nomination race: despite his participation in the 2005 ECT referendum campaign and successful bid in the 2010 regional elections in Auvergne, the latter suffered a notable deficit in popularity and media visibility at the national level. The relatively high degree of policy coherence within the FG coalition increased the salience of valence variables and the consideration by party members of the electoral viability of their presidential nominee.

The main line of division between the two FG presidential hopefuls was strategic – partisan vs non-partisan – rather than strictly ideological, particularly on economic issues where their main policy positions were for the most part aligned. Personality factors were equally manifest in the FN, where the significance of valence parameters was evidently both 'gendered' and generational, given Marine Le Pen's age (44) and profile as a divorced mother of three.

As noted earlier, in EELV, policy and strategic divergences, party identification and the radical vote by 'hard-core' supporters of the Greens were key factors in Hulot's failure to secure the nomination, which resulted in the selection of a candidate of more limited appeal to the general electorate in the person of Joly. Yet very scarce polling data showed some evidence of Hulot's deficit in valence, in particular in terms of economic credibility. The only comparative poll conducted by IFOP among supporters of the Greens in February 2011 showed that whilst Hulot had a significant lead over Joly on items of closeness to the electorate (60/38 per cent), honesty (69/58) or the ability to embody ecologist values and ideas (84/15), he nevertheless suffered from a lack of presidential credibility (only 43 per cent said he had 'the makings of a President' as opposed to 52 per cent for Joly) and, more importantly, the perceived incapacity to deal with crucial economic and social issues, a policy domain in which he was massively outperformed by his rival (27/71) (IFOP, *Journal du Dimanche*, 4 February 2011).

Finally, in addition to their strategic positioning and political marketing, what about the competitive allocation of valence and policy resources among the PS primary candidates in 2011? In the early stages of the nomination race, the crowning of DSK as favoured PS runner was essentially a choice of stature and competence over policy and left-wing credentials. Whilst benefiting from the international stature in his high-profile position as IMF managing director, DSK was nevertheless perceived by many inside the PS as a detached bourgeois-cosmopolitan liberal and subjected to harsh criticism by the Left wing of the party on account of both his personal distance from the 'realities' of French society and, more importantly, the austerity policies imposed by the Monetary Fund on a number of European countries under his authority. The political communication behind Hollande's official entry into the PS primary was without doubt intended to contrast with the public image of DSK. The decision by Hollande to announce his running for the PS candidacy from his town hall in the small rural city of Tulles reflected his positioning as an entrenched local *notable*, emphasising proximity and simplicity, which would eventually lead to his advocating a 'normal presidency' and a consensual approach to politics breaking away from Sarkozy's confrontational style.

With Hollande occupying the centre stage of the party, both Valls and Montebourg travelled a more centrifugal route towards the Right and Left of the PS, respectively. During the internal campaign, Valls promoted a Blairite economic platform, most notably criticising the 35-hour working week, combined with lay Republicanism and a distinctively tougher line on immigration and crime, which had become his political trademark as mayor of Evry since 2001. At the other end of the party spectrum, Montebourg entered the primary race in November 2010 advocating a more leftist and protectionist economic platform of de-globalisation and cooperative capitalism, in addition to his traditional project for institutional reform and new constitutional checks and balances embedded in his programme for a 'Sixth Republic'. This left little space available to Royal and Aubry, whose candidacies progressively organised more specifically along the partisan/non-partisan line which had structured competition five years earlier. While striving to overcome her public image as 'substitute' for DSK, Aubry was endorsed by the Left wing of the PS as guarantor of partisan and ideological orthodoxy. For her part, Royal found herself isolated on the fringes of the party by both her failure to win the leadership race in 2008 and the haemorrhaging of support for her Reims motion, denying her the resources to replicate her successful bid of 2006.

To a large extent, the strategic positioning by the various PS contenders was reflected in voters' perceptions and, more importantly, those of the primary selectorate consisting of left-wing supporters. Compiled data on all primary polls conducted between January 2010 and October 2011 allow the analysis of the distribution of policy and non-policy credibility factors in the Socialist primary voters' decision. Over the period of time considered here, a total of 36 polls were published covering a wide range of attributes in all main PS candidates across national samples of left-wing sympathisers. The data set includes a variety of items measuring candidate images, which fall into two main categories of 'policy' and 'valence'. On each item, the leading competitor can be identified. For obvious reasons, the data are disaggregated into two successive stages of the primary campaign, prior and subsequent to the arrest of DSK in May 2011 ($N = 10$ and 26 polls, respectively). The analysis is restricted to left-wing sympathisers following the assumption that the relevant population for the PS open primary of 2011 was Left-leaning voters rather than the general electorate or the smaller core

Table 4.5 Percentages of lead on policy and valence credibility polling items in the PS primary candidates among left-wing supporters by pre-/ post-arrest period

% Lead	Hollande	Aubry	Royal	DSK	
Pre-arrest (39)					
Policy	–	41	7	52	100
Valence	–	25	–	75	100
All	–	36	5	59	100
Post-arrest (61)					
Policy	54	46	–	–	100
Valence	74	26	–	–	100
All	66	34	–	–	100

Source: All 36 primary candidate evaluation polls published nationally between January 2010 and October 2011; number of individual items in parentheses; sub-samples of left-wing supporters.

group of PS supporters. The results of this analysis are summarised in Table 4.5.

What this table reveals is a clear reallocation of candidate valence from DSK to Hollande by left-wing supporters across the two critical periods of the PS primary season. In the early stage of the nomination campaign, DSK clearly established himself as a high-valence competitor, taking the lead in no less than 75 per cent of the ratings reported by pollsters. Unsurprisingly, favourable evaluations of the IMF director among Left-leaning voters were particularly high on stature- and competence-related attributes, as well as on his ability to defeat Sarkozy in the presidential election. However, the gap between DSK and Aubry was narrower on policy dimensions, where Aubry would lead in 41 per cent of cases. Perceptions by PS supporters were largely mirroring the portrayal of the two front runners in the French media, with DSK systematically winning the competition on the economy and the broad range of international issues, while Aubry would come ahead of her rival more often on social and environmental issues, her image being 'truly Left wing/Socialist', as well as on personality traits such as closeness to the people.

Comparable data for the post-arrest period show the replication with a moderate amplification of the initial structure of competition for both policy and non-policy variables, with Hollande immediately taking over DSK's status as the high-valence candidate. DSK standing down from the primary race did not significantly alter the image of Aubry among the PS selectorate, nor her ability to lead on crucial non-policy aspects, in more than about a quarter of the credibility ratings. Hollande topped the competition on non-policy capabilities and policy scores in 74 and 54 per cent of the items, respectively, particularly in competence, stature and plausibility as presidential runner where he outperformed his rival in more than 90 per cent of cases. The distribution of resources resembled that of the previous period, with Aubry winning support on social and environmental issues, closeness and left-wing identity, while Hollande would enjoy a more consistent lead on the economy and, perhaps as a more specific personality trait, being 'friendly'.

When contrasted with comparable data for the 2006 primary, the 2011 election displayed a very different pattern of competition over symbolic resources and candidate image constructs. Five years earlier, Royal had achieved high policy and valence scores throughout the whole nomination contest. Looking at the 16 credibility polls released during the year preceding the 2006 membership vote, she had taken the lead in no less than 90 per cent of the cases, with very similar results both in policy domains and in personality traits, leaving virtually no space for her primary rivals. It is striking that in 2011 Royal failed to replicate her victorious campaign of 2006, taking a very limited and short-lived lead in the pre-arrest period of the primary, essentially on social and environmental issues. Similarly, let us note here that Montebourg and Valls were unsuccessful in increasing the salience of their most favourable issue dimensions – for example, immigration and crime for Valls – at least in a way which would have allowed them to establish issue ownership more firmly.

* * *

In the simplest of terms, the identity and thereby personality of the Socialist candidate seems not to have mattered overly in the victory of the Left and the defeat of the UMP incumbent. Paradoxically, we have seen ample evidence that Sarkozy's own personality both did for his chances of re-election in 2012 and equally allowed him to go down with at least some dignity intact from a creditable second-round performance, especially in the light of the inflated polling differential a few months before the ballot. What allowed Hollande to secure victory, framed by an auspicious cooperative mood amongst the parties of the Left, was a programme which offered differentiation and change from that presented to the electorate by the UMP government over the previous five years.

Programmes and ideologies evidently matter in any electoral race for national government. Ostensibly, they mattered more in 2012 in the absence of a standout individual on the Left challenging for the Elysée, and in terms of offering an alternative to the austerity-driven cutbacks of the Right in the economic downturn, the importance of these policies lay in offering change and a brighter short-term future, even if the chances of success for such policies were self-evidently slim. How exactly the different issues and policies presented by the candidates in 2012 played out in competitive terms is what we now turn to in the following chapter.

5
Issues, Policy Debates and Candidate Valence

Any election is defined in part by the policies which attain salience as key decision points for undecided voters. Inevitably, the majority of voters will take the policy position of their favoured candidate through identification or ideological proximity. However, for a small but potentially key section of the electorate, candidate positioning and candidate credibility on these policies will matter. In 2002, the saliency of law and order and immigration, and the mainstream's ineffective positioning on this, ensured a strong enough performance by Jean-Marie Le Pen to progress to the second round. In 2007, the hard Right position adopted by Nicolas Sarkozy and the UMP was not a surprise in itself, but the extent to which this was embedded within the presidential ballot played a significant role in FN vote transfer.

Unsurprisingly, looking at the issue attention cycle and changes in the political agenda since 2007 points to the strength of economic and social issues in France's crisis-ridden polity, in a context marked also by the specific set of constraints imposed on the French presidential agenda by the unfolding of the Eurozone and sovereign debt crisis at the international level. This chapter examines the policy trajectories adopted by the main presidential contenders and the manner in which the latter have adjusted their strategies to this changing economic environment in order to address growing voter preferences for more egalitarian redistributive policies, while simultaneously placing their domestic economic agenda within the new European paradigm of public deficit reduction and fiscal discipline.

A specific focus is first on the strategic means employed by presidential parties to resolve the somewhat antagonistic goals of endorsing a common agenda of budgetary orthodoxy, on the one hand, while achieving the necessary amount of credibility and policy differentiation in the formulation of their economic platforms to maximise their appeal to voters, on the other hand. The former resulted predominantly in essentially symbolic – at times purely rhetorical – campaign acts on international finance regulation and fiscal consolidation. To avoid fragmentation, the established parties strove to downplay European issues which had been electorally costly in the past. In contrast, the campaign exhibited greater polarisation in fiscal and domestic economic policies, which helped Hollande spell out his agenda of 'social fairness' and redistributive demand-oriented economics against Sarkozy's incumbent track record of austerity and failure to deliver on his 2007 pocketbook promises.

The next section then discusses what was perhaps one of the paradoxes of the 2012 campaign. Whilst all minds – voters and elites alike – were almost exclusively set on the economy, the presidential arena saw a significant centrifugal shift on non-economic issues, and underwent what can be regarded as a progressive 'cultural' polarisation of the presidential arena. This pattern of opposition was due in particular to the increasing level of party competition over immigration and national identity resulting from the electoral revival of the FN on the Right of the political spectrum, as well as to the continuation of the move by the French Left – most particularly the PS – towards the libertarian pole of the cultural divide.

1. The primacy of economic issues: Voter expectations, candidate valences and positions

Analyses of campaign polling data show the gap which existed between the mix of domestic microeconomic issues that strongly influenced voter choice in the first round, on the one hand, and the international macroeconomic agenda of state deficit or sovereign debt reduction on the other hand. With respect to the latter, the 2012 campaign certainly presented the highest level of sophistication in the formulation of parties' economic policies, conceptualisation and expert analysis ever observed in French presidential elections, which contrasted somehow with the more 'trivial' pocketbook concerns expressed by voters. The increased specialisation of the campaign meant also that candidate competency and economic solutions took centre stage.

1.1. Popular demand for redistribution of wealth

Unemployment and purchasing power topped the presidential issue agenda, reflecting the deterioration of the labour market and the increasing pressure on household finances since the eruption of the 2008 financial crisis. An emergency 'social summit' was convened on 18 January 2012 to unveil – rather than effectively negotiate – a number of short-term measures intended to respond to the aggravation in the French labour market. This new set of measures comprised an 'employment package' totalling 430 million euros, including a special fund for partial unemployment and a cut in small companies' social charges for young employees, as well as a reinforcement of staff in the public employment-seeking services (Pôle Emploi). In the long run, this plan prefigured what was deemed to be a more radical reform of vocational training. This emergency package to quell unemployment was met by scepticism from the Left, labour representatives and the French public, and criticised by many commentators for its likely limited impact.

A brief glance at the IPSOS/CEVIPOF barometer survey conducted just before the first round shows the primacy of a triumvirate of personal welfare issues in egocentric voter motivations, with purchasing power ranking at 60 per cent followed with pensions (35 per cent) and taxes (32 per cent).[1] Pocketbook concerns were shared in equal proportion by all sectors of the French electorate, including the FN support where immigration only ranked second at 34 per cent. Sociotropically, now, the most prominent issues cited by voters were unsurprisingly the economic crisis (54 per cent), unemployment (43 per cent), public deficit (35 per cent) and purchasing power (29 per cent).

The issue agenda remained remarkably stable throughout the various stages of the campaign. Most notably, the profound shock caused by the Toulouse shootings and the subsequent development of the Merah controversy following the death of the terrorist, which we examine in Chapter 6, did not significantly alter the overall structure of issue priority and voter expectations, showing only a marginal increase in the lower collective prominence of immigration and security issues in the voting public's mind (Figure 5.1).

Looking at the attitudinal distribution of voters on the state–market axis of competition in 2012 suffices in corroborating the intensity of popular demand for more egalitarian economic policies of wealth redistribution, state intervention and protectionism (Table 5.1). Most strikingly, these polling data confirm the strong aspiration by voters to greater material well-being and the improvement of their economic fortunes, with over three-quarters (78 per cent) of the respondents expressing personal financial difficulties, while another two-thirds (65 per cent) would endorse the 'Robin Hood' principle of taking from the rich to ensure social fairness.

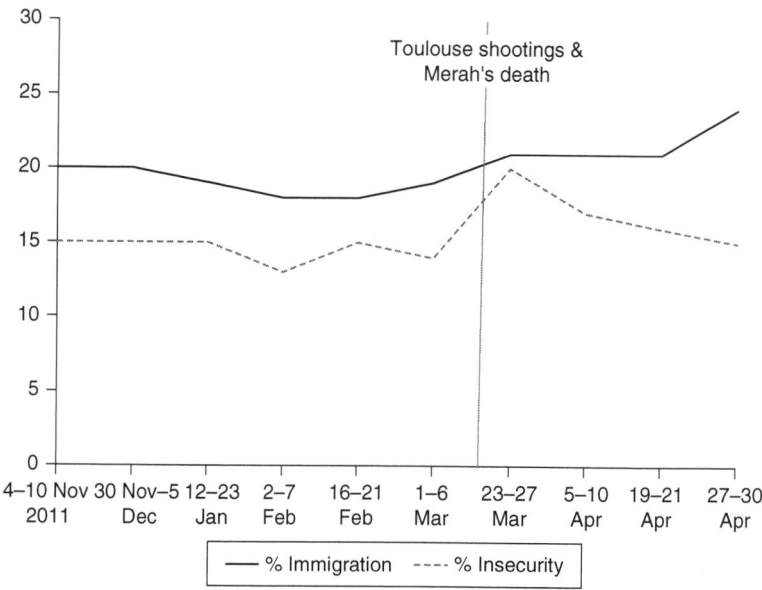

Figure 5.1 Salience of immigration and insecurity issues* before and after the Toulouse shootings

*% who said 'immigration'/'insecurity' was one of their three most important concerns.
Source: Présidoscopie – IPSOS/Logica Business Consulting pour *Le Monde*, le CEVIPOF, la Fondapol et la Fondation Jean Jaurès, wave 9, 19–21 April 2012 (*N* = 4,075 respondents nationally).

Table 5.1 Socio-economic attitudes in the presidential campaign

Item	% Do not agree	% Agree
Each month I wonder how I am going to pay all my bills	21	78
To ensure social justice, one should take from the rich to give to the poor	34	65
The economic consequences of globalisation are extremely negative for France	35	62
All things considered, equality between people is more important than freedom	37	57
Unemployed people could find work if they really wanted to	57	42
One should decrease the number of civil servants	58	40

Source: TNS-SOFRES–TriÉlec, Ministère de l'intérieur, Centre Emile Durkheim – Sciences Po Bordeaux, PACTE – Sciences Po Grenoble and Centre d'Études Européennes – Sciences Po Paris, 2–3 February 2012 (*N* = 1,008).

1.2. International finance as a valence issue in the presidential campaign

At party level, the presidential campaign was hampered by the international context, the unfolding of the debt crisis and the continuing turmoil in the Eurozone. Following the emergence of France's credit rating as a salient political issue during 2011, constraints of budget orthodoxy gained prominence in the economic agenda of the presidentials, as parties converged towards a common platform of fiscal discipline and public deficit reduction. The latter issues were in most cases articulated with elite rhetoric on the 'dangers' of unbridled economic globalisation under the yoke of international financial markets, certainly as a means of maximising their electoral appeal to voters in the post-2008 context. Whilst at the centre of public debates on fiscal consolidation, European integration largely remained, as will be argued, a 'sleeping giant' in the 2012 presidential campaign.[2]

1.2.1. Party convergence on budget deficit reduction

In the second half of 2011, the defence of France's triple A was made a national priority by the government, which announced a number of extraordinary budgetary measures to confront the sovereign debt crisis. On 13 January 2012, the downgrading by Standard & Poor's of France's credit rating by one notch represented a political blow for Sarkozy and was immediately slammed by the Socialist Party as the mark of failure of his economic and financial policies since 2007, notwithstanding an actual reduction in public deficit to 90.8 billion euros in 2011 (at 5.2 per cent of the GDP) down from 148.8 in the previous year.

Inevitably, the downgrade had an equally negative impact on the Socialist front runner and the other candidates' margins for manoeuvre. It clearly conditioned their ability to manipulate campaign promises of generous state spending after the election. With the exception of the extreme left, all presidential candidates were therefore forced to situate themselves within the framework of budget orthodoxy, and to offer credible plans to tackle public deficits while carefully avoiding any reference to austerity measures which would inevitably be electorally costly. Like in 2007, the latter issues were central to Bayrou's presidential bid and the definition of his issue profile. In mid-January, the centrist candidate lifted the veil on his strategic setting of 2015 as the target for elimination of structural deficit. His model included an immediate reduction of 10 billion euros during 2012, then 30 billion for each of the three following years.[3]

For his part, Sarkozy pledged to eliminate France's chronic budget deficit in 2016 and return the country to a budget surplus in 2017. His commitment to fiscal orthodoxy was further emphasised by his promise to enshrine his idea of a 'golden rule' of a balanced budget in the Constitution after the election. Although hardly a realistic plan given the existing balance of power in the French parliament, this was tactically intended to put the PS's vows of budget discipline to a more stringent political test. While rejecting the notion and attacking his UMP rival on his responsibility for the increase in France's public debt during his presidency, Hollande promised to match Sarkozy's plan to reduce the budget deficit to 3 per cent of gross domestic product in 2013, anticipating its elimination in 2017. On the far right, the FN sought to enhance its sectoral expertise and governmental credibility. In line with the party's strategy of 'normalisation', Marine Le Pen's campaign prioritised economic and financial issues and strove to formulate a set of more credible policy stances. These spanned an array of debt reduction measures which were intended to mark the party's difference with what was deemed a general move towards austerity by her presidential rivals. Besides taking the country out of the Eurozone, Le Pen's programme of budget deficit reduction included drastic cuts in the alleged cost of immigration, a plan to eradicate social fraud and cancelling France's general contribution to the European budget.

1.2.2. Waging the 'war on finance'

Party convergence towards budgetary orthodoxy was notably accompanied by the deployment of a repertoire of tools on economic globalisation, whereby most presidential candidates would endorse negative attitudes towards the global markets and the so-called 'world of international finance'. In France, economic globalisation has been traditionally regarded as a threat to the post-war model of social welfare (Meunier, 2003) and negative attitudes towards the internationalisation of the French economy have been widespread since the early 2000s. The symbolic construction of globalisation had been particularly evident from the deployment of elites' narratives on the world economy during and immediately after the 2005 ECT referendum campaign (Ivaldi, 2006).

The 2008 financial crisis certainly accentuated the connotation of the internationalisation of capital markets as a negative valence issue, both at the elite and the mass public level. During the course of the 2012 campaign, no less than 78 per cent of the French said globalisation was a 'bad thing' for their country, while another three-quarters of the respondents believed that it would have a negative impact on the number of jobs.[4] At the party level, this resulted in a *recitativo obbligato* of economic protectionism, moralisation of capitalism and international financial regulation, which was pervasive to all parties across the political spectrum. Without much surprise, the fiercest condemnation of the 'world of international finance' came of course from the radical Left, whose narratives of the imperative to break free from the 'domination of financial capitalism' would gradually infuse the political agenda of mainstream competitors. In his first public rally in Le Bourget on 22 January 2012, Hollande showed signs of shifting his campaign to the Left, in harsh criticism of the 'world of finance' while simultaneously stressing his love for 'people rather than money', reminiscent of Mitterrand's historic tirade against the 'power of finance that corrupts'. Emulating Mélenchon's concept of 'what is human first' (L'Humain d'abord), the Socialist contender had already addressed all those who have been 'abandoned, stigmatised or relegated' in his first official campaign meeting a few days before. In more concrete terms, Hollande would put forward a number of measures that were already in the party manifesto adopted by the PS in June 2011, such as pledges to separate the banks' loan-making businesses from their more speculative operations, to ban stock options or to impose stricter limitation on big bonus payouts.

The cross-cleavage propagation of the anti-finance agenda of the Left was revealed in a number of policy initiatives and proposals by candidates on the Right of the political spectrum. Most striking was perhaps the displacement of the FN in competitive space, a move caused primarily by the party's shift to the Left on the economic dimension under Marine Le Pen's leadership. Consistent with the progressive endorsement by the FN of anti-globalisation and protectionist policy features since the mid-1990s, the 2012 campaign by Le Pen participated actively in orchestrating the vilification of global market capitalism through a large array of anti-globalisation measures including temporary nationalisations of vital strategic companies, reinstating protectionist barriers, taxes on company relocations, a European tax on financial exchanges and the fight against corporate tax evasion by France's largest companies.

Similarly, the manipulation of anti-globalisation themes was discernible in Sarkozy's pledge to create a new minimum business tax on the largest companies – most particularly those listed on the CAC 40 – as well as his endorsement during the final stage of the campaign of Royal's 2007 proposal to suppress tax relief for companies relocating outside

France. Other attempts at issue triangulation were revealed in the reiteration by the UMP candidate of his 2007 promise to ban so-called 'golden parachutes', as well as his advocating a 'Google tax' on online advertising revenues and a somewhat symbolic promise of a crackdown on wealthy French tax exiles. The latter proposal, with a potential levy of 500 million euros according to Sarkozy, had originally been formulated by Mélenchon and met with the approval of a large majority (71 per cent) of the French.[5] The idea was then endorsed by Hollande, albeit in a more elusive way.

Finally, the positions taken by the main presidential contenders on a possible tax on financial transactions – the so-called 'Tobin' or 'Robin Hood' tax – revealed further the construction of a cross-partisan agenda of international finance regulation. This proposal had been on the Socialist programme since 2009 and re-emerged in Hollande's presidential platform in the form of a tax on all financial exchanges, including derivative products, which would be levied across the EU, based on the existing proposal made by the Party of European Socialists (PES). The Socialist proposal echoed the legislation voted by the right-wing parliamentary majority in February 2012, which imposed a 0.1 per cent tax on transactions in companies headquartered in France. During the campaign, Sarkozy pledged that he would also increase taxes on share dividends.

1.2.3. Still a 'sleeping giant': The pacification of the European cleavage

As had already been the case in 2007, European issues only interfered very partially with the party system dynamics of the presidential election, showing both the primacy of domestic economic debates and, more importantly perhaps, the strategic ability by mainstream actors to develop low-profile campaigns to downplay somewhat the otherwise potentially damaging issue of European integration. The presidential campaign saw therefore a low-magnitude and only temporary displacement of the main party divisions towards the more situational 'mainstream/periphery' line of division characteristic of the European dimension in the French party system.

The unfolding of the procedure for the ratification of the treaty establishing the European Stability Mechanism (ESM) revealed the convergence between the incumbent UMP and the PS within the traditional 'pro-EU cartel' against the disparate coalition of all other political forces in the system, with the extreme left (LO, NPA, FG), the Greens and the nationalist Right (FN, DLR) openly campaigning against the ESM. Parties of the mainstream were faced with the need to secure support from the more eurosceptic segments of their electoral clientele while simultaneously avoiding intra-party division and opening too wide a political space for protest actors on their flanks.

The French Left failed to present a completely united front, however, displaying the specific structure of inter-party competition on the European dimension together with internal dissent and factionalism in the PS – clearly reminiscent, albeit in a more attenuated form, of the disastrous episode of intra-party turmoil during the 2005 European referendum. In an effort to accommodate the Left wing of his party and to prevent too many Socialist supporters from turning to Mélenchon's anti-austerity position, Hollande made rather vague unilateral promises that he would seek to renegotiate the deal on the euro agreed in December 2011, stressing his demands for growth policies to be included in the battle to save the European currency. In January, a number of European leaders – including the newly elected Socialist president of the European parliament, Martin Schulz – criticised the position of the PS candidate[6] and deemed such renegotiating of the euro deal impossible, while pointing to the lack of political support for Hollande's proposal to create eurobonds. Nationally, the critical ambiguity in the PS position over Europe was revealed in the parliamentary vote on the ESM of February 2012, where the PS called for abstention yet failed to prevent a number of Socialist MPs from voting against the treaty.

Strategic ambiguity culminated on the Right of the political spectrum as Sarkozy strove to replicate his successful European campaign of 2007. Five years earlier, his promise of a new 'simplified treaty', combined with a soft eurosceptic stance and an anti-establishment appeal, had helped the UMP leader put the European giant back to sleep in spite of the fierce opposition which had developed in the 2005 ECT referendum. Despite his personal commitment to fiscal discipline and consolidation, the 2012 campaign witnessed yet another shift towards a more eurosceptic stance by the outgoing President in an effort to distance himself from the general move towards austerity policies in Europe – which he had previously supported – as a means to contain the electoral rise of the FN on his Right flank. A first significant protectionist turn occurred in the Villepinte rally in March, where Sarkozy publicly criticised the EU for its alleged 'laissez-faire' free-trade agenda, and demanded the passing of a 'Buy European Act', delivering an ultimatum to the EU by threatening to withdraw France from the Schengen agreements.[7] Presenting his electoral programme in April, Sarkozy called for a freeze on France's contribution to the European Union budget, reflecting the intensification of the presidential campaign. Repeating his 2007 strategic move of criticising the ECB's monetary policies, Sarkozy also reopened the debate over the role and power of the European Central Bank in (not) supporting economic growth, a controversial position which led Prime Minister Fillon to immediately reaffirm France's commitment to the independence of the ECB.

1.3. Compared economic credibility in presidential candidates

The growing characterisation of economic performance and public debt reduction as trans-nationalised valence issues[8] evidently increased the need for candidates to gain economic credibility, an area in which the outgoing President could assume an advantage, as revealed in the many attempts by the UMP to undermine Hollande's competence and capability to effectively confront a period of deep economic troubles. In the light of France's economic gloom, deep social pessimism and profound voter disenchantment with political parties from both sides of the spectrum, which we have addressed in Chapter 2, however, such efforts could have been deemed rather vain as a majority of voters seemed to give little if not no credit at all to the extensive economic platforms put together by parties in the presidential arena. According to a series of CSA campaign polls, only 40 per cent of voters said Hollande's economic programme was credible. Comparable figures were 44 and 37 for Sarkozy and Bayrou, respectively, and down to a mere 18 per cent for Le Pen.[9]

Within this general low-credibility framing of the campaign, a brief analysis of the competitive allocation by voters of candidate policy and non-policy credibility from the aforementioned IPSOS/CEVIPOF survey data shows nevertheless that Hollande would take a strong lead over Sarkozy on a number of selected personality traits – that is, being friendly, honest and sincere – as well as in terms of his perceived greater closeness to voters – 'he understands the problems of people like you'. The personality style emerging from Hollande's polling figures was certainly consistent with his previous portrayal by left-wing primary voters in 2011, and corroborated his strategic attempt to present himself as a 'normal' candidate. In contrast, Sarkozy had a clear advantage on his main rival in terms of 'presidential stature' (65 as opposed to 46 per cent for Hollande) and the perception by voters of his dynamic character (74 against 47 per cent). Both candidates presented very similar levels of general competence among voters, a valence attribute which they shared together with MODEM's president Bayrou, as opposed to the lack of perceived presidential capability in other third-party runners Mélenchon, Le Pen and Joly. As shown above, despite the wealth of technical financial and economic data in her economic platform, Le Pen was handicapped by her lack of credentials on the economy, while only a quarter (26 per cent) would support her plan to leave the euro, which had become the cornerstone of the FN presidential platform and a precondition of its generous redistributive policies.[10]

Looking more closely now at the various components of competence allocated to the two front runners from Table 5.2 shows distinct presidential credibility profiles. Positive endorsements of Sarkozy's capability were in the majority across all items of presidential and international stature. Some of the outgoing President's highest ratings were also found in the specific issues of immigration and insecurity, which have long served as strong political markers of his 'self-assertive' Right, echoing his shift further to the Right during the campaign (see below). Hollande on the other hand would come ahead of his UMP rival on the array of domestic socio-economic issues – education, welfare, health, pensions – as well as the anticipated ability to achieve greater social justice and fair redistribution. One interesting story here is the strong

Table 5.2 Compared components of presidential credibility in Hollande and Sarkozy

% *Is the most capable of* …	Hollande	Sarkozy	DK
Reducing social inequalities	70	26	4
Improving the educational system	69	28	3
Improving the health system	64	33	3
Conducting a fairer and more effective fiscal policy	61	35	4
Augmenting purchasing power	61	35	4
Reducing unemployment	59	37	4
Guaranteeing the future of pensions	55	42	3
Reducing public deficits	48	48	4
Protecting the French from the economic crisis	47	49	4
Confronting the economic and financial crisis	44	52	4
Improving the functioning of the EU	42	54	4
Taking a presidential stature	40	58	2
Making difficult decisions	39	58	3
Reducing insecurity	38	59	3
Confronting an international diplomatic or military crisis	35	62	3
Fighting illegal immigration	31	66	3

DK = Don't Know

Source: Présidoscopie – IPSOS/Logica Business Consulting pour *Le Monde*, le CEVIPOF, la Fondapol et la Fondation Jean Jaurès, wave 9, 19–21 April 2012 ($N = 4,075$ respondents nationally).

tendency to report uncertainty about future economic performances: both candidates would fail to garner a majority of support on the two key macroeconomic issues of public deficit reduction and protecting the French from the economic crisis. In contrast, Hollande would clearly outperform Sarkozy over the projected capability to augment their purchasing power and to reduce unemployment, which as suggested above represented the most crucial issues for vast sectors of the 2012 electorate.

1.4. Areas of Left–Right policy differentiation

Simultaneously, the prominence of microeconomic issues indicated that the respective qualities of presidential candidates would also be prospectively evaluated in their differential ability to entrench budgetary austerity measures in fiscal and economic policies which could effectively address voter preferences for social justice, as well as a fairer redistribution of wealth and increasingly scarce welfare resources. That specific credibility and valence profiles were found amongst the main candidates' programmes indicates that voters might have made their presidential evaluation not only in a strict valence sense but also on the basis of differences perceptible in the political positions taken by the main parties during the campaign. Within the boundaries of the budgetary orthodoxy paradigm imposed on candidates, Left–Right policy differentiation was discernible in party positions on the classic state–market dimension, with a strong focus on fiscal policies.

1.4.1. *Fiscal policies*

Whilst the commitment by all candidates to getting France's budget in order undoubtedly increased convergence across parties of the mainstream – with the two front runners endorsing tax rises of about 40 billion euros – fiscal policies served as a vehicle for policy differentiation both in positive and in negative terms. With respect to the latter, Sarkozy's Travail, Emploi et Pouvoir d'Achat TEPA fiscal package of 2007 had become the main target of the government critics in the French political debate and was regarded as further evidence of the outgoing President's incorrigible penchant for the wealthy. The continuation in particular of substantial tax cuts for the wealthiest after the 2008 financial crisis, together with some hard-hitting austerity measures which had been put forward just before the election, paved the way for Hollande's pledge for greater fiscal justice.

In policy terms, the Socialists defended a more egalitarian agenda of 'redistributive progressive taxation' (Clift, 2013), which revolved around prioritising economic and social 'fairness' with a claim of taking some of the burden away from the low- and middle-class households.[11] Redistribution of wealth was therefore central to the Socialist fiscal platform, which included a significant array of tax increases, most notably an additional 45 per cent tax band for the highest-income brackets, an increase in the inheritance tax, the return to higher and progressive rates for the wealth tax (ISF) which had been obliterated by the government reform of 2011, the suppression of Sarkozy's so-called 'fiscal shield' and '*TVA sociale*' (see below), the ceiling to family quotient in the richest households and a plan to align taxes on capital and assets with those on labour while reducing some of the existing loopholes in France's fiscal maze. Additionally, the Socialist candidate endorsed price control, pledging in particular to impose a ceiling on rents in costly urban areas, and suggesting that petrol prices should be temporarily blocked and that the government should reintroduce the defunct 'floating petrol tax' (*TIPP flottante*), a proposal which was opposed by the government and deemed both 'costly' and 'ineffective' (*Le Monde*, 19 January 2012).

Highly symbolic of the new fiscal trajectory set by the Socialists was of course Hollande's vow to enact a 75 per cent top marginal tax rate on earnings over 1 million euros. The latter came as a complete surprise in early March 2012 and soon became the focus of the presidential campaign as well as the subject of harsh criticism by the Right, the MEDEF employer association and a number of sports millionaires. Whilst probably debatable in terms of its effective financial impact and levy, the measure certainly had a strong political rationale as regards the development of the campaign. The announcement would allow Hollande to counter the electoral rise of Mélenchon on his Left flank while simultaneously helping him reclaim control of the presidential agenda. With over 60 per cent of the French approving his proposal, Hollande would also consolidate his first-round electoral performance and ensure stronger political support from the more leftist factions in the Socialist Party.[12] To his Left, the ideological escalation in the fiscal platform by the FG candidate increased policy polarisation, with Mélenchon putting forward proposals of a legal maximum annual income at 360,000 euros with a 100 per cent tax band for all earnings above that limit, together with massive rises in taxes on personal and corporate assets.

The package defended by the Socialist front runner would contrast sharply with the relative paucity of fiscal policies presented by his right-wing rival. Besides a negative campaign against the staggering tax blow (*matraquage fiscal*) that would allegedly result from implementing Hollande's programme, Sarkozy had little room for manoeuvre in his role as incumbent, and his re-election bid was significantly hindered by the already devastating impact of the unpopular pension and budgetary reforms conducted by his government in the months that preceded the election. In early January 2012, the UMP campaign took a first decisive turn after the announcement by Sarkozy of his intention to raise VAT in order to bolster the competitiveness of France's economy. Following the budget-cutting efforts of 2011, this appeared to be a very risky political move threatening to backfire on its instigator[13] and was fiercely opposed by all trade unions, with the notable exception of MEDEF, as well as by all opposition parties. In February, another significant political blow was delivered to Sarkozy's campaign by the revelation that the freeze on the income tax scale, which had been part of the austerity package of November 2011, would result in an additional 100,000–200,000 low-revenue households being liable for income tax.

That Sarkozy would increasingly find himself isolated to the Right of the fiscal spectrum was further evidenced by the FN's concomitant shift to the Left on tax policies, as Le Pen's party moved further away from its traditional neo-Poujadist core of tax cuts and small government policies, advocating higher income tax rates for the wealthiest at 46 per cent, a more progressive scale for the wealth tax as well as higher VAT rates on luxury goods.

1.4.2. Demand- vs supply-side economics

Hollande's strategy of fiscal redistribution was embedded in a general growth-oriented economic platform putting a stronger emphasis on state intervention through a set of measures which would at times be criticised for being incompatible with the candidate's pledge to otherwise achieve public deficit reduction. In a sense, policy coherence was somewhat higher in the microeconomics set out by the UMP candidate. Notwithstanding his tactical manipulation of the 'international finance regulation' repertoire of the Left, Sarkozy's programme could largely be regarded as the continuation, if not intensification of the supply-side economics upon which the Fillon government had relied since 2007, which of course reflected the narrowness of the opportunity structure available to the incumbent in the presidential race.

Consistent with his 'hard-Right' electioneering on cultural issues (see below), Sarkozy strove to frame his presidential bid with core values of the Right, most notably 'work' and 'effort', and a liberal labour market policy, resulting in promises to curb the alleged excesses of France's generous welfare system – the so-called *'assistanat'* – a theme which had been borrowed from the Droite sociale's agenda of putting the welfare 'bums' back to work. This was revealed in particular in Sarkozy's proposal to call for a referendum on his plan to make vocational retraining mandatory for the unemployed and force them to accept jobs accordingly, as well as in his proposals to enforce seven hours of compulsory work weekly for beneficiaries of the RSA and to reduce unemployment benefits over time. In line with the liberalisation agenda of the mainstream Right since 2007, Sarkozy's bid also included an additional stimulus by a cut in France's labour costs for those in the lowest income brackets, offset by a rise of 1.6 percentage points in VAT, as well as tax exemption for small entrepreneurs in cases of zero turnover, a programme of zero-rate loans to small businesses by the existing OSEO public investment bank and the exemption of social contributions in employment contracts for workers over the age of 55.

That the outgoing President was willing to continue deregulation policies was shown by his relentless criticism of the 35-hour working week and his promoting new competitiveness agreements which would allow for more flexibility in wage and work-time negotiations at company level. Simultaneously, Sarkozy showed his intention to extend the RGPP policy to regional administrations, most notably by imposing a reduction in the number of local civil servants similar in size to that implemented by his government at national level. Most strikingly, however, the former champion of purchasing power would fail to formulate credible policies of income growth similar to his 2007 'work more to earn more' mantra, preventing him from replicating his successful work-ethic strategy of five years earlier.

Hollande's economic platform was on the other hand shaped by the existing *rapports de forces* both inside the PS and at its margins. In line with the Colbertist tradition of the French Left, his economic stimulus package was based on state intervention and went as far as promising additional public spending to create jobs and bolster demand to reinvigorate France's slowing economy. Focus was on the establishment of a public investment bank to support small businesses (PME/PMI), a strategy of economic voluntarism which clearly resonated with the programmatic elements in the platform of re-industrialisation defended by Montebourg during the Socialist primaries, and whose call for 'de-globalisation' had garnered a substantial share of the vote by left-wing supporters. The multiplication of lay-off plans in the industrial sector, epitomised by the dramatic situation of the ArcelorMittal steel plant in Florange, led the Socialist candidate to advocate a law which would forbid closure in cases where there would be potential buyers, a pledge complemented by promises to make lay-offs more costly for profitable companies and to increase social contributions for those 'abusing' temporary work contracts. Finally, Hollande committed to enacting adjustable marginal rates for corporate tax according to company size, with a reduced rate for smaller businesses.

The main employment policies of the Socialist runner had been laid out in the PS's programme unveiled in June 2011. The party manifesto called for a new model of economic development to bolster France's economic growth and international competitiveness, which included a greater emphasis on education and training, as well as the plan to create 300,000 state-subsidised jobs for youths, a proposal which was reminiscent of the *'emplois jeunes'* by the *gauche plurielle* under Jospin's government in 1997. Hollande's approach to addressing in particular endemic under-employment of both youths and older people in France was subsumed in his own project for a 'generational contract' – with an announced target of 500,000 – and his campaign pledge to create 60,000 public service jobs in the educational sector through the redeployment of the systematic RGPP rules.[14]

Despite the constraints of fiscal discipline imposed on all parties of government, Hollande spelled out an ambitious agenda of public spending, which most notably included the PS's popular promise of a return to retirement rights at 60 for those with long careers. The Socialist front runner also called for a modest increase in both the annual school allowance and the minimum wage (SMIC) after the election, with a plan to index the SMIC on future economic growth. This certainly helped the Socialist candidate's more controversial move of repealing tax breaks on overtime, one of the most emblematic measures of Sarkozy's TEPA fiscal scheme in 2007.

Both Hollande and Sarkozy would find themselves under pressure from their more radical competitors. The leftist agenda of state intervention and wealth redistribution largely transcended the traditional delineation of the Left and the Right, to specify to some extent an increasingly converging populist agenda on the economy in the FG and the FN, due mostly to the displacement of the latter on that particular axis of competition. Mélenchon advocated generous redistribution measures, with promises of substantial increases in the SMIC and a pledge to abolish all the pension reforms conducted by right-wing governments since 2003. He also called for a ban on the so-called 'stock-market' lay-offs and for the state to intervene in strategic sectors. This was echoed by Le Pen's vow to augment all salaries in the lowest brackets of income and reinstate a return to retirement at 60 with a full pension, as well as by her endorsement of nationalisations and state interventions in sectors deemed of vital national importance.

2. The 'cultural polarisation' of the presidential agenda

Whilst there was a great deal of evidence that the economy would be decisive in the outcome of the election, the 2012 campaign saw crucial strategic shifts in the building of their issue profiles by the candidates, leading to a significant process of 'cultural polarisation' of the presidential agenda – that is, a displacement of party competition from the economic to the cultural dimension and its ideological polarisation.[15] In spite of their relatively low salience for voters (see above), cultural issues of immigration or national identity in particular came to occupy the front pages during the campaign, mostly as a consequence of the electoral resuscitation of the FN and the increased level of inter-party competition on the Right of the political spectrum. The endorsement by the PS of a libertarian agenda further increased ideological polarisation on the cultural dimension of conflict.

2.1. The mainstreaming of FN policies

Since the mid-1980s, the core themes of the FN have been central to party competition on the Right pole of French politics. Moves towards more repressive immigration and crime policies have been regarded as a response by the moderate right to the electoral entrenchment of the FN (Schain, 2006; Bale, 2008). In 2007, the tactical arrogation by Sarkozy of the cultural agenda of the far right was a key factor to his success (Perrineau, 2009). During his presidency, immigration and criminality issues continued to top the governmental agenda and gained unprecedented legislative salience, while the UMP was severely criticised for adopting postures of the extreme right (Marthaler, 2008).

The electoral revival of the FN in the 2010 and 2011 local elections accentuated further the salience of the far right's agenda, prompting the ruling majority to try and re-establish firmer control over immigration and law-and-order issues. As suggested earlier in this book, the polarising course taken by Sarkozy's strategy was embodied in his highly controversial Grenoble speech of August 2010. With the Right progressively moving away from the managerial labour-oriented *immigration choisie*, issues of national identity, Islam and multiculturalism became central to the immigration policy framework of the UMP majority, which ventured deeper into FN territory by linking immigration issues with crime or welfare provision.

In 2012, there were strong strategic incentives for Sarkozy to try manipulating the issue agenda of the presidentials by pushing polarising cultural issues. First and foremost, if successful, such a tactical diversion

stronger focus on Islam and issues of multiculturalism more generally – '*communautarisme*' in the French context. This was revealed for instance in Claude Guéant's statement on 'civilisations', Henri Guaino's definition of immigration as 'a problem' or Sarkozy's publicly reaffirming the 'Christian roots' of the country to denounce the 'communitarist pressure' by Islam.[16] Second, the UMP campaign progressively revealed Sarkozy's partial endorsement of the FN's traditional agenda of differential nativism, which until then had represented an un-crossable line of demarcation between the mainstream and the far right. One crucial element in the vilipending by Sarkozy of the Schengen agreements during the campaign was precisely the polemical articulation of immigration with social welfare provisions.[17] Symbolically, Sarkozy tried also to reach out to the *pieds-noirs* community – an estimated 3 million voters – by refusing to acknowledge France's responsibility for the Algerian war.

In 2012, Sarkozy's immigration platform continued to absorb the core policy preferences of the FN. The UMP candidate pledged to cut immigration by half over the next presidential term, impose stricter control on family reunions, limit welfare benefits for legal migrants and force a revision of the Schengen accords at the European level. In policy terms, this strong emphasis on restrictive measures represented a significant departure from the general framework of *immigration choisie* around which the making of immigration policies had revolved since 2003. In addition, Sarkozy marked his opposition both to giving voting rights to foreigners in local elections, and to what he deemed a plan of 'massive regularisation' by the PS. The demagogic escalation in the UMP candidate's immigration bid was revealed in his call for a national referendum on changing the administrative rules to facilitate repatriation of illegal migrants, a proposal which nevertheless received 59 per cent support in public opinion (TNS-SOFRES–i>Télé, 9 February 2012).[18] The proposal was embedded in the more general populist position taken by the UMP candidate, who endorsed the idea of extending the use of referendums to policy-making in order to 'give voice back to the French people…who have been dispossessed of their power by the elites, the trade unions and the political parties' (*Le Monde*, 15 February 2012).

In the early stage of the campaign, Sarkozy's tactical move on the libertarian-authoritarian dimension was facilitated somewhat by the relative downplaying by the FN of its own themes, as the focus of Le Pen's presidential bid was predominantly on gaining more visibility and economic credibility. The failure of the latter strategy, together with flatlining polls, led Le Pen, however, to promptly reorient her campaign and reassert issue ownership to conform to a more extreme position on the cultural axis. The FN's counteroffensive was launched at the Strasbourg meeting of February 2012, where Le Pen severely attacked Sarkozy's record on immigration and insecurity, while simultaneously repositioning her party more firmly on identity and Islam, as revealed in the short-lived halal controversy. In resuming her party's near-zero immigration policies, Le Pen advocated drastic cuts in legal immigration, a ban on regularisations, the suppression of free medical assistance to migrants and the conservation of her party's core principle of national preference. The Toulouse shootings, to which we return in the next chapter, provided Le Pen with the opportunity to point out the progression in France's suburbs of what she deemed a 'green fascism' fostered by 'massive immigration' and the 'hatred of the French people', and to pledge that she would 'put radical Islam down on its knees' (*Le Monde*, 25 March 2012).

The centrifugal shift revealed in Marine Le Pen's first-round score clearly accentuated further the rightward trajectory by Sarkozy in the run-off campaign. Immediately after the first round, the UMP candidate bestowed further legitimacy upon the FN (see Chapter 3) and emphasised key far right issues such as immigration, security and company relocations, while calling for the support of all 'patriotic' voters, who, he said, 'were concerned with preserving their way of life' (*Le Monde*, 23 April 2012). The UMP intensified the negative campaign against Hollande's promise to give voting rights to foreigners in municipal elections, evidently as a red flag for FN voters, while Sarkozy's partisans went as far as launching a claim that 700 mosques across the country had called for a vote in favour of the Socialist candidate. At policy level, Sarkozy publicly endorsed Le Pen's proposal to extend the presumption of innocence to police officers in their line of duty, in the form of a new 'presumption of self-defence'.

The ideological polarisation on the Right of the political spectrum contrasted with the permanence of a more balanced approach towards immigration in the Socialist Party, whereby the PS had certainly moved away from the more expansive control policies of the Mitterrand era while simultaneously managing to maintain a higher level of policy consistency in the area of immigrant integration. With regards to immigration control, first, Hollande distanced himself from the other candidates of the Left by advocating a reduction in the number of legal migrants admitted to France every year, together with the establishment by the French Parliament of immigration quotas for foreign workers. There was evidence on the other hand that the PS had not entirely removed its core integrationist preferences. In policy terms, this was revealed for instance in Hollande's intention to enact voting rights for foreigners, his pledge for more transparent criteria of eligibility in regularisation procedures, his promise to ban the detention of minors in migration transit zones and his commitment to repeal the Guéant memo on foreign students. Symbolically, the Socialist front runner called for the word *race* – an extremely controversial term in France – to be removed from the first article of the Constitution.

A similar conclusion applies to the positions taken by candidates on law-and-order issues, which as suggested earlier had only limited electoral salience in the 2012 presidential campaign. Hollande certainly strove to downplay a potentially harmful issue, which had cost the PS a severe electoral setback in the 2002 presidentials, while also addressing the traditional accusations of 'laxity' and 'naivety' by the Right. A first move to the Right had occurred in the 2007 campaign with Royal taking unorthodox positions on security and crime. The party could also expound its extensive experience of dealing with security issues at the local level, which was well embodied in Manuel Valls' 'tough on crime' personal profile during the primary campaign of 2011. Hollande's law-and-order platform was based upon principles of prevention and dissuasion, and included key measures such as the reinstating of Jospin's proximity police – albeit with more power of intervention – and the implementation of new Priority Security Zones (ZSPs). Departure from the repressive agenda of the Right was notable in the pledge by the Socialist runner to abrogate mandatory minimum sentences (*peines plancher*), to increase the number of educational juvenile detention centers and to fight racial profiling and prejudice in police ID checks.

Hollande's approach to security issues contrasted with the permanence of the populist repertoire in Sarkozy's campaign, whose political manipulation of emotional responses to crime and violence in French society had already been central to his 2007 presidential bid. While advertising the crime-cutting track record of his presidency, the UMP candidate accentuated his conservative and zero-tolerance programme. Sarkozy called for yet another reform of laws for youth offenders, the suppression of family allowances for school absentees, the generalisation of lay juries, the extension of the scope for minimum sentencing, life sentences for sexual crimes as well as a right of appeal for victims and their families both in criminal courts and during parole proceedings. During the campaign, the UMP parliamentary majority also adopted a provisional law reinstating the so-called 'double sentence', allowing for the deportation of foreign criminals.

2.2. The Left's agenda of cultural liberalisation

The polarisation on non-economic issues was increased by the position taken by Hollande and the Socialists on the cultural dimension of conflict, and their pushing an agenda of cultural modernisation which revolved around the two key issues of same-sex marriage and voting rights for foreigners, as well as including a number of gender equality policy proposals. This position was consistent with the polarising strategy pursued by the Left in France since the early 1980s, whereby the PS in particular had progressively moved towards the libertarian pole of the cultural axis (Bornschier, 2012), reflecting in part the structural change in its electoral support and the development of a more urban, younger, educated middle-class clientele – the so-called *bourgeois bohèmes*.

As in 1997, the PS entering into a coalition with the Greens certainly contributed to the perpetuation of the cultural liberalisation agenda in the 2012 campaign, although the Socialist candidate would keep his distance from some of the more controversial policies in the libertarian platform of the Greens, such as for instance the legalisation of cannabis. Finally, by increasing the salience of divisive positional issues on the cultural axis, Hollande incontestably achieved a higher degree of cohesion and ideological convergence among parties of the Left, while simultaneously revealing the more fragmented positions in the mainstream Right. The centrist segments of the UMP had already expressed their criticism of the so-called 'Grenoble strategy' of flirting with the FN in 2010, and would certainly be less than convinced on Sarkozy's uncompromising line on gay marriage or foreigners' voting rights during the presidential campaign.

At party level, the polarising impact of Hollande's backing of gay marriage and adoption, as well as the use of assisted reproductive technology for lesbian couples, was evidenced by the strong conservative and morally illiberal stance taken by the UMP on the issue, as revealed in Sarkozy's speech in Marseille where the outgoing President severely attacked his Socialist contender for 'putting a fad before France's identity [by] weakening the values of family and marriage which are deeply rooted in our collective consciousness' (*Le Monde*, 19 February 2012). However, public opinion polls displayed shifting attitudes about same-sex marriage and, more strikingly perhaps, adoption by homosexual couples. With respect to the former issue, 63 per cent of the French said they were in favour of gay marriage during the campaign (compared with 48 per cent in a survey conducted in 2000). Left-wing supporters would endorse the proposal by a 74 per cent majority, as opposed to 51 per cent on the Right, the latter figure showing the greater level of fragmentation in Sarkozy's electoral clientele. A more dramatic change was revealed in attitudes towards adoption, which received a 56 per cent public support, against 28 per cent in a 1998 poll (BVA–*Le Parisien*, 14 January 2012).

Similarly, party polarisation was high on the divisive issue of voting rights for foreigners in municipal elections. The latter proposal had formed part of the PS cultural agenda since 1972 but had failed to translate into actual legislation under periods of Socialist governments, due to a variety of political, institutional and public opinion factors. It had been the subject of a formal vote by left-wing majorities on two occasions in the National Assembly in 2000 and in the Senate in 2011. Voting rights for foreigners had been endorsed by the PS in its party manifesto in May 2011 and had progressed into Hollande's presidential agenda. During the campaign, the Socialist proposal received a 62 per cent majority support in the voting public (TNS-SOFRES–TriÉlec, 2–3 February 2012), but was met with fierce criticism by both the UMP and the FN, showing the ideological connivance between the far right and the rightist factions of the presidential party.[19] Whilst he had personally endorsed the measure twice in 2001 and 2005, Sarkozy strongly opposed the PS proposal during the presidential campaign, pointing to 'risks of communitarism', a position expressed in inflammatory terms by Guéant, who claimed for instance that 'voting rights would result in foreigners imposing halal food in school canteens' (*Le Monde*, 2 March 2012).

3. The end of Green politics?

Finally, the 2012 election was remarkable for the total absence of environmentalist themes, a situation which contrasted markedly with the salience gained by these issues in both the 2009 European and 2010 regional elections, where EELV had made significant electoral gains. The 2011 cantonal ballot, admittedly a difficult one for the ecologists traditionally, had already showed signs of voter realignment on the Left of the political spectrum, whilst nevertheless confounding expectations that the accident in the Fukushima nuclear plant in March 2011 would lead to a surge in popular support for Green candidates. A brief glance at the issue attention cycle in the year preceding the election corroborates that the accident had indeed only briefly disrupted the hierarchy of voter concerns. As can be seen from Figure 5.2, the Fukushima crisis had led to a very marginal increase in salience of environment issues in April 2011, with the effect waning rapidly in the following months.

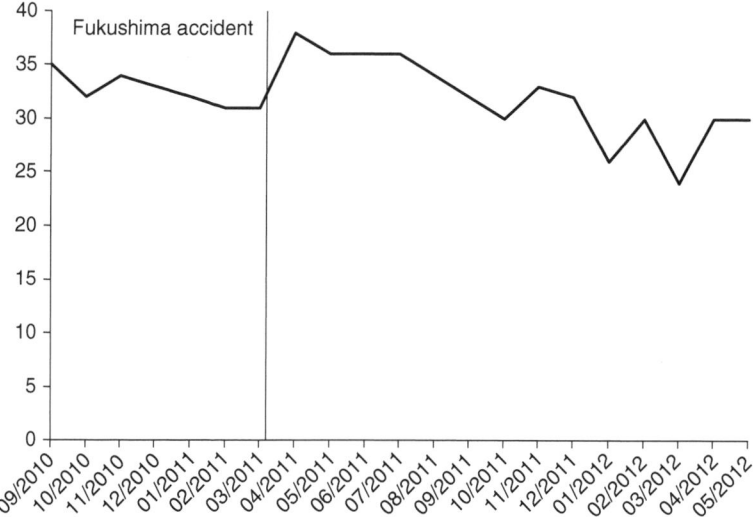

Figure 5.2 Salience of environmental issues* before and after the Fukushima nuclear plant accident
*% who cited 'environment' as one of their most important concerns.
Source: TNS-SOFRES Baromètre des préoccupations des Français (September 2010–May 2012).

In 2012, Joly failed to force crucial issues of climate change, nuclear safety or the push on renewable energies into the presidential campaign. Opinion polls exhibited an extremely low salience for green issues: items such as the 'environment' or 'the future of nuclear power' were for instance relegated to the bottom end of the list of voter concerns, with less than 5 per cent of citations. Most strikingly, environmental issues were put behind unemployment or social inequalities by Joly's supporters themselves, revealing a substantial shift in issue emphasis in the core electoral support for EELV.[20]

More importantly, unlike the presidential election of 2007 where Hulot had successfully channelled the environmental agenda into mainstream politics, the attempt to mobilise on green issues was also largely ignored by other candidates. In 2007, environmental issues had topped the governmental agenda of the Fillon government immediately after Sarkozy's election, as evidenced by the emphasis put on the role of the *Grenelle de l'environnement* in the formulation of ecological and sustainable development policies, as well as the status given to the Borloo's environment ministry in the governmental hierarchy. In the course of his presidential term, however, Sarkozy had progressively ceded to the political pressure exerted by both the agricultural and hunting lobbies – two mainstays of the electoral clientele of the moderate Right – against the expansive pro-environment agenda put forward by his government. In 2010, the President had clearly expressed his shift in preferences,[21] and also heralded his electoral pact with CPNT in 2012 and the disappearance of the ecology ministry after Borloo's departure from government. Similarly, on the Left of the spectrum, Hollande's distant personal relation to environmental issues represented a significant departure from Royal's pro-Green platform in 2007 and, to a lesser extent, from the more environmentalist policies formulated by the PS in 2011, in a shift back towards the more traditional productivist approach of the French Socialist Left.

Evidently, the economic context made ecology less of a potential winner, reducing also the ability by EELV to emphasise their own issues in a presidential arena dominated by socio-economic fears, a situation by no means peculiar to France – compare this with the 'climate silence' which hindered the environmental debate in the US presidential election of November 2012. The preparation by EELV of its presidential programme had acknowledged this change in the issue agenda of the voting public. While stressing Joly's personal anti-corruption profile, the 2012 manifesto incorporated a wide array of economic and financial policies, which showed that important efforts had been made to attain credibility, as well as to formulate a coherent set of redistributive and demand-oriented economic policies which placed Joly immediately to the Left of Hollande on the state–market axis of competition.[22]

Turning back to green issues *per se*, as we saw in Chapter 3, the policy trade-off which had formed part of the pre-electoral agreement between EELV and the Socialists in 2011 had also significantly diminished the potential electoral threat Joly could pose to Hollande. To some extent, in the eyes of many voters, the main policy debate over green issues had already taken place and been settled at elite level during the negotiation of the electoral pact with the PS, resulting in a minimum pro-environment platform by the Socialist runner, who signalled green supporters how far he was really prepared to travel to address their own policy preferences, leaving virtually no space for Joly during the campaign.

Finally, the EELV campaign was significantly weighed down by Joly's low valences and, overall, poor campaigning skills due to her relative lack of experience in national politics, which were of course mirrored in voting intentions and the candidate's popularity. Whilst Joly had the highest proportion of support for her 'programme and ideas' of all presidential candidates among her first-round supporters (at 88 per cent compared for instance with 67 and 78 per cent in Hollande and Sarkozy, respectively), her general valence profile was extremely low. Less than a fifth (19 per cent) of the voters held a positive opinion about her campaign and a mere 8 per cent would give her presidential credibility (as opposed to 28 and 31 per cent for the other third-party runners Le Pen and Mélenchon). In spite of her many efforts, she was perceived as the least 'friendly' of all candidates, a personal valence trait where she was outperformed even by her far right competitor.[23]

6
Campaign Events

The picture we have presented so far of 2012 is one of essential stability and in many ways predictability. A close following of elections since 2008, polling scores for the incumbent President and government and the issues at play in early 2012 all pointed with some degree of inevitability to a Socialist victory. Yet, there is no reason to believe that 2012 should have been determined months if not years before any more than other electoral races. Were elections to be entirely predictable, democracy would likely have failed. All voters have the possibility and opportunity to change their vote in line with the merest whim or fantasy. Anything which renders that element predictable, or worse redundant, removes the essence of competition. Often key to such unpredictability – electoral 'upsets' – are those events at various points before and during the campaign which may influence the final share of the vote. Indeed, as the US elections of 2000 showed, occasionally events after the election can equally influence the final share of the vote. Closer to home, the post-election UMP leadership race in November 2012 illustrated that French politics is just as prey to post-election manipulation and showdowns as any other system.

However, other French elections have shown the impact that such events can have on even the most important race. For example, in 1988 the Ouvéa hostage crisis in New Caledonia, where President Mitterrand ordered a military assault to free the hostages three days before the second round, undoubtedly reinforced some voters' view of him as a statesman able to take difficult decisions. Similarly, the attack on Paul Voise, a pensioner in Orléans, in 2002 was widely reported as having boosted Jean-Marie Le Pen's vote, as the candidate with the toughest stance on law and order. From an electoral analyst's point of view, significant campaign events at whatever point in the election cycle are a dual hazard. Prospectively, they are by definition unforeseeable. Any model, of whatever formality, can anticipate and include knowns in their respective equations. An unknown will alter the outcome, and usually by an unknown – and to some extent unknowable – degree. Anticipating such shocks may usually be impossible, but in any retrospective model, estimating their effect is essential to understanding the outcome.

It is worthwhile clarifying that 'shocks' would not include unexpected election results. In formal terms, results are outcomes and, whilst perhaps unexpected, may be the result to some degree or other of an exogenous shock, rather than one themselves. Moreover, by shock we certainly do not mean normatively inspired expectations being confounded, for instance the election of two FN deputies to the National Assembly.[1] In terms of the presidential elections, we look here at five very different events which could reasonably be defined as unforeseen and exogenous, and realistically expected to have an effect on the election outcome. However, as we shall see, in none of the five cases is there evidence of electoral impact of any magnitude. Each event certainly had impact – in some cases, personalised and tragic – but in terms of altering the election, there is more evidence that their impact was negligible than not. They remain an important part of the 2012 elections, however, as they did result in candidates taking positions, policy and otherwise, and oriented the focus and nature of the campaign. To that extent, their occurrence was influential, and it is important to recognise this role. We deal with them chronologically.

1. Dominique Strass-Kahn and the *affaire du Sofitel*

Undeniably, the first 'event' of the French election was Dominique Strauss-Kahn's arrest and indictment in New York for alleged sexual offences against a chambermaid in the Sofitel hotel. We have discussed the trend in polling support for DSK and the transfers to Hollande in the subsequent primaries in Chapter 4. Undoubtedly, in the immediate aftermath of DSK's arrest, his obvious removal from the presidential race appeared to constitute a significant blow to the Socialists' chances in the presidentials. Entering the summer before the primaries, the expected headline featuring Strauss-Kahn was meant to be his announcement that he would be running for his party's nomination, rather than the now notorious image of the director of the IMF doing the 'perp walk', handcuffed and on his way to Rikers Island. For a candidate who was for many the front runner in people's minds, not just for the primary but also for the presidential election itself 11 months later, to be removed so brutally from the race could not presage anything positive for the party left one leading candidate short.

In fact, it is unlikely that the Strauss-Kahn affair had any real impact on the eventual election. Had he competed in and won the Socialist primaries, a later scandal along these lines would have been deleterious to the Socialist Party. Occurring when it did, there was sufficient time for the affair to be rationalised as something separate to the presidential race, essentially as the criminal prosecution (eventually unsuccessful) it was. A simple glance at PS popularity around the time of the arrest shows that the image of the party had remained largely undamaged by the Sofitel scandal, exhibiting a rise in positive ratings of no less than 7 percentage points between March and September 2011,[2] which reflected the public's growing enthusiasm for the forthcoming primary campaign rather than the political aftershock of the New York events.

Furthermore, although for many DSK's entry into the Socialist primary seemed inevitable, and as we have noted in Chapter 4 even affected debates over the timetabling of the selection process, his certain victory in the primaries, let alone the presidentials, was not as certain as had been made out. Despite the intimations of DSK acolytes such as Pierre Moscovici that his mentor's participation was assured, and that consequently the point of someone like Hollande's candidacy was not necessarily apparent,[3] Hollande had made it clear over time that he would not simply be standing aside – *'une élection présidentielle, ce n'est pas un arrangement'* ('a presidential election isn't something you sort out amongst yourselves').[4] Martine Aubry and Ségolène Royal's candidacies had been less assured, having announced in late 2010 that neither of them would stand in the primaries were another candidate be better placed, namely DSK.[5]

It does seem unlikely that an untainted DSK standing would have been threatened by Hollande as the only principal competitor, unless Aubry had renounced a pact and stood anyway, thereby dividing the vote amongst three. As we have examined in Chapter 4, DSK's absence saw Hollande's support rise markedly, and in the presence of two other credible candidates in Aubry and Royal. What became evident in the presidentials was that DSK was not the only *présidentiable* in the PS. His replacement was manageable.

As we have already noted, to ask how a scandal-free Strauss-Kahn would have fared is a futile exercise in the counterfactual. Ideologically, the difference with Hollande's line is limited – Strauss-Kahn's vision of moving from *un socialisme de la redistribution* to *un socialisme de la production,* set out in his tract *La flamme et la cendre* (written two years after a previous run-in with the French justice system), confirmed his move towards the centre and an embracing of the logic of market economics – anathema, presumably, to the young militant of the 1970s at the heart of Chevènement's Marxist Centre d'études, de recherches et d'éducation socialiste CERES. The notion of social liberalism, reviving *'le goût du risque'* (Strauss-Kahn, 2002: 6) to introduce entrepreneurial dynamism supported by a state safety net, followed the trend in many European social democracies of a market-informed system of egalitarian opportunity.

Pierre Moscovici's eventual appointment as Minister of Finance brought his mentor's approach to the heart of the Socialist government, supported by other centrist Socialists such as Manuel Valls. Moscovici's continuation of DSK's line stopped at ideology however. After Strauss-Kahn's arrest, in line with Hollande's statement that this was a private matter, upon which he had no political take to offer, Moscovici highlighted that 'Anyone can see this has nothing to do with the Socialist Party'.[6] Such distancing could of course work both ways – a party dissociated from a scandal remains relatively untouched. Equally, an individual who has paid his debt could similarly claim that his return to the party fold should not be influenced by previous private 'affairs'.

DSK's return to politics in the Socialist Party and in France seems a very distant prospect. Charges linking him to prostitute rings in the so-called Carlton affair, subsequent revelations of his less than decorous behaviour towards a succession of female colleagues and journalists and separation from Anne Sinclair, his wife, who had stood by him throughout the New York scandal, have all revealed a man unlikely ever to present a credible face to voters again. Whether technocrat work to use his undoubted skills as an economic policy-maker appears again, or instead he simply fades into obscurity as many would prefer, remains to be seen. For the presidential elections of 2012, the Socialist Party will remain ever thankful that his demise came in May 2011, not six months later.

2. Eurozone and the AAA downgrading

Economic circumstances have been promoted as a key factor in election outcomes for as long as explanatory models of the vote have existed. As exogenous contextual variables, economic performance, together with electoral cycle and foreign intervention – war – was included in the very first VP-function models of vote and popularity (Mueller, 1970). As work on economic voting has noted, the relationship between a voter and the economy is not a simple one (Lewis-Beck, 1988). Voters may look at their own finances, the national finances, consider the past and estimate the future. They may even show varying level of emotion in their consideration, thereby conditioning the impact of the economy on their vote (Conover and Feldman, 1986).

As the forecast models discussed in the following chapter clearly show, there is a role for unemployment and GDP as classic economic indicators in any VP-function of the 2012 presidential and legislative elections. However, as known macroeconomic indicators, these are about as far from 'shocks' as it is possible to get. Immigration levels in the extreme right forecast model are unknowns, inasmuch as the finalised figures for the year are not released until many months subsequently (and are even prone to corrections months, if not years, afterwards). Again, however, these do not constitute shocks in the methodological sense.

The clear economic 'shocks', however, were the relatively rapid decline in the Eurozone, and the downgrading of the French economy from triple-A status on 13 January 2012. Since the banking crisis of 2008, the situation of the French economy in terms of GDP and unemployment had looked unstable (Figures 6.1 and 2.1, reported in Chapter 2). France's AAA credit rating had emerged as a salient issue in the public debate during 2011.[7] Before then, it had been largely absent from the

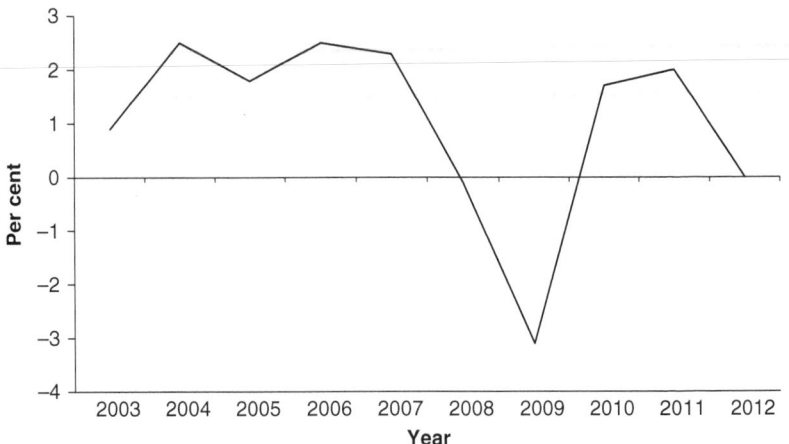

Figure 6.1   Real GDP growth rate (2003–2012)

Source: Eurostat key indicator database (http://epp.eurostat.ec.europa.eu/portal/page/portal/eurostat/home/).

French political arena and had remained confined to the world of financial experts and economists. The lowering by Standard & Poor's of its outlook for the American long-term credit rating in April 2011, followed by the downgrading of the country's AAA note in August, was the first significant event that brought the issue of creditworthiness to the attention of the French public. By December 2011, no less than two-thirds (66 per cent) of the French would deem the consequences of France losing its triple A rating 'serious'.[8] The role of international rating agencies was discussed for the first time ever in a French presidential campaign, with debates revolving around the idea of creating a public European counterpart to the three dominant private American agencies, a proposal which was endorsed by the Socialists but rejected by the ruling UMP.

Except for a small decrease between 2010 and 2011, the step change in unemployment from 2008 onwards was not reversed, and climbed steadily throughout the campaign and after to hit a 12-year high. Similarly, for 2008 and 2009, GDP shrank in France, and for the first time since 1999, dropped across 2008–2010, and by a significantly larger amount ($300 billion). For an incumbent President with a governmental majority, such figures would not predict a strong electoral performance, and indeed as we have noted this was one of the key reasons for Sarkozy's chances of re-election being rated so low. Within days of the triple-A downgrade by the credit ratings agencies, Sarkozy had announced a rise in VAT to bolster the French economy. Again, a direct tax on products and services within months of the election seemed destined to ravage Sarkozy's campaign, not least when members of the UMP coalition openly opposed the measure.[9] Correspondingly, the improvement in late November polls which the President had enjoyed on the back of his statesmanship through the Eurozone crisis promptly vanished.[10]

Given all of these events, the expectation would have been a crushing blow to Sarkozy and buoyancy for other candidates in the first round, and François Hollande in the second. Yet, whilst personal popularity declined in this period for Sarkozy, his vote intentions saw an inexorable rise. By less than two months later, he took for the first time a slender lead over Hollande in the polls. Whilst convergence across the main campaign had been widely expected, particularly in comparison with the enormous double-digit gap recorded in late 2011, at first sight this revival of the UMP candidate's fortunes sits awkwardly with what should have been negative shocks to his performance.

One explanation for this apparent contrary effect is simply that the 'economic effect' had kicked in by the beginning of the campaign.

Any voters who had sided against Sarkozy on the basis of economic performance had already done so by the time the campaign started. Additional bad news nearer the time had little effect on his support. Conversely, what the G20 summit and Eurozone crisis allowed was for him to demonstrate leadership through the presidential office – a role denied to François Hollande – and thereby convince voters of his aptitude and character for the position. Throughout polls from all institutes, Sarkozy continually outpaced Hollande on questions regarding *l'étoffe* – literally, the stuff of a leader – but fell short of the Socialist on other measures (Table 6.1).

By January following the elections, this desire for a strong, virtuous leader taking the helm in the socio-economic storm was brutally manifest in polls, with majorities of all party supporters agreeing that a strong leader was necessary to re-establish order, and that authority is too often criticised as a value in society.[11] Most tellingly, despite ongoing issues with de Bettencourt and rumours of Gaddafi-funded campaigns, still the most favoured UMP politician to run in the 2017 presidentials is Sarkozy, with 56 per cent, ahead of Fillon (17 per cent) and Juppé (9 per cent).[12]

In one sense, the economic crisis served Sarkozy well in showcasing his capacities as a statesman amongst the developed world's leaders. However, the effect was short-lived in terms of the polls, and not sufficient to see him overtake Hollande convincingly. The period of overtaking his rival was short, and the polls far from unanimous on this. Perhaps the strongest indicator that the statesman role was insufficient for re-election was Sarkozy's own return to domestic policy in the closing weeks of the campaign. A desperate play to the far right with a replication of 2007's appeal on issues of law and order and social authoritarian values implied that the President and his campaign team realised that the credibility factor was simply not enough to push him past Hollande.

Table 6.1 Importance of candidate attributes amongst supporters of run-off candidates

	Supporters of Sarkozy	Supporters of Hollande
Presidential stature	81	17
Change	8	65
Closeness to the people	9	29

Source: Table derived from Evans 2012: 129. Original survey – Ipsos, '2ème tour présidentielle 2012. Comprendre le vote des Français', 3–5 May 2012.

3. Afghanistan

On 20 January 2012, to the north-east of Kabul, a soldier in the Afghan National Army fired on French soldiers, killing four and wounding at least 15 others.[13] Immediately afterwards, President Sarkozy suspended all military operations of the French contingent of around 3,500 troops in the country originally due to remain until 2014. The Minister of Defence, Gérard Longuet, was despatched to the region to assess the conditions French troops were operating under, with a view to continuing or withdrawing from their mission. A week later, after a meeting with the Afghan President, Hamid Karzai, Sarkozy announced that all troops would be withdrawn by the end of 2013, a year earlier than anticipated, with 1,000 coming back during 2012.

Amongst the other presidential candidates, their reactions to the notion of an early withdrawal varied. Notably, François Hollande declared that he wished to bring all French troops home by the end of 2012. Other candidates on the Left, particularly on the radical Left, expressed similar sentiments, couched more explicitly in outright opposition to the NATO coalition involvement in Afghanistan. For the two centrist candidates, Bayrou and Morin, a more nuanced approach was encouraged, with French troops withdrawing once the military handover to the Afghan army had been completed. Elsewhere on the Right, the position reflected more that of the Left. Former Foreign Minister Dominique de Villepin restated his continued opposition to French involvement in the Afghanistan coalition and called for immediate withdrawal of troops. Marine Le Pen similarly denounced the entire plan, and demanded an immediate return of French troops.

The French contingent in Afghanistan would always have featured as a key element of debate on foreign affairs in the presidential race, with the French President's role as commander-in-chief of the armed forces necessitating a demonstration by each candidate of how they could be regarded as *présidentiable* in this respect. The focal point of foreign policy credibility comes in the debate prior to the run-off in the presidentials. The two candidates' positions – withdrawal in 2012 or 2013 – were both set out very clearly in this debate on 2 May, Hollande emphasising that in his opinion the combat mission in Afghanistan had been completed, Sarkozy questioning the possibility of effectuating an early withdrawal, and underlining the importance of staying true to the promises made to allies. Not for the first time in a presidential debate, the incumbent was able to demonstrate a hands-on knowledge that the inexperienced challenger would be unable to counter. However, polling after the debate produced no sign of any shift in voting patterns, so it is unlikely that the

Afghanistan issue produced any electoral change other than to confirm it as a salient policy area, and one firmly within the presidential domain.

Accordingly, the eventual position taken by the newly incumbent President was precisely that stated in January. At a NATO summit in Chicago in May, Hollande declared that the withdrawal of French troops by the end of the year was not up for negotiation, and visited Afghanistan a few days later with his foreign and defence ministers, Laurent Fabius and Jean-Yves Le Drian, to put his presidential stamp on the beginning of the withdrawal.[14]

4. Mohammed Merah

Mid-March 2012 witnessed a series of horrific shootings of members of the French armed forces in Toulouse and Montauban and, in perhaps the most traumatising incident, the murder of three Jewish children, as well as the father of two of these children, outside a school in Toulouse. The killer, Mohammed Merah, was killed by the French RAID firearms unit after an overnight siege. Merah was portrayed as a troubled individual with a history of mental illness, as well as a record of petty criminality. In phone calls to the media the night shortly before the siege, Merah ascribed the motivation of his attacks to defending Islam, and indicated he had links with al-Qaeda. At the time, authorities stated that there was no evidence that Merah had acted in conspiracy with anyone else, but his older brother, Abdelkader, was subsequently arrested and investigated for his possible involvement, as well as alleging the involvement of a third unnamed individual.

Initial politicisation of the Toulouse tragedy came before the identification of the killer. Because of the ethnicity of the soldiers killed in Toulouse and Montauban, enquiries were made amongst hardline extreme-right groupuscules.[15] Media reports discussed such enquiries as linking the attacks to a fanatic *identitaire*, and prioritised the possibility of extreme-right links over Islamic terrorism.[16] Social media were often less circumspect in their speculation over possible perpetrators. Similarly, foreign media highlighted the apparent role of attitudes to minority groups in France as a contributing factor to the attacks.[17]

Both Hollande and Sarkozy announced an interruption in their campaigns in the immediate aftermath of the killings. The only politician to expressly choose not to, in order to change *'le ton et le fond'* ['tenor and basis'] of the campaign, was François Bayrou, although he too was careful to note the collective solidarity of candidates on all sides paying tribute to the victims.[18] An interesting parallel may be drawn between Sarkozy's moratorium on campaigning in the direct aftermath of the murders and President Obama's similar decree subsequent to Hurricane Sandy's landfall in October. For the US President, the interruption of campaigns during the national emergency led to a drop in his opponent Mitt Romney's momentum, which, in the wake of the first televised debate, looked capable of unseating a Democratic incumbent campaigning in lacklustre fashion. For Sarkozy, stepping out of the campaign, for legitimate and laudable reasons, could only have a similar effect, but having cast himself in the role of challenger, it was his own momentum which suffered. Hollande's baseline position as expected victor was not affected by a relatively immobile campaign; a suspension of this self-same campaign would then not hamper his efforts.

Sadly, this was not the first time that such an attack had preceded an election. In 1995, the RER station at Saint-Michel was bombed by Algerian terrorists – the first of a wave of attacks over the summer – shortly before legislative by-elections, where, as a result, the FN saw its vote increase. Almost exactly a decade earlier, Richard Durn had opened fire at a council meeting in Nanterre killing eight people. The tributes paid by all candidates to the victims were however marked out in this case, unlike Merah, by a statement by Jacques Chirac on law and order that was critical of his cohabitation partners and seen by the Socialists as a means of making political capital out of the tragedy.[19] Whilst some fringe commentators raised suspicions that Sarkozy felt able to continue to campaign by other means despite announcing an interruption in the presidential campaign, as well as conspiracy theories of political manipulation due to inconsistencies in the police reports of the manhunt and siege,[20] a more tempered politicisation was the norm, and certainly there was little evidence of overt manipulation of the event evident on the political stage.

In some ways, French politicians were unsure how to react to the tragedy in terms of the election.[21] For the Left, the violent criminalisation of a small number of young French people was evidence of a failing in the socio-political system. For Sarkozy, the threat derived from the radical socialisation of extremism. Within a few days of the shootings, he had announced a tightening (*renforcement*) of penalties for those accessing terrorism or hate websites or travelling abroad for the purposes of radicalisation.[22] However, none of these politicised any aspect of the crimes themselves – they acted simply to position candidates' policy stances more clearly.

Of perhaps all the candidates, Marine Le Pen was the most overt in highlighting the political effect of the event. She openly stated that

'*L'affaire de Toulouse va recentrer la campagne sur des thèmes que je défends depuis plus d'un an et demi*' ('the Toulouse shootings will reorient the campaign around issues I've been fighting on for over 18 months').[23] Marine Le Pen's stance on the atrocity was to combine calls for a war on 'politico-religious fundamentalism' with law and order more specifically, calling for a referendum on the restoration of the death penalty[24] while simultaneously denouncing the government's 'laxness' in dealing with the threat of Islamic terrorism in France, as well as playing 'victim' of the unfounded accusations of which the FN had been subject immediately after the Montauban shootings. This would be the expected line of the FN leader, combining its two key issues of authoritarianism and anti-Islamism.

The rhetoric on the latter issue clearly revealed the ambiguity in Le Pen's strategy, as she would undoubtedly seek to exploit the opportunity offered by the Toulouse events to appropriate the presidential agenda, while striving to avoid accusations of overt political manipulation on the other hand. Le Pen made certain to identify a specific group, rather than broadly 'Muslims'. Whilst for many *frontistes* the distinction will have been redundant, from Le Pen's perspective the positioning of the issue mattered in terms of appealing to voters turned off by general xenophobia or ethnocentrism, but still concerned by specific threats from extremist groups. As suggested earlier, however, the reorientation of her campaign was not entirely devoid of controversial statements, as revealed for instance in her denouncing the danger of 'green fascism' or the 'gangrene of radical Islam' (see Chapter 5). In a late March meeting, Le Pen would also further attempt to trigger fears of Islamic fundamentalism, by connecting terrorism to immigration, crime and what she would deem the failure of France's model of integration: 'Merah', she said, 'is perhaps the tip of the iceberg... How many Mohamed Merahs come to France every day in boats and planes full of immigrants? How many Mohamed Merahs among the children of those unassimilated immigrants?' (*Le Monde*, 25 March 2012).

The Toulouse events also gave the FN the opportunity to return to one of its cornerstone policy areas. Five years earlier, crime and security were headline areas of candidate programmes, together with immigration. In 2012, however, the focus remained tightly on the economy for the majority of the campaign, relegating law and order to second-tier status. Conscious of the need to focus on bread-and-butter issues, Marine Le Pen's most publicised programmatic event was the launch of the economic programme in mid-January, in an attempt to win credibility in an area often perceived as weak, or at best *ad hoc*, for the FN. This attempt met with little success – two months after the launch, less than 20 per cent of the electorate found the programme convincing.[25]

In the final electoral account, the impact of these events turned out to be limited. As Ipsos polls one week later demonstrated, there was evidence that Sarkozy's actions in the aftermath of the attacks were rated highest by voters, with Hollande some way behind, and only a minority of respondents judging the three trailing candidates to have found the *ton juste*; voting intentions hardly shifted as a result. No politicians in the race won or lost from their respective stances,[26] while the public's mind remained firmly set on social and economic concerns of unemployment or purchasing power (see Chapter 5).

Looking at the unfolding of the campaign, two minor events helped Hollande in particular in reorienting the campaign towards more propitious economic themes, as security and immigration issues threatened to monopolise the presidential agenda. A first event was the release by INSEE of the unemployment statistics for February, which showed another deterioration in the French labour market, putting the campaign's spotlights back on Sarkozy's track record. The second significant event was the revelation by the press that the CEO of the Publicis advertising company, Maurice Lévy, would collect 16 million euros in deferred remuneration in 2012, which triggered passionate debate among candidates and certainly contributed to the progressive fading of the Toulouse events in the media.

5. Trierweiler and Twitter: The first scandal of the Hollande presidency

Throughout the coverage of the Socialist Party (rather than of François Hollande) in the presidential and legislative elections, a large proportion of articles on the former presidential candidate, candidate for First Secretary of the party and president of the regional council of Poitou-Charentes, Ségolène Royal, apparently felt compelled to add two other roles, namely former partner of the Socialist presidential candidate and mother of his four children. In a system where gender parity has been legislated but has largely fallen prey to the pragmatics of financial cost – for its avoidance – and where suspicions of nepotism by many of its politicians have been widespread, it seems that even a high-ranking Socialist Party *notable* is unable to divorce herself entirely from her private life in public view.

In the legislative elections, her defeat by the Socialist Party dissident Olivier Falorni in La Rochelle at the second round (as described in

Chapter 8) would have been painful enough, even had it not been accompanied by a widely publicised tweet by François Hollande's current partner, Valérie Trierweiler, in support of Falorni – *'Courage à Olivier Falorni qui n'a pas démérité, qui se bat aux côtés des Rochelais depuis tant d'années dans un engagement désintéressé'* ('Good luck to Olivier Falorni who's done nothing wrong, and who has fought for La Rochelle for so many years with a disinterested commitment.').[27] The Prime Minister, Jean-Marc Ayrault, was quick to underline that Ségolène Royal was the official candidate and that he and the party endorsed her and her alone in that respect. François Hollande, most importantly, had done likewise, but one day before his partner sent the tweet. Inevitably the press speculated that Trierweiler's message was motivated at least in part by jealousy of Hollande's support for his former partner.[28] Given Trierweiler's career as a high-profile political journalist, it seems unlikely that she would not be aware of the publicity and impact that her message of support would have.

Whilst it would be tempting to see the publicity surrounding the event as playing a role in the eventual outcome in the run-off in La Rochelle, it is very unlikely that it played a decisive role. Already in the constituency, the campaign *'Tous sauf Ségolène'* had received significant support from UMP sympathisers, and Falorni was already receiving well over 50 per cent of the intended vote in polls after the first round. As Table 8.4 in Chapter 8 shows, this campaign was entirely successful – the increase in Royal's vote in the second round was marginal compared with her opponent almost doubling his score. In net terms, Falorni collected the vast majority of all other candidates' votes, as well as benefiting from the increased turnout. At most, we can say that Royal's humiliation before the second round simply underlined the apparent depth of feeling against her candidacy from many quarters.

The principal effect of the Trierweiler tweet was to place a very early question mark next to the newly installed President's claims to a 'normal' presidency. One of Hollande's apparent advantages over Sarkozy was his less ostentatious, blander approach to politics and to life in general. The success of this portrayal, and the evident problems which Sarkozy's previous flamboyance had caused, had led the latter to emulate the humility and 'man of the people' stance of his opponent in the latter days of the campaign. Yet, by June, the sight of Hollande's current partner undermining his ex-partner's bid not just for a seat in the Palais Bourbon but the presidency of the chamber had opened up the President to jibes of a 'Dallas' presidency from the UMP.[29]

Despite extensive coverage of her new role as First Lady in the days following the presidentials, Valérie Trierweiler withdrew very quickly from media coverage after the tweet scandal, and maintained this until well after the legislatives were completed – a return to the discretion highlighted in pre-election features.[30] Since then, Trierweiler has returned more noticeably to the limelight, for example as an ambassador for the Fondation Danielle Mitterrand, but also less helpfully in some robust confrontations with cameramen following her husband.[31] In the end, it is unlikely that a First Lady can remain entirely beyond media scrutiny. More specifically, the role of the presidency in France, particularly during an economic crisis, means that the actions of Hollande's partner are likely to be blurred out by the focus on the executive's own actions.

Despite the apparent lack of effect of these five events on the outcome of the presidential and legislative elections, we are speaking only of course of the net result. Undoubtedly some individual voters will have been motivated to change their vote on the basis of this – vote for Sarkozy due to his demonstration of leadership during the euro crisis summits; move to a candidate with a stronger law and order position in the wake of the Merah shootings; even deciding to turn out in the run-off in La Rochelle to bandwagon on the anti-Royal campaign. But in aggregate, there is nothing to suggest in the play-out of these events, the candidate responses or other dynamics of the election that they did anything beyond embedding voter choices and confirming candidate positions on the various axes of competition.

In closing, it is worth returning to the personality assessments of voters for the two lead candidates in Table 6.1. The difference between Hollande and Sarkozy on presidential attributes could not be more stark regarding presidential stature – how the person fills the presidential shoes – and embodiment of change and their closeness to the people. For the vast majority of Sarkozy supporters, the first was vital. For Hollande supporters, only a small minority cared. What they cared about was change. For Sarkozy, then, the Eurozone crisis, Merah and Afghanistan all confirmed his ability to act as France's statesman. Despite the woeful polling scores from early in his presidency, and an openly criticised presidential style, the last six months gave him three opportunities – as it turned out, final ones – to lead France. In that sense, the closing of the gap between him and Hollande as the campaign entered its final phase will certainly not have been hurt by these events, but to the extent that the gap closed but never disappeared, they were not sufficient to change the outcome of the election.

Finally, we should remind ourselves that the campaign was not devoid of any events other than those highlighted in this chapter. The susurration of illicit party and campaign finance allegations continued through yet another election campaign. On the Right, the first rumours of campaign funding for Sarkozy in 2007 from Muammar Gaddafi emerged in mid-March. On the Left, the Pas-de-Calais affair laid open by Montebourg embarassed the Socialist Party well before the campaign proper commenced. Both sides managed to stifle any real progress in investigations for the period of the campaign.

Libel threats as usual emerged throughout the long campaign – Jack Lang against Arnaud Montebourg for perceived smears in the leaked Pas-de-Calais letter; Yannick Noah against Marine Le Pen, after she called him a 'tax exile' with 'money stashed away abroad' (*planqué son argent à l'étranger*); Le Pen against Mélenchon's team and vice versa (a surprise, given the virulence of the fight between the two, that this took until the legislatives to occur). However, this was the sum of the scandals to enliven the campaign. Indeed, the level of interest in the campaign appeared so low by the end of March that many feared the return of record low turnout, and the skews this could produce in the outcome.[32] In the end, such fears were unfounded, and as we shall see in Chapter 8, even record abstention in the legislatives did not work against the mainstream. In a pivotal election, then, for a re-ascendant Left and an ousted Right and its one-term President, the direction of travel of the outcome could not be diverted by *faits divers*, no matter how striking. For an election forecaster, whose work we turn to in the next chapter, 2012 seems to represent a stable case for prediction.

7
Polls and VP-Functions: Forecasting the Elections

One important underlying premise of this book is that the final outcome of the 2012 elections in France was largely predictable. Looking at the institutional, political and economic conditions under which the elections were fought, the chances that Sarkozy could avoid a 'negative referendum' were slim. His position as unpopular incumbent contrasted sharply with the political and electoral dynamics displayed by parties of the Left in the lead-up to the presidential election, while aggravation over unemployment and the first 'austerity cure' imposed on the French by the Fillon government threatened to kill any last chances of re-election for the President.

In the preceding chapters, however, the proposition that a victory by the Left and, consequently, an alternation in national office were somewhat inevitable outcomes has been examined mostly in qualitative fashion, based upon the identification of factors which were likely to shape party competition and voter preferences in the elections. Another manner in which the degree of predictability of the 2012 elections can be gauged is by looking at forecasts and polling analyses for the presidential and legislative races. In Chapter 4 we already borrowed some useful information from national voting intention polls, showing the exceptionally low level of electoral support for Sarkozy in the run-off, compared to the Socialist contender(s) who took a strong and remarkably consistent lead in the projected second-round vote. Of course, individual polls do not predict by themselves the outcome of the election. They are simply an estimation of public opinion at a point in time – why *informed* use is important. Since perhaps the nadir of polling in America, mispredicting Truman's defeat against Dewey in the 1948 election, polling methods have steadily improved to the point that informed use can provide a strong indication of the likely victor, and the margin of confidence around a predicted score. This does not mean that polls predict the outcome in deterministic fashion – and, self-evidently, less so for close races – but it does provide an empirical benchmark of likely outcome.

In a more sophisticated fashion, the 'inevitable alternation' hypothesis can also be put to more stringent examination by looking at evidence-based forecasts for the 2012 elections. Indeed, predicting elections goes beyond simply the use of polls in the political science literature. Of perhaps greater interest in terms of long-range forecasts are forecasting models which use socio-economic indicators as well, broadly included under the vote-popularity (VP-) function literature. Two of the most crucial variables to which we have repeatedly referred in our analyses of the 2012 elections so far – namely incumbent popularity and the state of the national economy – are fundamental component parameters in the traditional vote-popularity equations which form the core of econometric models. France provides a propitious case for running such models of various specifications testing outcomes for incumbent, opposition and minor candidates, although this approach is still far from the mainstream compared with other countries.[1]

Nevertheless, a series of forecasts of both the presidential and legislative elections were produced in anticipation of the 2012 elections, which we examine below to look at both their accuracy as well as their usefulness – the two not being synonymous in election forecasting – in understanding the respective races. France's presidential election with a two-candidate run-off clearly has parallels with the US leadership race, and indeed across time has led to famous two-country comparisons (Converse and Dupeux, 1961; Lewis-Beck, 1997; Pierce, 1998) reflected in more recent work taking US concepts and testing them on the French case (Adams and Merrill, 2000; Stimson et al., 2010). Whilst most prevalent in the US case, and also well suited to the two-party system there, France has provided a European case with a growing literature on forecasting. This has often focused on forecasting incumbent/opposition performance, whether at national or sub-national level (Jérôme and Jérôme-Speziari, 2004; Lewis-Beck and Nadeau, 2004). There are also examples, however, of forecasting third-party performance, particularly of the FN (Jérôme and Jérôme-Speziari, 2003; Auberger, 2005; Evans and Ivaldi, 2008).

This chapter then turns to the examination of the French polling results to look at how close these were to the actual outcome of the 2012 presidential race, and the extent to which polls did provide a useful tool for understanding the French elections. In keeping here with the transatlantic comparison, two major national elections enjoyed very different outcomes in terms of opinion polling in 2012. The first election – in France – saw polling organisations once again the target of criticisms from politicians and commentators that their polls were biased, in particular for under- or overestimating minor party performance.[2] The second election – in the USA – saw polling organisations roundly condemned by many commentators (mostly from the Republican side) as deliberately biased towards Barack Obama, at best misleading voters and at worst influencing them. In the end, if the polls were being deliberately manipulated to influence voters, this turned out to be the most successful exercise in mass mind control ever carried out, and indeed most critics have since chosen silence over conspiracy theory. That the polls correctly predicted Obama's victory was down to robust method and intelligent interpretation of polls.

As we shall discuss, the French case is a little more complicated. As a multiparty system, any assessment of polling accuracy is more involved. A number of smaller candidates in both Left and Right blocs make individual candidate polling estimates more unstable, except generally at the block level. Moreover, in the case of extreme candidates, such as the FN or to a lesser extent the radical Left candidates, socially acceptable responses may underestimate support. With respect to the latter in particular, French polling institutes are less forthcoming about the collection and adjustment of their polling scores, making the reliability of the polls more difficult to assess than in countries such as the US and the UK, where there are strict standards for reporting raw data, weighting and adjustments – certainly, beyond those required by the French Commission des Sondages. 'Informed' use of polls is therefore by definition less obvious.

Having then looked at how the polling estimates relate to our understanding of the election outcome, we turn to a final and perhaps ambitious test of ex post forecasting for the legislative elections, to examine the extent to which they fit a previous model of legislative outcome, derived for the 2007 elections, and thus follow dynamics that are something other than a six-week plebiscite on the presidential outcome.

1. Ex ante forecasts

One of the key criticisms of much forecasting is that it occurs in an ex post environment. That is, researchers fit statistical models to elections where the outcome is already known. In mid-electoral cycle, this is almost unavoidable – either a model makes an unreasonably long-range forecast, or it needs to be applied retrospectively in order to assess its accuracy. The criticism of ex post approaches is that they inevitably allow the possibility that independent variable selection and coding is based not upon first principles, but upon model performance. In short, ex post models can be as much an exercise in data-fitting as in identifying a stable 'true' forecast model. In the end, the only recourse researchers have to countering such accusations is to apply the identical model to a future election, and for the eventual forecast to be accurate.[3]

Perhaps understandably, vote forecasters are often reticent about publishing ex ante estimates of election outcomes. Within French political science, there is a tradition of using polling data (which we explore later) to estimate likely results, but some suspicion of econometric models perhaps due to the enforced simplicity of causation which such approaches require.[4] Happily, the 2012 elections witnessed a number of ex ante forecasts, many of them included in a symposium of *French Politics* (2012), with estimates of presidential outcomes (winners and vote shares) and legislative results. In the tradition of previous reviews of forecast success (Lewis-Beck, 2005; Campbell, 2008), Table 7.1 presents a summary of the forecasts provided before the election, and their eventual success.[5]

Encouragingly, most of the forecasts were successful at the top level, predicting a left-wing victory, largely corroborating the 'foreseeability' of the 2012 election outcome which we have developed in the previous chapters of this book. The only model which provided a forecast of a Sarkozy victory – that by Jérôme and Jérôme-Speziari (2012a) – did so under strict terms which in the end did not apply. The economic downturn and the continued low personal poll ratings for Sarkozy meant that these conditions were not met, resulting in a (predicted) Hollande victory.

Nadeau, Lewis-Beck and Bélanger (2012a) also encountered a common forecast issue, namely correct winner but overstated margin of victory. Predicting 53.2 per cent of the vote for the Left bloc, this turned out to be 44 per cent. As the authors themselves discuss (2012b), part of the issue in forecasting first-round vote is how to classify the Centre. In the past, François Bayrou and the MODEM have been clearly situated in the Right camp. However, in 2012, Bayrou's opposition to Sarkozy and his apparent rapprochement with Hollande and the Socialists brought him closer to the Left. Including Bayrou's score in the Left group would correct the forecast left-bloc vote for Nadeau and colleagues, but unfortunately this throws the parameters from the previous elections – where Bayrou was of the Right – into disarray. Their conclusion? That only the independent variable, immigration. Contrast this with the Jerôme and Jerôme-Speziari model which wrongly forecast a Sarkozy victory, but still managed another degree of accuracy – the vote share it forecast was superior to later polls' – and also provided an insight into the relative chances of Sarkozy's victory or defeat – simply, strategic choices made during the campaign, namely moving rightwards to appeal to a *frontiste* voter in the second round who would not vote Sarkozy, whatever his ideological position (Jerôme and Jerôme-Speziari, 2012b: 376). Such a model confirms our initial view of the 2012 election, namely that a repeat of 2007's strategy was bound to fail, given disappointment amongst extreme right voters at the paltry returns from their support.

Whilst the majority of the pieces focus on 'the main event', that is the presidential winner, two take a different stance, one (already mentioned – Evans and Ivaldi, 2012a) looking at the third-party performance of Marine Le Pen, the other forecasting the legislative election results (Foucault, 2012). As we have repeatedly stated throughout this book, and will study further in the following chapter, the legislative elections are definitively second-order races, inasmuch as they are strongly conditioned by the presidential outcome. This does not mean, however, that no variation in the legislative result will be possible (Foucault, 2012: 69). Moreover, the extent to which the elections are forecastable from previous legislative races is of relevance. As in any electoral system, the political 'traditions' of constituencies are important inertial predictors which need to be used as a baseline. As we will examine further in the next chapter, the regional colouration of politics has shifted notably over the past quarter-century, not least in the re-Socialisation of the West. However, these are secular trends across a number of years – incumbency effects (whether of candidate or simply party) should be observable as a norm.

From a forecasting perspective, Foucault's approach provides an interesting corollary to the presidential–legislative relationship. Finding the Left likely to win a majority in the 2012 legislatives implies through this model specification a victory of Hollande in the *preceding* presidential race. A strong model forecasting legislative outcomes can therefore give insights into the likely outcome of a presidential race (2012: 80).

In common for all the full-election forecasts (as opposed to party-specific ones) is the use of a dichotomous coding of competitors into incumbent (Right) and opposition (Left). Specifically for the French case, the possibility of including the FN in the Right bloc has been the subject of some debate, as we have noted elsewhere, whereas Mélenchon's location on the Left appears on the other hand to be much less debatable.

Similarly, the positioning of Bayrou's MODEM on the political spectrum has become increasingly problematic, as revealed by changes which have occurred in the party's cooperative and competitive strategies, as well as in the transformation of its electoral support over the past ten years. More broadly, whilst block inclusion of a number of parties or presidential candidates may resolve successfully in a system with a two-candidate run-off, the loss of information through such amalgamation should be avoided if possible. After all, forecasting is not simply about predicting a winner. Very few approaches to forecasting employ multiparty measures which take into account each competitor. In the sections which follow, we report a new method of looking at polling data which does precisely this, and in the final section provide a legislative forecast, based upon a previous attempt (Arzheimer and Evans, 2010), which represents a first multiparty forecast using a single model for more fine-grained block definitions than the Left/Right dyad.

2. Polls: Accuracy and artefact

In a modern democratic election, a campaign without polling estimates has become unthinkable, and France is no exception. The majority of individuals have no active participation in a campaign; their election information is restricted to traditional media, the internet, and peer conversation. Whilst this can provide local knowledge, the use of sampled polling estimates is effectively the only potentially reliable estimate we have of trends in likely vote and therefore the expected outcome. With respect to the 2012 elections, the story told to voters was primarily one of political change: as early as May 2008, voting intention polls had begun to frame the future defeat of Sarkozy as the most likely outcome of the then distant presidential race.[6] Leaving aside a brief relapse in polls during 2009, the main scenario presented to the French public by pollsters in the second half of the presidency was that the ruling UMP President would quite simply be ousted come 2012.

Yet, the precise role of polls is fuzzy. They are not 'scientific' in terms of constituting a precise forecast of the election outcome, and the further out from the election they are made, the less accuracy they will enjoy. Instead they reflect the likely vote 'if the election was held tomorrow' – which self-evidently it generally is not. Moreover, in the French case, polls do not all report key information: (a) some report undecideds, that is people who cannot yet indicate how they would vote, but this is not the case for all pollsters; (b) with the exception of the newly constituted YouGov panel, no polling organisation reports the unadjusted data upon which the final, adjusted polling estimates are based. Polling organisations in France have vigorously defended their right to protect unadjusted data as an 'industrial secret', which if revealed would put them at a commercial disadvantage in revealing their adjustment techniques – a position upheld during the campaign by the *Conseil d'Etat*.[7] Equally, pollsters and their defenders claim that reporting the unadjusted data would backfire. The perceived inaccuracy due to inherent biases for which standard correction procedures exist would provide ammunition for politicians to decry polls unjustly: what is reasonable statistical adjustment could be portrayed to a non-technical audience as manipulation.

Precisely such a political explanation for these adjustments has been put forward in particular by Marine Le Pen and the FN, namely that there is a conspiracy to underestimate her true scores in a bid to damage her election chances, even calling for the directors of polling institutes to bet their salaries against the accuracy of their polls.[8] It is clear that the far right expect their scores to be higher in the adjusted data. The fact that in previous elections polls have both underestimated (2002) and overestimated (2007) the FN candidate's score suggests that the adjusted polls to date have been unstable, rather than consistently biased. For 2012, as Table 7.2 shows, the final polls of each of the eight main polling institutions did all underestimate Le Pen's first-round score at 15.8 per cent of the vote. However, the majority were within the margin of error, showing also a reduction in the level of uncertainty in predicting the extreme right: in absolute terms, their average 2012 error (2.1) was smaller than both their 2002 and 2007 misforecasts (respectively 3.3 and 3.4). Are the pollsters then able to claim that their adjustments are

Table 7.2   Final-week polls and official results

Pollster	Date	Hollande	Sarkozy	Le Pen	Bayrou	Mélenchon
OpinionWay	17/04/2012	27.5	27.5	16	10	13
LH2	18/04/2012	27	26.5	15.5	10	15
IPSOS	19/04/2012	29	25.5	16	10	14
CSA	19/04/2012	28	25	16	10,5	14,5
BVA	19/04/2012	30	26.5	14	10	14
TNS-SOFRES	19/04/2012	27	27	17	10	13
IFOP	20/04/2012	27	27	16	10.5	13.5
	Mean	**27.9**	**26.4**	**15.8**	**10.1**	**13.9**
	1st round	28.6	27.2	17.9	9.1	11.1
	Difference	*0.7*	*0.8*	*2.1*	*−1.0*	*−2.7*

indeed valid? A possible counter to this argument is that polling scores influence voters, and the dampening effect that may be being employed is acting to reduce electoral support through a negative bandwagon deterrent.

A more likely scenario for Le Pen's polling is that pollsters make the best estimate of adjustments based upon demographic profile weighting of respondents and previous performance, but are haunted by previous issues of polling accuracy with Jean-Marie Le Pen's performance in 2002. At that election, even the last polls before the first round failed to anticipate his score of 16.9 per cent. By 2007, pollsters anxious to avoid a repeat of not anticipating a strong performance by the FN leader *over*-estimated his eventual score. Given Le Pen's poor performance, and a 'democratic' run-off between the Socialist and UMP candidates, little was made of the polls' repeated failure. In March 2011, Harris Interactive published a now-infamous Internet poll giving Le Pen victory in the first round, with 23 per cent of the vote.[9] That polling institutes are playing a highly complex game of voter manipulation, first raising the prospect of a Le Pen victory to discomfit the electorate, then downgrading her scores to try to prompt a moderating bandwagon effect – without risking an underdog effect backlash – seems unlikely given the continued problems pollsters inevitably have in getting accurate results, even on the night of the election (see below).

One means of assessing polling accuracy is to consider how well they performed in the later stages of the campaign as predictors of the eventual vote outcome. Again, we should remember that polls are not formal forecasts of an election result. However, throughout a campaign, a reliable set of polling estimates should converge towards the eventual result. The 2012 acid test in French elections was the release of the results at 8 pm on France's news channels.

How did French polls perform? Looking back at Table 7.2, in the last week of polling, the seven main polling institutes predicted the final order of the five top-ranked candidates. The average of the seven polls published in the campaign's final week gave a very close estimate of the balance of the two front runners with a 0.8-point variation in both Hollande and Sarkozy, whereas the main source of error was found in the two peripheral 'protest' candidates, namely Mélenchon (−2.7) and Le Pen (+2.1). One way of roughly assessing the level of accuracy can be taken from the sum of absolute errors for all candidates (we use a more sophisticated method later in this section). In 2012 the total of errors gave an 8-point error for the ten candidates in the presidential race, as opposed to 12.2 across all 12 contenders in the

2007 election. In sum, the global performance by France's pollsters has slightly improved compared with five years earlier. Moreover, pollsters could legitimately claim that even the largest differences are within the margin of error.

Polling on the night produced rather less salutary results, inasmuch as the expectation is polls which reflect the result with a very low margin of error (Table 7.3). As the Observatoire des Sondages notes, the exit polls on election night have generally been expected to produce highly accurate results, with the results likely to change very little once the actual results from a small number of polling stations have been used to adjust the estimates. Whilst for many of the candidates the results proved very reliable, two in particular caused major headaches – Marine Le Pen, for whom scores as high as 20 per cent were given, and Nicolas Sarkozy, whose score was underestimated by a similar margin. It is impossible to know the reason for these two errors, which, as the table shows, are not necessarily linked: for example, TNS-Sofres which overestimated Marine Le Pen's score by over 1 point produced almost exactly Sarkozy's eventual score. Only IPSOS produced results for both candidates which exceeded 1.5 points of error. Certainly in no case did the error change the predicted result of the election.

A second, more innovative method of assessing polling accuracy is to try to look at the global accuracy of any poll. Our examination of polls throughout the book so far has looked at their individual scores for the ten candidates. For individual polls, this provides the snapshot of public opinion at a particular point in time. However, as graphs of the polls across time make clear, the variation in each candidate's score makes it well nigh impossible to assess clearly how well each poll fares overall. In other words, taking into account deviation from each candidate's eventual result on 22 April, can we summarise the overall accuracy of that poll?

Again we should remind ourselves that polls are not forecasts, and particularly for surveys carried out some weeks or months ahead of the election, there would be no reasonable expectation that they should reflect the actual result precisely. Were they to do so, this would be merely coincidental. Polls closer to election day should converge upon the actual result, if they are representative of public opinion, however. Dynamically, then, a measure of global accuracy is useful to understand trends in the development of public opinion, looking for movement amongst individual polling organisations, as well as 'critical junctures', such as the confirmation of a certain candidate or a key election date, such as to understand if they had any effect on public opinion.

Until recently, no effective global indicator of accuracy existed for multiparty systems. For two-party systems, the exercise is relatively trivial. With only two competitors, the accuracy score is simply the divergence of one candidate from their actual score – by definition, the other candidate's accuracy will be the same, simply signed differently. In that sense, there is a ready indicator of overall polling accuracy.[10] However, on moving to three or more competitors, the data become *compositional* – that is, no single candidate difference score necessarily conveys all the information about the polling accuracy, but all differences duplicate some of the same information (similarly to if we reported both candidates' accuracy scores in a two-competitor race[11]).

A recently developed indicator, B, building upon a more sophisticated summary measure of polling predictive accuracy for two-party races (Martin et al., 2005), now allows us a practical index for multiparty settings (Arzheimer and Evans, 2013). Based upon a multinomial statistical measure of the relative odds of voting for each party or candidate, the B index is a summary of the overall accuracy of the poll predicting the multiparty race.[12] A weighted version of the index can be calculated which takes into account the share of the vote for each candidate. This way, variations in the leading candidate scores – which matter more in the overall outcome of the election – can be given greater weight than similar variation for smaller candidates.[13]

Returning to the full polling data we have since July 2011, and taking into account the information available from polling institutes for their polls, including sample size, we can plot the (un)weighted B_w (B) scores across time. Figures 7.1 and 7.2 provide these plots, including only polls ($n = 95$) for which the two measures could be calculated.[14] A couple of words about the plots are in order. First, each plot has four lines – these correspond to the possible codings of the candidates. For software reasons, the maximum number of candidates we can include is nine. With ten candidates to cover, we therefore need to code Nathalie Arthaud and Jacques Cheminade (just over 0.8 per cent of the national vote) as 'other'. This coding is mapped by the B8 and B_w8 line. However, we are also able to collapse together increasing numbers of minor candidates to assess the effect of focusing on just the leading two, three and five candidates, reflecting the run-off candidates ($B2/B_w2$); the increase in inaccuracy when including Le Pen ($B3/B_w3$); and the overall accuracy for the candidates identified as influencing the competitive dynamics of the election ($B5/B_w5$). Second, as critical junctures, we include two reference lines by date. The first is 16 October 2011, when François Hollande was identified as the Socialist candidate after the primary run-off; the second

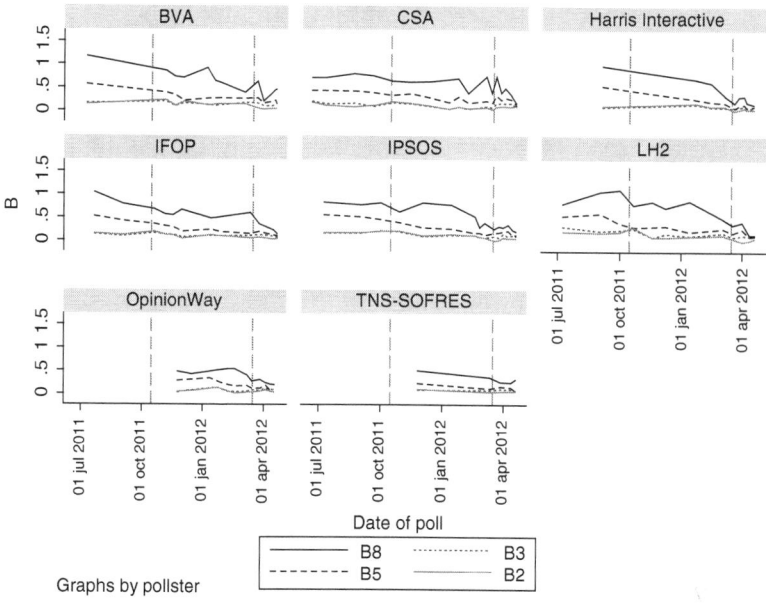

Figure 7.1 Polling accuracy across time (unweighted)

is 16 March 2012, when candidates had to register their candidacy, accompanied by the requisite 500 signatures.

Across time, there appears to be a consistent decrease in B_w as the election approaches. With regard to the two critical junctures, four of the six polling organisations for which we have data at this stage demonstrate inflections on or shortly after the announcement of Hollande's definitive candidature. BVA's change occurs too long after the date, and is an artefact of the single preceding poll. Similarly the gap between polls for Harris Interactive is too long to allow any analysis. For the four others, however, there is evidence of a shift in public opinion towards the eventual result once the Socialist candidate is identified. In Chapters 4 and 6, we confirmed that the identity of the Socialist candidate was in many ways immaterial to the final result. However, the confirmation of the identity of the candidate is still important in the polls as it stabilises the polling estimate.

There are divergent trends in the data after the 16 March split. Once the final roster of candidates had been identified, one might expect opinion to stabilise around voters' final choices. BVA, CSA and IFOP show this. However, for LH2, Harris Interactive and OpinionWay, quite

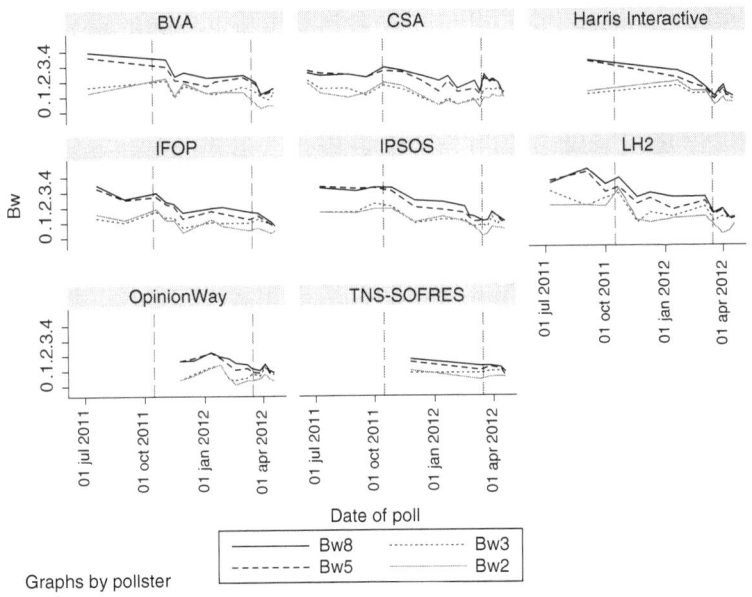

Figure 7.2   Polling accuracy across time (weighted)

the opposite is seen – a divergence from the eventual result occurs in the post-500-signature period. There is one interesting exception across these three – the two-candidate coding for LH2 drops significantly, unlike the other three codings. In other words, the accuracy for the two main candidates plus the others is much higher than when these candidates are left separate. If a true depiction, this suggests that for the LH2 sample in this period, opinion had stabilised for the leaders but not amongst the other candidates. Of course, this dynamic is not reflected by the other polling organisations, so it may be an artefact of sampling or house effect.

What is clear, however, is that more nuanced codings including eight separate candidates shows the highest B_w. As more candidates are collapsed into an 'other' category, so a degree of individual bias is confounded, thereby apparently increasing overall accuracy. There is an evident divide between the three-candidate coding (which tracks the two-candidate counterpart for the most part) and the five-candidate coding (which tracks the eight-candidate version). Part of this is predictable – the vote share of the five- and two-party 'other' category varies only by a small number of percentage points, whereas there is a shift of over 20 per cent between the three- and five-candidate codings.

In particular, the post–16 March period shows interesting differences between polling institutes. We need to be aware that ostensibly greater fluctuation nearer the election is an artefact of the higher frequency of polls. All institutes show converged B and B_w estimates for their last poll, but the 'route' to convergence differs. LH2 for instance shows quite substantial bias in its eight-candidate coding – suggesting significant accuracy issues with minor candidates – until very close to the poll. CSA on the other hand has strikingly stable accuracy estimates over the entire period, but again with oscillations in the eight-candidate coding in the final weeks. OpinionWay shows probably the most sustained and convergent set of B_w biases (the TNS-SOFRES scores being largely due to a small number of data points).

Looking at average B and B_w scores using the eight-candidate coding (Table 7.4), TNS-SOFRES enjoys the highest degree of overall accuracy in 2012, with BVA showing the greatest bias. From the available reported results, TNS-SOFRES has markedly fewer polls, with the majority held much closer to the election than other institutes. The change in candidates looking to run would suggest that polling accuracy should increase after the 16 March cut-off (Table 7.5). Both BVA and TNS-SOFRES scores improve after this date. However, looking at the average B and B_w scores by each institute, this is not the case for all. For CSA, IFOP and IPSOS – three of France's leading polling organisations – as well as LH2, polling accuracy did not improve, or worsened, after the cut-off. Nor had this anything to do with polling method – there is no evident relationship between telephone or Internet polls and accuracy. Indeed, IFOP and IPSOS enjoy markedly similar polling averages using the distinct methods.

Overall, then, polling institutes performed adequately as indicators of the 'state of play' in the 2012 campaign. Whilst there were some poor episodes – and a couple of red faces on election night itself – the

Table 7.4 Average polling accuracy by polling organisation

	B	B_w	No. of polls
BVA	.28	.20	15
CSA	.27	.17	18
Harris Interactive	.20	.13	9
IFOP	.23	.16	13
IPSOS	.21	.15	16
LH2	.26	.19	14
OpinionWay	.21	.14	12
TNS-SOFRES	.17	.11	5

Table 7.5   Polling accuracy across electoral campaign

	B (pre-16/03/12)	B_w (pre-16/03/12)	B (post-16/03/12)	B_w (post-16/03/12)	Method
BVA	.32	.23	.28	.20	CATI
CSA	.26	.17	.30	.18	CATI
Harris Interactive	.25	.17	.25	.15	CAWI
IFOP	.26	.18	.28	.18	CAWI
IPSOS	.24	.18	.28	.18	CATI
LH2	.30	.23	.33	.23	CATI
OpinionWay	.25	.15	.21	.14	CAWI
TNS-SOFRES	.20	.13	.17	.11	CATI

stabilisation of estimates across time brought the majority of institutes' forecasts into line with the result. To that extent, there is no reason to castigate them for poor performance or manipulation. Only when expectations are too high of their performance do they disappoint: a forecast of Marine Le Pen support near one-quarter of the electorate over a year before the ballot should be read only as an indicator of rising support, not of eventual outcome. This comes with one caveat: whilst French pollsters continue to refuse to release their unadjusted data, a proof of the validity and robustness of their work on providing a valuable benchmark for election dynamics will remain indirect and speculative. Whatever the concerns regarding political manipulation, the full original data can serve to reinforce, not weaken, their contribution.

3. Legislative forecasts

The principal focus for forecasters in 2012, as in previous elections, was to forecast the presidential result. As Table 7.1 showed, only one author concentrated on the legislative race, and did so for the second-round prediction (Foucault, 2012). Far less common are forecasts for the first round, and where these exist they generally follow a multi-model format, with separate estimators for different party groupings. Here we employ a single multiparty model previously constructed for the 2007 legislative elections by Arzheimer and Evans (2010). Using a statistical technique called seemingly unrelated regression, the model estimates the likelihood of vote for one party or grouping compared with a common reference category, according to the explanatory variables of interest. Once these likelihoods are converted back to proportions of vote, the predicted estimate for each party can be compared directly with the actual vote share.[15]

The model faces a significant challenge to its accuracy. Despite being multiparty, the level of measurement – the departmental level of vote – requires relatively stable party groupings to be used, to ensure representation across all 96 metropolitan territories. Some groupings are obvious: extreme right, for instance, combines FN and other extreme right candidate votes together. As an anti-system group on the Right still cut off by the *cordon sanitaire*, we may safely assume this forms a single unit. Similarly, the main competitive unit of the radical Left, the Communist Party and its running partners in Mélenchon's formation, also forms a self-contained unit. However, where to place the other radical Left candidates is more problematic. As low-scoring candidates unevenly spread across the French political landscape, but nevertheless in competition with the PCF, we relegate these to 'other'.

Similarly, the main competitive blocs are complex. The moderate left inevitably forms around the Socialists and their political symbiont, the PRG. Other independent and dissident Left (*divers gauche*), sharing greater or lesser shares of the moderate left electorate, are also included. However, EELV poses a time-series problem. For elections between 1981 and 1997, the Greens were clearly independent competitors to the Left. The forecast model has been built around this coding, and similarly in 2002 and 2007, Greens were put in the 'other' category. This does however lead us to risk underestimating the moderate left vote. On the moderate right, a similar dilemma emerges. The UMP and precursor RPR forms the core, together with minor right-wing movements formerly in coalition with the predominant governing party. As discussed earlier in this chapter, the MODEM presents a similar issue. Its historical umbrella UDF belonged in the moderate right group. However, since 2007, the MODEM has formed a significant competitor to the UMP, with the aspirations of Bayrou to lead a Centre formation, and in 2012 one that increasingly leaned to the Left. In 2007, the MODEM was already coded as 'other', a decision we retain here. Other also contains regionalist parties and blank and spoilt ballots. A final abstention category forms our reference – we include them as we wish to forecast the choices of the entire French electorate (*électeurs inscrits*), including the spoilt and blank ballots in the 'other' category, not just the *bulletins exprimés* (valid votes cast). These groupings' vote share is measured at the departmental level, giving 96 observations per legislative election since 1981.[16]

As far as the predictors are concerned, we include two economic variables – growth in GDP in the year of the election, and absolute rate of unemployment by department in the quarter of the election, in other words Q2.[17] We also include an incumbency dummy variable (left-wing government) to estimate the effect of a further penalisation on the government in power, particularly in the presence of poor unemployment figures (which we identify using an interaction between incumbency and departmental unemployment). Finally, to pick up any other specificities by department including political tradition, we include a series of dummies which work as fixed effects for each department. Lastly, in keeping with standard practice for time-series data, we use robust standard error estimators to correct for any autocorrelation in error not picked up by the fixed effects (Huber, 1967; White, 1982).

Table 7.6 presents the parameters of the model run on ex post data, in other words the elections between 1981 and 2007. The coefficients when 2007 is included are generally similar to those found in the original model (Arzheimer and Evans, 2010: 24, table), although in most cases the size of the effect has diminished. In particular, rises in unemployment still penalise mainstream parties, but not to the same degree, especially for the moderate left group, where the relative effect (compared with abstention) is now identical to the moderate right, reflecting perhaps the consolidation of the PS in its role as the main opposition party since 2002, less likely therefore to be 'blamed' for poor economic performances. Looking at the R^2 for each contrast, however, it is clear that the introduction of the 2007 data into the ex post baseline does not improve the overall fit. As was noted in the original forecast, the 2007 election encountered some significant issues, not least the removal of the MODEM from the moderate right grouping into the 'other' group – as we saw earlier in this chapter, a problem also encountered in other

Table 7.6   Parameter estimates for full model forecasts (1981–2007)

	Communist	Mod. left	Mod. right	Ext. right	Other
Unemployment (U)	0.08 (.01)	−0.05 (.01)	−0.05 (<.01)	0.40 (.02)	0.40 (.05)
Left incumbency (I)	−0.76 (.13)	−0.30 (.08)	−0.25 (.09)	2.39 (.25)	3.50 (.59)
ΔGDP	0.03 (.01)	0.13 (<.01)	0.05 (<.01)	0.24 (.03)	−0.82 (.11)
UxI	0.08 (.01)	0.05 (.01)	0.07 (.01)	−0.11 (.02)	−0.34 (.06)
R^2	0.43	0.52	0.56	0.57	0.29
Recall R^2 (2007)	0.59	0.61	0.57	0.61	0.36
Root MSE	0.70	0.37	0.25	0.90	2.79

Notes: – All contrasts with abstention baseline.
– Departmental dummies not shown.
– All coefficients significant at p <.05 or lower.

forecast models (Nadeau et al., 2012b) – as well as the somewhat unexpected magnitude of the post-presidential deflation in the FN legislative score. A necessary coding choice for the statistical model does not sit well with contemporary political reality.

This is confirmed when we turn to the predictive strength of the models (Table 7.7). For 2007, the model had had mixed success. Whilst it predicted the winner of the race, and came close to the extreme right score – even *under*-predicting what had been seen as an unexpectedly low score – the overall error in prediction was much higher for this election than for ex post predictions of all the other legislative ballots between 1981 and 2002 (Arzheimer and Evans, 2010: 26–28). For 2012, through incorporating the 2007 'weak case' into the foundation, there are some improvements. The model, for example, over-predicts the Communist vote much less severely. The PC's performance in 2012 as part of the FG is more in keeping with its historical performance and its traditional role as a protest force in French politics, subject to contemporary economic conditions and executive incumbency. With regard to the mainstream governing blocs, the over- and under-prediction is inverted – this time, the losing moderate right are over-predicted, and the moderate left under-predicted, by roughly the same margin. As we might expect for a model that does not control for personality effects or other contextual influences, the victorious party's premium post-presidentials are not accounted for. Finally, the extreme right forecast performed well in 2007 because it anticipated the poor performance of the FN – in 2012, conversely, it fails to pick up the significant boost

Table 7.7 Predicted and observed vote outcomes in 2012 (% of total voters registered and of votes cast)

	% Registered voters		% Votes cast (incl. spoilt and blank)	
	Observed	Predicted	Observed	Predicted
Communists	4.0	6.0	6.7	9.2
Moderate left	20.8	16.6	34.7	25.3
Moderate right	20.5	26.2	34.2	39.9
Extreme right	8.1	2.3	13.5	3.5
Other	6.5	14.5	10.9	22.1
Abstention	40.1	34.4		

Note: The percentages refer to proportion of registered votes for metropolitan France, thereby excluding DOM-TOM and *Français d'outre-mer*.

to the legislative score from Marine Le Pen (albeit, as we shall see in Chapter 8, a boost below expectations for the party). As we discuss elsewhere (Evans and Ivaldi, 2012a), one crucial issue to forecasting the FN vote in 2012 was the extent to which a probable Marine Le Pen's personality effect could be first measured and then incorporated into any given set of estimates derived otherwise from the long period of uninterrupted reign by her father.

Can 2007, then, be regarded as an outlier which degrades the forecast potential of the model for 2012? Table 7.8 also reports the forecast for 2012 if the 2007 data were excluded, as well as the individual differentials. It certainly appears to be the case that a number of the party grouping forecasts improve. The moderate left forecast improves almost threefold, with a very small change in moderate right accuracy, and 0.5 deterioration in the extreme right forecast. The 'other' category improves noticeably. The main deterioration is in the Communist forecast, which is an improvement on the 2007 forecast but double the error of 2012 with 2007 included. In real-world terms, then, the MODEM's move to the 'other' category, whilst artificially boosting this group by including a relatively successful former centre-right grouping in 2007, thereby pushed expectations of the MODEM much too high in 2012. Had 2007's purple patch not occurred, the redistribution of votes to other parties, and the parties' subsequent catastrophic performance would have been much more in line with the historic trend for 'other' parties. The Green inclusion would also be in line.[18]

Similarly, the model's accurate prediction for the extreme right in 2007 worked only because of the collapse of FN turnout in the light of Jean-Marie Le Pen's poor presidential performance. A revivified FN under

Table 7.8 Comparison of individual errors in 2007 forecast and 2012 forecasts

	2007	2012	2012 (2007 excluded)
Communists/FDG	+6.1	+2.0	+4.5
Moderate left	+9.7	−4.2	−1.5
Moderate right	−3.6	+5.7	+5.9
Extreme right	−1.7	−5.8	−6.3
Other	−4.9	+8.0	+3.3
Abstention	−5.3	−5.7	−5.9

Note: The percentages refer to proportion of registered votes for metropolitan France, thereby excluding DOM-TOM and *Français d'outre-mer*.

Marine Le Pen's leadership and with strong regional footings cannot be anticipated by the model, even under the terms of the historic trend only. In short, the return of the FN's electoral success is not simply the same mechanism as its success in the 1990s and early 2000s, an observation which is corroborated by some of the changes which have taken place in the electoral support for the party in the 2012 elections, most evidently the erosion of the traditional 'radical Right gender gap' (Mayer, 2013). Nevertheless, abstention remains stable in its underestimation. However, whether this is direct evidence of the effect of the *quinquennat* is suggested but not provable by this model – fluctuations in accuracy of the model's prediction for the other elections are within ±5 per cent. Certainly, however, neither 2007 nor 2012 is wildly out of line with the historic trend.

Overall, given the issues identified in the model for 2007, and the difficulties a single model for a multiparty system imposes, the results are a useful confirmation of some of the trends in the electoral arena in 2012 and previously. As with any forecast specification, there remain a number of alternative specifications to test, using different predictors to the unemployment and GDP variables used here. Whilst one of the main 'known' conditions identified in Chapter 2 was based upon precisely these two economic variables – certainly with a primacy of unemployment – other predictors such as crime, immigration and even European position, which have been used in other forecasting contexts (e.g. Evans and Ivaldi, 2010), may also be appropriate, particularly for elections such as 2007 and 2012 where hard-line social policy characterised the Right of the spectrum. Work remains to be done, then, to explore the potential power of this approach, but 2012 confirms this to be a worthwhile venture.

*   *   *

Perhaps the main confirmation of the legislative model has been that, whilst the presidentials can be successfully predicted using a variety of approaches, one of the issues with 'independent' prediction of the legislatives is precisely that it now follows the presidentials in a way that was not previously the case, particularly for legislative elections in years apart from presidential races. Bayrou's performance undoubtedly added to the over-prediction of the MODEM's performance. Le Pen's personal success buoyed the FN support. However, in the relatively sterile environment of a panel time-series model, the manifestation of these

8
The Legislative Elections of June 2012

Under the Fifth Republic, elections to the National Assembly have always ceded primacy, constitutionally and institutionally, to the presidential race. Charles de Gaulle ensured that political parties received little or no mention within the Constitution, to suppress the divisive factionalisation of political representation which had proved so deleterious to the Third and Fourth republics (Wright, 1989: 4). The elections which would empower these parties in identifying the governing coalition fared little better constitutionally, receiving a single line in Article 24 noting that they should be by direct universal suffrage, as compared with the presidential election's more substantial definition in Article 7.

So much for the founder's intentions: the three successive post-presidential legislative elections of 2002, 2007 and 2012 in fact represented a return to the secondary role of the legislative function after a period in which the National Assembly elections attained a higher saliency, which enabled them to act as a block to, if not parity with, presidential ambition, resulting in two periods of cohabitation starting in 1993 and 1997. In 1986, when for the first time a government was appointed which did not come from the presidential camp, some commentators doubted the ability of the Republic to survive a bicephalous executive with antagonistic heads. Right-wing domination and Left fragmentation had ensured de Gaulle, Pompidou and Giscard all inherited broadly aligned governments, with legislative elections sorting out some internecine clashes but with no real executive implication.

Two years proved that the imminent collapse some feared was an exaggeration. However, the periods of cohabitation which followed did demonstrate the legislative deadlock to which divisive policies would give rise. As the governmental partners to a right-wing President for the later five-year period of cohabitation between 1997 and 2002, a Socialist

Party with its eye on occupying the Elysée Palace with a supporting majority and coinciding elections for the new presidential *quinquennat* returned the system to the *status quo ante*, where a President governing without a legislative majority was not only constitutionally, but also rationally, unthinkable.

In a system where the election to the Assembly now follows within weeks of a presidential election, the likelihood of an outcome providing anything other than a supportive majority for the elected incumbent is small. The legislative elections can therefore reasonably be described as a plebiscite of endorsement for the President. In short, we no longer look to legislative elections to provide a macro-outcome other than continuity for a successfully returned incumbent, or *alternance* to reflect an opposition presidential victory.

Since 2002, the reduction of the presidential term to five years, with legislative elections immediately coming after the presidentials, has affected both the mechanical and psychological forces that shape responses by parties and voters. The new institutional setting has intensified the effect of the '*vote utile*', or the tendency to avoid wasting votes on minor peripheral parties with little chance of getting seats. The accentuation of this form of strategic voting shapes the party system, increasing its degree of presidentialisation and reducing fractionalisation. Moreover, voting intentions for legislative elections are altered by the perception of what happened in the presidentials to affect the overall political regime, one assumption being that voters would tend to support the newly elected President in the legislative ballot to avoid another period of divided government.

In this chapter, we will first look at the competitive strategies on both the Left and the Right, strongly determined by the outcome of the presidentials. Having then looked at the overall outcome of the two rounds of the legislative race on 10 and 17 June, we will then look to understand what micro-outcomes – constituency-level results – tell us about the context in which these ballots took place, and most importantly what indications of future dynamics in the party system and political competition more generally could be discerned at the close of the fourth ballot in three months.

1. Competitive strategies in the legislatives

The dynamics and outcome of the presidential election did not significantly change as they moved to collective rather than personalised competition in the legislatives. Following Hollande's election, a victory of the Left was the most plausible scenario for the June legislatives, the crucial issue being whether the PS could secure an overall majority by itself or would need to rely on parliamentary support from other left-wing actors, most particularly EELV, the PRG and – worst-case scenario for the PS, barring the slim possibility of defeat – the FG. Nevertheless, the danger of the extremes was more immediate on the Right of the spectrum, where a groggy UMP would now confront an electorally reinvigorated FN.

Under such conditions, which are certainly not new to 2012, parties therefore have very strong incentives to cooperate in semi-permanent electoral cartels or, as was demonstrated by the formation of the UMP in 2002, to enhance their competitiveness through organisational transformation. The logic is one of consolidation. A quick glance at the total number of candidates in the legislatives over the past ten years shows a decline, from an average of 14.8 contenders per metropolitan constituency in 2002 down to 11.4 in 2012 (see Table 8.1). Over the *longue durée*, the tight competitiveness during the famous bipolar quadrille of the 1970s and 1980s gave way to a profusion of minor party candidacies in the 1990s, the blossoming of the extremes reaching its zenith in 2002. That the competitive structure has become less

Table 8.1 Candidates per constituency in legislative elections (1958–2012)

Year	Constituencies*	Candidates	Mean
1958	465	2.8	6.0
1962	465	2.2	4.6
1967	470	2.2	4.6
1968	470	2.3	4.8
1973	473	3.0	6.3
1978	474	4.2	8.9
1981	474	2.7	5.6
1986**		769 departmental lists	
1988	555	2.8	5.0
1993	555	5.1	9.3
1997	555	6.2	11.2
2002	555	8.2	14.8
2007	555	7.4	13.4
2012	539***	6.2	11.4

Notes: *Figures are for metropolitan France; **1986: Proportional representation; ***Following redistricting in 2011.

complex over the past decade is mostly accounted for by the persistence of strategies of accommodation in the mainstream of the French party system, although with a higher degree of party fragmentation continuing on its fringes.

1.1. The Left in the legislatives

Within the Left bloc, parties very much followed the patterns observed in the presidential race, with a high level of mainstream cooperation and continued party fragmentation on the extreme left. Despite a poor showing in the presidentials, and the strong institutional incentives for collaboration in the legislative arena, the parties of the extreme left failed to present a united front in the June elections, partly as a result of differing strategic objectives but also partly as a result of a psychological rejection of the reality of narrowing opportunities offered by 'confirmatory' post-presidential legislative ballots in the French political system.

Consistent with the party's traditional position as a revolutionary anti-system force, LO ran independently across 552 constituencies – one short of the 553 candidates in 2007 – refusing to negotiate stand-down agreements with the other parties of the Left. The persistence of strategic disagreements vis-à-vis the PS also stymied most electoral pacts between the NPA and the FG despite overlap and convergence amongst sections of their respective leaderships. The two parties only reached formal unitary accords in 25 constituencies, whereas the NPA candidates stood in another 339 locations – nonetheless an indication of the diminishing organisational strength of the movement, which in 2007 had managed to field a total of 487 candidates under the old LCR label. The salience of internal splits increased during the legislative campaign, eventually leading to yet another schism in the NPA, which resulted from the defection by the anti-capitalist Left (*gauche anticapitaliste*) faction of Pierre-François Grond and Myriam Martin to the FG in July 2012.

The FG exhibited a more conciliatory position in the legislatives, as a consequence of the increased electoral pressure by the FN and the somewhat disappointing presidential performance by Mélenchon, as well as the more pragmatic attitude by the communists, dictated by the imperative of safeguarding their pool of outgoing deputies by avoiding overt confrontation with their hegemonic Socialist counterparts. Still, diverging political goals came to the forefront of the debates held at the PC's national conference in June 2012. They manifested themselves principally through the juxtaposition of Mélenchon's widely publicised bid to confront Le Pen in Hénin-Beaumont with the lower-profile and more conciliatory line by communist candidates across most constituencies.

Mélenchon's key tactic throughout the campaign was to attack the FN candidates persistently on the campaign trail, and in particular in the television studio in the pre-election debates on *Des Paroles et Des Actes*. But this was an asymmetric battle: Le Pen was entirely reluctant to spend time debating a minor candidate looking to capitalise on anti-FN feeling, and thereby lose time for herself attacking mainstream Left and Right candidates, who offered easier targets and potentially larger electoral returns. Indeed, the difficulty of Le Pen's position became clear in the televised debate, where she made it clear she would not engage with Mélenchon, whom she described as 'la voiture-balai de [François] Hollande' (Hollande's broom wagon). To debate the PG candidate on equal terms risked being beaten in a debate; but not to debate him potentially gave ammunition to critics claiming she was threatened by a credible populist alternative, and demonstrating the same ostracisation tactics of which she accuses the political mainstream.

The continuation by Mélenchon of his presidential strategy of distancing himself from the PS, although a useful counter to Le Pen's accusations, was decidedly at odds with the communists' main objective of preserving their ability to influence policy-making through their integration into the new left-wing majority. The radicalisation and hard anti-PS stance of Mélenchon during the presidential campaign narrowed the scope for electoral cooperation with the mainstream Left and precluded tactical agreements between the FG, the PS and EELV across constituencies where the FN threat was deemed to be most serious. The realisation by the FG of the need to tone down their attacks on Hollande became visible in the joint efforts by Pierre Laurent (PC) and Martine Billard (PG) to broker a pre-election deal with the Socialists in those constituencies having an FN threat. It did not succeed. Overall, the various constitutent parties of the FG stood independently in 556 constituencies. As part of the original presidential trade-off with the FG, and because of the existing organisational and grass-roots resources of the communists, the PCF represented the coalition in no less than 415 constituencies (about three-quarters), compared with 102 and 22 for the PG and the Gauche Unitaire GU, respectively.

Following Hollande's success in the presidentials, the PS maintained its position of dominance within the Left bloc, a position which was likely to be strengthened further by the institutional and psychological effects described above that are inherent in the legislatives. That the PS refused to consider electoral pacts with the FG was testimony to the growing estrangement provoked by Mélenchon's policy shift to the Left and his denigration of Hollande's leadership skills. As in 2007, either the PS or the MRC ran candidates against all outgoing communist deputies.

Socialist intransigence also revealed the importance of the 2011 EELV–PS agreement, whereby the PS had already made substantial concessions to their environmentalist partners in the allocation of single-candidate constituencies, as well as Hollande's willingness not to appear to have been taken hostage by the more radical policy preferences of the FG, thereby giving the UMP the opportunity to raise the spectre of the 'Reds' being about to return to power. The EELV–PS platform was intended to provide the environmentalists with the opportunity of forming a parliamentary group through the allocation of 63 constituencies. The analysis of the size of the electoral support for the Left – as measured by Hollande's score in the second round of the presidentials – showed that EELV had effectively been allocated a number of safe-seat constituencies: on average, Hollande had received 49.1 per cent in the constituencies where EELV were running as unitary candidates, compared with 47.7 per cent where the PS was representing the alliance. Whether the Socialists felt better placed to defend less safe seats against the Right than their EELV partners, or simply 'gifted' a relatively small proportion of safe seats to their minor allies is moot. One definite consequence of the above electoral pact was to reduce the number of candidates put forward by both parties, with a relatively even distribution of 462 and 472 contenders for the Greens and the Socialists.

1.2. Re-composition of the Right?

Turning to the Centre and the Right of the political spectrum, important changes occurred in the structure of competition, some of which had already been embedded in the configuration of the presidential arena. The legislative campaign confirmed the isolation and electoral marginalisation of the MODEM, a much higher level of fragmentation of the centre-right camp on 2007, and individually the diminishing strength of the UMP. In strategic terms, the legislatives saw a notable change in the FN's position vis-à-vis the mainstream Right, and confirmed that the episodic tactic of the Republican front which had been put under significant pressure in 2011 had indeed come to an end.

Following Bayrou's mediocre performance in the presidentials, the MODEM entered the legislative campaign as a largely irrelevant political force, lacking coalition and blackmail potential on either side of the political spectrum. To the Left, a newly incumbent President had made clear that a Left–Centre alliance was out of the question, whatever the MODEM leader's personal inclination in his second-round presidential choice. To the Right, that choice had pushed the UMP yet further away and despatched any possibility of a MODEM-saving alliance to the realm of the absurd. In 2012, his party ran 400 candidates under the new Centre pour la France umbrella (of which 345 were members of the MODEM), as opposed to 529 five years earlier, reflecting the organisational impact of the series of electoral misfortunes experienced by the party over the 2008–2012 period. Symbolically, the decision by the PS to field a candidate against Bayrou in his stronghold of Pau confirmed that the political space for an independent centre was slender, and that there was very little chance of survival in the highly bipolarised competition dominating the legislative arena, outside forming a tactical alliance with one of the two main ideological blocs – an option that had been taken off the table long before.

The imminent collapse of the MODEM coincided with a significant reshuffling of the centre-right, resulting from the growing political autonomy of some of the former confederated parties of the UMP, in particular Borloo's radicals and Morin's NC. The strategy of right-wing clarity that Borloo at least had championed had failed in the presidentials, and the legislatives thereby represented an ideal opportunity to now mark out a territory for a new centre-right formation. Indeed, this strategy of differentiation from the mainstream Right stretched back to the building of the ARES in mid-2011. Whilst Sarkozy's ability to maintain credibility and thus electoral viability had eventually deterred a number of rival presidential candidacies on the centre-right in April, his eventual defeat, and more importantly his official retirement from national politics, plunged the UMP into a severe leadership crisis and decreased intra-party discipline, lessening its ability to avoid centrist fragmentation in the legislatives. Borloo's PR ran independently in 98 constituencies, competing against its former right-wing ally in 75 of these. The NC fielded 108 candidates, including 66 where the UMP was also standing. Additionally, Jean Arthuis' Alliance centriste ran in 55 constituencies.

The diminishing legislative strength of the UMP was well in evidence, despite the extension of the electoral agreement with Nihous' CPNT, and the disappearance of de Villiers' MPF on its Right flank.[1] Overall, it fielded 502 candidates as opposed to 548 in the 2007 elections. In nearly 300 constituencies, the UMP candidates found themselves running alongside Dupont-Aignan's DLR, whilst there was a sizeable increase in non-partisan 'other Right' candidates, from 291 in 2007 up to 489 in June 2012. Of greatest concern to the former governing party, however, was the FN, which ran a total of 572 candidates under the new Marine Blue Rally (*Rassemblement Bleu Marine*, RBM) franchise. Due mostly to the collapse of Mégret's MNR after 2008, the FN was in a position to further assert its political hegemony over the far-right camp, despite the attempt by rival minor organisations to join forces with the Parti de la France (PDF) and Robert Spieler's Nouvelle Droite Populaire (NDP). The UDN ran a total of 70 legislative candidates, but was to have virtually no impact whatsoever on the FN's electoral performance.

Perhaps most importantly, although probably as a mark of future dynamics rather than impact on the 2012 race, these legislatives saw a momentous transformation in both the mobilisation and potential for inter-party cooperation on the far right. A first signal was sent through the building of the RBM as a new electoral umbrella for the FN, which carried a message of change in the competitive strategies by the far right and its opening to party outsiders, as well as potentially to the mainstream. In sharp contrast with Le Pen's anti-establishment strategy in the presidentials, which was important to coalesce national support for a candidate *pas comme les autres*, the FN publicly envisaged negotiating mutual stand-down agreements with candidates of the more established parties. Immediately after the presidential ballot, Le Pen called explicitly upon UMP representatives in the field to 'break the *cordon sanitaire*' while simultaneously encouraging RBM candidates to foster talks with local leaders of the UMP.

At the national level, political ostracisation of the far right dominated the UMP's strategic agenda, with clear indications that the mainstream Right would maintain the cordon that had been built against the FN in the late 1990s. Locally, however, a number of right-wing hardliners – mostly in the Droite Populaire – expressed their disagreement with this uncompromising stance of the UMP leadership, and called for tactical pacts with the FN in the course of the legislative campaign, reminiscent of the profound trauma caused by the FN–Right collaborations of the 1998 regional elections. Furthermore, it turned out not to be beyond a number of vulnerable UMP *notables* to make more or less explicit appeals for FN voter support in tight races – mostly in vain, and to gloating media comment. Whilst there were virtually no formal FN–UMP alliances, the attenuation in the far right's anti-system strategy will undoubtedly bear important implications for the future of party competition on the Right, even more so when considering the decision by the UMP ultimately to renounce the 'Republican front' strategy, which will increase the FN's competitiveness in future fragmented three-way legislative contests.

In the lead-up to the legislatives, polls showed that public support for cooperation on the Right was on the rise, with 59 and 64 per cent of the

UMP and FN sympathisers respectively supporting a political alliance of the mainstream and the far right (OpinionWay–*Les Échos*, 24 May 2012), adding to the symbolic significance of Sarkozy's acknowledgement of the democratic nature of Le Pen's party before the presidential run-off. According to an IPSOS poll conducted before the second round of the presidentials, no less than 70 and 68 per cent of the UMP and FN supporters, respectively, said they were in favour of mutual stand-down agreements to block the candidate of the Left in legislative run-offs (IPSOS–*Le Monde*, 5 May 2012). Finally, the analysis of the questions employed occasionally in IFOP election polls since the late 1990s showed that the percentage of UMP sympathisers in favour of tactical pacts with the FN in local elections had risen from 36 per cent in 1998 to 54 per cent in May 2012 (IFOP–*Paris Match*, 6 May 2012).

2. The principal outcomes of the legislative elections

Hollande's victory in the run-off and the political momentum given by French voters to the Left sealed the likelihood of alternation in power at the June elections. On the Right, the brief era of Sarkozy's flamboyant leadership coming to an end, together with the electoral resuscitation of the FN, threatened to damage severely the UMP's parliamentary presence, even potentially amplifying the impact of electoral swings to the Left if the FN managed to make it as far as the second round and exercise its historic 'nuisance power' in splitting the right-wing vote. As had already been the case in 2002 and 2007, voter turnout was anticipated to play a crucial role in shaping party competition in the run-offs.

2.1. 'Des Français à nouveau démobilisés' – again[2]

Whatever the strategic incentives for cooperation and standing down, the political offer only apportions the votes cast. The outcome of legislative elections in France (as elsewhere) is heavily determined by turnout. However, perhaps more strongly than in other countries with different institutional set-ups, the positioning of the legislative elections directly after the presidentials has worked to depress turnout subsequent to a trend when legislative turnout was already dropping.

Figure 8.1 tells a story very different to the presidential outcome of a month earlier. Despite presidential turnout remaining above 80 per cent and the watershed return of a Socialist President, by June a significant proportion of the electorate had lost interest or were unwilling to cast their vote. The 2012 legislatives exhibited the highest abstention rates ever since the beginning of the Fifth Republic, with 42.8

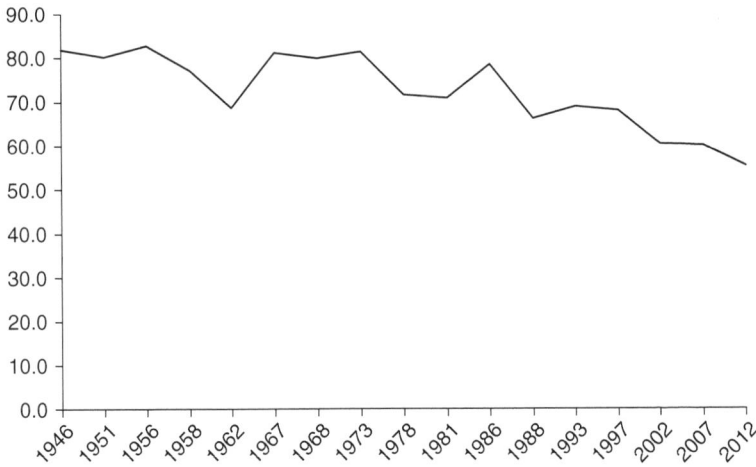

Figure 8.1   Legislative turnout in post-war France

Source: Institute for democracy and electoral assistance (IDEA), http://www.idea.int/vt/countryview.cfm?id=53.

and 44.6 per cent in the first and second round, respectively – to which one should add blank and spoiled ballots amounting to 0.9 and 2.1 per cent – confirming the declining trend in legislative turnout since the late 1980s. The simplest interpretation of this is that the record low turnout combined a level of fatigue for elections seen as confirmatory, rather than truly competitive, together with individuals actively deciding against voting in elections for the parties of candidates who had disappointed in the presidentials. Opinion polls tapping campaign interest in the legislatives showed that the enthusiasm for the presidential election had waned: one week before the legislatives, 59 per cent of the French were expressing interest in the campaign, compared with 74 per cent in the presidentials.[3] Media coverage of the legislatives notably framed competition by looking at individual political personalities and highly symbolic constituencies across the country rather than the substance of the parties' policies, which had been examined in the presidentials. Simultaneously, campaign news focused predominantly on the future developments of the main party actors – for example, Aubry's successor as First Secretary of the PS, or the anticipated leadership crisis within the UMP.

Looking more closely at the profile of abstainers partially confirms this (Table 8.2). An IPSOS survey including the sociological profile of the abstentionists indicates a number of reasons for this record abstention.

Table 8.2 Sociological and political profile of abstainers in 2012 legislative elections (first round)

TOTAL	Voters	Abstainers
	57.2	42.8
Gender		
Men	55	45
Women	59	41
Age		
18–24	34	66
25–34	43	57
35–44	50	50
45–59	62	38
60 and over	75	25
Occupation		
Self-employed	58	42
Professionals, managers	60	40
Middle management	56	44
Routine non-manual	48	52
Blue-collar workers	51	49
Retired	71	29
Education		
No education	61	39
BEPC/BEP/CAP/CEP	60	40
Baccalaureat	54	46
Bac + 2	55	45
Bac + 3	58	42
Vote in first round, presidentials		
J.-L. Mélenchon	62	38
François Hollande	68	32
François Bayrou	54	46
Nicolas Sarkozy	65	35
Marine Le Pen	54	46
Party proximity		
FG	75	25
PS	69	31
Greens	50	50
MODEM	54	46
UMP	65	35
FN	54	46
None	37	63
Left/Right position		
Left	67	33
Right	60	40
Neither	33	67

Source: '1er tour des élections législatives. Comprendre le vote des Français', IPSOS–Logica Business Consulting for France Télévisions, Radio France, *Le Monde*, *Le Point*, http://www. ipsos.fr/sites/default/files/attachments/rapport_svv_leg_1er_tour_-_11_juin_2012_-_10h.pdf.

First, the standard sociological explanations of turnout are valid (Evans, 2004: 151). Abstention is strongest amongst predominantly younger males, and represented particularly amongst manual and routine non-manual occupational strata. However, this does not extend to education – the *bac* group sees the highest proportion of abstention followed by those with some level of university education. The differences are not large, but they are certainly not in line with other social indicators, or indeed with previous elections (Héran, 2004: 363).

Other noticeable differences can be seen in the political profile of abstainers. Abstention peaked among the more politically alienated sections of the electorate, with over two-thirds of those with no ideological affiliation in particular saying that they had not voted in the legislatives (67 and 69 per cent in the first and second round, respectively). With the exception of Mélenchon's voters, who were probably keener to consolidate the presidential victory of their camp, abstention was also higher than average among supporters of other third-party candidates. From the first round of the presidential election, François Bayrou and Marine Le Pen supporters were almost as likely to abstain as to vote in the legislatives. In contrast, voter turnout was higher in the mainstream parties, Hollande's supporters being perhaps unsurprisingly most likely to turn out. The legislatives focus on the dominant parties in each bloc maximising their legislative return across the vast majority of constituencies where they fielded candidates. Minor parties see significant support in constituencies where their candidates enjoy the chance of victory, but elsewhere unwinnable seats only mobilise smaller parties with difficulty.

UMP sympathisers were more likely than on average to vote, so there is no evidence that the defeat of Sarkozy left his close supporters feeling disenfranchised – at least, only a couple of points more than the victorious PS, and far less than the coin-toss Green supporters. Looking at general political affiliations in the electorate on the other hand provides some evidence of differential turnout, albeit of limited amplitude, with right-wing voters being more likely to abstain than left-wing supporters (40–33 per cent). A brief glance at the relationship between Sarkozy's first-round vote and abstention shows that abstention was generally higher in the departments where Sarkozy had achieved his best scores in the first round of the presidential election (Figure 8.2). The relationship is significant, and particularly strong if the two outliers – Seine-Saint Denis (93), where massive abstention accompanied one of Sarkozy's lowest votes, and Lozère (48), where turnout for the legislatives was well above average – are excluded.

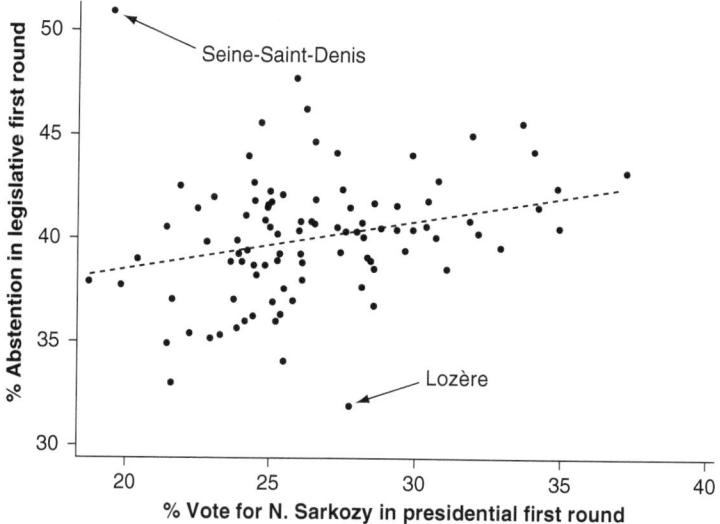

Figure 8.2 Relationship between Sarkozy first-round vote and first-round legislative abstention by department

Note: Pearson correlation (96 departments) = .270 (p < .01); Pearson correlation (94 departments, Seine-Saint-Denis and Lozère excluded) = .403 (p < .001).

Source: Ministry of the Interior.

Quite aside from the inputs to abstention, turnout has a very significant impact upon the shape of electoral competition itself. Growing abstention rates in legislative elections since the late 1970s have significantly raised the threshold for participation in second rounds, with a substantial increase in the average share of the valid vote needed to take part in the decisive round, from about 15 per cent up to nearly 22 per cent in the 2012 ballot (given the existing institutional requirement that a candidate must win over 12.5 per cent of registered voters to progress to the run-off) (see Figure 8.3).

Consequently, in constituencies where notably the FN expected to reach the run-off stage of the election through a reasonable, but third-placed first round performance, the opportunity to exercise its nuisance potential was denied because low turnout – paradoxically, often cited in elections as a bonus for far-right parties (Evans and Ivaldi, 2012b: 854) – prevented it from reaching the requisite proportion of the registered electorate. Of course, it was not just the FN who were to suffer from the high threshold. Most notably in the eliminations which might have been avoided with higher turnout was to be Jean-Luc Mélenchon in perhaps the highest-profile constituency of the election (see below).

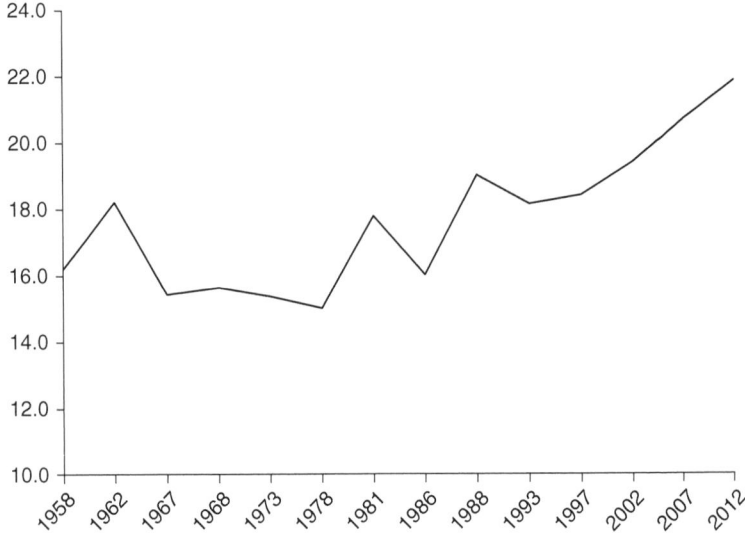

Figure 8.3   Theoretical electoral threshold* for legislative run-offs (1958–2012)
Note: *In per cent of the valid vote cast based on rule of 12.5 per cent of all registered voters, estimated from national turnout in first rounds of legislative elections.

2.2. A reversal of the balance of power

Turning to party performances, the 2012 legislatives corroborated the drop back towards bipolarisation of France's politics and the consolidation of a two-pole system oriented around the PS and the UMP, yet simultaneously exhibited a higher degree of polarisation from the electoral resurgence of peripheral protest parties on both extremes of the political spectrum, together with the marginalisation of the independent Centre embodied by Bayrou's MODEM. In June, the parties of the mainstream totalled only just over three-quarters (76.3 per cent) of the vote compared with 84.5 per cent five years earlier.[4]

Despite increasing polarisation, the 2012 elections showed no significant departure from the general trend towards the simplification of the more 'formal' party system, which is discernible in the relative strength of political actors in the parliamentary arena. As can be seen from Figure 8.4, the effective number of parties in the National Assembly shows a pronounced decrease in fractionalisation between 1978 and 2012. Overall, the number of parliamentary parties has dropped to a 2.8 average since the mid-1980s. The trend is even more marked in the Senate, where the effective number of parties has been halved from 6 down to 3 since the late 1950s. Enduring difficulties confronted by

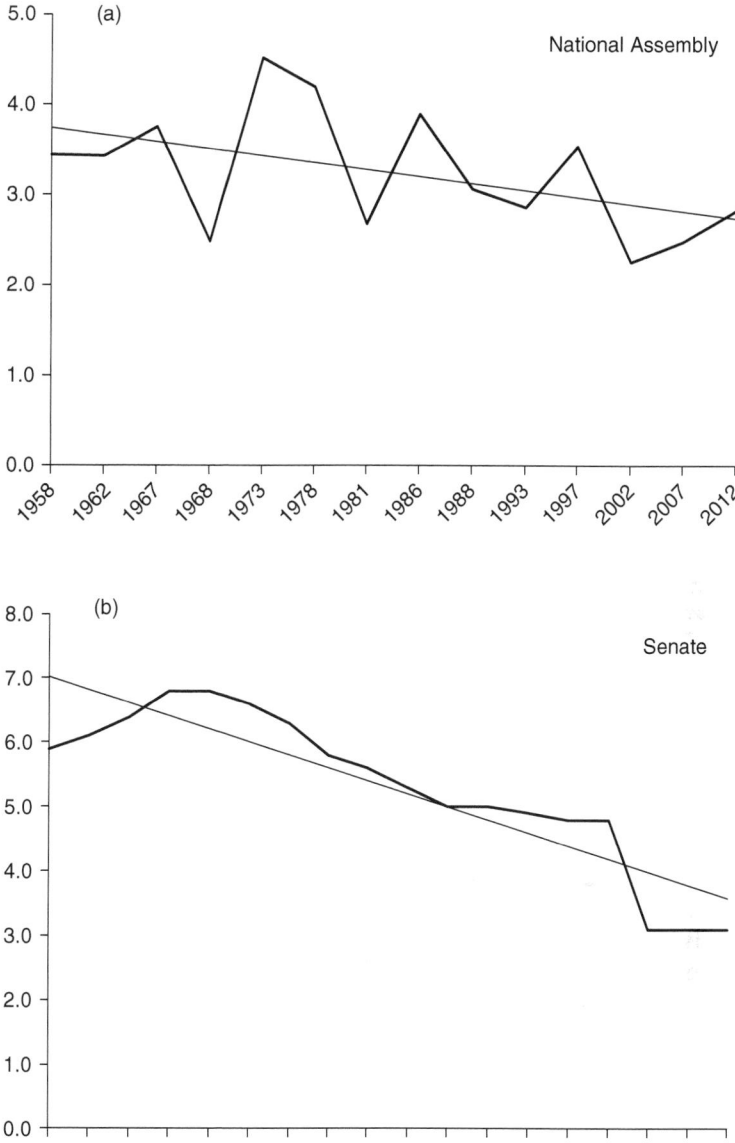

Figure 8.4 Effective number of parliamentary parties* in the French National Assembly and Senate (1958–2012)

Note: *Effective number of parliamentary parties calculated from seats (Laakso & Taagepera, 1979).

Source: Ministry of Interior, National Assembly & Senate.

parties outside the mainstream in gaining parliamentary representation are also revealed in levels of disproportionality, with an increase in the least squares index (LSI) (Gallagher, 1991) from 13.6 in 2007 up to 17.7 in 2012.

More importantly, the outcome of the 2012 legislative elections exposed the profound alteration in the general balance of power between the Left and the Right, with the former clearly reaping the electoral benefits of Hollande's presidential victory. This process of 'amplification' resulted first in an increase in the total vote share of left-wing parties in the first round of the legislatives, at 47.8 per cent up from 44 per cent in the presidential ballot. Compared with 2007, however, the Left camp progressed by 8.8 percentage points while the share of the right-wing vote fell simultaneously by 10.9 points. In terms of the parliamentary balance of power, then, the Left won a total of 341 seats against 229 for the mainstream Right; five years earlier, the UMP and its allies had totalled 345 seats as opposed to 227 for the Left.

Parties of the Left continued to gain momentum in the second round as the UMP largely failed to regain control of the electoral agenda. Unlike 2007, where the Left had been successful in generating a controversy around the alleged plan by the Fillon government to increase VAT, the 2012 campaign was devoid of such divisive issues which would have allowed the UMP to limit the electoral damage, although the UMP's very aggressive campaign on immigration and cultural issues certainly played a part in ensuring sustained mobilisation of core right-wing voters. Moreover, the new Ayrault government had been careful to put forward a number of highly popular reforms such as the partial return to retirement at 60, a modest increase in the minimum wage (SMIC) or imposing a pay ceiling for CEOs' salaries in the public sector, which certainly contributed to enhance the electoral attractiveness of the Left in the legislatives.

At the governmental level, the contrast between incumbents and challengers was stark. Before the first round of the legislatives, Prime Minister Jean-Marc Ayrault followed his predecessor Fillon in 2007 by making it clear to his government that any of them who stood for election in the legislatives and lost would be compelled to relinquish their ministerial portfolio as well. Twenty-six ministers, including Ayrault himself, nevertheless stood in the first round. Only two – Najat Vallaud-Belkacem, Minister for Women's Rights, and Christiane Taubira, Minister of Justice – withdrew from the election to avoid the possibility of a costly defeat. By the end of the second round, all 26 had won,

Table 8.3   Results of the 2012 legislative elections

Party	First-round vote	Second-round vote	Number of deputies
Extreme left	0.98	–	–
FDG	6.91	1.08	10
PS	29.35	40.91	280
PRG	1.65	2.34	12
Other Left	3.40	3.08	22
EELV	5.46	3.60	17
TOTAL LEFT	**47.75**	**51.01**	**341**
MODEM (Centre pour la France)	**1.77**	**0.49**	**2**
Centrist Alliance	0.60	0.53	2
Radical Party	1.24	1.35	6
NC	2.20	2.47	12
UMP	27.12	37.95	194
Other Right	3.51	1.81	15
TOTAL RIGHT	**34.67**	**44.11**	**229**
FN	13.60	3.66	2
Other extreme right	0.19	0.13	1
TOTAL EXTREME RIGHT	**13.79**	**3.79**	**3**
Regionalist	0.56	0.59	2
Other ecologist	0.96	–	–
Others	0.52	–	–

Source: Ministry of Interior.

with six of them (Ayrault, Fabius, Lurel, Cuvillier, Batho and Cazeneuve) elected at the first round.[5]

With 280 out of 577 seats in the National Assembly, it is clear that the Socialist Party victory in no way constituted utter domination of the legislative forum (Table 8.3). Easily the largest party and therefore unarguably fit to form Hollande's majority, the PS itself did not win an absolute majority of seats. Contrast this with the 313 seats won by the UMP in 2007, without *divers droite* and *majorité présidentielle* allies, which gave the party a hegemonic status no doubt responsible for the high level of stability enjoyed by the Fillon government across its five-year tenure. Too much emphasis can be placed on this 'diminished' plurality, however. Most importantly, the Socialist Party's pact with EELV and PRG assured it a total of 309 seats in coalition, more than ample for a working majority. An additional 22 *apparentés*, including a number of dissident candidates, in the parliamentary group pushed that majority even higher.

For the EELV, the stand-down pacts with the PS allowed it to win its largest ever tranche of seats, sufficient even to form a parliamentary group. This stresses the continuing process of institutionalisation in the Green party. Together with their 17 legislative seats, the ecologists have also made significant inroads in the Senate (ten seats) and the European Parliament (14 MEPs) while simultaneously entrenching themselves at the sub-national level with over 2,000 local and regional councillors. Its garnering two ministerial positions, with former *porte-parole* Cécile Duflot (Les Verts) as *Ministre du Logement* and Pascal Canfin (Europe Écologie) as *Ministre délégué au Développement* in the Quai d'Orsay, provided further legitimation for a party whose USP on environmental issues has long since been copied by mainstream parties, and whose governing credentials lie in providing differentiation – rather than radicalism – in a broad Left coalition.

It is clear that a Socialist Party unwilling to ally itself and gift seats to EELV would have managed to win most, if not all, of the *circonscriptions* it surrendered to the environmentalists. However, in maintaining the governing coalition which had proved intermittently troublesome for the Jospin administration between 1997 and 2002, the plural agenda of a dominant party looking to promote an alternative to austerity in its response to the economic crisis of 2012 was worth the loss, relatively speaking, of a handful of seats. Moreover, with EELV owing its position to the Socialist generosity, the likelihood of coalition fractures for anything short of outright policy deadlock is slim. In passing, a PRG which owes its continued existence since even the 1980s to Socialist indulgence, and conscious of its role in the 2002 presidential debacle, is even less likely to break ranks. The unwillingness of Christiane Taubira to risk standing in what was a relatively safe seat, for fear of losing the *Garde des Sceaux*, illustrates the premium placed on power.

To the Left of the PS, the isolationist position resulting, whether intentionally or not, from Mélenchon's populist stance saw a further blow to the PCF's political fortunes. With 6.9 per cent of the national vote, the result for the FG coalition proved to be a rather disappointing result for the anti-liberal camp, and only a marginal improvement on the PC's showing in 2007 (4.3 per cent). At party level, the legislative outcome revealed the limits of the anti-PS stance adopted by Mélenchon during the presidential campaign, precluding electoral cooperation with the Socialists. Electorally, the *'vote utile'* delivered a severe blow to the FG's national leadership: together with Mélenchon himself, Martine Billard, François Delapierre and Éric Coquerel were all defeated in their respective constituencies.

The campaign certainly exposed further the precarious strategic equilibrium achieved by the PCF within the FG coalition, further away from their former Socialist partners. In the legislatives, the communists made limited electoral gains from collaborating with Mélenchon – in 2012 the FG won just over 600,000 votes more than the PCF five years earlier – which could hardly compensate for their losses suffered in the French Assembly. Indeed, the PCF saw its parliamentary strength diminish further, with the number of communist deputies moving down to ten – including PG's Marc Dolez – from 15 in the previous legislature, and compared with 21 immediately after the 2002 elections (Figure 8.5). The governing Left running in all constituencies with outgoing deputies barred the PC from progressing into the run-off in no fewer than seven of 12 cases. Only four outgoing deputies eventually secured re-election, owing largely to the benevolence of the other parties of the Left with the PS and EELV standing down in five constituencies allowing for the re-election of outgoing FG MPs – most notably Marie-George Buffet, as well as Dolez. That the surviving communist deputies had then to seek *ad hoc* alliances with a number of independent deputies from the overseas territories in order to safeguard their parliamentary group was testimony to the institutional decline of the PCF.

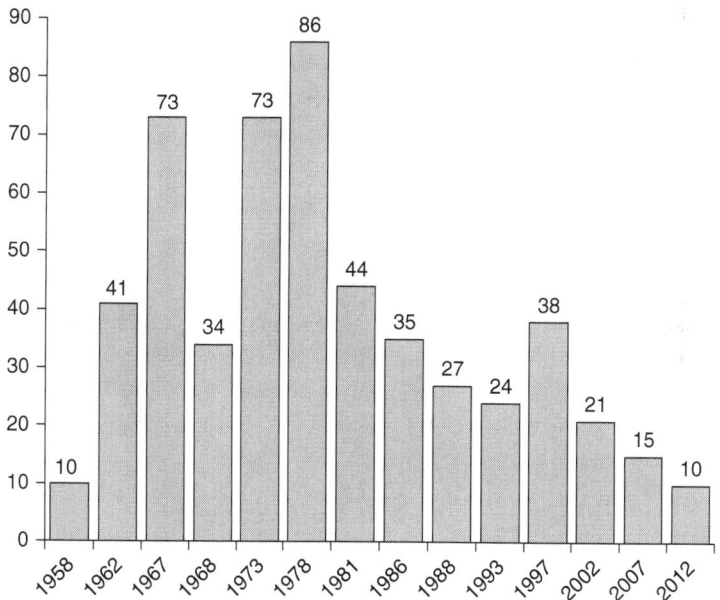

Figure 8.5 Number of communist deputies (1958–2012)
Note: In 1958, ten MPs in the group of *'non inscrits'*.
Source: National Assembly (http://www.assemblee-nationale.fr/elections/historique.asp).

On the Right of the political spectrum, the situation of the UMP in the legislatives mirrored that of the PS five years earlier. The former presidential party had to confront both a crisis of leadership after Sarkozy's retirement from politics, and the imperative to renew its policies to adapt to the changing mood of the French public. The legislative campaign showed very little deviation from the 'hard-line' cultural strategy that had prevailed in Sarkozy's presidential bid. The UMP embarked on yet another 'crusade' against immigration and the 'welfare bums', while simultaneously advocating public debt reduction and traditional right-wing values of authority, family and work.

In the first round, the UMP candidates polled 27.1 per cent of the vote nationally, down from 39.5 per cent in 2007. Altogether, parties of the moderate right – UMP, NC, PRV, PCD, MPF, CPNT – won 34.7 per cent of the vote share, showing an improvement of about 7.5 points on Sarkozy's first-round performance in the presidentials. Their progression was most notable in the rural areas, where Marine Le Pen had made significant gains in the presidentials, and where the mainstream Right was represented by well-entrenched local *notables* in the legislatives. The second round was marked by a severe electoral setback for the outgoing parliamentary majority with 44.1 per cent of the vote and 229 seats, as opposed to 345 five years earlier.

The departing UMP government saw significant losses amongst its ranks. High-profile names from both Sarkozy's campaign and the Fillon government were ousted from their parliamentary seats (department – *circonscription* in parentheses). Amongst the highest were Nadine Morano (54–5), Claude Guéant (92–9), Michèle Alliot-Marie (66–6), Valérie Rosso-Debord (54–2), Hervé Novelli (37–4), Renaud Muselier (13–5), Georges Tron (91–9) and Frédéric Lefebvre (FFE Amérique du Nord). Nevertheless, a number of key UMP politicians survived, including most notably the two main pretenders to future UMP leadership, Jean-François Copé and former Prime Minister François Fillon, who had narrowly avoided a dissident challenge from former minister Rachida Dati.

2.3. Changes from 2007 to 2012

How did changes in support for the main competitors in the race distribute regionally across France? Maps 8.1 to 8.3 show the change in support for the PS, UMP and FN at the first round of the 2012 election from 2007. Of course, some individual constituencies will see large change due to desistment pacts and other tactical changes, but patterns in the broader aggregations are unlikely to be biased by this.

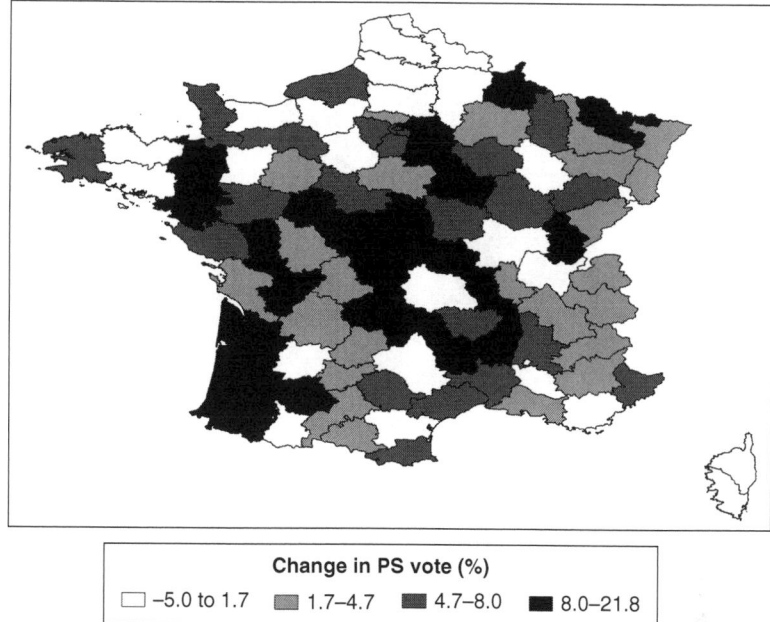

Map 8.1, 8.2 and 8.3 Change between 2007 and 2012 first-round vote in the legislative elections for the PS, UMP and FN by department
Note: Choropleth maps are shaded by quartile of vote change.

Unsurprisingly, the two main rivals saw changes in line with the overall result. The Socialists saw rises in the vast majority of the departments, the significant exceptions being some northern departments, where often dissident candidates were responsible for split votes and electoral failure – Eure, where a three-way split between Socialist dissidents and the official EELV candidate in the 5th *circonscription* led to a left-wing disaster (see below); Morbihan, where Hervé Pellois eventually defeated the official Socialist Claude Jahier; Jean-Pierre Kucheida in the 12th *circonscription* of the Pas-de-Calais and Aisne, which experienced the largest decline (5 per cent) in part due to the presence of the dissident René Dosière in the 1st *circonscription*. One of the largest declines – Corse du Sud – is a product of the Socialists not fielding a candidate in either of the constituencies, in the presence of local *divers gauche* candidates. One stronghold, Puy de Dôme in the Massif Central, saw a 3-point decline, principally due to a stand-down pact with EELV in one constituency, and competing candidates between the governmental partners in the other four. Otherwise, the Socialist Party won increases

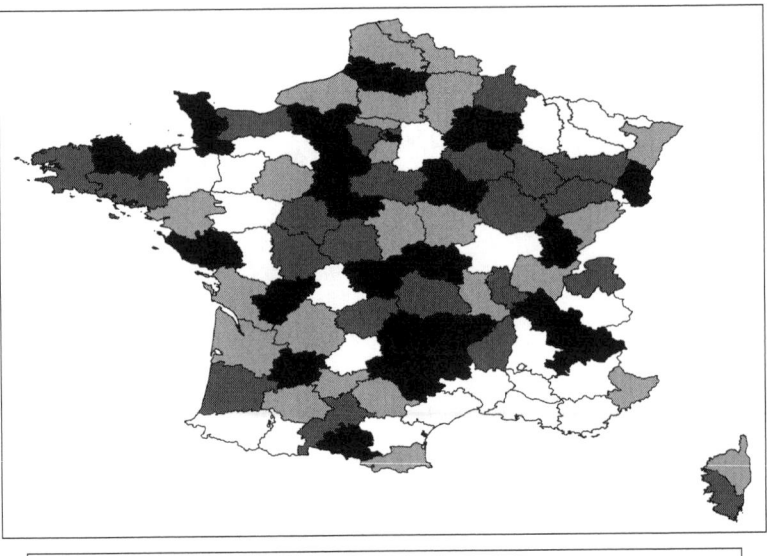

Change in UMP vote (%)

☐ −30 to −15.4   ▨ −15.4 to −11.8   ▦ −11.8 to −8.3   ■ −8.3 to −2.0

Map 8.1, 8.2 and 8.3   (Continued)

in all other departments. There is little evidence of a regional pattern, beyond a cluster of strong improvement in the south-west and centre, as well as the north-eastern border departments of Ardennes and Moselle.

Conversely, the UMP saw drops in support in every department, of at least 2 per cent, and in the worst case, Deux-Sèvres, of over 30 per cent. The latter case was due to the redistricting of constituency boundaries (see below), with the one incumbent UMP deputy, Jean-Marie Morisset, losing his constituency. However, numerous other departments had double-digit drops simply through competitive decline in vote. The largest cluster of losses occurred in the non-coastal north-west, around the Calvados–Pays de la Loire–Bretagne border triangle, and most markedly in the decidedly coastal Midi. Across the western regions, the diminishing number of seats netted by the UMP is striking – most evidently in Bretagne, Basse-Normandie, Aquitaine, Poitou-Charentes and Pays de la Loire.

Finally, whilst losing ground from Marine Le Pen's presidential performance nationally (−4.3 percentage points), the FN proved more resilient across a number of constituencies clustered mostly in the southern regions, with a concentration of the extreme right vote in its traditional

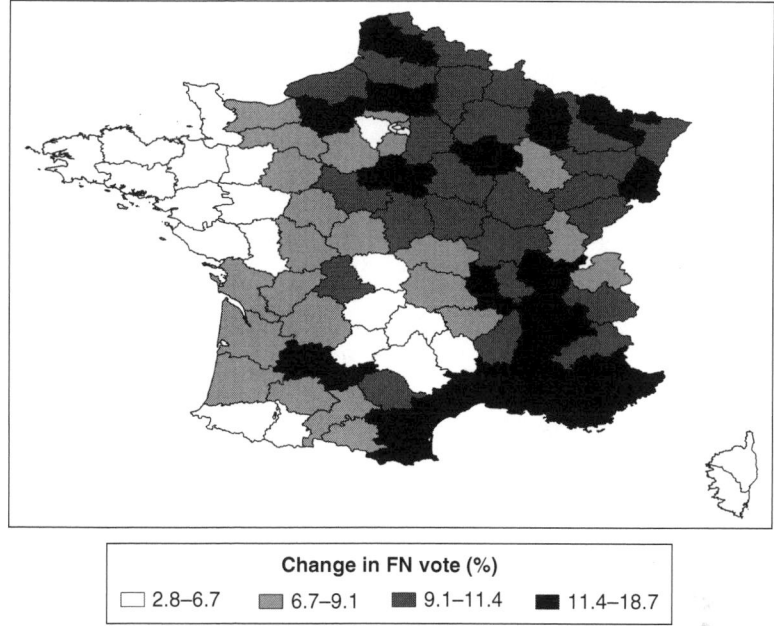

Map 8.1, 8.2 and 8.3 (Continued)

bastions of Gard, Vaucluse and Bouches-du-Rhône. The territorial consolidation of the FN shows a clear 'Mediterranean tropism': 36 out of
59 run-off constituencies are located in the southern regions, with 23
of them in Provence-Alpes-Côte d'Azur only, while another 20 constituencies are found in the north-east, making it the second regional
stronghold of the party. This pattern of regional polarisation reflects
the heterogeneous political make-up of the FN electorate, drawing from
both the Left and the Right: in the second round of the legislatives, vote
transfers from the FN back to the UMP were more ample for instance in
the south, where the sociological and ideological porosity between the
mainstream and the extreme right had historically been higher (Ivaldi,
2012).

Not for the first time in French electoral history, the clearest pattern
in vote change is to be found in the FN's results (or, more accurately, the
results of the RBM). As the area where they came closest to winning –
and in two cases, won – deputies, the south saw the most significant rise
in votes, with the highest increase of almost 19 per cent in the Gard
department – the location of Gilbert Collard's victory, and where five of
the six constituencies saw FN candidates progressing to the run-off.

Besides these increases in the heartlands of FN support, there are noticeable 'cool spots', namely the north-west and the rural Massif Central, traditionally a Socialist bastion, but one less prey to the anti-establishment rhetoric so powerful in the former industrial heartlands of, say, the north. But very clearly the eastern half of the country still represents the core support which was evident even in the 1993 legislatives (Birenbaum et al., 1996: 346). A revived FN with Marine Le Pen at the helm has established its threat once again in the same regions as her father before her, with the partial exception of a new stronghold in the Nord-Pas-de-Calais.

As we noted in Chapter 2, this variegated pattern to mainstream support is a shift away from the traditional delineation around the north–south axis, particularly for the Gaullists and moderate right in the rural west of the country. The Socialists have now firmly redressed the balance to the west, leaving little competitive space there for the FN (Fourquet, 2012: 88). In another geographical perspective, the difference is even more striking for all three parties, as for their presidential candidate. The PS now sees its heartlands in the major cities of France – Lyon, Strasbourg, Bordeaux, Paris. A younger educated middle-class elite moving into large urban milieus has socialised these cities (Fourquet, 2012: 57).

To some extent, the PS's legislative victory can also be regarded as the 'end product' of the growing local entrenchment by the party over the past ten years, reflecting both the development of a vast network of over 60,000 representatives[6] across the country and the progressive transformation of the PS into a *'parti d'élus'* since the mid-1980s (Sawicki and Lefebvre, 2006). This is exemplified by the situation of the party in Bretagne for instance where the Socialist candidates in the legislatives capitalised on the local strengths of the party to outperform Hollande's first-round presidential score by nearly 8 percentage points.

Conversely, the UMP finds its heartlands in rural areas at a distance from the cities – a more conservative, parochial tranche of French society (although not the very depths of the countryside, at least in 2012, which saw much higher support again for the Socialists). Overall, the UMP continues to dominate in the eastern regions of the country and in the Côte d'Azur. The FN occupies the hinterland between the two – *le grand péri-urbain*, distant from the gentrified cities, in many cases priced out of the now-expensive urban centres, but still focused inwards in suburban exile.

The 2012 legislatives were fought under the new constituency boundaries which had resulted from the readjustment of 2010. The latter had been enforced to take into account demographic changes and the increasing distortion in the proportionality of representation since the last redistricting carried out in 1986. While the total number of deputies was preserved, the readjustment led to a redistribution of seats across the departments, and the suppression of 33 old constituencies, mostly in the northern and central regions, of which 18 and 15 were held by the Left and the Right, respectively. The main innovation was the creation of 11 new legislative constituencies for the French living overseas[7] – an estimated 2.3 million, of whom 1.1 million were registered voters – who would be offered the possibility of voting electronically.

Despite criticism and short-lived accusations by the PS of gerrymandering by the right-wing government, the redistricting had little visible effect on the final outcome of the legislatives in metropolitan France, as well as in the overseas territories (DOM-TOM). The main impact was anticipated to be found, however, in the newly created *'Français de l'Etranger'* constituencies, as some commentators suggested these would advantage candidates of the mainstream Right.[8] In the end, there was little empirical evidence to support such claims. The 2007 presidential vote by French expats had returned an outcome very similar to that of the rest of the country, with 54 per cent of the vote in favour of Sarkozy in the second round. More importantly, perhaps, what was revealed in the electoral returns from the French living abroad was their dramatically low turnout – in the second round of the 2007 race, only 42.1 per cent had voted as opposed to 84 per cent nationally, a trend corroborated in the 2012 presidentials with a 42.2 per cent participation rate in the run-off.

While confirming the extremely low level of voter mobilisation (with an average turnout of 20.9 per cent), the results of the 2012 legislatives displayed mostly a replication of the re-balancing of power which had occurred nationally, with eight out of the 11 foreign constituencies won by the Left. Most notable were the defeat of former UMP spokesman Frédéric Lefebvre in the first constituency (USA/Canada) and that of a former member of the Fillon government, Marie-Anne Montchamp, in the fourth (Benelux), and the victory of former transport minister Thierry Mariani in Asia and Oceania (11th constituency).

3. Symptoms of a hesitant *alternance*

At the individual level, there were a number of high-profile media 'stories' which characterised the election while simultaneously showing important contextual effects and, at times, exposing some of the flaws or limitations inherent in the mobilisatory and competitive strategies adopted by French parties. The Socialists of course did not have the legislatives all their own way, despite their overall victory. In Hénin-Beaumont, the 'battle of the extremes' certainly revealed Mélenchon's weaknesses, while the election in Pau gave what could be a final blow to Bayrou's political endeavour at the centre of the spectrum. For the FN, despite bright post-presidential prospects, the performances by the new RBM failed to substantiate the anticipation by the party's leadership of yet another 'Marine blue wave' in the legislatives.

3.1. Socialist upsets and irritations

Ostensibly contrary to the win-win scenario described above, the PS–EELV pact had led to a number of dissident Socialist candidates (about 20 against official EELV runners), disgruntled at losing their seat to an EELV junior partner in the constituency-mongering preceding the legislatives. A number of these led to lost constituencies. However, of the original 47 dissident Socialists standing against official PS or EELV candidates, 15 progressed to the second round, and 13 of these cases at the expense of the official candidate.[9] The parliamentary group subsequently welcomed most of the victorious dissidents as *apparentés*, with certain exceptions – Royal's nemesis, Olivier Falorni, being the highest profile, who instead joined the Radical, républicain, démocrate et progressiste group.

Most strikingly, the spectre of Hollande's former partner returned yet again to haunt proceedings. As we have already examined in Chapter 6, despite an independent career as a successful politician and credible presidential candidate in 2007, Ségolène Royal has been seemingly unable to cast off her profile as the ex-Madame Hollande. Whilst ill-concealed ambition to become the first female President of the National Assembly did not enamour her to many commentators, the media coverage of the tweet by Hollande's partner, Valérie Trierweiler, supporting Oliver Falorni in La Rochelle to defeat Royal undoubtedly sealed the latter's fate at the hands not only of some Socialist voters disenchanted by what they regarded as a patent parachuting (despite Royal's presence as president of the Poitou-Charente regional council), but also of many other voters happy to discomfit the new Hollande executive by helping oust one of his party's *notables*. A quick glance at the raw voting figures (Table 8.4) shows the second-placed Falorni more than doubling his share of the vote at a run-off where turnout rose by over 1,500 votes.

The justification for Royal's candidacy in La Rochelle had been an apparent requirement of the Socialist Party's bid for parity in the

Table 8.4 Actual vote counts in the first and second rounds of 1st *circonscription*, Charente-Maritime

	First round	Second round
Turnout (incl. spoilt ballots)	59,904	63,247
Olivier Falorni	17,155	38,545
Ségolène Royal	19,005	22,661
Spoilt and blank	570	2,041
Other	23,174	–

National Assembly, despite the absence of a primary race between Royal and other female candidates. This was not the only constituency to cause the Left problems due to the parity requirement, even if the party only reached just over 45 per cent of female candidates. For example, the PRG found themselves putting a member of Génération Écologie, France Gamerre, into the 11th *circonscription* of Rhône given to them through the Socialist pact, to respect the parity laws. In the end, with a low-profile candidate parachuted in, the constituency went to a run-off between UMP and FN. Similarly, electoral pacts between the Socialists and EELV left a number of Socialist candidates without a seat to contest, at least under their official party label, for example Hélène Ségura and Anne Mansouret in Eure – again, a dissident candidacy which resulted in a UMP–FN run-off.

3.2. The battle for Hénin-Beaumont: The invisible winner

Of any constituency in the legislative race, the 11th constituency of Pas-de-Calais attracted the most column inches, at least until the 'Trierweiler affair' in the second round. As a coal-mining constituency in the industrial heartland of the north of France, the constituency which came to be known by its eponymous main town had a leftist tradition which, in keeping with bastions particularly of the Red Left, declined throughout the 1980s and 1990s as the industrial core dwindled, and gave way to a strong anti-establishment momentum. In 2009, the Socialist list had been beaten into third place by an FN list led by Steeve Briois and Marine Le Pen in the first round of a municipal by-election called after the suspension of the Socialist mayor Gérard Dalongeville for misuse of public funds. The FN list polled 39.3 per cent, with the two main left-wing lists only managing just over 37 per cent.

In circumstances of such disarray for the Left, the chances for a high-profile candidate such as Le Pen, already a municipal councillor in the town, to build upon the 2009 municipal performance and win the constituency appeared very high. Continuing in his anti-*frontiste* and anti-Le Pen campaign, Mélenchon announced he would stand against the FN candidate in this constituency, despite the presence of a strong Socialist candidate, Philippe Kemel. Hénin-Beaumont marked a turning point in perceptions of Mélenchon's populist Left revolution, and demonstrated that his strong presidential performance had come at a price. The battle of the extremes undoubtedly damaged Mélenchon as party leader (rather than presidential candidate) further. The focus on his duel with Le Pen in the Hénin-Beaumont constituency threatened to eclipse all other aspects of the party's legislative campaign.

Competitively, Mélenchon's apparent obsession with facing off Le Pen was almost counterproductive, if his party is part of the Left. Rather than acting as a radical Left foil, Mélenchon's rhetoric had moved the party into a position hostile to both the extreme right and to the Left majority. By the close of the legislatives, Jacques Rigaudiat, one of the party's key economic thinkers, had resigned, and in December 2012, the PG's only deputy, Marc Dolez, had followed suit: '*Ne donnons pas le sentiment que l'adversaire du Front du gauche, c'est le PS*' ('Let's not give the impression that the Front du Gauche's opponent is the PS').[10]

In the legislatives, the Socialist candidate, Philippe Kemel, whose presence became somewhat of a footnote to the Mélenchon–Le Pen rematch, at least in media coverage, eventually won the *ballottage* by just over 100 votes against Marine Le Pen.[11] The failure by Mélenchon to outperform his Socialist opponent in the first round certainly reflected the collapse of his last-minute political 'self-parachuting' and his personal deficit in local support, which contrasted with Marine Le Pen's more patient strategy of gaining a foothold in the region since 2007. More importantly, his electoral setback in this crisis-ridden industrial heartland shows the disconnect between the PG and the working class electorate, whose interests Mélenchon claimed to articulate during the campaign. In particular, the strong pro-immigration stance taken by the PG leader must have been at odds with the exclusionist preferences that have become pervasive to some sections of the lower social strata in France, and which are now 'best' represented by the FN in the party system.[12]

3.3. The FN's disappointment

Marine Le Pen's narrow defeat in the Pas-de-Calais came as a disappointment to her personally, mirrored by her party's showing at the national level. Whilst the election of two deputies appeared cause for celebration in the extreme right party, in the end, the FN's performance with 13.6 per cent of the vote, whilst well above the dismal showing in

2007 (4.3 per cent), was below what the party had set as its own target. This was particularly true with regard to the projected number of three-way contests[13] and their anticipating a handful of deputies in the new National Assembly. Instead, the June elections confirmed once again the difficulty for protest fringe parties to carry presidential momentum over into the legislative arena. As indicated earlier, Le Pen's voters were over-represented among abstainers in the legislative ballot, and, among those who turned out, the party failed to some extent to prevent a *'vote utile'* in favour of the UMP. Moreover, this 'semi-success' reflected the enduring organisational weaknesses of the party in the field and, since the electoral debacle of 2007, serious financial difficulties.

The FN appeared to have resurrected only very partially its nuisance potential. In many cases, the mechanical raising of the electoral threshold barred the extreme right from progressing into second rounds, as evidenced by the presence of 59 candidates at the run-off, with 28 of them in three-way *triangulaires* and another 31 in duels (22 and 9 against the Left and the Right, respectively). A marked improvement on the disastrous situation of the party in 2002 and 2007, these first- to second-round successes nonetheless came nowhere near the heights of 1993 and 1997, when the FN had managed to get 101 and 132 candidates through to the second round, respectively – but still won no deputies. Unlike 1997, the increased presence of the FN in three-way contests had a very limited impact on the final distribution of seats between the Left and the Right, showing no clear nuisance effect.[14]

In the end, the FN fell short of breaking the *cordon sanitaire* and only two deputies were returned to the Assembly – Marion Maréchal Le Pen, in the 3rd *circonscription* of Vaucluse, and Gilbert Collard in the 2nd *circonscription* of Var, both of whom were political neophytes and, in the case of Collard, located at the periphery of the FN. In contrast, all the party's national leaders – beginning with Marine Le Pen herself but including also Steeve Briois, Louis Aliot and Marie-Christine Arnautu, for instance – failed to win a parliamentary seat even if by a very narrow margin in some cases – for example, Florian Phillipot in the 6th *circonscription* of Moselle. Almost paradoxically, then, the electoral future of the FN may lie with a new generation of candidates with a much less marked profile or personal history at the extreme right and, at times, weaker ties with the party.[15]

3.4. The MODEM's swansong?

Following Bayrou's misfire in the presidentials, the legislative elections sanctioned the failure of the 'independent centre' strategy, unquestionably casting a shadow over the political future of the MODEM and its ability to establish leadership over the centre ground of French politics. At national level, the MODEM's candidates polled a mere 1.8 per cent of the first round vote cast, returning only two deputies to the Palais Bourbon. The vast majority of Bayrou's presidential supporters seem to have returned to their natural 'homes' of the Left and the Right, 33 and 42 per cent, respectively, according to IPSOS, whereas only 16 per cent remained loyal to the MODEM.[16]

After Bayrou's personal endorsement of François Hollande, his own seat and those of his party were seriously jeopardised. Bayrou's failure in the three-way contest in the 2008 municipal election of Pau had already shown the narrowness of the political corridor running between the Left and the Right. Having made clear the centre route designated for his party, the chances of any MODEM candidate involved in competition with either the Left or the Right – and worse, both of them in three-way run-offs – were slim. Bayrou's own seat in the Pyrénées-Atlantiques was the archetype, beaten by the Socialist candidate alongside a UMP candidate who could legitimately claim to be the only *ballottage* candidate of the Right. Whilst the UMP had stepped down to clear the way to the MODEM leader in 2007, it was clear this time that they would push Bayrou all the way back onto the ropes. Let us note that this strategy of 'retaliation' was endorsed by voters as well, as there was evidence of heavy losses by the MODEM in some of the traditional strongholds of the Right and centre-right such as Haute-Savoie or Alsace.

Only two candidates – Jean Lassalle, in the neighbouring 4th *circonscription* of Pyrénées-Atlantiques, and Thierry Robert in the overseas constituency of Réunion – managed to win. Four others did not – along with 393 who did not progress beyond the first round. This contrasted sharply with the electoral fortunes of the NC, whose tactical alliance with the UMP helped return no less than 12 parliamentary seats in spite of a mere 2.2 per cent of the national vote in the first round of the legislatives.

9
Conclusion

In the immediate aftermath of the presidential and legislative elections, the results appeared remarkably coherent with the expected progression of the four ballots. In the face of a deeply unpopular right-wing President and a country experiencing a significant deterioration of its economic position, the opposing left-wing candidate was elected by a clear majority, and went on to secure a strong legislative majority to support his government. The homogeneous bicephalous executive, which the Right had enjoyed for a decade since 2002, had now alternated. On the extremes of the political landscape, the social and economic problems which neither Left nor Right had successfully addressed had given two radical presidential candidates significant shares of the vote, and in both cases their potential blackmail of the moderate parties had drawn votes away from the centre as clear ideological alternatives were put before voters.

In that sense, the working of the electoral system and political competition, and the resultant outcomes were 'textbook'. Some distance before the elections were held, the generally anticipated results were correct. The political landscape that emerged in the presidential election in particular was certainly one of higher ideological polarisation on both the economic and cultural dimensions. In ideological and policy terms, however, the French parties largely took their expected positions with respect to both the economic and cultural axes of conflict, with the notable exception perhaps of the FN, whose leftward shift on the economy after 2010 resulted in a rotation of its location towards the egalitarian-authoritarian quadrant of the competitive space. This aside, all the other competitors in the party system were found in their natural homes, although the imperatives of the campaign and the changing mood of the post-2008 voting public would lead at times to substantial adjustments to their core policy preferences. Finally, cooperative and competitive strategies by the presidential and legislative parties showed only marginal departure from the patterns of cooperation which had been discernible on both sides of the political spectrum across all intermediary elections since 2007.

However, 'textbook' does not indicate an untroubled system. Since the elections, the dynamics on the Left and the Right have indicated anything but stability or normality. Ostensibly, the political landscape in France a year after the election appeared remarkably stable. The Ayrault government was still in power. The priorities which the President had underlined as part of his programme and which had appeared in the legislative manifestos as well had started promptly. The minimum welfare income (SMIC) had been raised by 2 per cent. The retirement age had been lowered back to 60 for those with longer careers. A number of new hires for primary education, including special needs teaching, had been made. Despite an unfortunate initial rejection by the Constitutional Council over legislation to implement the change, ministerial salaries were finally lowered by 30 per cent. On the Right, the UMP remained the main party of the mainstream – the threatened collapse subsequent to the legislative defeat did not occur – with a number of centre-right formations emerging from the strictures of electoral discipline to assert their independence: Borloo's and the centrist UDI, looking to coalesce all of the centre-right *courants*, looked likely to offer a post-UMP umbrella *à l'UDF*, in light of the diminished strength of the MODEM.

Such an analysis demonstrates the limits of a party system perspective. Despite a stable structure to the system, the intra-block and intra-party dynamics are on the contrary highly unstable, and in the approach to the main sub-national elections of this presidential cycle – the local and European elections of 2014 – the possibility of a cataclysmic result for the political mainstream appear a strong possibility, if not highly probable. The principal, and expected, outcome of the 2012 elections was the opportunity for the Left to form a unified executive for the first time since 1993. Ironically, this victory could probably not have come at a worse time. Opposition parties often accede to power at times of economic or social crisis – if the *status quo ante* had been positive, the incumbent may well have remained in power. But for the Socialists in 2012, the economic situation they inherited from Sarkozy and the UMP was of course peculiarly hostile.

First, and most obviously, the President and his government have already 'enjoyed' a decline in popularity worse than the scores which

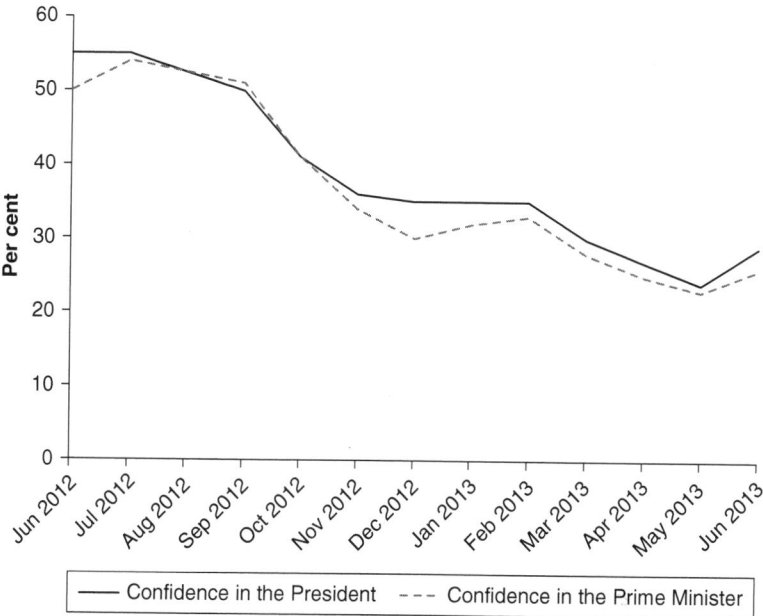

Figure 9.1 Confidence ratings in François Hollande as President and Jean-Marc Ayrault as Prime Minister
Source: Baromètre TNS Sofres/*Figaro Magazine*.

heralded the very demise of the executive they replaced (Figure 9.1). By May 2013, François Hollande's personal confidence levels were at a record low of 24 per cent, with his Prime Minister 1 point below that. The Prime Minister's decline was steeper in the autumn of 2012, as the government was widely reported as being effectively 'frozen' – inactive in the face of a worsening economic situation, and, despite a relatively auspicious start, legislation to address the two key problems of budget deficit and unemployment was largely absent. Eventually such accusations pushed the Ayrault government to lay out its timetable for policies to address the economic situation upon return from the summer recess – hardly the emergency measures that some were demanding. Moreover, soon similar criticisms were being aimed at the President. His initial grandstanding of a tough line on German-led austerity in the Eurozone in reality had produced an almost unchanged European Treaty on Stability, Coordination and Governance (ETSCG), which the majority of Greens and all the Front de Gauche deputies in the National Assembly opposed, together with a handful of Socialist rebels.

The PS and the UMP opposition both voted in favour of the eventual ratification.

Given the worsening economic situation, France expected Hollande to take the lead for the nation in uniting the country in the face of adversity, even if solutions which had seemed simple and effective in his manifesto were not necessarily as apparent in the real political world. Some economic problems were coincidental in their timing – for example, the announcement of the closure of the Peugeot factory at Aulnay (although this was not helped by the backtracking of Industrial Development Minister Arnaud Montebourg from promising to save the factory to admitting his inability to do so). Yet, unlike his Socialist predecessor in 1981, a sense of driving through fundamental change in the spirit of *Le changement, c'est maintenant* was simply nowhere to be found. It was very soon apparent that domestic reforms were to be left to Ayrault and his government – Hollande was focusing on the presidential domains, in particular foreign policy. Within weeks of assuming power, Hollande had made a number of overseas visits to world leaders, most notably Angela Merkel in the very first days of his presidency. But as the unchanged limits on state spending and relatively anodyne new paragraph committing to growth as part of Europe's economic strategy in the ETSCG showed, the value of these visits, beyond the standard introduction of a new statesman, was very limited.

Cynics would say that his remaining above domestic policy was with a view to protecting himself from the criticisms of poorly performing economic policy, which was inevitable in the current context of the Eurozone crisis and growing budget deficit. A more generous interpretation would be that Hollande wished to sustain the notion of 'normal' presidency – not an executive leader interfering in all manner of domestic policy, as the previous occupant of the Elysée had done, but staying within the bounds of the presidential remit and leaving the day-to-day running of the country to the government. Even if this were the case, many in France believed that what the country needed was not a mild-mannered, modest leader, but someone to take charge. Where government ministers were perceived to be damaging business interests, in the manner of Montebourg attacking the ArcelorMittal steel company with threats of nationalisation, and thereby discomfiting foreign investors and the German government, such a leadership role was surely vital.

Some of the presidential lead which then followed did not help reassure the electorate of a leader with a clear vision. For example, the introduction of the notorious 75 per cent tax band for high incomes received more coverage for the adverse reaction of some of France's richest individuals, including the actor Gérard Depardieu, who moved first to Belgium and then to Russia to escape the tax, as it did for any economic benefit that would accrue. Its first implementation was knocked back, again by the Constitutional Council, because it exceeded the established level of permitted taxation. A number of other issues with its focus on households led Hollande to shift the burden in March 2013 to businesses rather than their employees – a significant symbolic shift away from the notion of France's wealthy paying back into the French economy towards what would be perceived as a state control on business and enterprise.

Perhaps the most significant and divisive issue to emerge from the early months of the Socialist incumbency, however, was the introduction of same-sex marriage. As set out in Hollande's *60 engagements pour la France*, the law passed on 23 April 2013 set out to legalise marriage for same-sex couples, but was referred to the Constitutional Council by its opponents. Within the National Assembly, the vote split the chamber almost entirely along a Left–Right division – the governmental majority voted almost unanimously in favour, the Right opposition against, with around ten opposition deputies voting in favour. However, unlike most legislation, the divisiveness of the bill was felt more strongly outside the legislature, in street protests both in favour of and against same-sex marriage, and public opinion which suggested France was split down the middle on the issue.

For a European country portrayed by opinion surveys as becoming increasingly liberal across time, the outcry by certain sections of the community against the bill was striking in its vehemence. Whilst in part criticisms of the bill were based upon individuals claiming to be concerned that the Socialist government was focusing on 'unimportant' issues at the expense of, or deliberately to divert attention from, economic matters, such views were largely expressed by those opposing same-sex marriage anyway. Reports of homophobic attacks increased during the campaigns on the issue, but seemingly had no impact on opposition politicians' rhetoric against the bill.

Potentially, such a situation could present ample opportunity for the opposition to assert itself very early in the Socialist incumbency. The same-sex marriage bill in particular would allow the mobilisation of a large section of French society by the parliamentary opposition. Yet, the mainstream Right, whilst largely united on this issue, was nonetheless deeply divided on the leadership of the UMP, and by extension the policy priorities of its two possible leaders. After the stepping down of

Sarkozy from politics in the wake of his presidential defeat, a leadership contest which had been bubbling under for many months, if not years, prior to the presidential contest turned into a fiasco which came close to destroying the UMP. The more moderate social liberal and former Prime Minister, François Fillon, stood against the hard-line former parliamentary group leader and current General Secretary Jean-François Copé. Whilst opinion polls suggested Fillon would win by a large margin, the eventual result was extremely closely tied, and was announced for both candidates – wrongly – on the night of the election. Electoral fraud, manipulation of party resources and a strangely impotent system of internal appeals led to the two candidates eventually agreeing, after a series of increasingly hostile press releases, to the holding of a fresh ballot in September 2013.

In the meantime, a party in dire financial straits after its loss of a substantial proportion of state funding following the legislative defeat, as well as a rejection of the financial accounts for reimbursement of its presidential campaign, was left with a politburo (run by *Copéistes*) shadowed by an alternative politburo of *Fillonistes*. Having announced his willingness to stand aside from a re-ballot, were that to ensure unity for the UMP, Fillon announced in May 2013 that he would stand for President in 2017 'come what may' (*quoiqu'il arrive*). The risk of a dissident candidacy was somewhat reduced in late April 2013 after the two camps agreed on the principle of an open presidential primary to take place in 2016, and to which all potential presidential hopefuls, including Fillon and Sarkozy, should submit. But in preparation for the 2014 locals and Europeans, let alone the 2017 race, the party was not oriented towards coherent campaigning as an opposition party looking to benefit from governmental unpopularity. In passing, it is worth noting here that the Socialist Party's own leadership 'race' after Martine Aubry's stepping down in September 2012 saw the highly criticised 'undemocratic imposition' of Harlem Désir subsequent to Aubry and Ayrault's endorsement before the party congress. As party leader, Désir found himself increasingly marginalised as voice of the grass roots in a governing party led top-down by presidential and governmental priorities. The need for unity and the imperative of building a strong coherent presidential majority faction in the party – in direct relation to Hollande's incumbency and the PS governmental responsibility – has taken the leadership election back into the smoke-filled room, away from the members' power of decision.

The party which has undoubtedly benefited from such problems in the mainstream is the Front national. Whilst the elections of 2012 presented a mixed bag of results – two deputies, but not as many as anticipated; a strong presidential performance which resulted in no tangible outcome beyond the 17.9 per cent recorded – its renewed reputation as a political force to be reckoned with has allowed it to present itself as a unified right-wing party untarnished by broken election promises, leadership crises or – importantly for its strategy as an anti-system party – ongoing corruption scandals. The resignation of Jérôme Cahuzac, budget minister, over accusation of financial impropriety; continuing allegations of illegal party funding for right-wing presidential campaigns in 2007 – both allow the FN to portray itself as above such corrupt practice.

More generally, perhaps, the presence of the Left in national office has been traditionally propitious to ideological polarisation on the Right of the party spectrum, resulting in centrifugal shifts by subsectors of the mainstream Right's electoral clientele. Let us recall for instance that the first electoral success of the FN in 1984 was precisely built upon its ability to attract substantial numbers of politically disappointed UDF/RPR voters who were willing to demonstrate their hostility towards the expansive immigration policies of the first years of Mitterrand's presidency, and to punish the right-wing opposition for their perceived lack of responsiveness. The evolution and competitive positioning of the UMP in late 2013 will certainly tell whether a similar structure of opportunity will be offered to Marine Le Pen and the FN. Judging from recent polls showing an alarming crystallisation of anti-immigration and anti-Muslim attitudes in French public opinion,[1] and with Hollande's promise of voting rights for foreigners still looming as a potential hackneyed subject for the rest of his presidency, the FN's immediate future looks bright.

This will be particularly true of the 2014 municipal elections. With both mainstream parties in disarray, no sign of recovery on the employment and economic fronts and ever-strengthening municipal power bases particularly in the south of the country, these elections look likely to benefit the far-right party to record levels. The municipals have historically been a tougher proposition for the FN, relying as these elections do on *notables*, who have usually been backed by mainstream parties. With the successes of Marion Maréchal-Le Pen and Gilbert Collard in the Midi, however, the prospect of enhanced performance for the FN at the local level becomes more likely. Were there to be any sort of split in the UMP, especially from hard-Right members of the Droite Populaire, the potential for more explicit cooperation between the UMP's (former) Right wing and the FN – already attempted at electoral levels where proportional representation is used, that is regional elections – would become more compelling for breaching the *cordon sanitaire*. At national level, Marine Le Pen will also be likely to hold the floor of the June 2014 European elections, where her strong anti-EU message will undoubtedly resonate with the anger and concerns by many French voters about the continuation of austerity policies across Europe.

The thorn in Le Pen's side – Jean-Luc Mélenchon – continued his attacks on the FN whilst the possibility of a rerun of the legislative ballot in the Pas-de-Calais existed. With that possibility overruled by the courts, Mélenchon focused his campaigning on the same-sex marriage issue (which indirectly kept him in conflict with the FN) but increasingly as an even more vocal critic of the Socialist government. The inevitability of austerity in the government's policy provided ammunition for Mélenchon, though less so for more conciliatory FG members and communists, to attack the failed promises of Hollande and his programme. For Mélenchon, the Socialists have acted as *escrocs politiques* in promising an innovative programme predicated upon growth, but delivering something in line with austerity. In particular, the failure to amend the European Growth and Stability Pact or to include significant complementarity on social protection has been highlighted as a failure of the Socialist government in diverting Europe from its austerity-oriented path. On 5 May 2013, a march through Paris to demand the removal of the Socialist executive, and furthermore the instigation of a Sixth Republic – a cornerstone of radical reform for the previous decade – underlined the movement's firm anti-system agenda on the Left.

To return to the party system perspective, the current array, whilst evidently bipolar in its format, represents a potentially highly unstable situation with weakened moderate mainstream parties flanked by two strong anti-system elements. Even in the 1970s, the party system array was more stable than this, with a PCF slowly but gradually moving out of its cold war position and closing the gap with the Socialist Party, and a still weak FN flanking the RPR. The Front de Gauche under Mélenchon is moving away from the Socialists, and the FN flanking the UMP is anything but weak. Finally, whilst Borloo represents a possible *rassembleur* for the Centre, the tendency is definitively centre-right: the 'true' Centre of Bayrou is to all intents and purposes moribund. The success of the extremes is not guaranteed, however. Since Mélenchon's success in the 2012 presidentials, the FG coalition has for instance become more precarious in major part due to his outspoken attacks, revealing the changing balance of power internally and the more asymmetric allocation of resources across its two main components. Diverging coalition strategies in preparation for the 2014 municipals have surfaced, which might bring the PCF closer once more to the Socialists. Similar dynamics look less likely for an FN looking to exploit a divided UMP.

As the first year of the Hollande presidency closed, one politician's popularity appeared to be in the ascendancy once more – Nicolas Sarkozy. Despite having resigned from politics, his endorsement for leading the Right into the next presidential race was higher than any other right-wing politician. Whilst his ousting in 2012 represented an alternation for identifiable and predictable reasons, in the presence of a strong degree of protest, the resultant instability in the French political landscape has, perhaps perversely, highlighted the positive elements (at least, retrospectively) of Sarkozy's incumbency. In a period when both mainstream Left and Right, empowered by the institutional framework but simultaneously enfeebled by challenges to their actions and competencies, look vulnerable, the capacity of individuals to inspire confidence at the mass level, and to mobilise and unite at the militant level, is of greater importance. The extent to which governing parties manage to identify such individuals and exploit these over the next electoral cycle will determine whether 2017 results in alternation once more, or an ever stronger challenge from protest.

Notes

1   Introduction

1. Indeed, even without such confounding factors, a 'pure' bipartisan system would not be predictable any more than an imperfect, realistic one. Knowing the equilibrium number of parties in a system does not guarantee knowing who votes for them or why. Even under Downsian rationality, ideology for the two parties acts as a signpost, not a GPS.
2. Those more enthused by cycle race or chess analogies should refer to commentary on the 2012 elections on our blog: 500signatures.com.

2   Knowns and Unknowns: Identifying the Critical Spaces of the 2012 Elections

1. 'Deux riches familles ont payé les vacances des Sarkozy', *Libération*, 18 August 2007, http://www.liberation.fr/politiques/010119427-deux-riches-familles-ont-paye-les-vacances-des-sarkozy, accessed 4 February 2013.
2. 'Quand le président cajole ses (généreux) donateurs', *Le Parisien*, 9 December 2009, http://www.leparisien.fr/politique/quand-le-president-cajole-ses-genereux-donateurs-09-12-2009-737945.php, accessed 4 February 2013.
3. As we shall see in Chapter 8, perversely for the FN, low turnout – so often a bonus for far right parties – dampened their ability to play kingmaker in a large number of constituencies.
4. Drees (2012) *Suivi barométrique de l'opinion des français sur la santé, la protection sociale, la précarité, la famille et la solidarité*. January, 67 p. (http://www.drees. sante.gouv.fr/IMG/pdf/synthese2011_barometre_drees_bva.pdf).
5. We examine this further in Chapter 8.
6. This is revealed by the positive correlation that can be found between the FN vote and the subsequent rise in blank ballots ($r = .62$) across all metropolitan cantons ($N = 3, 883$), which becomes non-significant for other candidates such as Bayrou or Mélenchon.
7. http://www.lefigaro.fr/politique/2012/02/10/01002-20120210ARTFIG00586-nicolas-sarkozy-mes-valeurs-pour-la-france.php, accessed 14 March 2013.
8. Polling averages, rounded figures. 2007 presidential election, second round (6 May 2007): CSA–*Le Parisien*, exit poll ($N = 1, 030$); IPSOS–*Le Point*, exit poll ($N = 3, 609$); LH2–*Libération*, exit poll ($N = 1, 003$); TNS-SOFRES–*Le Figaro*, exit poll ($N = 1, 200$). 2012 presidential election, second round (6 May 2012): TNS-SOFRES–*TriElec*, exit poll ($N = 1, 521$); IFOP–*Paris Match*, exit poll ($N = 1, 968$); IPSOS–*Le Monde*, pre-election poll ($N = 3, 123$).

3 Party Cooperation and Conflict: Actors' Competitive Positioning

1. Besancenot's Ligue Communiste Révolutionnaire notably refused similar alliances.
2. Looking at the 862 Left–Right second-round duels, the total score of the Right and the FN was above 50 per cent in 358 cantons. In the run-offs, however, the candidates of the mainstream Right were in a position to secure a majority in 247 (69 per cent) of those cases.

4 Candidate Selection Processes and Effe

1. In November 2006, Ségolène Royal had swept the nomination with 60.6 per cent of the vote against her rival candidates Dominique Strauss-Kahn (20.7 per cent) and Laurent Fabius (18.7 per cent).
2. It is also significant that a number of prominent personalities within the UMP (Fillon, Juppé, Hortefeux) called for a similar candidate selection process in anticipation of the 2017 presidential election, a proposal which was supported at the time by a 56 per cent majority of UMP voters (TNS-SOFRES–Canal+, 16 October 2011).
3. In the final stage of the internal campaign, opinion polls showed that Le Pen was considered the best embodiment of the party by 69 per cent of the FN supporters, against 23 per cent for her father and a mere 5 per cent for Gollnisch (BVA–Canal+, 10 December 2010).
4. In the run-off, Voynet eventually won the candidacy over Cochet with a relative majority of 46.2 per cent.
5. Let us recall that in December 2006, an overwhelming majority (81.1 per cent) of the party members had chosen to endorse Marie-George Buffet as the presidential candidate, which had then led to a split within the anti-liberal coalition and José Bové running independently to represent the whole range of non-communist partners in the anti-ECT movement. Buffet and Bové subsequently polled a disastrous 1.9 and 1.3 per cent of the vote nationally.
6. The attempt by Royal to evade the power and influence of the Solferino headquarters was probably facilitated then by the fact that the party had been severely damaged by internal strife over the European constitution referendum of 2005. To many observers, however, Royal had been subsequently handicapped by the lack of support from the party apparatus and national establishment in the 2007 presidential campaign, which triggered her attempt to take over the PS in the aftermath of the election.
7. Following his appointment as IMF managing director in September 2007 and because of the increasingly crucial role played by the fund in the international management of the 2008 financial crisis, DSK had returned to the top of French opinion polls as 'providential leader' for the Left and odds-on presidential favourite to defeat Sarkozy in the 2012 election.
8. www.opinion-way.com/pdf/le_figaro-lci_le_barometre_des_primaires-vague1_14_avril.pdf, accessed 14 March 2012.

9. A quick glance at PS popularity shows a moderate increase in favourable ratings from 40 per cent in March 2011 up to 46 per cent immediately after the nomination race, and 51 per cent in the final stage of the first-round campaign (TNS-SOFRES).

10. Five years earlier, pollsters had very well anticipated Royal's success but had already failed to predict primary support for Fabius. The latter had been underestimated by 10 points, inflating DSK's score by a similar proportion, pointing to variation in primary support across party members and Socialist sympathisers.

11. This contrasted with the balance of power that had emerged from the 2007 Bordeaux party congress, which had placed Gollnisch ahead of Le Pen in the central committee delegates' vote.

12. If we simply compute the effective number of motions – using the classic index proposed by Laakso and Taagepera (1979) – it is noticeable that there were as many as 4.1 effective motions in Reims compared with only 2.3 and 2.6 in the 2003 and 2005 party congresses, respectively.

13. The latter underwent dramatic fragmentation in 2011 following DSK's giving up the primary bid, which pointed to the lack of organisational cohesiveness in this otherwise ideologically consistent group of elites. Most of them endorsed Hollande – Pierre Moscovici, Gérard Collomb, Marisol Touraine or Jérôme Cahuzac for instance, with only Jean-Christophe Cambadélis lending his support to Aubry.

14. With the exception of a handful of her most loyal followers such as Jean-Louis Bianco, Jean-Jack Queyranne, Najat Vallaud-Belkacem and Delphine Batho, many of Royal's supporters defected to Hollande in the primary campaign (e.g. Malek Boutih, Julien Dray, Aurélie Filippetti, Vincent Peillon and François Rebsamen). The former PS presidential candidate had also to confront the decision by Valls to run individually.

15. Over 400 in total including daily presidential tracking polls during the 2012 campaign as opposed to 293 in 2007, 193 in 2002 and 157 in 1995 (*Le Monde*, 20 April 2012).

16. A CSA–*Marianne* survey revealed for instance that 20 per cent of voters would consider voting for Le Pen in 2012, as opposed to only 7 per cent for Gollnisch (*Marianne*, 14 January 2011). A month earlier, a BVA–Canal+ poll had shown that Le Pen and Gollnisch would receive 17 and 8 per cent, respectively, in the presidential election.

17. With only 4 per cent of right-wing supporters saying that 'they would feel closer to the FN' under Gollnisch as opposed to 25 per cent under Le Pen's leadership (BVA–Canal+, 10 December 2010).

18. A position which she subsequently lost in early 2007.

5   Issues, Policy Debates and Candidate Valence

1. http://www.ipsos.fr/sites/default/files/attachments/rapport_presidoscopie_vague9.pdf, accessed 7 May 2013.

2. We borrow the expression from Van der Eijk and Franklin (2004).

3. This would be achieved by tax raises – most notably a 2 per cent increase in VAT, the re-establishment of taxes on extra working hours and an additional 50 per cent band in the income tax for the wealthiest households – a freeze

on government spending and the continuation of the current RGPP policy of 2007 albeit in a what would be deemed a less automatic and better prioritised approach.

4. IFOP–*La Croix* poll, 11 April 2012, http://www.la-croix.com/Actualite/ Economie-Entreprises/Economie/Les-Francais-veulent-relever-les-barrieres-douanieres-_NG_-2012-04-11-791901, accessed 10 May 2013.

5. IFOP–*L'Humanité*, 14 March 2012.

6. There were speculations that a united 'front' of conservative European leaders had been formed by Angela Merkel, Mario Monti, Mariano Rajoy and David Cameron, whereby they agreed not to meet with the Socialist candidate before the election.

7. To quote the French President: 'I want a political Europe that protects its citizens … We need a common discipline in border controls … We can't leave the management of migration flows to technocrats and tribunals' (*Le Monde*, 11 March 2012, http://www.lemonde.fr/election-presidentielle-2012/article/2012/03/11/suivez-en-direct-le-meeting-de-nicolas-sarkozy-a-villepinte_1656 131_1471069.html, accessed 10 May 2013).

8. Stokes (1963) defines valence issues as those 'on which parties or leaders are differentiated not by what they advocate but by the degree to which they are linked in the public's mind with conditions or goals or symbols of which almost everyone approves or disapproves'.

9. Source : series of CSA-M6 polls : 'Les Français et le programme économique de Marine Le Pen', 5 February 2012; 'Les Français et le programme économique de François Bayrou', 4 March 2012; 'Les Français et le programme économique de François Hollande', 11 March 2012; 'Les Français et le programme économique de Nicolas Sarkozy', 18 March 2012.

10. CSA–M6, 'Les Français et le programme économique de Marine Le Pen', 5 February 2012, http://www.csa.eu/multimedia/data/sondages/data2012/opi20120201-les-francais-et-le-programme-economique-de-marine-le-pen. pdf, accessed 10 May 2013.

11. According to Hollande: 'people know the country is facing considerable problems and challenges … Another big change will be a focus on fairness. That's the condition people will require for making further effort, and that's been discarded and forgotten under Sarkozy. That isn't a question of style. It has to do with priorities and values' (Interview, *Time*, 13 April 2012, http://world.time.com/2012/04/13/time-interviews-french-presidential-front-runner-francois-hollande/, accessed 10 May 2013).

12. 61 and 65 per cent of public opinion support according to TNS-SOFRES–i> Télé and BVA–RTL polls, respectively.

13. Inside the UMP, this strategy met with strong resistance from the Droite Populaire, whose members publicly expressed their doubts about 'a hardly understandable and highly unpopular measure' (*Le Monde*, 18 January 2012) that would fuel public discontent. A few days later, Lionnel Luca called it 'political suicide' (*Le Monde*, 25 January 2012).

14. In his first public rally in Le Bourget in January, Hollande confirmed his intention to put an end to the systematic RGPP rule of not replacing one in two civil servants going into retirement.

15. We refer here to a classical conceptualisation of party competition as a two-dimensional space formed by the intersection of economic and cultural issues (Kitschelt, 1994). The cultural dimension of conflict summarises

non-economic issues – immigration, crime, identity, authoritarian values, etc. Marks et al. (2006) define this axis of competition as GAL/TAN – green, alternative and libertarian vs traditional, authoritarian and nationalist. Kriesi et al. (2006) argue also that issues such as globalisation and European integration form part of the cultural dimension of conflict.

16. The risk of escalation in such a strategy was revealed in the controversy stirred by Sarkozy after he coined the idea of a 'Muslim appearance' in a radio interview, referring to a physical look to identify Muslims.

17. 'At a time of economic crisis', Sarkozy said, 'if Europe doesn't pick those who can enter its borders, it won't be able to finance its welfare state any longer' (*Le Monde*, 11 March 2012, http://www.lemonde.fr/election-presidentielle-2012/article/2012/03/11/suivez-en-direct-le-meeting-de-nicolas-sarkozy-a-villepinte_1656131_1471069.html, accessed 10 May 2013). Earlier on French television, Sarkozy had stated his opposition to 'immigrants whose sole motivation would be their desire for social benefits...because the welfare state is more generous in France' (*Le Monde*, 7 March 2012).

18. Within the presidential party, the Droite Populaire also demanded a revision of the nationality law, with a return to the provisions of the controversial Pasqua laws of 1993.

19. In October 2011, the Droite Populaire had for instance launched a national petition against voting rights for foreign citizens, which was immediately followed by a similar initiative by the FN.

20. Présidoscopie – IPSOS, wave 9, 19–21 April 2012.

21. During his visit to the agriculture salon in Paris, Sarkozy had simply declared: 'enough with all those environmental questions!' (*Le Monde*, 25 February 2012).

22. Most notably, the EELV platform pledged for instance to create a million new jobs in ten years, including the recruitment of 20,000 civil servants in the education sector, while repealing Sarkozy's RGPP and pension reforms to allow for retirement at 60. It advocated tax raises with new marginal rates up to 70 per cent above 500,000 euros, price controls on rents and energy as well as a 50 per cent increase in all minimum social benefits over a five-year period.

23. All polling figures are from Présidoscopie – IPSOS, wave 9, 19–21 April 2012.

6   Campaign Events

1. Given media coverage of the FN's legislative performance in the first round, the colloquial shock here was perhaps that Le Pen's party did not win more seats.

2. Source: TNS-SOFRES–*Le Figaro*, Baromètre politique, http://www.tns-sofres.com/popularites/cote3/choixdate.php?parti=ps, accessed 10 May 2013.

3. 'Primaires PS: François Hollande ira "jusqu'au bout"', *Le Point*, 1 May 2011, http://www.lepoint.fr/politique/primaires-ps-francois-hollande-ira-jusqu-au-bout-01-05-2011-1325353_20.php, accessed 11 April 2013.

4. 'François Hollande: "les pactes, ça vaut pour ceux qui les signent, pas pour ceux qui n'en sont pas"', *RTL*, 25 November 2010, http://www.rtl.fr/

actualites/article/francois-hollande-les-pactes-ca-vaut-pour-ceux-qui-les-signent-pas-pour-ceux-qui-n-en-sont-pas-7638719241, accessed 17 April 2013.

5. 'DSK, Royal et Aubry "proposeront une candidature ensemble"', *L'Express*, 25 November 2010, http://www.lexpress.fr/actualite/politique/dsk-royal-et-aubry-proposeront-une-candidature-ensemble_939888.html, accessed 17 April 2013.

6. 'DSK mis en examen, Hollande marque sa distance', *Le Monde*, 27 March 2012, http://www.lemonde.fr/election-presidentielle-2012/article/2012/03/27/dsk-mis-en-examen-hollande-marque-sa-distance_1676268_1471069.html, accessed 17 April 2013.

7. The notion was first expounded by the newspaper *Le Monde* in an article entitled 'Outlook, downgrading, credit rating: The manual' on 21 April 2011 ('Surveillance, dégradation…notation mode d'emploi', *Le Monde*, 21 April 2011).

8. IFOP–*Sud Ouest Dimanche*, 15–16 December 2011.

9. 'Le projet de TVA sociale ne passe pas auprès de certains députés UMP', *Le Monde*, 18 January 2012, http://www.lemonde.fr/election-presidentielle-2012/article/2012/01/18/le-projet-de-tva-sociale-ne-passe-pas-aupres-de-certains-deputes-ump_1630980_1471069.html, accessed 25 January 2013.

10. 'Sondage: Sarkozy replonge, Bayrou décolle', *L'Express*, 17 January 2013, http://www.lexpress.fr/actualite/politique/sondage-sarkozy-replonge-bayrou-decolle_1072354.html, accessed 25 January 2013.

11. 'Les crispations alarmantes de la société française', *Le Monde*, 24 January 2013, http://www.lemonde.fr/politique/article/2013/01/24/les-crispations-alarmantes-de-la-societe-francaise_1821655_823448.html, accessed 25 January 2013.

12. IFOP survey for Atlantico.fr, 27 February–1 March 2013.

13. One of the wounded soldiers subsequently died of his injuries.

14. 'François Hollande en Afghanistan pour préparer le retrait français', *Le Monde*, 25 May 2012, http://www.lemonde.fr/international/article/2012/05/25/francois-hollande-en-afghanistan-pour-preparer-le-retrait-francais_1707328_3210.html, accessed 12 April 2013.

15. 'Tuerie de Toulouse: retour sur les événements', *Le Monde*, 23 March 2012, http://www.lemonde.fr/societe/article/2012/03/23/tuerie-de-toulouse-retour-sur-les-evenements_1674320_3224.html, accessed 12 April 2013.

16. For example, 'Tuerie de Toulouse et Montauban: la chasse à l'homme est ouverte', *Le Point*, 20 March 2013, http://www.lepoint.fr/societe/tueries-de-toulouse-et-montauban-la-chasse-a-l-homme-est-ouverte-20-03-2012-1443194_23.php, accessed 13 April 2013.

17. 'Tuerie de Toulouse: la presse étrangère blâme le climat délétère français', *Rue89*, 20 March 2013, http://www.rue89.com/2012/03/20/la-fusillade-de-toulouse-vue-de-la-presse-etrangere-230362, accessed 12 April 2013.

18. 'Bayrou souhaite que le "ton et le fond" de la campagne changent', *Le Monde*, 21 March 2012, http://www.lemonde.fr/election-presidentielle-2012/article/2012/03/21/francois-bayrou-souhaite-que-le-ton-et-le-fond-de-la-campagne-change_1673645_1471069.html?xtmc=bayrou_campagne_toulouse_tuerie&xtcr=2, accessed 18 January 2013.

19. 'Chirac dit que l'Etat va mal', *Le Parisien*, 29 March 2002, http://www.leparisien.fr/politique/chirac-dit-que-l-etat-va-mal-29-03-2002-2002937142.php, accessed 13 April 2013.

20. 'Affaire Merah, voyage au pays des conspirationnistes', *Le Monde*, 19 June 2012, http://www.lemonde.fr/societe/article/2012/06/19/affaire-merah-voyage-au-pays-des-conspirationnistes_1717409_3224.html, accessed 14 April 2013.

21. 'Les candidats perplexes face au drame de Toulouse', *Le Monde*, 24 March 2012, http://www.lemonde.fr/election-presidentielle-2012/article/2012/03/24/les-candidats-perplexes-face-au-drame-de-toulouse_1675118_1471069.html, accessed 17 April 2013.

22. 'Sarkozy veut renforcer les sanctions contre l'extrémisme', Reuters, 22 March 2012.

23. 'Marine Le Pen fait campagne sur l'affaire Merah', *Le Monde* 26 March 2012, http://www.lemonde.fr/election-presidentielle-2012/article/2012/03/26/marine-le-pen-fait-campagne-sur-l-affaire-merah_1675493_1471069.html, accessed 8 July 2013.

24. 'Toulouse: Marine Le Pen suggère à nouveau un référendum sur la peine de mort', *Le Monde*, 21 March 2012, http://www.lemonde.fr/election-presidentielle-2012/breve/2012/03/21/toulouse-marine-le-pen-suggere-a-nouveau-un-referendum-sur-la-peine-de-mort_1673058_1471069.html, accessed 18 January 2013.

25. 'Moins de 2 Français sur 10 jugent crédible le programme économique du FN', *Le Point*, http://www.lepoint.fr/economie/moins-de-2-francais-sur-10-jugent-credible-le-programme-economique-du-fn-03-02-2012-1427185_28.php, accessed 28 January 2013.

26. 'Intentions de vote: l'effet limité de la tuerie de Toulouse', *Le Monde*, polling blog, 27 March 2012, http://sondages.blog.lemonde.fr/2012/03/27/intentions-de-vote-leffet-limite-de-la-tuerie-de-toulouse/, accessed 12 April 2013.

27. 'Valérie Trierweiler encourage Falorni contre Royal', *Le Monde*, 12 June 2012, http://www.lemonde.fr/politique/article/2012/06/12/valerie-trierweiler-encourage-falorni-contre-royal_1716981_823448.html, accessed 14 April 2013.

28. See for example 'Valérie Trierweiler, le ministère de la jalousie', *L'Express*, 12 June 2012, http://www.lexpress.fr/actualite/politique/valerie-trierweiler-le-ministere-de-la-jalousie_1125784.html, accessed 14 April 2013.

29. ' "Dallas à l'Elysée": la droite jubile après la sortie de Trierweiler', *Le Nouvel Observateur*, 12 June 2012, http://tempsreel.nouvelobs.com/legislatives-2012/20120612.OBS8319/dallas-a-l-elysee-la-droite-jubile-apres-la-sortie-de-trierweiler.html, accessed 17 April 2013.

30. 'Valérie Trierweiler, la femme discrète', *Le Point*, 24 February 2011, http://www.lepoint.fr/politique/valerie-trierweiler-la-femme-discrete-24-02-2011-1302271_20.php, accessed 17 April 2013.

31. 'Agacée, Valérie Trierweiler tire un caméraman par la capuche', *Le Parisien*, 9 April 2013, http://www.leparisien.fr/actualite-people-medias/video-agacee-valerie-trierweiler-tire-un-cameraman-par-la-capuche-09-04-2013-2710629.php, accessed 8 July 2013.

32. 'Le spectre de l'abstention guette', *Le Monde*, 9 April 2012, http://www.lemonde.fr/idees/article/2012/04/09/le-spectre-de-l-abstention-guette_1682628_3232.html, accessed 15 April 2013.

7 Polls and VP-Functions: Forecasting the Elections

1. Indeed, there is a suspicion of econometric models manifest in many commentaries on such approaches, which generally remain the preserve of econometricians rather than political scientists. No doubt due to the harsh criticisms in 2002 and 2007 of polling accuracy, this clash has been particularly notable between pollsters and econometricians in 2012.

2. For some, election night saw some embarrassing errors in polls normally confident of very precise estimates after only a few polling stations had returned. The announcement, in particular, of Marine Le Pen above the psychological bar of 20 per cent was a watershed moment. Granted, a number of other polling institutes provided much more accurate estimates for Le Pen as the polling booths closed. CSA for instance estimated 18.2 per cent, and Harris 18.5 per cent. It is unfortunate however that the company chosen by French state media to announce the outcome turned out to have the most wayward forecast.

3. Although it should be noted that forecast models that perform at one election are still not out of the woods – successive elections would need to be forecast accurately to increase certainty that it is indeed validity, rather than coincidence, which is responsible. Given the infrequency of elections, this is a time-consuming proof, and one reason why forecasters often move to other national, or the same sub-national, cases.

4. Such concerns over econometric approaches are not restricted to France, either. Many quantitative researchers are unhappy with the notion of fitting regression lines to sparse data. Others, for instance the PollyVote team, prefer to combine multiple indices to average forecasts. Most notably, political markets such as the Iowa Electronic Markets derive estimated outcomes from a market trade of political shares based as much upon the so-called 'scouts' gut reactions – and ideological biases – as upon any 'stats' objectivity.

5. Both Lewis-Beck's and Campbell's approaches are more formalised with criteria ranking each forecast model – lead time, parsimony, etc. This is possible because with the US elections only one result is forecast – the eventual presidential winner. In the French case, as Table 7.1 shows, a number of different approaches and ballots can be tested.

6. According to an LH2 poll, Royal would defeat Sarkozy in the run-off with no less than 53 per cent of the vote (LH2–*nouvelObs.com*, 2–3 May 2008, $N = 1,004$).

7. CE, 8 February 2012, M. Mélenchon, no. 353357, http://www.conseil-etat.fr/node.php?articleid=2565, accessed 17 May 2013.

8. 'Le Pen lance un défi aux instituts de sondage', *Europe 1*, 3 April 2012, http://www.europe1.fr/Politique/Le-Pen-lance-un-defi-aux-instituts-de-sondage-1019501/, accessed 3 January 2013.

9. 'Le Pen donnée en tête du 1er tour: le PS charge Sarkozy', *Le Parisien*, 5 March 2011, http://www.leparisien.fr/election-presidentielle-2012/le-pen-donnee-en-tete-du-1er-tour-le-ps-charge-sarkozy-05-03-2011-1344715.php, accessed 3 January 2013.

10. Nevertheless, the different measures developed by Mosteller and his team indicates that even two-party systems can be analysed in a number of ways (Mosteller et al., 1949).

11. We ignore here the complications which can affect even two-party elections, such as undecided voters and measures that focus on the two leading candidates when there are even minor third parties running. See Mosteller et al. (1949) and Martin et al. (2005) on these.

12. To calculate B, a Stata package, 'surveybias', is available from Boston College Statistical Software Components (SSC) archive.

13. Whether 1 per cent variation for a candidate with 2 per cent of the vote is more or less important than 1 per cent variation for a candidate with 20 per cent of the vote is answerable mathematically (the proportionate change is an order of magnitude greater for the former) but depends on perspective for analytical purposes. All the researcher can do is consider polling scores in their electoral context, and decide accordingly.

14. In a small minority of polls, particularly earlier ones, candidates who eventually stood in the election were omitted.

15. For more details of the statistical procedure, please refer to the original article, as well as Tomz et al. (2002).

16. A more fine-tuned coding at constituency level would obviously encounter the issue of boundary changes which took place before the 2012 elections, and therefore break the time series.

17. Growth data are taken from Eurostat (http://epp.eurostat.ec.europa.eu), forecasted at a clear 0.0 per cent for 2012. Unemployment data for 1981 and 2007 were taken from INSEE (http://www.bdm.insee.fr/bdm2/do/accueil/AccueilAppli), and for 2012 from the new French government data portal, http://www.data.gouv.fr. All data and syntax are available for replication in Stata from http://dvn.iq.harvard.edu/dvn/dv/arzheimer.

18. A model where Greens are included under moderate left yields similar accuracy in results. Overall, the Green forecast is in line with the model's expectations.

8   The Legislative Elections of June 2012

1. In 2007, the MPF had managed to field 410 candidates.
2. We take our inspiration here from Muxel (2008: 111).
3. Harris Interactive, Les Français et les élections législatives de 2012, 5–7 June 2012, http://www.harrisinteractive.fr/news/2012/08062012.asp, accessed 30 March 2013.
4. The revival in particular of the FN resulted in a greater number of three-way run-offs across 34 constituencies – out of 46 possible cases before mutual *désistements* – as opposed to only ten and one in the 2002 and 2007 legislatives, respectively.

5. Only Pierre Moscovici in his Doubs constituency found himself in a *triangulaire* with the FN and UMP at the second round, missing an absolute majority by less than 1 per cent of the final vote after the right-wing vote split.

6. According to statistics by the Fédération Nationale des Elus Socialistes et Républicains (FNESR).

7. 1st *circonscription* (USA/Canada), 2nd *circonscription* (Central America/South America/Caribbean), 3rd *circonscription* (UK/Ireland/Scandinavia), 4th *circonscription* (Benelux), 5th *circonscription* (Iberian Peninsula/Monaco), 6th *circonscription* (Switzerland), 7th *circonscription* (CEE/Balkans), 8th *circonscription* (Italy, Greece, Turkey, Cyprus, Israel), 9th *circonscription* (North and West Africa), 10th *circonscription* (Africa and Middle East), 11th *circonscription* (CIS/Asia/Oceania).

8. An OpinionWay poll conducted among French expats in March 2012 indicated that Sarkozy would win a 51 per cent majority against Hollande in the run-off, while he would lead the first-round vote with 37 per cent (http://www.opinion-way.com/pdf/bj8239-etude_aupres_des_francais_de_l_etranger-mars_2012-vf.pdf, accessed 16 May 2013).

9. Contrast with this the six EELV dissidents, all of whom were defeated in the first round.

10. http://www.lepoint.fr/politique/marc-dolez-quitte-le-parti-de-gauche-19-12-2012-1603528_20.php, accessed 21 December 2012.

11. Although Marine Le Pen won the town of Hénin-Beaumont itself by more than a 10 per cent margin.

12. During the legislative campaign, an anonymous tract was circulated in Hénin-Beaumont, which quoted Mélenchon declaring: 'There is no future in France without Arabs and Berbers of the Maghreb' (http://www.lemonde.fr/politique/article/2012/05/30/tension-a-henin-beaumont-autour-d-un-tract-anonyme_1709505_823448.html, accessed 30 March 2013).

13. Forecasts immediately after the presidentials anticipated no less than 345 *triangulaires* based on Marine Le Pen's scores across the constituencies: 'Législatives: vers 345 triangulaires?', in *Le Figaro*, 23 April 2012, http://www.lefigaro.fr/flash-actu/2012/04/23/97001-20120423FILWWW00688-legislatives-vers-345-triangulaires.php, accessed 23 March 2013.

14. Three-way run-offs contributed nevertheless to UMP losses in a number of constituencies. In Arles, Roland Chassain placed third in the 16th *circonscription*, and stood down in favour of the Socialist Michel Vauzelle, to allow the defeat of the FN's Valérie Laupies. In the Bouches-du-Rhône's 8th *circonscription*, the UMP's Nicolas Isnard fell prey to a classic *triangulaire* against the FN's Gérald Gerin, with the PS' Olivier Ferrand winning with only just over 40 per cent of the vote. A similar defeat occurred for Richard Mallie, this time at the hands of EELV's François-Michel Lambert, in the neighbouring 10th *circonscription*. In Marion Maréchal-Le Pen and Gilbert Collard's constituencies, a refusal to put together a *front républicain* ensured the FN's own victory.

15. A third extreme-right deputy, Jacques Bompard, was a former FN member who left in 2005.

16. IPSOS poll, 7–9 June 2012, http://www.ipsos.fr/ipsos-public-affairs/actualites/2012-06-10-sociologie-et-motivations-l-electorat, accessed 29 April 2013.

9   Conclusion

1. An IPSOS poll conducted in January 2013 showed a 70 per cent majority of French agreeing with the statement that 'there are too many foreigners in France', while another 62 per cent said 'they didn't feel at home any more'. No less than three-quarters (74 per cent) also said that 'Islam was intolerant' and 'not compatible with French society' (http://www.lemonde.fr/politique/article/2013/01/24/les-crispations-alarmantes-de-la-societe-francaise_1821655_823448.html, accessed 17 May 2013).

References

Adams, J. and Merrill, S., III (2000) 'Spatial models of candidate competition and the 1988 French presidential election: Are presidential candidates vote-maximizers?', *Journal of Politics*, 62:3, 729–756.

Andersen, R. and Evans, J. (2002) 'Values, cleavages and party choice in France, 1988–1995', *French Politics*, 1:1, 83–114.

Andersen, R. and Evans, J. (2005) 'The stability of French political space, 1988–2002', *French Politics*, 3:3, 282–301.

Arzheimer, K. and Evans, J. (2010) 'Forecasts of the French legislative vote from regional economic conditions', *International Journal of Forecasting*, 26:1, 19–31.

Arzheimer, K. and Evans, J. (2013, forthcoming) 'A new multinomial accuracy measure for polling bias', *Political Analysis*.

Auberger, A. (2005) 'Forecasts of the 2004 French European election', *Swiss Political Science Review*, 11:1, 61–78.

Bale, T. (2008) 'Turning round the telescope: Centre-right parties and immigration and integration policy in Europe', *Journal of European Public Policy*, 15:3, 315–330.

Bartolini, S. (1984) 'Institutional constraints and party competition in the French party system', *West European Politics*, 7:4, 103–127.

Bell, D. and Criddle, B. (2002) 'Presidentialism restored: The French elections of April–May and June 2002', *Parliamentary Affairs*, 55:4, 643–663.

Bergounioux, A. and Grunberg, G. (2005) *L'ambition et le remords: les socialistes français et le pouvoir. 1905–2005* (Paris: Fayard).

Bornschier, S. (2012) 'Why a right-wing populist party emerged in France but not in Germany: cleavages and actors in the formation of a new cultural divide', *European Political Science Review*, 4:1, 121–145.

Birenbaum, G., Mayer, N., Taguieff, P.-A., Viard, J. and Ysmal, C. (1996) 'Le FN dans la durée', in Mayer, N. and Perrineau, P. (eds) *Le Front national à découvert* (Paris: Presses de Sciences Po), pp. 343–379.

Bréchon, P. (2008) 'Un nouveau centrisme électoral?', in Perrineau, P. (ed.) *Le vote de rupture. Les élections présidentielle et législatives d'avril–juin 2007* (Paris: Presses de Sciences Po), pp. 175–195.

Brouard, S., Appleton, A. and Mazur, A. (eds) (2009) *The French Fifth Republic at Fifty. Beyond Stereotypes* (Basingstoke: Palgrave Macmillan).

Bussi, M. and Fourquet, J. (2007) 'Élection présidentielle 2007', *Revue Française de Science Politique*, 57:3, 411–428.

Campbell, J. (2008) 'Editor's introduction: Forecasting the 2008 national elections', *PS: Political Science & Politics*, 41:4, 679–682.

Cautrès, B. and Muxel, A. (eds) (2009) *Comment les électeurs font-ils leur choix?* (Paris: Presses de Sciences Po).

Clift, B. (2005) 'Dyarchic presidentialization in a presidentialized polity: The French Fifth Republic', in Webb, P. and Poguntke, T. (eds) *The Presidentialization of Politics – A Comparative Study of Modern Democracies* (Oxford: Oxford University Press), pp. 219–243.

Clift, B. (2013) '*Le changement?* French socialism, the 2012 presidential election and the politics of economic credibility amidst the Eurozone crisis', *Parliamentary Affairs*, 66:1, 106–123.

Cole, A. (1989) 'Factionalism, the French Socialist Party and the Fifth Republic: An explanation of intra-party divisions', *European Journal of Political Research*, 17:1, 77–94.

Cole, A. (2003) 'Stress, strain and stability in the French party system', in Evans, J. (ed.) *The French Party System. Continuity and Change* (Manchester: Manchester University Press), pp. 11–26.

Conover, P. and Feldman, S. (1986) 'Emotional reactions to the economy: I'm mad as hell and I'm not going to take it anymore', *American Journal of Political Science*, 30:1, 50–78.

Converse, P. and Dupeux, G. (1961) 'Politicization of the electorate in France and in the United States', *Public Opinion Quarterly*, 26:1, 1–23.

Cordell, J. (2005) 'Unity and plurality in the French Right', *South European Society and Politics*, 10:2, 191–206.

Dolez, B. and Laurent, A. (2007) 'Une primaire à la française: la désignation de Ségolène Royal par le Parti Socialiste', *Revue Française de Science Politique*, 57:2, 133–161.

Dolez, B. and Laurent, A. (2010) 'Strategic voting in a semi-presidential system with a two-ballot electoral system: The 2007 French legislative election', *French Politics*, 8:1, 1–20.

Dupoirier, E. and Sauger, N. (2010) 'Four rounds in a row: The impact of presidential election outcomes on legislative elections in France', *French Politics*, 8:1, 21–41.

Elgie, R. (2004) 'Institutions and voters: Structuring electoral choice', in Lewis-Beck, M. (ed.) *The French Voter: Before and After the 2002 Elections* (Basingstoke: Palgrave Macmillan), pp. 110–125.

Elgie, R. (2006) 'France: Stacking the deck', in Gallagher, M. and Mitchell, P. (eds) *The Politics of Electoral Systems* (Oxford: Oxford University Press), pp. 70–87.

Evans, J. (2004) *Voters and Voting: An Introduction* (London: Sage).

Evans, J. (2012) 'Normalising the French presidency: Explaining François Hollande's victory in 2012', *Renewal*, 20:2/3, 123–129.

Evans, J. and Ivaldi, G. (2008) 'Forecasting the extreme right vote in France (1984–2007)', *French Politics*, 6:2, 137–151.

Evans, J. and Ivaldi, G. (2010) 'Comparing forecasts of radical Right voting in four European countries', *International Journal of Forecasting*, 26:1, 82–97.

Evans, J. and Ivaldi, G. (2012a) 'Forecasting the FN presidential vote in the 2012 elections', *French Politics*, 10:1, 44–67.

Evans, J. and Ivaldi, G. (2012b) 'Deriving a forecast model for European election turnout', *Political Research Quarterly*, 65:4, 854–866.

Evans, J. and Mayer, N. (2005) 'Electorates, new cleavages, social structures', in Cole, A., le Galès, P. and Levy, J. (eds) *Developments in French Politics* (Basingstoke: Palgrave Macmillan), pp. 35–53.

Foucault, M. (2012) 'Forecasting the 2012 French legislative election', *French Politics*, 10:1, 68–83.

Foucault, M. and Nadeau, R. (2012) 'Forecasting the 2012 French presidential election', *PS: Political Science and Politics*, 45:2, 218–222.

Gallagher, M. (1991) 'Proportionality, disproportionality and electoral systems', *Electoral Studies*, 10:1, 33–51.

Fourquet, J. (2012) 'Le sens des cartes. Analyse de la géographie des votes à la présidentielle' (essay), Fondation Jean Jaurès.

Grunberg, G. and Haegel, F. (2007) *La France vers le bipartisme? La présidentialisation du PS et de l'UMP* (Paris: Presses de Sciences Po).

Grunberg, Gérard and Florence Haegel (2008) 'Le bipartisme imparfait en France et en Europe', *Revue Internationale de Politique comparée*, 14:2, 325–339.

Grunberg, G. and Schweisguth, E. (1997) 'Vers une tripartition de l'espace politique', in Boy, D. and Mayer, N. (eds) *L'électeur a ses raisons* (Paris: Presses de Sciences Po), pp. 179–218.

Grunberg, G. and Schweisguth, E. (2003) 'French political space: Two, three or four blocs?', *French Politics*, 1:3, 331–347.

Gschwend, T. and Leuffen, D. (2005) 'Divided we stand – Unified we govern? Cohabitation and regime voting in the 2002 French elections', *British Journal of Political Science*, 35:4, 691–712.

Haegel, F. (2004) 'The transformation of the French Right: Institutional imperatives and organizational changes', *French Politics*, 2:2, 185–202.

Héran, F. (2004) 'Voter toujours, parfois ... ou jamais', in Cautrès, B. and Mayer, N. (eds) *Le nouveau désordre électoral. Les leçons du 21 avril 2002* (Paris: Presses de Sciences Po), pp. 351–367.

Huber, P. (1967) 'The behavior of maximum likelihood estimates under non-standard conditions', in *Proceedings of the Fifth Berkeley Symposium on Mathematical Statistics and Probability* (Berkeley: University of California Press), pp. 221–233.

Ivaldi, G. (2006) 'Beyond France's 2005 referendum on the European constitutional treaty: Second-order model, anti-establishment attitudes and the end of the alternative European utopia', *West European Politics*, 29:1, 47–69.

Ivaldi, G. (2007) 'Presidential strategies, models of leadership and the development of parties in a candidate-centred polity: The 2007 UMP and PS presidential nomination campaigns', *French Politics*, 5:3, 253–277.

Ivaldi, G. (2012) 'Législatives: un bilan en demi-teinte pour le Front national', *Revue Politique et Parlementaire*, 1063–1064, 175–189.

Jérôme, B. and Jérôme-Speziari, V. (2003) 'A Le Pen vote function for the 2002 presidential election: A way to reduce uncertainty', *French Politics*, 1:2, 247–251.

Jérôme, B. and Jérôme-Speziari, V. (2004) 'The 2004 French regional elections: Politico-economic factors of a nationalized local ballot', *French Politics*, 3:1, 142–163.

Jérôme, B. and Jerôme-Speziari, B. V. (2012a) 'Forecasting the 2012 French presidential election: Comparing vote function simulations and vote intention polls', *French Politics*, 10:1, 22–43.

Jérôme, B. and Jerôme-Speziari, V. (2012b) 'Forecasting the 2012 French presidential election: Lessons from a region-by-region political economy model', *French Politics*, 10:4, 373–377.

Katz, R. (2001) 'The problem of candidate selection and models of party democracy', *Party Politics*, 7:3, 277–296.

Kitschelt, H. (1994) *The Transformation of European Social Democracy* (Cambridge: Cambridge University Press).

Knapp, A. (2002) 'France: Never a golden age', in Webb, P., Farrell, D. and Holliday, I. (eds) *Political Parties in Advanced Industrial Democracies* (Oxford: Oxford University Press), pp. 107–150.

Knapp, Andrew (2003) 'From the Gaullist movement to the President's party', in Evans, J. (ed.), *The French Party System* (Manchester: Manchester University Press), pp. 121–136.

Kriesi, H., Grande, E., Lachat, R., Dolezal, M., Bornschier, S. and Frey, T. (2006) 'Globalization and the transformation of the national political space: Six European countries compared', *European Journal of Political Research*, 45:6, 921–956.

Laakso, M. and Taagepera, R. (1979) 'Effective number of parties: A measure with application to West Europe', *Comparative Political Studies*, 12:1, 3–27.

Lavabre, M.C. and Platone, F. (2003) *Que reste-t-il du PCF?* (Paris: Autrement).

Lewis-Beck, M. (1988) *Economics and Elections* (Ann Arbor: University of Michigan Press).

Lewis-Beck, M. (1997) 'Who's the chef? Economic voting under a dual executive', *European Journal of Political Research*, 31:3, 315–325.

Lewis-Beck, M. (2005) 'Election forecasting: Principles and practice', *British Journal of Politics and International Relations*, 7:2, 145–164.

Lewis-Beck, M. and Nadeau, R. (2004) 'Dual governance and economic voting: France and the United States', in Lewis-Beck, M. (ed.) *The French Voter. Before and After the 2002 Elections* (Basingstoke and New York: Palgrave Macmillan), pp. 136–154.

Lewis-Beck, M., Nadeau, R. and Bélanger, E. (2012) *French Presidential Elections* (London: Palgrave Macmillan).

Marks, G., Hooghe, L., Nelson, M. and Edwards, E. (2006) 'Party competition and European integration in East and West. Different structure, same causality', *Comparative Political Studies*, 39:2, 155–175.

Marthaler, S. (2008) 'Nicolas Sarkozy and the politics of French immigration policy', *Journal of European Public Policy*, 15:3, 382–397.

Martin, E., Traugott, M. and Kennedy, C. (2005) 'A review and proposal for a new measure of poll accuracy', *Public Opinion Quarterly*, 69:3, 342–369.

Mayer, N. (2002) *Ces Français qui votent Le Pen* (Paris: Flammarion).

Mayer, N. (2013) 'From Jean-Marie to Marine Le Pen: Electoral change on the far right', *Parliamentary Affairs*, 66:1, 160–178.

Mergier, A. and Fourquet, J. (2011) 'Le point de rupture: Enquête sur les ressorts du vote FN en milieux populaires' (essay), Fondation Jean Jaurès.

Meunier, S. (2003) 'France's double-talk on globalization', *French Politics, Culture and Society*, 21:1, 20–34.

Mosteller, F., Hyman, H., McCarthy, P., Marks, E. and Truman, D. (1949) *The Pre-Election Polls of 1948: Report to the Committee on Analysis of Pre-Election Polls and Forecasts* (New York: Social Science Research Council).

Mueller, J. (1970) 'Presidential popularity from Truman to Johnson', *American Political Science Review*, 64:1, 18–34.

Muxel, A. (2008) 'Le retour de la participation électorale?', in Perrineau, P. (ed.) *Le vote de rupture. Les élections présidentielle et législatives d'avril–juin 2007* (Paris: Presses de Sciences Po), pp. 99–118.

Nadeau, R., Didier, T. and Lewis-Beck, M. (2012) 'Leader images and election forecasting: French presidential elections', *French Politics*, 10:1, 11–21.

Nadeau, R., Lewis-Beck, M. and Bélanger, E. (2012a) 'Proxy models for election forecasting: The 2012 French test', *French Politics*, 10:1, 1–10.

Nadeau, R., Lewis-Beck, M. and Bélanger, E. (2012b) 'Choosing the dependent variable: Sarkozy's forecasting lesson', *French Politics*, 10:4, 364–368.

Oesch, D. (2006) *Redrawing the Class Map: Stratification and Institutions in Britain, Germany, Sweden and Switzerland* (Basingstoke: Palgrave Macmillan).

Parodi, J. L. (1997) 'Proportionnalisation périodique, cohabitation, atomisation partisane: un triple défi pour le régime semi-présidentiel de la Cinquième République', *Revue Française de Science Politique*, 47:3–4, 292–312.

Pelizzo, R. and Babones, S. (2007) 'The political economy of polarized pluralism', *Party Politics*, 13:1, 53–67.

Perrineau, P. (1995) 'La dynamique du vote Le Pen: le poids du "gaucho-lepénisme"', in Perrineau, P. and Ysmal, C. (eds) *Le vote de crise* (Paris: Presses de Sciences Po), pp. 243–261.

Perrineau, P. (2009) 'La "défidélisation" des électeurs de Jean-Marie le Pen', in Cautrès, B. and Muxel, A. (eds) *Comment les électeurs font-ils leur choix?* (Paris: Presses de Sciences Po), 201–220.

Perrineau, P. (2011) 'Défiance politique' in TNS-SOFRES, *L'état de l'opinion* (Paris: Seuil), pp. 47–60.

Pierce, R. (1998) *Choosing the Chief: Presidential Elections in France and the United States* (Ann Arbor: University of Michigan Press).

Ravenel, L., Buléon, P. and Fourquet, J. (2003) 'Vote et gradient d'urbanité: les nouveaux territoires des élections présidentielles de 2002', *Espaces, Populations, Société*, 3, 469–482.

Sartori, G. (1976) *Parties and Party Systems: A Framework for Analysis*, vol. 1 (Cambridge: Cambridge University Press).

Sauger, N. (2007) 'Le vote Bayrou. L'échec d'un succès', *Revue Française de Science Politique*, 57:3–4, 447–458.

Sawicki, F. and Lefebvre, R. (2006) *La société des socialistes. Le PS aujourd'hui* (Bellecombe-en-Bauges: Editions du Croquant, coll. Savoir/Agir).

Schain, M. (2006) 'The extreme-right and immigration policy-making: Measuring direct and indirect effects', *West European Politics*, 29:2, 270–289.

Shields, J. (2006) 'Political representation in France: A crisis of democracy?', *Parliamentary Affairs*, 59:1, 118–137.

Stimson, J., Tiberj, V. and Thiébaut, C. (2010) 'Le mood, un nouvel instrument au service de l'analyse dynamique des opinions: Application aux évolutions de la xénophobie en France (1999–2009)', *Revue française de science politique*, 60:5, 901–926.

Stokes, D. (1963) 'Spatial models of party competition', *American Political Science Review*, 57:2, 368–377.

Stone, W. and Abramowitz, A. (1983) 'Winning may not be everything, but it's more than we thought: Presidential party activists in 1980', *American Political Science Review*, 77:4, 945–956.

Stone, W., Rapoport, R. and Atkeson, L. R. (1995) 'A simulation model of presidential nomination choice', *American Journal of Political Science*, 39:1, 135–161.

Strauss-Kahn, D. (2002) *La flamme et la cendre* (Paris: Editions Grasset et Fasquelle).

Strudel, S. (2007) 'L'électorat de Nicolas Sarkozy: "rupture tranquille" ou syncrétisme tourmenté?', *Revue Française de Science Politique*, 57:3–4, 459–474.

Tomz, M., Tucker, J. and Wittenberg, J. (2002) 'An easy and accurate regression model for multiparty electoral data', *Political Analysis*, 10:1, 66–83.

van der Eijk, C. and Franklin, M. (2004) 'Potential for contestation on European matters at national elections in Europe', in Marks, G. and Steenbergen, M. (eds) *European Integration and Political Conflict* (Cambridge: Cambridge University Press), pp. 33–50.

Villalba, B. (2008) 'The French Greens: Changes in activist culture and practices in a constraining environment', in Frankland, E., Lucardie, P. and Rihoux, B. (eds) *Green Parties in Transition: The End of Grass-Roots Democracy* (Farnham: Ashgate), pp. 45–60.

White, H. (1982) 'Maximum likelihood estimation of misspecified models', *Econometrica*, 50:1, 1–25.

Wright, V. (1989) *The Government and Politics of France* (London: Unwin Hyman).

Young, L. and Cross, W. (2002) 'The rise of plebiscitary democracy in Canadian political parties', *Party Politics*, 8:6, 673–699.

Index

Printed and bound in the United States of America